FEEDBACK

Peter Cawdron

Twenty years ago

Rain lashed the windows of the aging Sea King helicopter. The wipers on the windscreen rocked back and forth, vainly trying to clear the sea spray whipped up by the helicopter's rotor blades. The craft flew barely thirty feet above the choppy ocean, its searchlight illuminating the darkness. White capped waves stretched into the night. The swell of the ocean rose and fell beneath the fuselage, rolling beneath the aging helicopter, making Captain John Lee feel small in the darkness.

"We're not normally this far north," Lee said, turning sideways and glancing at the US Navy SEAL leaning into the cockpit.

Lieutenant Andrews wore a nondescript black wetsuit with the skintight hood hanging down his back, ready to be pulled over his head to seal him off from the ocean below. A small red light on the side of his headphones added to the muted hues within the cockpit, allowing Andrews to read from a high-contrast map as he replied to Lee.

"Get us as close as you can, Captain. We'll take it from there."

Lee understood why the Navy SEAL was so nervous. Being South Korean, Lee could hear the radio chatter with the North Koreans in Sunwi-do, but for Andrews, hearing the harsh, clipped words in a language he didn't understand must have been unnerving.

Lightning rippled through the storm clouds.

Co-pilot Josh Park was seated next to Lee. He set the microphone in his helmet to transmit externally and spoke in Korean, saying, *"We are Search and Rescue Foxtrot Echo Sierra Four Zero out of Incheon, responding to a Mayday call from a downed Piper Cub LAJ 357, that is Lima Alpha Juliet Three Five Seven. We are Foxtrot Echo Sierra Four Zero, conducting a grid search south of Pup'o-ri. Over."*

The North Korean response crackled through the headphones set in Lee's helmet.

"Foxtrot Echo Sierra Four Zero you have entered our airspace. You do not have permission to pass through the Democratic People's Republic of Korea. Change heading immediately or you will be fired upon. Over."

Technically, both sides of the 38th Parallel North spoke Korean. In practice, they spoke separate languages. Both Lee and Park had to concentrate carefully to distinguish the North Korean's intent. Years of training drills had them prepared for such interactions, and even then it took considerable focus to understand what the North Koreans were saying. The possibility of miscommunication added to the tension of the moment.

Lee checked his channel, being particularly careful to ensure he was not broadcasting externally as he spoke to the Navy SEAL.

"They're not buying it; they're calling our bluff. It's the usual bluster. Go home or we'll send you home in a coffin."

"How long before they escalate?"

"Usually, we turn around about now," Lee replied. "But we've probably got a good five to ten minutes before they start targeting us. And in this weather, it will take them longer to respond. If we turn east and make like we're starting a long, slow arc to the south we can get you and your men a little closer, but I doubt we'll get you within less than a couple of kilometers offshore. Sorry, boys, it's going to be a long swim."

"Roger that," Lieutenant Andrews replied.

American servicemen were a mixed bag, Lee thought. Lee had run into every conceivable type, from the John Waynes of the world to those with blistering intelligence. Sometimes they could be condescending to a civilian pilot like Lee, but Andrews was a good man. Lee had been on several training runs with Andrews and always found him balanced and considerate. Whether US or South Korean, Lee's experience had been that most commanders abused their power, wielding it like a club, but not Andrews. If ever Lee went to war, he would want to serve under someone like Andrews. The Lieutenant exuded competence without being cocky.

Park took his cue from Lee. Using a combination of his foot pedals and the cyclic control rising up between his legs, he eased the helicopter around to a new heading, one which took advantage of the rugged, irregular coastline hidden in the darkness, bringing them closer to land while ostensibly turning back toward South Korea.

Lee keyed his microphone to transmit externally and spoke in Korean, saying, *"This is Foxtrot Echo Sierra Four Zero to Sunwi-do. Foxtrot Echo Sierra Four Zero is complying with instructions from Sunwi-do, conducting one last sweep to the south and returning to Incheon. Over."*

Strangely, there was no reply. Lee barely registered the silence, he was focused intently on the instruments before him.

Park fought to keep the Sea King steady as they struggled through the storm. Gusts buffeted the craft. The cyclic control was a steel rod set into the floor of the cockpit, controlling the direction in which the helicopter faced. The control stick shook in his hand as the storm raged around them.

Lee double checked his instrumentation. He understood the concept of target fixation and the tendency for pilots to drift into anything they stared at for too long. Although he could see the breaking caps of the waves rushing beneath them, to focus on the ocean would be a mistake. The wave height was misleading. In the dark of night, all either pilot could rely on was their instruments. Night flights were particularly taxing, and with the weather, Lee couldn't afford to let his concentration drift. He switched from external coms to internal.

"Bring us up to fifty meters and take us to a hundred knots," he said to the co-pilot, looking at the radar and the fluorescent green outline that marked the shore several kilometers off in the distance. "They know we're here. There's no point in trying to hide anymore. Let's hope they buy our course correction as legit."

Lee was speaking in English as a courtesy to the Navy SEALs listening in on the cockpit chatter. English was the de facto norm for aviation, and should have been the accepted language for communication with Sunwi-do, but the North Koreans were nothing if not belligerent. International standards were of no concern to them. They preferred forcing the South Koreans to use Korean over the airwaves.

The churning ocean may as well have been featureless. The flashing strobe lights on the chopper reflected off the waves, breaking through the night briefly every few seconds. Their searchlight lit up a patch of sea out in front of the helicopter, but the light was for show. They weren't looking for anyone.

Although the Sea King was carrying eight US Navy SEALs, this flight would be logged as a search and rescue mission, with the manifest noting only four South Koreans onboard: Lee, Park, the loadmaster and a rescue swimmer.

Lee knew well enough not to ask about the purpose of the American military operation. The South Korean Coast Guard had been used for several other unofficial missions in the past few years. Their regular patrols and the occasional rescue of fishermen aboard a swamped trawler or the need to ferry medicines to merchant ships gave them a veneer of credibility with the North Koreans. The Coast Guard was a known entity, nothing out of the usual even at the most unusual of times, but somehow the North Koreans smelled a rat on this cold, dark night.

The Sea King helicopter had a pronounced radar profile, but that didn't seem to bother the Americans. They could have used one of their stealth helicopters, but even within the restricted zone inside their military base, keeping a top secret helicopter under wraps was no easy feat. It might have been invisible in the dark of night, but on the ground such a helicopter attracted too much attention. There were too many curious civilians and service personnel. The potential for compromising a mission was too great, and the US military had long known the simple options were often the best. Paranoia was rampant within the North Korean military. All it took was a few loose words in a bar or a leak to a reporter and tensions could escalate. Piggybacking off the coast guard was a natural fit. There was nothing out of the ordinary about their daily ops.

The coast guard was the first resident at the new international airport outside of Incheon. For the most part, it was little more than a construction zone, with the airport's completion not due for years to come. Construction work made it easy for the SEALs to come and go as US engineering contractors without attracting unwanted attention. There was no official policy of course, but the US Navy SEALs liked hitching a ride with the South Korean Coast Guard, as their presence with the Guard was unnoticed.

The SEALs were dressed in civilian wetsuits; which Lee knew was to give them deniability should they be caught during whatever clandestine activity they were undertaking. He didn't want to know. He just wanted to fly. He and his crew got a monthly stipend for being on standby for these supposed training runs, and performing an actual training run brought a bonus that doubled their monthly salaries. Besides, it felt good to be needed, to be surreptitiously part of the team.

Lee kept his mind in the present.

"Lieutenant. We are five minutes out from our closest approach to the coast, approximately three kilometers south by southwest of the original drop point."

"Roger that," came the reply from Lieutenant Andrews. "We'll be fine. We are ready to drop."

A warning light flashed on the cluttered instrument panel.

"The storm's really screwing with the radar," Park said. "But there's definitely something out there. We're not alone."

"Another chopper?" Lee asked.

"Negative. Moving too fast."

Lee was about to suggest the blip was a radar ghost, an artifact of the storm misleading their instruments, when Park called out, "It's coming straight at us."

"Heading?" Lee asked, trying to remain calm. His mouth ran dry. Adrenaline surged through his veins.

"From due north, our nine o'clock."

"Can we drop below radar?" Andrews asked.

"You're not helping," Lee replied tersely, already bringing the Sea King lower as they raced along, dropping to barely thirty feet above the crest of the rolling swell. "If that's a MIG, we'll never get low enough because he's got look-down radar. We might be able to play hide and seek with land-based radar, but he's going to light us up like a goddamn Christmas tree."

"I've lost him," Park cried. Seconds later, Park slammed his hand against the upper windscreen, pulling against his five-point harness as he watched a dark shape streak by overhead. "FUCK!"

Lee struggled with the control stick as the wash from the jet rocked the helicopter, causing the Sea King to skew sideways and twist in the air. He fought with his foot pedals to correct the yaw introduced by the buffeting winds from the MIG, fighting to keep the helicopter on course.

Park cried, "Damn that was close. I could see his fucking flight lights."

"His radar is probably as fucked up as ours is in this weather," Lee said. "I doubt if he saw us until he was right on top of us. Probably scared him as much as us."

Lee keyed his microphone to broadcast and spoke rapidly in Korean, saying, *"Sunwi-do. This is Foxtrot Echo Sierra Four Zero. We are an unarmed civilian aircraft complying with instruction to leave North Korean airspace. Over."*

There was no reply.

"Sunwi-do. This is Foxtrot Echo Sierra Four Zero. We are Search and Rescue helicopter returning to Incheon. Over."

"Will he be back?" the Navy SEAL asked.

"He'll be back," Lee replied grimly. "His turning circle is worse than a destroyer, it will take him out a couple of miles, and that will buy us some time, but he's got the smell of blood, he'll be back."

Lee applied steady pressure to the rudder with his foot, watching as the compass heading turned to due south.

"We need to get that little girl," Andrews said. "Drop us anywhere you can."

Girl? That was the first time Lee heard the SEALs mention their target that night. In the years to come, he would look back on that moment as a pivotal point in his life. From then on, everything had been about that mysterious child. Even then, in his mind's eye, he struggled to understand why the US military would be interested in a young North Korean girl. Was she really worth risking the lives of a dozen SEALs and aircrew? Was the life of one little girl worth the risk of provoking war?

Lee was rattled. As he leveled the Sea King, he wondered about the girl. Who was she? What had she done? Why was she so important to the US government? Did she even know about the maelstrom of covert activity unfolding around her?

As a rescue pilot, Lee risked his life for complete strangers several times a month, but he'd only ever rescued a child on one occasion. A yacht had capsized in heavy weather. The GPS distress beacon had guided his team to the stricken vessel. When they arrived on the scene, all Lee could see were bodies floating face down in the water. It had been the loadmaster that spotted the child, a young girl of eight clinging to a large cushion that had been washed overboard.

The rescue swimmer had gone down on the winch to effect the rescue. He'd grabbed her on the first try, bundling her into a recovery basket.

After spending four hours in the water, the young girl was in shock. Once she was onboard, the loadmaster wrapped her in a thermal blanket, coaxing her body temperature back to normal while the rescue swimmer continued to retrieve the bodies. The chopper remained at the scene for several grueling hours, recovering the bodies of her father, her mother, her brother, her sister and her grandmother.

The rescue helicopter touched down at the airport a little after midnight the following morning. Lee could still remember the look on her face, her cold clammy skin and dilated pupils. She lunged for him as he reached out to help her down from the chopper. The girl threw herself into his arms and clung fiercely, as if she were still in danger of dying alone in the water instead of safe on dry land. He'd tried to comfort her, but there was no comfort to give.

It was four in the morning before Child Services arrived to take her away, and in the intervening time she never spoke a word. She cried as she left. It was the first time he'd seen her cry since they fished her out of the ocean. The elderly lady from Child Services was kind and soft spoken, but that didn't matter. The young girl reached out for Lee. Her eyes flooded with tears, and Lee found himself crestfallen as she was pulled away.

The incident left Lee shaken. There was nothing more he could have done, and yet he felt the weight of guilt bearing down on him. To see a child so distraught left him devastated.

In the back of his mind, Lee struggled to reconcile the words of the US Navy SEAL; *We need to get that little girl.* Those words cut through to his heart. He breathed deeply, steeling his mind to focus on the present. He had no idea who this girl was, but right now she had to take second place. He hated himself for the decision he had to make, but he had no choice. The safety of his crew came first.

"I'm sorry," he said to Lieutenant Andrews. "There will be no drop. You'll have to find another way into North Korea."

"Son of a bitch!" Andrews yelled, thumping the steel bulkhead of the helicopter.

Andrews had no idea how hard that decision was for Lee. Looking into the darkness, Lee felt physically sick.

"That MIG must have been on an exercise," Park said. "There's no way they could have scrambled a MIG that quickly in this weather."

"Go dark," Lee replied.

Park flicked a bunch of toggle switches and the strobe light and spotlights turned off. The backlit instruments in front of him cast a soft red glow throughout the cabin. With no external lights, the night closed in on them. Lee kept his eyes on the altimeter and elevation bubble. He eased the Sea King slightly higher, wanting to compensate for their blind view.

"He's coming around again," Park said. "Fucker's coming straight at us from six o'clock. Two miles out. Flying right up our tail."

Lee keyed his microphone and pleaded for their lives, again speaking in Korean as he cried, "*Sunwi-do. This is Foxtrot Echo Sierra Four Zero. We are heading to international waters. Disengage, I repeat, disengage. Over.*"

Again, there was no reply.

Lee switched to internal coms, asking, "Guns or missiles?"

"Sorry?" Park replied.

"What do you think he's carrying? Guns or missiles? If you're right, and he was on night exercises, what armament would he carry? Guns, missiles or both?"

"Guns," Andrews offered, injecting himself into the conversation. "Bullets are cheaper than bombs and missiles."

"Is he left handed or right?" Lee asked.

"I don't know," Park snapped.

"Which way did he break last time? To the left or the right?"

"Left."

"Then he's right handed. When we break, we go right, we turn against his natural lean. We try and force another fly-over."

"What are you going to do?" Andrews asked.

Lee ignored him. "Distance?"

"Half a mile," Park snapped.

"Hold on," Lee cried. He raised the collective control, arresting the forward momentum of the Sea King and adjusting the angle of the blades so the helicopter climbed swiftly.

The Sea King shuddered.

The airframe of the helicopter groaned under the strain. Lee could feel the blood draining from his head as he snatched at the collective, rapidly altering the pitch of the blades. He pulled back on the cyclic stick, forcing the helicopter to pitch back with its nose raised. The Sea King's initial momentum fought against the screaming engines driving them higher.

Within twenty seconds, the helicopter approached vertical and began to stall. With its nose pointing toward the clouds, the helicopter's engines stuttered in the air. Lee slammed the stick forward and pressed hard on his right foot pedal. The aging helicopter was sluggish, slow to respond. Eight and a half tons of metal began falling from the sky, plummeting under the pull of gravity. Lee could feel himself lifting out of his seat as they plunged back toward the ocean. His stomach moved up into his throat. A burst of lightning lit up the night, illuminating the raging sea hundreds of feet below them. The engines whined.

"Come on, you bitch!" Lee yelled, dropping the collective control while pulling on the control stick, fighting to level the Sea King as she plunged toward the ocean. Lee executed a 180 degree turn and had the helicopter racing north toward the MIG.

"What the hell are you doing?" Andrews yelled, gripping the side of the cabin for dear life.

"Reducing his angle. Cutting down his response time. Limiting his options."

The Sea King leveled out barely twenty feet above the waves, its engine whining as it tore through the storm.

The helicopter shook with the impact of incoming rounds striking the airframe. The windscreen shattered. Soldiers screamed in agony. The MIG raced screaming overhead. Lee eased the cyclic control stick to one side, turning the helicopter back to the south as the cabin filled with acrid smoke.

"Mayday, Mayday," Park cried into his microphone. Although he was broadcasting externally, this time he was speaking in English, knowing the frequency was being monitored from Incheon. "This is Foxtrot Echo Sierra Four Zero declaring an emergency. We have a cockpit fire."

"Losing hydraulics," Lee called out.

"Losing hydraulics," Park repeated, relaying their predicament over the radio.

A calm voice replied over the airwaves, saying, "Foxtrot Echo-"

"We've lost flight controls," Lee barked as the power surged and the radio cut out.

"Brace for impact," Park yelled. "Brace—"

Lee thought he was ready, but he wasn't.

The ocean seemed to reach up and snatch them out of the air, pulling them violently into the murky depths. The left float of the Sea King caught the top of the waves, causing the helicopter to wrench to the side as the float was sheared off by the initial impact. Although the front of the Sea King was designed as a boat, with a broad, curved, flat front, the angle the helicopter came down at was awkward, at almost thirty degrees, negating any design considerations as the chopper caught on the waves.

The Sea King shuddered as it slammed into the ocean swell. To Lee, it felt as though he'd driven into a brick wall. His head snapped forward. His body strained against the harness holding him in his seat, while his seatbelt dug into his hip. His arms were flung out in front of him, striking the instrument panel.

Water poured in through the shattered windscreen.

The Sea King listed to one side as it was buffeted by the waves.

For a moment, Lee couldn't see anything, but not because of the loss of cabin lights. Although he was conscious, his vision had blacked out. Hazy red dots flickered before his eyes. His head pounded. Slowly, his eyes focused on the dim, flickering instruments before him.

Ice cold water flooded the cabin, swirling around his legs and up over his thighs. He struggled with his harness release, but the lock was jammed. In a panic, Lee fought with the locking mechanism. His gloved fingers slipped on the slick metal clips. Water rose over his chest, soaking his uniform.

Lee tugged at the seatbelt, but the more he pulled, the tighter the harness seemed to hold him. He could feel the icy cold water creeping through his trousers and into his boots. The shock of the water running from his neck down his chest and around his waist caused him to gasp.

The sinking helicopter continued to twist, leaning heavily to one side, leaving him with a triangular pocket of air around his head as the canopy began to slip beneath the waves.

Lee struggled to keep his head above water as he yelled out, "Park? Andrews? Anyone?"

The wind howled outside. Rain pelted the sheet metal, but there was no sound of life, human or mechanical.

"I need help!" he cried. "Is there anyone there?"

Waves broke against the sinking hull of the Sea King.

"I'm stuck! I can't get loose!"

The frigid water swirled around his chin, forcing him to take a deep breath as the salt water lapped at his mouth. Within seconds, the ocean claimed him entirely, covering his eyes, his forehead and his helmet. Lee tried not to panic. He had to stay calm. If he could remain calm, he had a good minute or so to get out of his seat. If he panicked he'd be dead in seconds, burning up what little oxygen there was in his lungs.

A light flickered beneath the water. Through the murky gloom, Lee could see that his co-pilot was dead. Park's lifeless body was pinned in his seat. Blood blossomed in the water from a shard of glass embedded in the side of his neck.

Seconds were the enemy.

He had to get out of his seat.

Lee pushed himself back against the cushion, relieving pressure on the belt. He twisted the release as gently as though he were sitting in the cockpit on the tarmac back in Incheon, having just finished his shift.

Deep inside the steel lock he felt something click and give. Pushing off gently with his feet, he drifted out of the harness. Lee reached out with his hands, pulling himself through the sinking wreckage.

The side cargo door was submerged, but open. His lungs were burning. He kicked toward the door, pushing off the bulkhead and reaching for the opening, but his boots were heavy, his helmet was bulky, and his clothes weighed him down.

Lee fought to clear the wreckage as the Sea King slipped into the depths. He managed to get his helmet off. His ears stung with the pressure of the water weighing down on him, telling him he had to be at least twenty feet below the surface already. He tried to equalize his ears by stretching his jaw out into a forced yawn, but the pressure of the water around him was changing too quickly as the chopper slipped into the depths.

In the darkness, Lee had no way of knowing how deep he'd been dragged beneath the waves. Feeling with his hands, he tugged at the drawstring on his life vest. Immediately, a tiny gas cylinder inflated his vest, propelling him toward the surface.

His ascent seemed never ending.

Lee convulsed.

He couldn't stop himself. He was suffocating, dying. He had to breathe. The urge was primal, instinctive, overwhelming. His lungs demanded air. They would be deprived no longer. A reflex reaction took over and he inhaled, coughing on a mouthful of sea water.

In those final few seconds, with his brain starved of oxygen, Lee's mind drifted. Memories flashed before him in muted scenes. Far from seeing his life in miniature, Lee saw only one image, that of a young girl terrified of leaving him. Her arms were outstretched. She was frozen in time, etched in his mind. Bereaved of her entire family in a single night, and now forcibly taken from her rescuers. Her eyes begged for compassion, for understanding, for respite, but the past could not be undone.

The surface never came.

Darkness washed over him.

Present Day New York

Jason loved New York. He sat at an old wooden desk overlooking the intersection of Columbus and West 67th, barely a block from Central Park. His rundown apartment was small—a single room with a kitchenette and a bathroom/shower barely larger than a closet. The carpet was worn and paint peeled off the walls, but it was home.

From the second floor, he looked out across the street at an Italian deli on the far corner. He could hear an old woman singing some archaic, operatic song as she set up a wooden stall outside the deli, loading it with bagels and freshly baked sourdough bread. Her voice carried on the wind, drifting above the cars and trucks speeding by. She was irrepressible, and he loved the sense of character she brought to the neighborhood.

The smell of coffee drifted up from an independent coffee shop on the ground floor below his apartment. Originally, the shop had been a Starbucks and the smells had been predictable, but there were so many other independent stores and restaurants in the area that they could encourage consumers to boycott big name chain brands. It was Jason's claim to fame. That he lived above a failed Starbucks. Thankfully, the 7-11 across the street had fared better or he would have had a three block walk to the nearest grocery store.

The new owners of the coffee shop were Moroccan. Hints of cinnamon, cloves and cardamon floated on the breeze. The allure of freshly roasted Arabica coffee beans brought customers in from miles around. The line for a morning cup of coffee stretched around the corner. Jason smiled. Although it was the smell of the dark coffees, the espressos and cappuccinos that brought people in, most customers left with a latte or some other weaker coffee. For him, the smell was enough to get his synapses firing. He sipped at his generic brand instant coffee, smelling the Moroccan coffee wafting through the open window, trying to fool his taste buds.

Jason looked at his phone: 7:10am and already 85 degrees. It was going to be another scorcher.

Jason was a first generation Korean-American. His parents adopted him from an orphanage in Seoul. He was too young to remember anything other than their warm, smiling faces, but on coming to America they never let him forget that they regularly endured humid summer temperatures of 100 degrees without air conditioning. In Jason's family, you weren't allowed to complain about how hot it was until you'd baked under a ceramic tile roof on the Korean peninsula.

He was doodling when his cellphone rang. Jason was absentmindedly drawing symbols and equations on a scrap of paper. He put down his pen and picked up the phone. Before he could say anything a deep, husky voice said, "Hey, baby."

Jason didn't bite.

A male voice that sounded like Barry White with a chest cold asked, "What are you wearing?"

Jason shook his head without saying a word.

"Come on, baby," the caller continued, speaking with slow deliberation. "Talk dirty. Tell me what you're wearing. Don't make me come over there. I swear, I'll bring riding whips and chains."

Finally, Jason laughed, saying, "You are sick. You know that, don't you? You need professional help."

The voice on the other end of the phone laughed. "You know you love it, you gigolo!"

Jason couldn't help but grin as he replied, playing along with the charade as he added, "Whore!"

"You sexy minx!"

Through tears of laughter, Jason forced a reply with, "Tramp!"

"I know your kind," the rough voice continued, "You need a good spanking!"

Jason was out. He'd been beaten. He had nothing else to come back with. The provocative voice on the phone added, "I'm going to slap some fluffy cuffs on you and stretch you out naked on the table."

"So what's up, man?" Jason asked, fighting through his laughter. "Why did you call?"

"Sugar daddy doesn't need a reason to call. So what are you wearing?"

"All right," Jason replied, sitting there wearing gym shorts and a Nike T-shirt. "I'm naked."

"Liar," the voice said in rough, sexy tones. "You're wearing leathers, aren't you? Skin tight black rubber latex?"

"All right. You win, Mitch!"

Mitch loved playing the fool. Anyone listening in would probably have been offended, but Mitchell was just being silly. A little banter between friends kept things lighthearted.

The voice on the phone lightened, no longer dark and mysterious. "Hey, so are we on for our wild Fourth of July weekend down in Atlantic City?"

"I can't, Mitch," Jason replied. "I'm doing Fifty Shades of University Catch Up over here. I've got to finish this paper on M-Theory."

"M-Theory my ass," Mitchell replied. "It's a goddamn national holiday tomorrow; birth of a nation and all that crap. Don't tell me that bully Lachlan has you working through your Independence Day! What would Thomas Jefferson say?"

"It's my fault," Jason confessed. "I missed the deadline. He gave me an extension, but I've got to have my paper on his desk by noon tomorrow."

As he spoke, Jason's attention wandered. He found himself staring at a beautiful Asian girl across the street by the deli. She was standing on the street corner by the lights, but she didn't cross as the lights cycled through. She had been standing there for a while. She must have been lost.

"Tell me you're sticking to the study material," Mitchell said. "Tell me you're not going off on your own theories again."

Jason screwed up the piece of paper he'd been doodling on, feeling guilty and tossing it in the wastepaper basket beside his desk. That he didn't answer seemed to tell Mitchell what he wanted to know.

"You can't keep doing this," Mitchell continued. "You've got to walk before you run. You can't go proposing some J-Theory just because you don't like M-Theory."

"Yeah, I know," Jason replied sheepishly.

"And quit with the doodling," Mitchell continued. "Lachlan will flunk you. He doesn't care how smart you think you are. He cares about the curriculum."

"Yeah, I know," Jason repeated, staring at the scrap of paper in the bin. The crumpled paper was covered in multiple formulae and calculations, hastily scribbled over the top of each other.

"OK, listen," Mitchell said, "Forget Atlantic City. Let's do breakfast at Mario's Diner tomorrow."

"Sure."

"And no more distractions. Promise?"

"Promise," Jason agreed.

"All right, catch you later, *bitch!*"

Jason smiled as he ended the call. Mitchell was right. He needed to knuckle down and finish his assignment. He grabbed his notes, pulled out his laptop and got to work.

After several hours, a rumble in his stomach told him it was time for a break. The aging clock on the wall of his rundown kitchenette surprised him with 1 PM. He'd made good progress, having cranked out seven pages of theoretical discussion points.

Beside his computer, though, sat a pad of legal paper covered in symbols and drawings. Jason was barely aware he'd been scrawling on the pad as he immersed himself in the assignment. To the casual observer, his scribbles would be meaningless, just a bunch of Greek letters and math symbols. Even Professor Lachlan would have struggled to comprehend his notation, as it was an abstract representation. A bunch of placeholders he'd arbitrarily assigned to explore different physical properties of subatomic particles. Ultimately, he knew calculus was a means of quantifying relationships, the only problem was that no one agreed with his notation.

Sweat dripped from his forehead. He got up and grabbed a Coke from the fridge and made a peanut butter and jelly sandwich for lunch. As he sat down, he noticed the girl again, still standing on the far corner of the intersection.

The sun was relentless, baking the city. Heat shimmered from the scorching concrete.

There was no shade on that corner, but there she stood looking the wrong way down a one-way street like she was waiting for someone to drive like a salmon against the flow of cars and pick her up. Her dark hair, pale skin and petite body seemed to be wilting in the heat like flowers left out of a vase.

Jason bit into his sandwich, wondering about her, curious about where she was from and where she was going. She clearly wasn't a local. What was she doing in New York? Who was she waiting for? Why didn't she stand back in the shade? Curious, he wondered what the story was behind her vacant stare. He popped open the can of Coke and sipped at the cool drink, enjoying the brief respite from the heat.

Jason had work to do. Staring at eye candy wasn't going to help him get his master's degree in physics. He focused his mind, having enjoyed the brief distraction, and got back to work.

Hours drifted by unnoticed.

The sun was setting when he next glanced out the window. Although he expected she would be long gone by then he half hoped to see her again. She had sparked his curiosity. For today, at least, she was his mystery woman.

Several pages of legal paper lay strewn on the ground, covered in apparent gibberish.

There she was. She looked like she hadn't moved from the one slab of concrete he'd seen her on earlier that morning. In the back of his mind, he'd been vaguely aware of her standing there throughout the day, catching her occasionally out of the corner of his eye.

Jason checked his phone. It was half past six in the evening. He'd completed an intellectual marathon, or so he felt. His paper was finished. Well, he mused, physics revolved around relativity and uncertainty, and finished was a relative term, one that in his case carried a high degree of uncertainty.

He knew he needed to spend at least a couple of hours reviewing his work before he was really finished.

Looking at her, he knew she had been out there for the better part of twelve hours. She must have moved, he thought. She couldn't have stood there all day in the unrelenting sun. She had to have had something to eat, something to drink. She must have gone to the bathroom at some point, but if she had, he hadn't noticed.

Jason stared down the road, wondering who she was waiting for. Whoever it was, they were really late.

Since traffic only went one way down the street and she was looking in the direction the traffic was traveling, he decided she must be waiting for someone on foot. He wondered if she would make a scene when they finally arrived. She must have been mad as hell standing there all day. That would make a good show, he thought, smiling to himself.

Storm clouds started to gather over the city. The temperature began to drop, bringing some welcome relief from the heat.

Jason grabbed some left over Chinese take out from his fridge and heated it in the microwave. He sat on the edge of his bed and ate as he watched the evening news, giving his mind a break from study. There were reports of a UFO sighting over Manhattan. Damn, he thought, it must have been a slow news day for that garbage to make it into the broadcast.

Jason knew what was coming before the phone rang. Sure enough, the news shifted to sports and Mitchell called.

"Did you see it?"

"I saw it," Jason admitted, knowing he'd regret the discussion that was coming.

"I'm telling you, man. Aliens are real. UFOs are real. They're buzzing Manhattan!"

"UFOs *are* real," Jason countered, accentuating the word 'are,' agreeing with Mitchell while not agreeing at all. "By definition, UFOs are unidentified. But just because something is unidentified doesn't mean it's a flying saucer from Mars with little green men."

Mitchell countered, saying, "Weather balloons, huh! You know, that's getting a little old now."

Jason laughed. "Venus rising, experimental military aircraft, and shimmering stars viewed through swamp gas are far more plausible explanations than aliens. Think about it. If someone can traverse dozens of light-years to get to Earth, why would they hide? How is that intelligent? They are supposed to be intelligent, remember?"

Mitchell took the bait. "Over fifty thousand Americans have experienced an abduction event."

Jason smiled, trying not to laugh as he added, "And all of them live on remote farms in West Virginia."

Rain began to fall outside, gently at first, but slowly building to a crescendo as the storm broke. Lightning crackled across the sky. The rumble of thunder drowned out the traffic.

Mitchell laughed. "I'm telling ya, aliens are real. This year marks the twentieth anniversary of the Incheon incident when a UFO crashed off the coast of North Korea. Anniversaries are like magnets to these guys. They'll be back, mark my words. They will be back."

Jason replied, saying, "Anniversaries are like magnets to those with tinfoil on their heads!"

"You'll see. One day, you'll see I'm right."

"I doubt it," Jason said, distracted as he wondered about the girl across the street. He got up from his bed and sat at the desk. She was still standing there in the rain, making no effort to shelter from the raging storm. The news switched to the weather forecast, distracting him. High nineties, low hundreds for the next five days, with evening storms. New York was going to be a sauna over the long weekend.

"Catch yah tomorrow," Mitchell replied, ending the call.

A welcome breeze blew in through the open window. Jason found the sound of falling rain soothing, stunting the sounds and smells of the city, replacing them with a crisp scent of life and renewal. The temperature dropped considerably. Suddenly, the inside of his apartment was like the walk-in cooler at the liquor store.

Looking out into the night, he could see her still standing there staring down the road. The street was empty. With most of the city clearing out for the holiday weekend, the neighborhood was unusually quiet.

Jason stared at her for a few seconds. She glanced up at him and he was embarrassed. From her perspective, it must have looked like some creep was staring down at her from a window. In the darkness, she probably only saw a silhouette, but Jason still felt stupid, self-conscious. She was pretty. She probably had guys hitting on her all the time and hated the unwanted attention. She was probably staring at him thinking, "What the hell are you looking at, weirdo?"

Jason wasn't sure why, but he waved. In a way, he felt connected to her, as though they shared something in common having endured the unbearably hot day together. It was silly, and must have looked creepy, but he waved anyway, just wanting to be friendly. She waved back, but not enthusiastically. Just a slight shake of her wrist, never raising her hand above her waist.

Jason turned away from the window and shook his head. He couldn't believe he was going to do this, but he felt chivalrous, as though she were some damsel in distress in need of rescue by a knight in shining armor. He grabbed an umbrella and headed out of his apartment and downstairs. Within minutes, he found himself standing in the rain with the umbrella limp by his side, telling himself he was crazy.

Lightning rippled through the sky. Thunder broke around him. The heavens opened and rain fell in a torrential downpour. Water rushed through the streets, swirling in the gutters.

Jason looked for traffic. The streets were empty. He ran diagonally across Columbus Ave, cutting across the intersection toward her. In the back of his mind, he hoped there were no cops around to bust him for jaywalking.

She was smiling.

Like him, she was dripping wet.

He opened his umbrella and held it over her head, saying, "Hi."

"Hi," she replied, pulling her wet, heavy hair away from the side of her face and behind her ear.

"I'm Jason."

"Lily."

She offered him her hand. He shook it, noticing how limp her fingers were. She felt unusually cold.

Lily was soaked. Her dark, black hair clung to the side of her neck. She was petite, wearing a plain white tank top and a short, floral skirt. A small purse hung over her shoulder, hanging by a thin strap.

"Thank you," she said, looking up at the umbrella.

Standing there, it struck him that the umbrella was useless, or at least too late to be of any real use.

"Ah," he said, smiling and trying not to laugh at how ridiculous he felt. He hadn't thought through what he was going to say to her beyond hello. Now that he'd said hello, his mouth went dry and he struggled, not knowing quite what to say next. Impulsively, he blurted out, "Would you like to come in out of the rain?"

"I'm waiting for my father," she said, ignoring his invitation. She pointed down the street. Jason looked down the street, following her gesture. There was no one there; no cars, no pedestrians, no buses.

"You've been waiting a long time," he replied. "Would you like to come inside, dry off and warm up? I mean, I'm a nice guy. I'm not trying to hit on you or anything. I'm not some weirdo, honest. I just thought you might–"

"Sure," she said, cutting him off and sparing him further embarrassment. Lily wasn't wearing any makeup. Even so, her face radiated warmth. Despite the rain, her high set cheeks were rosy. Her teeth were pearly white and perfectly straight, at least they seemed to be at the glance he had when she smiled. Although she was soaking wet, Jason thought she looked beautiful.

They started walking across the street, with Jason trying to keep the umbrella over her. Lily laughed and he got the hint, dropping the umbrella to his side and surrendering to the rain.

"Rain is good," she said. "Rain brings life."

Jason was fascinated by her. There was a simple elegance to Lily, an understated beauty that seemed more than skin deep.

"Rain is fun," Jason decided, jumping in a puddle. Water splashed up her legs. She laughed, jumping in the next puddle and splashing him back.

"Yes, it is," she said, and they hopped and skipped through the puddles, splashing each other playfully as they made their way to his building.

Jason shook himself off in the entranceway of the building as Lily wrung her hair out, still laughing with him as she let her hair drip on the mat. He led her upstairs with giddy excitement. He wasn't sure why, but he felt comfortable with her already. They'd barely spoken a dozen words between them, but Jason felt as though he could be himself in front of her, as though there was no need to try to impress her. He felt as though she accepted him for who he was. Although she was a complete stranger, Jason felt like he'd finally caught up with a long lost friend.

As he opened the door to his apartment he was horrified to see his unmade double bed immediately in front of him. A half-eaten box of Chinese take out sat on the messy sheets. Clothes were strewn across the floor. Lily didn't seem to notice. She raised her eyes, as though she were surveying art work in a gallery. She was looking at the posters and pictures covering his walls. There were several striking images of Mars from the HiRISE camera on NASA's Mars Reconnaissance Orbiter along, with an image taken by COBE: a map of the cosmic background radiation that still saturated the universe as the afterglow of the Big Bang. A tattered poster of the Andromeda galaxy hung next to the kitchen, while the wispy filaments of the Sloan Digital Sky Survey, mapping the location of millions of galaxies in deep space, was proudly displayed next to his desk.

Jason kicked some of the clothes to one side.

Lily squeezed around the bed, moving to the only open area within the cramped apartment, a section of worn linoleum between the desk and the kitchenette.

"I'm … I'm sorry it's such a mess," Jason spluttered. "I don't normally have people over."

"No. It's wonderful," she said, gesturing at the walls. "I love looking at scenes from outer space."

Scenes, he thought curiously, that was an unusual way of describing posters. Scenes implied stories, actions, events. He liked that. Scenes were a better description of these images, given the timespan captured by each of the posters and the stories they told.

"Puts things in perspective, doesn't it?" he said.

"Yes," she replied, smiling. "In each of these scenes, you see beyond the confines of this small planet."

In the bright light of his apartment it was apparent Lily wasn't wearing a bra under her t-shirt. Jason wasn't sure if he blushed, but he suddenly realized he was staring at her wet t-shirt while she gazed at the posters. The thin white cotton was all but transparent when wet, clinging to her body and accentuating her curves.

"I'll get you a towel to dry off," he said, his eyes dropping to the floor as he turned and grabbed a towel from the bathroom.

Lily shivered as he wrapped the towel around her shoulders. She sat down on a small loveseat jammed between his desk and the kitchenette, sitting sideways so she could stare out the window at the intersection as they talked. Jason sat on the bed, hurriedly straightening the covers.

"So, where are you from?"

"Korea," she replied.

"Really? My parents are from Incheon, just west of Seoul."

He wasn't sure, but she seemed to blush as she replied, "I am from a small fishing village south of Sunwi-do."

Jason hadn't heard of Sunwi-do. He had only been to South Korea once to visit his grandparents, and only for a week. His recollection was of jet lag, thousands of people bustling along the sidewalks, and an astonishing assortment of neon lights and signs that put Times Square to shame. Seoul was the New York City of the East, a dazzling city that never slept.

"What's your dad's name?" he asked, picking up his phone and opening a browser to search for her father's contact details. "I can look him up and we can give him a call. Let him know you're OK."

"Lee."

"Is that his first name or his last name?"

"His name is Lee," Lily insisted.

"OK," Jason said, a little confused. "Do you have an address?"

"Columbus and West 67th."

"Ah ... that's where we are," Jason replied. "Do you have an address for Lee?"

Lily started to speak, but he cut her off, saying, "Columbus and West 67th, right?"

"Yes."

Well, he thought, this isn't quite what I expected.

"How long have you been in America?" he asked, shifting on the bed. Somehow, her uncertainty made him feel a little more at ease. He relaxed.

"I arrived this morning," Lily said, still shivering a little. Her words were stilted. She was a FOB: Fresh Off the Boat, as Jason's Korean-American friends would say, but he'd never say that to her. Although her English was good, her words were heavily accented, with a distinctly Korean feel to the consonants.

Jason stood up. He looked past Lily at the intersection. The street was empty.

"Listen," he said, opening a drawer and pulling out some clothes. "Why don't you go and have a shower? You'll feel better if you warm up a bit."

He handed her a shirt and a pair of shorts, adding, "I'll keep watching for Lee."

In reality, he had no idea who he was watching for and would have felt pretty stupid calling out to a stranger down on the street, but he resolved to do it nonetheless. This wouldn't be the first time he'd made a fool out of himself over a girl.

Lily bowed slightly, thanking him as she took the clothes. She left her purse hanging on the back of the chair and disappeared into the bathroom.

Within seconds, the sound of the shower competed with the rain. Steam wisped out around the gaps in the door jamb. The landlord was supposed to have reframed the door a month ago, but he'd forgotten and Jason kept forgetting to hound him about it.

Jason didn't know what to do with himself. No one was coming down the road, that much was obvious. If Lee had failed to show after eight hours, the likelihood of him showing in the next few minutes was negligible.

He sat on the edge of the bed for a moment, wondering what he should do next. Staring at her purse, curiosity got the better of him. She had to have a passport or a driver's license. Perhaps if he knew her last name he could track down her father. Jason felt guilty, but he told himself a quick peek was justified. He was trying to help her. He opened her purse and was surprised to find it empty. There was no money, no credit cards, none of the normal junk that accumulates in a bag, not even scraps of lint. The purse looked brand new.

The shower had stopped but he hadn't noticed. He was too busy looking to see if there were any compartments inside the purse he might have missed. He felt the lining, looking for a zipper, wondering if there were any hidden sections. Even with his limited knowledge of woman's fashion accessories, the purse seemed basic, no pockets or dividers, just a simple bag.

Jason heard the door handle turn behind him and his heart sank. He scrambled to put Lily's purse back, turning rapidly and looking as guilty as sin when Lily stepped back into the apartment.

Lily looked stunning. With her hair carefully combed and slicked back, a smile on her face and bright, intelligent eyes, she looked like she'd stepped from the covers of a glamor magazine. The t-shirt he'd given her was baggy on her small frame, but she'd rolled up the sleeves so they rested on her shoulders. Standing in front of him, she tied a knot in the front of the shirt, pulling it tight and exposing her hips, accentuating her figure. Even the shorts looked good on her. Lily's long, smooth, thin legs looked as though they had been sculpted from rose colored marble. Jason could have stood there staring at her all night. He wasn't sure what he expected when she came out of the shower, but he hadn't expected her to look so beautiful in his clothes.

"Are you hungry?" he said, more to distract himself than to offer her something to eat. There wasn't much in the fridge, and only some breakfast cereal and ramen noodles in the cupboard — they were hardly a meal at the best of times.

"No. I'm fine," Lily replied, and he wasn't sure if she was just being polite.

"Coffee?" he asked.

"Sure."

Jason turned his back on her and put the kettle on. All he had was instant coffee—a shot in the arm for a student in desperate need of a quick fix. He liked fancy coffee as much as the next person, but as foul as instant coffee was, it worked miracles when pulling an all-nighter studying. At times like that, quantity took precedence over quality. He opened a packet of plain crackers, silently berating himself for being such a tight ass and not splurging on Oreos.

"Milk and sugar?" he asked as the kettle came to a boil.

"Just black," Lily replied.

As he poured the coffee into two cups he noticed her staring at the posters again.

"Tell me about them," she asked.

And that was all he needed. Jason turned on the lava lamp sitting on his desk as he handed her a cup of coffee. He grabbed his cup and turned off the main light. His apartment was a poor substitute for an astronomical observatory, but he could dream. The red light from the lava lamp set the mood, allowing his imagination to carry him across the universe as he gazed at each picture. To him, it was as though he was recalling a summer vacation from photographs.

Lily stood. A distant street light behind her cast a faint shadow on the wall, making her thin, lanky body look even more extended. As he looked at her shadow, Jason realized that Mitchell would have pointed out that the shadow she cast was a close match to the grays, mythical aliens that had supposedly been visiting the Earth since the Roswell Incident. Jason shook any such notion from his mind, scolding himself for even thinking anything remotely similar to Mitchell and his wacky conspiracy theories.

The way Lily stood there silently looking at his tatty posters was reminiscent of someone in an art gallery staring at one of the great masterpieces, being mesmerized by Gauguin or Monet.

His mind raced with the possibilities. Was she really that interested in his geeky posters? Or was she just being polite? Where should he start?

Lily gazed around the room, apparently waiting for him to say something to break the silence. She seemed particularly interested in a large poster of Earth set against the pitch black void of space.

"Oh, I love this one," he said, getting up and walking over to the poster. "Most astronomers spend their time looking at other planets, stars, nebulae and galaxies, but I never get tired of seeing the Earth from space. This is—"

"A blue marble," Lily said, walking over and reaching out to touch the poster-size print. Her fingers hovered above the image, running over the outline of the Sinai, Africa and Madagascar.

"Yes," Jason replied. "This photograph was taken by Apollo 17 on their outbound journey as they headed to the Moon. For me, it's an image full of wonder and sadness."

Lily turned to him, her head tilted slightly in surprise. He could see she wanted him to clarify his comment.

"This was the last manned lunar mission in the Apollo program. NASA called this image *The Blue Marble* because Earth appeared to sit against the backdrop of space like a marble glistening in the sunlight, but Earth would have appeared much larger to the astronauts. Perhaps the Blue Basketball or the Blue Beach Ball would have been more accurate, but not quite as poetic. I often wonder what it must have felt like to stare out through that cold glass, looking at a planet you could hold in your hands."

"It's upside down," Lilly said.

"Ah, no," Jason replied tentatively. "That swirling mass of white at the bottom is the cloud cover over Antarctica. You can see Africa stretching out to the north, with that distinct green band of jungle giving way to the sands of the Sahara."

Lily turned her head to one side, leaning over and looking at the image sideways as she spoke softly, saying, "I remember it differently."

Jason laughed.

"Only a handful of astronauts have ever seen Earth quite like—" He stopped mid sentence, changing tack. "You know, I do remember reading that the command module was inverted relative to Earth when the crew took this photo."

He walked over beside her and pulled the poster from the wall. The tape came away easily.

"You're right," he added, turning the poster upside down and sticking it back on the wall. "There's no reason to choose any one orientation over another. If anything, this picture should be viewed the way Cernan, Evans and Schmitt saw it. Looks kinda strange, though, doesn't it? We're so used to seeing north as up we assume that's the way it should be."

"It looks better," Lily said, smiling.

Jason stood there for a second, examining the poster of Earth set on a jet black background. Thinking about it, he added, "With the Sahara desert encircling the bottom of the world and the lush greens of South Africa rising up toward the top, Earth looks like an alien world."

Lily said, "Earth is an alien world."

Jason raised an eyebrow in surprise at her comment. He started to say something, but Lily spoke first.

"And this one?"

"Oh," Jason replied, losing himself in another poster. "Those are sand dunes on Mars, but it's the dark fuzzy sections that are most intriguing. Current thinking is they're the result of subterranean aquifers bursting through to the surface during summer."

The two of them sat on his bed and talked into the early hours of the morning, talking about stars and planets, about

Korea and America. Jason found Lily captivating, intoxicating. At times she seemed to barely grasp English, at other points she showed a surprising depth of intelligence, as though she knew far more than she was letting on.

There was something about Lily. Jason felt like he'd known her for years. He wasn't one for concepts like déjà vu, but he could have sworn they'd met before.

When the conversation finally started to slow, Jason offered her his bed. Regardless of how much he protested, Lily insisted on sleeping on the loveseat. She said she wanted to keep watch over the intersection. She sat there, curled up with her head on a pillow, staring out the open window. Jason draped a blanket over her, promising he'd help her look for her father in the morning. He wasn't sure how he was going to keep that promise, but it seemed to be the right thing to say.

"Jason," she said, as he turned off the lava lamp and hopped into bed.

"Yes?"

"Thank you for being such a gentleman."

Λlive

Lee woke to the sound of waves crashing and gulls squawking overhead. He was drifting with the tide. He could feel himself bobbing on the waves with his head kept out of the water by the headrest on his lifejacket. A chill ran through him. His feet were numb. Blood oozed through the cracks in his chapped lips.

Dawn was breaking. The sky was grey. Rain drizzled in the early morning breeze.

Lee felt his body spasm, jerking itself awake. He turned and saw a jagged cliff looming overhead. Waves broke at the base, crashing on the rocks. Looking around, he could see sand dunes not more than a mile away. Clumps of grass leaned to one side with the prevailing winds, but the beach below the dunes wasn't visible over the choppy waves.

He tried to swim against the tide, but he was too weak. His chest hurt where bruises had formed following the crash. The seatbelt harness in the Sea King had bitten into his waist and upper chest. It had saved him from being impaled on the control stick during the crash, but that salvation had come at a price.

The rolling swell dragged him toward the rocks. Over the next few minutes, he watched as the surge washed over the jagged rocks before pulling out briefly, and then swirling in again, crashing on the shore, throwing brilliant white spray thirty to forty feet in the air.

Waves pounded the rocks.

Seaweed wrapped around his legs.

How long had he spent floating at sea? Just one night? Could it have been more? He felt as though he'd been drifting for days, but this had to be the morning after. His head ached from dehydration.

Lee kicked to free himself and began mentally timing his swim. If he could drift in on one of the surges, hold himself near the shore and then climb onto the rocks as the swell retreated briefly, he could scramble up beyond the waterline. Lee didn't like his chances, but he didn't have a choice. One way or the other, he was going to end up on those rocks, and soon. It was just a matter of in what condition.

Salt spray flew through the air as another large wave broke over the rocks.

Waves surged and crashed, pounding the rugged cliff base.

Lee felt his body being lifted on the swell. He fought to get close to the rocks, drifting to within a few feet of their jagged, black edges. Barnacles and seaweed littered the shore. In the back of his mind, he felt the rhythm of the sea. To anyone watching, it would have seemed like suicide, but he could feel the might of the ocean subsiding briefly as he struck out for the rocks.

As a child, Lee had hunted lobster in the turbulent water off the Chungnam coast in South Korea. He and his father would each don a snorkel, mask and flippers and fish at the top of the tide, taking advantage of the slack and change in currents. Drifting just a few meters from the rocky shoreline, they could easily avoid being thrown onto the rocks. Lobster would scuttle around the rocks beneath the swell, anywhere from ten to fifteen feet below the surface. Their spidery legs and spindly antenna would waver with the current. With a burst of speed, they would pump their tails and shoot through the water, escaping at the first hint of a threat. His father taught him to be decisive, not to hesitate when grabbing at these small monsters of the deep. As long as he grabbed the carapace of the lobster, its massive claws couldn't reach him.

"Just like the old days," Lee muttered. He'd never tried this before, but he knew it was possible. Normally, he and his father would swim to a sheltered area or to a waiting boat, but he'd seen other fishermen clamber up onto the rocks.

Lee felt the moment come in the wash of the waves and the rise of the swell. The rising swell lifted him up as his boots scrambled for a hold. He kicked hard at the water, grabbing at the slick rocks, managing to catch hold and climb up. Within seconds, he was level with the base of the cliff, escaping just as a wave pounded the rocks behind him, soaking him in white spray.

Lee was breathing hard as he cleared the lower, wet rocks, surprised by the rush of adrenaline and the tingling sensation in his fingers. He was shaking.

"Ha!" he cried, stopping for a moment and looking around, enjoying the excitement of escape. The rush of adrenaline faded, leaving him feeling spent.

As the adrenaline wore off, Lee found the world spinning around him. He felt sick. A burp brought the taste of salt water to his mouth. Seconds later, the raging sea seemed to follow and he vomited, spewing into a tidal pool and gagging as bile stretched from his mouth to the rocks beneath his feet.

A bitter, cold wind whipped along the face of the cliff, chilling him. Lee staggered closer to the cliff, wanting to find a wind break.

Rocks gave way to boulders. Landslides marked where the weather had washed away sections of the embankment.

Lee walked on, wiping the spew from his face. His hands were numb. The water in his boots squished between his toes as he struggled over the uneven rocks. His focus seemed narrow as though he had tunnel vision. The world had been reduced to the sharp, jagged rocks and boulders in front of him. He was suffering from the early stages of hypothermia. Try as he might, he couldn't shake the feeling that he was going to die on those rocks.

The wind howled.

Lee climbed higher.

Gulls glided on the wind above him, casually watching him.

He was alive. For a moment, he stopped and let that realization sink in. Furthermore, if he'd survived, others could have survived as well. His mind flashed to thoughts of his crew, the US Navy SEAL Lieutenant Andrews and his team, and he wondered if any of them had made it to shore. Were they huddling somewhere among the sand dunes, trying to survive the cold? He looked out across the ocean, hoping to make out the sight of a Day-Glo orange lifejacket bobbing on the swell. The sea rolled away from him, dark and foreboding, unrelenting and unforgiving.

Making his way around the side of the cliff, Lee headed toward the beach he'd caught a glimpse of in the distance, wanting to get into the warmth of the sun. From his vantage point, he could see a rugged coastline, windswept and barren, stretching for miles as it curved into the haze of sea spray.

There was someone down there on the beach, not more than a couple of hundred yards away.

"Hey," he yelled, waving his hands over his head in excitement, but his cries were drowned out by the crash of the waves.

Was it Andrews? He couldn't be sure.

Lee was buoyed. It never occurred to him he was stranded in North Korea, in a hostile country intent on destroying its southern neighbor.

He waved his hands again, but the dark figure didn't respond. Whoever it was, they were pointing at the low cliffs running along the edge of the beach. The man jogged a few feet and then turned and pointed again, which confused Lee. It was only then he heard the crack of gunfire over the pounding surf. The unrecognizable man shot at someone, but he was so far away the vision of the handgun firing and the smack of the shot echoing through the air were disconnected in time. The crack of gunfire arrived a second or so after the the man's arm recoiled with each shot.

Several dogs burst onto the beach, running down from the sand dunes. The man was shooting at them with a handgun. The dogs attacked him, knocking him to the ground and tearing at his body. Lee stood there stunned, watching as a pack of dogs savaged the man, tearing at his arms and legs.

Several North Korean soldiers ran onto the beach, following hard behind the dogs. They were shouting and waving their arms, but Lee couldn't make out what they were saying. It was only then he realized he was standing there in the open wearing a Day-Glo orange life jacket. Had they turned, they would have seen him instantly.

Lee dropped behind a weathered, worn boulder and pulled his life jacket off, tossing it on the rocks. Peering out from behind the boulder he watched as the soldiers kicked at the body lying on the wet beach. From where he was, Lee could see blood running on the sand, mixing with the waves rolling across the gentle slope leading down to the ocean.

More soldiers came running down from the dunes, their indistinct cries carried on the wind.

Lee turned away. Sitting down on his haunches, he held his hands up to the side of his head, pulling at his hair as he groaned, saying, "No, no, no."

For a brief moment, he had felt a surge of adrenaline at the excitement of not only being alive, but in seeing that someone else had survived. He'd forgotten where he was. He was stranded on a North Korean beach. This could have been one of the craggy beaches on the Taean peninsula south of Incheon, but the cruel reality of his physical location was brought thundering home to him by the body lying on the sand.

More soldiers poured onto the beach.

Dogs strained at their leashes, trying to pull free and savage the fallen American.

The man had to be one of the SEALs, Lee figured, as he was wearing a black wet suit. The American didn't move. None of the North Korean soldiers rendered any assistance. They stood around the body. A couple of them sheltered their faces from the wind with their hands, and Lee guessed they were lighting cigarettes. That they could be so callous, so indifferent to the American's slow, painful death stunned him. The American must have been shot, as the dogs alone wouldn't have killed him. Lee could see he was beyond help, and he found himself hoping the man wasn't suffering, hoping that death would be mercifully quick.

Rotor blades beat at the wind. Lee could hear a helicopter passing by out of sight beyond the cliff. The engine sounded wrong. It was too rough to be either South Korean or American. The North Koreans were hunting for survivors from the air. They were looking for him, and that realization personalized the danger he felt. If they found him, they'd kill him.

The sound of rotor blades grew louder, echoing off the rocks, making it hard for him to identify where the chopper was coming from. Within seconds, the helicopter would be on top of him. He had to hide.

Lee scrambled into a gap beneath a couple of boulders. Crabs scurried out of sight. He wedged his body in a narrow gap, with his boots resting in water.

A helicopter hovered overhead. It was an old Russian Hind. Its rotor blades thrashed at the air in a vicious tempo. The chopper was almost directly above him. To one side, his discarded life jacket fluttered across the ground under the downdraft. Lee panicked seeing the orange material flapping, knowing it would give him away. He scrambled out of hiding, not sure whether he was too late. His knees and shins scraped painfully on the rocks as he grabbed for the jacket. Above, he caught a glimpse of the tail boom on the Hind as it turned, sweeping over the area. Lee knew there would be at least two spotters onboard, one looking to port, the other to starboard. He rolled back under the boulder, catching his elbow on a rocky outcrop and tearing his jacket. His heart pounded in his chest as he slid back into the gap in the rocks.

The Hind hovered overhead for several minutes, and Lee expected dogs and soldiers to descend on him at any moment and drag him out of hiding, but the chopper left, racing away along the beach before turning inland.

Lee lay there in the cold, shivering. His mind felt lethargic, sluggish. Hypothermia was setting in and he struggled to care. What would it matter if he died here? What would it matter if he slipped into an unconscious state never to awake again? He wanted to care, but his body was shutting down, telling him this was a better death, a kinder death, one free from pain.

Sunlight broke through the clouds, glistening off the wet rocks beyond the shadows.

Lee reached out his hand, resting his fingers on the sharp, jagged rocks, marveling at the warmth soaking into his wrist. The sun coaxed him out with the promise of life. Slowly, he crept forward until he was lying in the sun, sheltered from the wind. He wasn't sure how long he lay there, but his mind began to clear and his survival instincts took over.

He crept around the base of the cliff until he found a gully leading to the cliff top. The gentle slope led him away from the beach.

The sun had risen high in the sky.

The storm clouds had passed, revealing the azure blue dome of heaven.

Lee couldn't help but wonder if this was the day he'd die; such a beautiful day.

He looked around from the top of the hill, some three hundred feet above the raging sea. From what he could tell, the tides had swept him onto the headland of a vast peninsula. Various coves and inlets stretched out on either side, with a mountain range dominating the hinterland.

Crouching down, Lee used the waist high brush for cover, watching as a line of North Korean soldiers walked abreast of each other in the marsh behind the cove. They were moving away from him, sweeping the area, whacking the bushes with sticks, flushing out the game, except that their quarry was men. With rifles slung over their shoulders and a couple of dog handlers leading the way, the line of soldiers stretched for almost a kilometer inland. No more than a couple of feet separated any of them.

The helicopter returned, searching the ground in front of the advancing troops. Lee could see a couple of military jeeps parked on the road that wound into the hills. They had to be spotting for the troops, using binoculars to scan the marshland for any sign of movement.

Lee crept backwards, down to the edge of the cliff, staying out of sight. From there, he headed in the opposite direction, although that meant marching north, away from the border. He had no idea where he could go or what he should do. For now, surviving from one moment to the next was all he could think about.

The wind howled across the cliff and out over the ocean, which was good, as that would disperse his scent, carrying it out to sea, making it harder for the soldiers to pick up on his trail with the dogs.

Lee was worried about the helicopters. There were at least three of them. If they caught him in the open, the game would be over.

He struck up a light jog, avoiding the temptation to run madly, wanting to put some distance between himself and the search party but knowing he had to pace himself.

By mid afternoon, he estimated he'd covered roughly ten to fifteen kilometers. The helicopters had long since disappeared. Occasionally, he'd catch a glimpse of one climbing high above the plateau behind him, flying inland. That several helicopters had come and gone by the same route suggested their base was in that general direction. Hopefully, that's where the soldiers were from as well, he thought.

The windswept coast gave way to rugged bushland with little in the way of walking tracks, slowing his progress. His clothes were damp and began chafing against his neck, underarms and thighs.

Lee came across a clearing bathed in sunlight. He stopped, stripped down to his underwear and hung his clothes out to dry as he rested in the warmth of the sun. For a moment, lying there with his eyes closed, he could almost imagine he was safe.

The clearing was on the leeward side of a hill overlooking one of the numerous inlets along the rugged North Korean coast. With the sound of birds calling in the trees and the wind gently rustling the leaves, Lee drifted off to sleep, exhausted.

He woke, shivering.

Clouds covered the sky. The temperature had dropped. Another storm loomed overhead.

Lee dressed and continued on his way. Across the bay, he could see a fishing village. Several boats were docked against a rough wooden pier. Fishermen tended to their nets, stringing them up on poles and repairing any tears or holes in the fine mesh. Women toiled in fields beyond the village, gathering crops. Children played on the muddy ground, kicking around what looked like a soccer ball.

He had to escape. Crossing the most heavily guarded border in the world, with two armies separated by the largest minefield ever devised was suicide, but if he could steal a fishing boat in the dead of night he stood a chance. Having a plan encouraged him. For the first time since he washed up on shore, Lee felt as though he was going to make it home.

As he followed an animal trail he came across a muddy track winding its way up from the coast. Creeping through the undergrowth, he walked parallel to the track for a few minutes before hearing the neighing of a horse in distress.

Lee froze and hid behind a fallen tree for several minutes, waiting to see if someone was coming along the worn track.

The animal's cries were muffled by the wind rustling the leaves. The anguished neighing faded with the shifting breeze, and he wondered if the cries he could hear were his imagination toying with him.

The bush track had been cut into the steep hill in several places, and sections of the embankment had collapsed, blocking the path. Lee could see the slips were old, with horseshoe prints and cart tracks climbing over them. Further down the slope, fresh mud and rocks spread out, having slid down from above.

Lee could hear a woman's voice, crying out for help, barely audible over the ghostly howl of the coming storm.

Cautiously, he stepped down onto the track and peered over the edge. There, pinned beneath a shattered wooden cart, lay a young woman.

She saw him.

Instantly, she reached out with both hands, pleading for him to help her, and Lee found his mind flashing back to the young girl he'd rescued months before. This woman had the same look in her eyes; a plea for pity. He couldn't turn away. He had to do something, even if it meant risking capture. He couldn't leave this woman to die.

"Hold on," he called out, starting to negotiate the slippery terrain.

The cart must have slid off of the side, dragging the horse down with it. Clumps of dirt had been dug out of the side of the hill, marking where the horse had fought to stay upright. The mare lay on her side some thirty feet below the makeshift road. Her front leg must have broken in the fall. Blood pooled and clotted from a gash on the shoulder of this once proud horse.

Darkness descended.

Rain fell.

Thunder rumbled in the distance.

Lee grabbed at the thin tree trunks and branches as he slid down the steep, muddy bank, his boots sliding on the loose rocks and stones. He dug in his heels, slowing his descent. A small avalanche of pebbles and dirt followed behind him, covering his boots.

"Hang in there," he cried. "You're going to be fine."

As he came down beside her, he saw a look of terror sweep across her face.

"No," she cried.

"Hey, it's OK," he said, holding out his hands in a gesture to demonstrate he meant no harm. He realized his uniform, his South Korean accent, and the mud and grime covering his face must have terrified her.

She wriggled, trying to free herself, trying to pull away from him.

"I'm not going to hurt you."

There was so much misinformation, so much distrust, so many myths. She had probably never seen anyone from South Korea before, but she would have heard the propaganda, the lies intended to isolate the North Koreans from the outside world.

Lee wasn't one to cling to ideologies. Back in the 50s, merely attending a communist meeting in the south was enough to have someone lined up before a firing squad, even if they'd only gone there for the free rice. For decades, both sides had lived in fear of each other. Lee hated how his country had been cut in half by something as arbitrary as a line on a map. The North had been taught to fear outsiders, to fear the differences regardless of how irrational that was. To Lee, fear was the real enemy.

In that moment, he saw the realization in her eyes. She understood he just wanted to help. She must have seen the compassion of one human being for another, regardless of ideology. She took a deep breath, relaxing.

Lee crouched down, looking at the cart. Her leg was pinned under the rear wheel. He tried lifting the cart, but the horse was lying on the front corner, pinning the shattered wooden frame. The horse shifted its weight, but was in danger of dragging them all further down into the gully. Water poured down from above, running in a stream over the hind flanks of the crippled beast.

Looking around, Lee found an uprooted tree, a sapling not more than six feet in length. He wedged one end of the slender trunk beneath the cart and pried at the frame, trying to gain some leverage on a large rock. Slowly, the cart lifted and the woman pulled herself from beneath the wheel.

Lee was breathing hard has he dropped down beside her. She was grimacing in pain, but she forced out two words, "Thank you."

From the awkward angle her foot was at and the swelling below her knee, he knew she had broken her fibula bone, but the break hadn't broken through the skin, which was good. Hopefully she'd avoid infection.

"Please, don't be afraid. My name is John Lee. I am a captain with the South Korean Coast Guard."

The woman nodded. He'd expected her to introduce herself, but she didn't. He wasn't sure if she was shy, if she felt intimidated by someone who was ostensibly her enemy, or if this was some kind of cultural protocol between men and women in North Korea, but she looked away as though she were embarrassed. On thinking about it, he realized any South Korean would probably feel as confused and dazed if they were suddenly rescued by a North Korean soldier, so her response was understandable.

"Listen. Your leg is broken. I need to make a splint or I'm going to cause more damage when I move you. Do you understand?"

She nodded.

Lee had a knife with a saw-tooth back in his survival kit. He used the jagged blade to cut through two branches, trimming them to roughly a foot long. It was tiring work as each stroke spanned only a couple of inches. Even in the cold, sweat beaded on his forehead as he sawed at the wood. He spoke as he worked. Talking made him feel better.

"We crashed off the coast last night. My helicopter was damaged and sank. I thought I was dead. The last thing I remember was swimming through the wreckage, trying to get to the surface. I must have blacked out, but my life jacket kept my head above water and somehow I survived. I was washed ashore about fifteen kilometers south of here."

Lee should have been more guarded with his words, but he had to speak. Talking broke down the artificial barriers between them. He wondered how much she understood, wondering if she would recall his words to the North Korean soldiers and betray him, and yet he felt he had to trust her. From the moment he decided to help, he knew he'd have to trust her to do the right thing, just as he'd done the right thing in coming to her aid. What was greater? Loyalty to one's country, or kindness to a stranger?

"We were searching for someone," he continued. "A girl, a young girl."

"The girl from the stars?" she said, and he stopped sawing.

"Yes, the girl from the stars," he replied, his heart pounding in his chest.

Lee was surprised by the emotion stirred by her words. Her description of a girl from the stars took him off guard, but that had to be who the US Navy SEALs had come looking for. How did this woman know about her? What made her talk about this girl as coming from the stars? How was that even possible? He had so many questions, but he felt prudence was the best tactic and finished sawing at the wood without saying any more.

"I have seen her," the woman added, breaking the silence. "She was rescued by one of the fishermen in my village. I will take you to her."

Lee was surprised by the woman's openness. There was something in the tone of her voice, in the conviction with which she spoke, as though she had been bold enough to speak out against taboo. He nodded, saying, "Thank you."

Although what could he do to help this child? He had no idea who she was, where she was really from, or why she was so important to the Americans. And he had no way of rescuing the young girl, no way of rescuing himself. For now, however, that could wait.

"First, we need to get you out of this ravine," he said, kneeling beside her and placing sticks on either side of her leg. He took off his jacket and removed his shirt. Then, using his knife, he tore the shirt into long strips of cloth. "I'm sorry, but this is going to hurt."

He could see her gripping the roots of the tree she was leaning against. Her knuckles were white with anticipation. She nodded, and Lee got to work, trying to move as swiftly and deliberately as possible as he straightened her leg and bound sticks on either side. She cried out in pain, but held herself still.

"You're doing good," he said, as her head jerked to one side. Lee understood what she was doing. She wanted to pull away, to remove herself from the pain, but she had to know how important it was to keep her leg still. Her pent up anguish and pain manifested itself in tension in her arms, shoulders, neck and head, but she kept from moving her legs.

He hated seeing anyone in pain, much less being the one inflicting the pain, but this was necessary. With fourteen years in the Coast Guard, Lee had seen his fair share of grisly injuries, but they were normally tended to by the medics. Necessity demanded precision, to be cruel to be kind. She was gritting her teeth as he fed the strips of cloth under her leg and bound them to the sticks, tying them tight.

He finished and let her rest for a few minutes, knowing that the pain from setting her leg would take some time to subside. Already, there was considerable swelling around the leg.

"You were very brave," he said as rain dripped from his face.

"I bet you say that to all the girls," she replied, trying to joke with him. This was good, he knew. She looked pale and had begun shivering in the rain, and he was worried about the effect of shock and the impact of the temperature drop as night settled. To hear her joke relieved him and allowed him to gauge her resilience. She was tough.

Lee helped her stand, pulling her arm up over his shoulder. The horse had fallen silent, but it wasn't dead. It craned its head, looking over at them, perhaps sensing rescue. There was nothing to be done for the animal. If he had a sidearm, he would have been tempted to put a bullet in its brain, even if it would have attracted unwanted attention. In any case, there was nothing he could do for the suffering mare.

"Easy, girl. Easy," he said to the mare, speaking in a soft tone. If the horse became spooked and started lashing out with its legs the crushed remains of the wagon could come loose and slide further down the gully, taking them with it. The horse craned its neck, turning its head and looking back at him with the whites of its eyes exposed in terror.

"Easy," he whispered, sensing the fear running through the distressed animal.

The horse turned its head away, staring out into the darkness. He could see it was exhausted. The water running across its back and flanks must have been chilling its core. For a moment, Lee thought about dragging the woman out of the gully and then returning to put the poor animal out of its misery, but with a knife he'd only ensure the horse died in agony. The horse rested its head in the mud, resigned to its fate, and Lee decided hypothermia was the kindest death it could have.

Lee helped the woman up, keeping one eye on the mare.

The woman stood on her good leg, keeping the knee of her broken leg bent, trying to avoid touching the ground.

"I am Sun-Hee," she said, and Lee smiled, realizing how culturally difficult this was for her. With her arm around his neck for support, she seemed to struggle with being uncomfortably close to him. Such close proximity didn't bother him, but she appeared to be pushing through a mental barrier. He recognized that and wanted to show warmth and friendship in response.

"It's nice to meet you, Sun-Hee, although I wish it were under different circumstances."

"Me too."

It took over an hour to climb out of the gorge as night fell. Lee picked his way up the side of the slope, moving at an angle. He dragged Sun-Hee with him, helping her from one tree to the next, resting often. Occasionally, she'd cry out in pain as her broken leg knocked against the ground or caught on a rock. Her screams pierced the quiet of night, but there was no reply. No one was looking for her.

"What were you doing out here in the forest?" he asked as they staggered out onto the darkened track.

"I was returning from the markets in Koh-Soh. I live with my grandfather, a fisherman in the village below."

"Yes, I saw the village from the ridge," Lee replied, relishing how their conversation had warmed.

With the rain falling in a drizzle, they hobbled down the muddy track toward the distant village.

Mario's

"Dude, you scored! Come on. Tell me. Who is she?"

Mitchell wasn't subtle at the best of times, thought Jason. With his hair buzzed close to the scalp on the sides and back of his head and an excessive amount of hair gel sticking up the remaining crop on top, Jason imagined Mitchell's hair style came from sticking his fingers in an electrical socket. He kept that thought to himself.

"Her name's Lily," he replied.

Ordinarily, Jason wasn't one to get caught up with infatuations, but Lily had an uncanny effect on him. Just the mention of her name was a delight, which was a strange sensation for someone who normally kept himself aloof and saw relationships as a luxury rather than a necessity.

Earlier that morning, Jason had taken Lily's photo with his smart phone and printed the image on paper, making a flyer with his cellphone number on it. He used tape to stick several copies to the traffic lights on the corners, as that was the only way he was going to get Lily away from the intersection and over to Mario's Diner for breakfast. Even then, she had asked if she could hold onto his phone as she didn't want to risk missing the call.

Jason and Lily had met up with Mitchell and his girlfriend Helena outside Mario's. Mitchell hadn't stopped grinning. He'd been waiting to drop that pearl on Jason as soon as the girls were out of earshot.

Jason and Mitchell slid into a booth overlooking Central Park while Helena and Lily went to the bathroom. Helena had insisted on having Lily come with her, and Jason figured she was grilling Lily on all the juicy details of what she imagined had gone on last night. There was nothing, of course. Lily had sat there staring out the window into the night as Jason had drifted off to sleep. He'd woken a couple of times, which was unusual, but each time he'd seen her still sitting there staring out into the night. When he awoke with the dawn, Lily looked like she hadn't moved all night. Helena wouldn't believe a word of it.

"How did you meet her?" Mitchell asked. "How long have you guys been going out? And how the hell did you keep her secret from me?"

Jason opened his pill case and took a swig of water, swallowing a red capsule followed by two dull blue tablets. He suffered from a rare genetic disorder known as Cander's Syndrome and needed to watch his meds to avoid ending up in the hospital. He slipped the case in his pocket as Mitchell continued.

"Where is she from?"

Jason wasn't sure which question he was supposed to answer first, but he decided the last one was the simplest.

"She's Korean, from some place called Sun-Way-Do."

"Sunwi-do," Mitchell replied. "You're fucking kidding me!"

Jason shrugged. He wasn't sure why Mitchell was so excited.

"Dude," Mitchell said, opening his backpack and pulling out his tablet computer. "That's the peninsula from the Incheon Incident. Sunwi-do is in North Korea."

"Isn't Incheon in South Korea, just outside of Seoul?" Jason asked, knowing he was going to regret asking.

Mitchell switched on the tablet, saying, "It's called the Incheon incident because that's where the rescue helicopter was based, but if you want to be technical about it, it's the Yellow Sea incident, although that's confusing as well, as the Chinese weren't involved."

"Weekly World News? Seriously?" Jason said, catching a glimpse of several poorly photo-shopped images as Mitchell opened an application and flicked through virtual pages.

There was an image of a man with three heads, or was that three people with one body? Another shot showed a classic, bug-eyed, hairless alien with a bulbous head sitting behind the President's desk in the Oval Office. In another, UFOs sat outside the departure gate of some anonymous midwest airport.

"This stuff is gold!" Mitchell said, overacting, knowing he was goading Jason. "It's serious investigative journalism."

Jason shook his head, trying not to laugh.

As Mitchell flicked through the pages, Jason spotted an image of a hairy man running through a child's playground.

"Hey, that's a monkey suit," Jason cried, but Mitchell kept running his finger back and forth over the glass display, turning pages.

"Oh," Mitchell replied. "You gotta separate the wheat from the chaff, but there's some great stuff in here. Most of this stuff has been classified top secret for decades!"

"Yeah," Jason replied dryly, pretending to agree with him. "It's real Pulitzer Prize material."

Mitchell turned to a page near the back of the virtual newspaper and pointed at a grainy picture. He slapped his finger on the screen, exclaiming in triumph.

"There!"

From what Jason could make out, the image showed someone pulling a young child from the ocean into a rickety old fishing boat. There was something beneath the water directly below the boat, but it was impossible to make out what the object was. He reached over and touched the glass screen, pinching with his fingers and enlarging the image.

Lights appeared to glow from beneath the waves, but he thought they looked like they'd been added to the photograph.

Jason read the caption beneath the photo.

"Two decades have passed since the Incheon Incident, when a UFO crashed into the sea off the coast of North Korea. The only known survivor of this extraterrestrial contact was a young girl of three or four, rescued from the ocean by North Korean fishermen as the UFO took on water and sank."

"I don't see what this proves," Jason said.

Mitchell turned to another virtual page, crying, "Look at that!"

He pointed at an image of a UFO flying past the Empire State building. Apart from the appalling lack of chromatic balance, Jason didn't see anything noteworthy in the picture.

"It's the same UFO," Mitchell announced.

"It's the same poor photoshop skills," Jason conceded. He pretended to peer closely at the screen, taking the computer tablet from Mitchell and holding absurdly close to his face until the glass touched his nose. He squinted, adding, "Oh, yeah. That's definitely been doctored by the same guy!"

Mitchell laughed as Jason gently placed the tablet back on the table.

Jason loved Mitchell like a brother, ever since they'd met during their first year at college, but his gullibility for the outlandishly absurd was astonishing to Jason's rational mind.

Mitchell said, "Look at the facts: twenty years ago, a UFO crashes and a young girl survives. Today, you meet a roughly twenty year old woman from the same province. What are the odds that they are one and the same person?"

Jason thought about it for a second and said, "Zero. One's fictitious, the other's real. There's no chance they're one and the same person."

"Come on," Mitchell pleaded. "Think about it. All life on Earth follows circadian rhythms, with a day/night wake/rest cycle, but by your own admission little old Lily sat up all night. How do you explain that?"

"Two words," Jason said, watching as Helena and Lily walked over to join them. "Jet lag."

Lily smiled. She slid around into the booth and sat next to him. For someone who had dropped into his world barely a day ago, having her beside him felt both comforting and refreshing. Jason couldn't express why, but it felt natural to be with her, as though they belonged together. He wasn't one for the old cliché of love at first sight, but Lily was different from any other girl he'd ever met. She seemed almost disinterested in a physical relationship, and he found that strangely appealing. Perhaps it was the lack of expectation that disarmed him, the absence of any pressure was welcome. Rather than trying to make something happen between them, it felt like it had already happened years ago.

Was this déjà vu, he wondered? Jason wasn't one to buy into superstitions. He preferred to think of the two of them as somehow complementary at a hormonal level. Yes, he thought, compatible chemistry, that was a better explanation.

"Are you guys ready to order?" a waitress asked, standing there with her plastic stylus poised above a digital tablet ready to take their order.

"Blueberry pancakes," Jason said.

"I'll have the deluxe omelet," Helena said.

"Trucker's breakfast," Mitchell said.

Lily looked overwhelmed by the choices on the menu. Each meal had a glossy, color image associated with it, and Jason could see her eyes darting around the menu without settling on anything.

"What do you normally have for breakfast in Korea?" he asked.

"Rice."

"And lunch?" Mitchell asked.

"Rice."

"And dinner?" Helena asked.

"Fish … With rice."

"Whatever you do," Helena said, addressing the waitress, "do not give this girl any rice."

Lily laughed.

Helena turned to her, saying, "You can have anything on here you want."

That didn't help, Jason noted.

Finally, Lily said, "I'll have what he's having," pointing at Jason.

The waitress wandered off.

Mitchell leaned across the table, addressing Lily as he said, "So, what do you remember from your childhood? Say, when you were about three or four?"

Jason kicked him beneath the table.

Lily looked confused.

"Don't worry about him," Helena said. "Mitch was born with his foot in his mouth. That's what I love about him."

Lily blushed, and Jason wondered what was running through her mind. Here she was, thousands of miles from home, in a strange culture, surrounded by three Americans she didn't know, unable to find her father. The poor girl must have been terrified, but she kept a brave face.

"You are all very kind," she said. "I am lucky to have found you."

Helena spoke in a serious tone, saying, "You need to be careful, Lily. New York is a dangerous place for a girl on her own."

"Yeah," Mitchell added, kicking Jason's feet. "You never know what weirdos you'll meet."

Jason smiled, shaking his head as Mitchell laughed.

Lily picked up on their banter and rested her hand on Jason's knee, saying, "Jason is a gentleman. I feel safe with him."

Jason turned his head slightly to one side and grinned at Mitchell. Mitch would know precisely the retort Jason wanted to utter to him at that point, something along the lines of, 'Take that, *Bitch!*' Mitchell smiled knowingly.

Lily pointed at the computer tablet lying on the table and asked, "What's in the news?"

"The news?" Mitchell replied, sounding innocent. "Oh, funny you should ask."

"Mitch, Honey," Helena said, resting her hand on his forearm.

Jason jumped in with, "Mitch thinks New York is about to be invaded by aliens."

"Really?" Lily asked, and Jason saw some of the naiveté he'd noted the night before. She seemed intelligent, but was easily led.

The waitress arrived carrying all four plates. She set them down and left.

"The odds are against it," Jason said, pouring maple syrup over his pancakes. Lily copied him.

"Space is absurdly large," he added, picking up a tiny speck of dust between his fingers and holding it up, examining it in the morning light, somewhat lost in thought. "If this was the sun ... Well, actually, even this is a bit too big. If our sun was a single blood cell, visible only under a microscope, then our galaxy, the Milky Way, would be the size of the Continental US."

"And the nearest star?" Lily asked.

Jason looked out the window of the restaurant and across the street at Central Park. From their first floor booth, he could see over the tops of the trees. There were some kids throwing a Frisbee in an open grassy patch by the lake.

"About there," he replied, pointing at them. "Roughly two hundred yards away, perhaps a little more. And it too would be no more than a microscopic speck of dust."

"What about Voyager?" Mitchell asked. "It's left the solar system and is headed toward the stars, right?"

"Well, yes and no," Jason replied. "It all depends on how you define the solar system."

Jason pulled a quarter out and put it on the table in front of him, with his finger resting in the middle of the coin.

"If the sun was the size of a blood cell, most of the planets, including Earth, would orbit inside this quarter. Voyager would be just marginally beyond our quarter. Voyager is beyond the most distant, recognized planet, and well beyond the heliopause, where solar winds buffet against interstellar space, but it's not really the edge of our solar system, not if you consider the solar system as the system directly affected by the sun."

Jason pointed across the street at a man walking his dog through the park, just visible through the trees. He'd only just walked his beagle across the street.

"He's probably at about the right distance. Surrounding our sun almost a light year away is the Oort cloud containing billions, if not trillions of comets all held loosely in check by the sun's gravity, just waiting to start their long slow fall in toward the inner solar system and put on a show. That's the real edge of the solar system, at least from a gravitational perspective."

Lily had stopped eating. She sat there with her elbows on the table, her head resting on her hands, listening with rapt attention.

"Space is mind-bogglingly huge. There's a whole lot of nothing out there. Imagine New York City as an empty void. You'd have maybe a couple of hundred microscopic specks of dust scattered around as stars. Perhaps one of them would be on top of the Empire State Building, another might be on the Statue of Liberty, and so on. But there would only be a couple of hundred tiny specks broadly scattered around the place.

"If the Milky Way were the size of the Continental US, there would be a massive black hole at the center, just outside of Lebanon, Kansas, up by the border with Nebraska. But it too would be no larger than a few grains of sand. As for us, the tiny speck we call the sun would probably be in St. Louis."

"I like St. Louis," Helena said, grinning as she sipped some coffee.

"Black holes in Kansas!" Mitchell cried. "Sounds like you've been reading News of the World."

Jason laughed, saying, "There's just too much empty space out there. Interstellar travel is impractical. It will take Voyager 30,000 years just to reach the Oort cloud, let alone any of the stars. Thirty to forty thousand years ago, Homo sapiens had just reached Europe and discovered Neanderthals and Cro-Magnon man. Imagine where we will be in thirty thousand years time!

"One day we'll travel to the stars, and that will be the greatest act of exploration ever undertaken, but make no mistake about it, we're traversing an arid desert, a desolate Arctic wilderness, an oxygen-starved mountain far more dangerous and inhospitable than Everest. The distances involved and the difficulty of maintaining life in outer space should not be underestimated."

Helena seemed more interested than Mitchell, saying, "But we've been traveling into space for decades. We've been to the Moon. We've got a space station."

"Honestly," Jason replied. "That's like playing in a duck pond, never being more than an arm's length from shore. If space travel was swimming, we'd be comfortable in a kiddie pool. Getting to the Moon would be like swimming a few lengths in an Olympic size pool, while traveling to Mars compares to swimming from Cuba to Florida. Going to another star, well, now you're taking on a distance that makes crossing the Pacific look like your kiddie pool."

Mitchell disagreed, saying, "And just because we haven't done it, you think no one can? That makes no sense. There's no reason to think aliens would be at the same technological level as us. They could be millions of years more advanced."

"Or billions of years behind us," Jason added.

"So you don't believe in aliens?" Lily asked.

"Oh, it's not that I don't think there are aliens. I just don't think they're surreptitiously visiting Earth every couple of years to probe the rectums of a select few rednecks.

"That life exists in outer space is undeniable. Just look at us. We're in outer space and we're alive. Sounds strange to consider, I know, but our perspective is so narrow and prejudiced toward seeing Earth as unique. We naturally assume our Earth-centric view of the universe is reality, as though the Sun, Moon and stars really do revolve around us, but they don't. Copernicus and Galileo proved that over five hundred years ago, but in practice it's very hard not to think of sunrise and sunset. Try picturing Earth-turn instead. You'll give yourself a migraine!"

"You're such a geek," Helena said. "Only you could take a perfectly romantic notion like a sunset and turn it into something weird."

Jason laughed, saying, "Well, reality is weird, and that's the problem: it's our notions that are distorted, not reality."

Helena just shook her head as she finished her breakfast. "Listen," she said, checking the time on her phone. "I don't know what you boys are up to today, but how about I take Lily with me. We can't have her running around the city in your baggy clothes. I've got some spare clothes I can give her."

"I've got plenty of spare clothes," Jason said, feeling a little affronted by Helena assuming she could lay claim to Lily.

"Have you got any spare bras?" Helena asked, raising an eyebrow.

"Ah, no."

"I didn't think so."

Jason couldn't help but smile. Helena liked to be right. She got up, motioning for Lily to follow.

Lily looked a little bewildered. She glanced at Jason so he said, "Have fun."

"But what about your phone?" Lily asked, holding it out in front of her. "What about my father?"

"I'll call Helena if I hear anything," Jason replied, taking the phone gently from her.

"We'll let you boys pick up the tab," Helena said, taking Lily's arm and winking at them as they left.

"She's a wild one," Mitchell said, but it took Jason a moment to realize Mitchell was talking about Helena not Lily, and that surprised him, exposing how much he'd taken a shine to Lily.

"Dude," Mitchell continued, seemingly reading his mind, "you realize this can't go on, right?"

"Huh?" Jason said, lost in thought for a moment. Sitting there in the booth, he could see the girls outside waiting at the lights, getting ready to cross the street.

"She's going to find her dad, and then she'll be out of here."

"Yeah, I know."

Jason was doodling, drawing equations and ratios on a napkin, barely aware his mind was running through a physics calculation. Dark strokes outlined various Greek letters and scientific notation. He'd written one equation several different ways, reversing and inverting portions of the equation but always arriving at the same result.

"You are such a weirdo," Mitchell said, pointing at his scribbled notation. "When most people are distracted, they bite their nails, they don't reframe Schrodinger's equations."

Jason laughed, "Yeah, funny one, that. Just the way my mind works, I guess. I find math soothing."

"Oh, it's a cure for insomnia," Mitchell added, pretending to agree. "So, Mr. Good Samaritan, what are you going to do when she leaves you?"

"There's nothing between us," Jason confessed, "Just a passing fascination, I guess. But if she's still around tonight, I thought we'd go to the fireworks in the park."

"You and a couple of hundred thousand other people," Mitchell quipped. That was the thing about New York, even when it seemed empty over a long weekend, there were still millions of people around. Empty was a relative term in New York.

Down at the intersection, Helena turned and pointed, directing Lily's gaze up to the second floor window where the two young men were seated. Lily waved. She had one hand on her purse with the strap sitting comfortably over her shoulder. To anyone else, it would seem perfectly rational for a young woman to want to keep her purse secure, but Jason knew otherwise.

"It's empty, you know," Jason said, his mind still dwelling on that fact.

"What is?" Mitchell asked, sipping some coffee.

"Her purse. There's no money, no passport, no credit cards, no ID, no names and addresses, nothing."

"You looked?"

"I looked," Jason confessed.

"Dawg," Mitchell replied. "I'm telling you, she's about the right age to have been plucked out of the water by those fishermen."

Jason shook his head. "You're an idiot," he said affectionately, unable to suppress the grin on his face.

"You laugh, but I'm telling you, this shit is real. I saw lights over Manhattan last night."

"What would an alien be doing in my apartment?" Jason asked, humoring him. "Why would an alien come all this way to sneak around disguised as a young asian woman?"

"I don't know," Mitchell replied. "Maybe it's like those nature documentaries. You know, where they film animals in the wild. Yeah, that's it, they're doing a special on the mating habits of Homo sapiens and are looking for some live footage."

"You really are an idiot," Jason repeated, finishing his coffee.

Mitchell put on his best English accent, impersonating Sir David Attenborough as he said, "The mating call of the wild physics student can be heard for miles, echoing through the concrete jungle."

Jason punched him playfully on the shoulder, saying, "Let's get out of here."

But Mitchell wasn't finished. He kept his voice in a style that could only be described as BBC English, giving his words a crisp, clipped tone as he added, "The call of the Asian American is distinctly different from that of the African or European American, earning these fascinating creatures the title of the Great Warbling Bed Thrasher."

Jason laughed.

Sunny

Night had fallen in North Korea.

Lee staggered in the rain.

Blisters had formed on the sides of his feet where his boots had rubbed the skin raw. The pain caused him to hobble, but he had to push on.

Rocks and pebbles crunched under his stiff rubber soles.

Torrential rain blurred his vision, running down over his forehead, across his eyes and down his cheeks. Blinking and squinting, he raised his hand to shelter his eyes from the rain. The rain sounded like a jet engine warming up, thrashing the leaves, splashing in puddles, and slapping at his shoulders.

The young North Korean woman slipped on the muddy track so Lee braced her against himself, catching her before she fell. Although her arm was draped over his shoulder, her body felt limp.

"I can't do this," Sun-Hee said as Lee struggled to keep her from slipping to her knees. "I can't go on."

She was shivering. Her clothes were soaked. Rain ran down her face like tears. Her straggly black hair was as wild as the darkened tangle of trees and vines around them.

A stream ran down one side of the track, cutting its way into the trail, curling around rocks and over boulders, washing away sections of the track. The rain pounded the leaves of the trees hanging over the path.

In the darkness, Lee couldn't see more than a couple of meters. The trail seemed as though it would never end.

"Please," she whimpered. "It is too much. I must rest. Let me rest."

If they stopped, she would die from hypothermia, Lee was sure of it. He had to get her to the village, but the look in her eyes pleaded for mercy.

A thicket of bushes provided some relief from the rain.

Lee helped Sun-Hee sit on a gnarled root beneath an old tree holding the embankment together. He tried to get her out of the worst of the weather, but the rain dripped relentlessly upon them, washing over his eyes and cheeks, running down his neck.

He stepped back, arching his head toward the sky and allowing the rain to wash over his closed eyes and fall into his mouth. After a few seconds, he cupped his hands, catching what rain he could and drinking, trying to quench his thirst.

"You should leave me," she said.

Lee put his hands gently on either side of her head as he crouched before her, looking deep with her dark eyes as he spoke.

"Hey, it's going to be OK. You'll get through this. In the weeks and months ahead, all this will seem like a bad dream. A year from now, you'll laugh as you tell this story to your friends and family, relaxing around the warmth of a fire."

Sun-Hee smiled, but her smile was forced. Lee couldn't be sure, but he thought she was crying. Her tears mingled with the rain. Her blank stare told him she had given up. She couldn't go on.

It wasn't until he pulled his hands away from the side of her hair that he realized she was bleeding from a head wound. She must have taken a knock to the back of the head when she'd fallen from the track. In the darkness, he hadn't noticed before now. Gently, Lee reached around, his fingers touching gingerly at her matted hair. Sun-Hee winced in pain.

"I feel ... I feel sick."

The muscles in her neck felt weak. Her shoulders sagged.

"Hey," Lee said. "Stay with me. Think of your grandfather. Think about seeing him again. Think about the sunshine. Think about a warm summer's day. We're going to make it."

Lee pulled her to her feet, determined to continue on, but it was as though he was dragging a sack of coal. She had no strength with which to stand. Even with a broken leg, she seemed barely aware of the world around her.

Sun-Hee collapsed in his arms, her legs dragging on the ground behind her.

Lee crouched, placing both arms under her frail body. He lifted her up, holding her in a cradle before him.

"This night will end," he said softly. "There is always a dawn. There is always a new day ahead."

Somehow, their fates seemed entwined, and he felt as though he were destined to save her. Lee had never been fatalistic, had never been into horoscopes or fortune tellers, and would have ordinarily dismissed such a notion as bogus, but on that dark, cold night he felt vulnerable. Perhaps it was his own impending demise he felt so acutely. Having watched one of the SEALs being murdered on the beach, he knew his own prospects of survival were next to nil.

Lee had been through evade and escape scenarios and one thing they made very clear was that the chances of escape were like winning the lottery. In the exercises, everyone got caught. It didn't matter how fit you were, how smart you thought you were or how cunning you could be, nobody escaped.

Perhaps saving Sun-Hee would make up for his loss. Perhaps that's why he felt so drawn to help her. If he couldn't survive, maybe she could and in that he'd find some hollow victory.

"My grandfather," she mumbled. "Not my brother ... Don't let my brother see you."

She was deteriorating quickly, becoming delirious. Lee had seen this before on too many occasions, the cumulative effect of shock and the onset of hypothermia. The solution was always the same: get the patient warm and dry. He had to get her to that village.

Her head rolled to one side as he staggered back onto the track and continued down the hill, focusing on one step at a time. His ankles felt as though they had lead weights strapped around them. His boots scuffed at the loose stones as he stumbled along.

"Talk to me," he said. "Tell me, how I will know your grandfather? Where does he live in the village?"

It didn't really matter, and he knew that. He could leave her with any of the villagers and they'd care for her and find the old man, but he wanted to keep her talking, to keep her conscious.

Sun-Hee rested one hand at the nape of his neck, touching him gently. Her fingers were cold, but that she could touch him filled him with hope. Such tenderness was overwhelming to a man on the run, fighting for his life. With all he'd gone through, surviving both the crash and the raging sea, seeing his fellow man brutally murdered, running for his life and the physical exhaustion of a forced march over the best part of thirty kilometers, enduring the cold and wet, after all this, her touch was incongruous, disarming. Feeling her soft touch spoke to him of compassion, a reminder that beyond the calloused enmity of two nations on the verge of war, humanity was only ever one isolated soul reaching out to another.

"Look for the diesel tank ... He lives by the tank."

"That's good," he said. "And you, tell me about yourself."

"I ..." But that was all she could manage.

Lee had to keep talking. Already, the muscles in his arms were burning under her weight. It wasn't that she was overly heavy, but that he had her in front of him, forcing him to lean backwards slightly to distribute the weight and maintain his center of gravity. If he favored one side and then another, he found he could alternate the stress on his arms, giving them a brief sense of relief.

Talking helped Lee to shuffle on down the mountain, pushing through his own exhaustion.

"What do you do in the hinterland? Do you trade seafood with the farmers?"

Sun-Hee didn't reply. Her head lolled to one side, falling limp. The rain eased, softly tapping at her bare neck, running beneath her wet clothes.

"Oh, stay with me," he said, tears running down his cheeks. Normally, Lee kept himself distant from any emotional attachments with strangers in distress. His ingrained professionalism allowed him to be detached, almost as though he were interacting with a video game rather than a real person in real life. Yet when it came to Sun-Hee, he couldn't help but feel as though their fates were somehow intertwined, as though it was his life hanging in the balance, not hers.

Pebbles crunched beneath his boots. The sound of the rain faded, signaling that the heart of the storm had passed.

"I was raised in the city," he said, knowing she couldn't hear him, but needing to talk. "We rarely ever went into the countryside. Why would we? We had everything we needed. Malls, movies, nightclubs. And the food, oh, you'd love the food: cold soup noodles and kim bap, almost like sushi, spicy rice cakes, oxtail soup and pig's feet, oh, but it's the deep fried chicken that is the best."

Those words and the memories they brought carried him to another place, another time. Physically, he was exhausted, trudging through the mud, dragging one foot after the other. Mentally, Lee was at home in Seoul, going out for a bite to eat with friends. He could picture the bench in the kitchen beside the back door of his apartment.

In his thoughts, Lee grabbed his wallet and keys, slipping them into his jacket as he opened the door, making sure he thumbed the lock as he stepped through the doorway, listening as the lock clicked in place behind him. Garbage bags lined the alleyway, but neither the sight nor the smell bothered him. His eyes saw beyond the shadows, seeing the flickering neon lights in the distance. A truck roared past the end of the alley. There was the sound of a siren in the distance. A woman's voice laughed from somewhere upstairs, while a feral cat skittered away as his shoes splashed in a puddle.

Lee's boot caught on a loose rock, causing him to stumble and twist his ankle. He avoided a sprain, but the stabbing pain dragged him back to the present. His legs faltered. With each step, he fought not to slip and fall.

Slowly, the ground leveled out. The trail no longer wound back and forth, opening out onto a crooked path. Mud gave way to coarse gravel. The forest surrendered to freshly plowed fields surrounding the village. In the darkness, they looked lifeless and inhospitable, as though they were a source of death rather than life.

Lee felt his thighs cramping, but he pushed on. He desperately wanted to be back in Seoul. In a strange way, the darkened village represented those glittering lights in his mind. He wondered if he'd ever see those bright lights again.

"I'll take you to Seoul one day and show you where I was raised. The air is not as crisp. The city is dirty, and the noise can be overwhelming, but for me, it's home.

"Oh, the lights. You'll love the lights. Everyone does, the first time they see them. Sure, you've got the beauty of the stars out here in the country, but our neon constellations are a sight to behold: a galaxy of man-made stars. They're like rainbows, dazzling the eye."

In his delirious state, he imagined a conversation with her. He felt as though he were replying to her as she questioned if anything could be as beautiful as the North Korean sky on a clear night or a field of wildflowers in the spring.

"Flowers?" he mumbled. "Flowers may look pretty for a day, but their beauty fades. City lights have no season. And the surge of the people. Ha, you'll probably find it all a bit too much at first, but I love the bustle, I love the noise, the sense of purpose everyone has, whether they're going to or from work, heading out to the mall or off to the theatre. There's a symphony of humanity. Seoul never sleeps."

Thin strands of light broke through from the shutters of the huts in the village.

A dog barked, but no one seemed to care.

Oxen stood in the fields, silently enduring the drizzling rain.

Lee fought to change his hold on Sun-Hee, wanting to give his arms some relief. She was completely limp. Her arm swung down as he shifted his hands and he almost dropped her as her weight shifted. Clutching at her frail body, he pushed on.

The diesel tank was easy to spot as it was mounted on a raised platform visible above the rooftops. The village must have used gravity feed instead of a pump when refueling tractors and fishing boats. The tank was next to the pier and he saw that boats could be refueled with ease. Yet the fishing boats at rest by the dock all had masts with wrapped sails tightly bound against the storm. Lee wondered if the tank had held any diesel in years.

Flecks of paint peeled off the aging tank. Spots of rust marred its legs. Steel rungs ran up one of the legs to a hatch on top. A wooden hut sagged beside the tank, its roof bowed with age. Smoke rose from the chimney. Light glinted out around the cabin's window shutters.

Stumbling, Lee stepped up onto the porch of the hut. The wind blew the rain into his back. There was no handle on the door, no lock, just a rough wooden bolt set into the vertical wooden planks. Lifting the bolt and shifting it to one side would be easy. From there, the wind would probably blow the door open, but then reality struck him.

Up until this point, no one knew he was this far north. All the searches he'd seen by North Korean troops had been to the south. He was about to expose himself to the villagers, and that thought struck him like a bolt of lightning, sobering him.

This was one of the amateur mistakes they talked about in his evade and escape training: never trust the locals, their loyalty will always be with the defenders. He was risking detection by walking through the village, as any boot prints not washed away by the rain would reveal the presence of a stranger.

He should leave her.

Perhaps, he thought, he could lie her on the porch, knock on the door and run. No, just put her down and run. He needed to get out of the village before being spotted. Someone would find her in the morning. Would she last till morning?

Lee wondered what the grandfather would do. Would he betray him to the authorities? Perhaps he would help him? It was wishful thinking, but Lee wasn't thinking straight. He was tired, hungry. Would the old man turn a blind eye? Lee needed food. He needed shelter. He needed to rest. Stealing a boat sounded like a good idea until he was down beside the dock, looking at the fishing boats with their rigging and their old-fashioned sails. Could he sail single-handed? What if they removed the rudder or locked the wheel at the helm overnight? Lee felt his mind struggling with the unknowns. What had seemed like a clear idea on the ridge, now felt like a disaster.

Standing there, he couldn't think clearly. He was bitterly cold. His body ached. He could smell the distinct aroma of a stew wafting through the air. Temptation was the enemy.

There were voices inside the hut. Compassion must prevail, he thought. He'd saved Sun-Hee's life. That had to count.

Lee fumbled with the wooden bolt, reaching blindly for it as he held Sun-Hee in his arms.

The door swung open and he was met with a rush of warm air. The dim glow of a fire flickered within the cabin. Lee staggered in, unsure what to say. An old man sat at one end of a rough hewn wooden table next to a young man facing the door. A gas lantern rested on the table, casting long shadows around the hut. A series of bunks had been built onto one wall, maximizing the space in the one room hut. Ragged curtains hung to one side, sectioning off part of the cabin.

At first, Lee didn't realize that the young man sitting next to Sun-Hee's grandfather was dressed in a uniform, but his eyes picked out the old bolt action rifle leaning against the wall by the rear door, barely a couple of feet from the soldier.

Silence descended on the hut.

The drab olive green lapels, red shoulder boards made from coarse wool, and polished brass buttons looked out of place inside the rundown cottage.

Lee froze.

He locked eyes with the young soldier, not sure what would happen next. He stood there with Sun-Hee in his arms. Water dripped onto the floor. The old man pushed away from the table and the legs of his chair scraped on the rough wooden floor.

"Sunny," the aging man said softly, using a term of endearment for his granddaughter, or perhaps it was that Lee mistook his accent and this was how he pronounced Sun-Hee.

The grandfather hobbled to the door, his frame bent from arthritis. Although he was balding, with thin wisps of grey hair clinging to the side of his head, his eyebrows were dark and bushy. The leathery skin on his arms and hands looked cracked and worn. He reached out for Sun-Hee, saying, "My poor Sunny. What happened to you?"

Lee stepped forward, turning toward the bunks. He tried to crouch, but fell awkwardly to one knee as he placed her on the lumpy cotton mattress. There were no sheets, no pillows. The mattress stank of piss and sweat, but it was dry. Sun-Hee moaned. As gently as he could, Lee pulled his arms away, laying her on her side so her broken leg lay on top of her good leg. His crude splint had held, but the swelling and bruising on her lower leg looked severe.

Her eyes flickered.

The old man rested his hand gently on her forehead.

"Oh, my dear Sunny."

Lee held onto the side of the bunk as he got to his shaky feet. Spasms rippled through his lower back muscles, causing him to grimace.

The soldier hadn't moved. He had to be the brother. Lee could see the young man's hands trembling but he kept them in sight on the table. There must have been some significance in keeping his hands in sight, Lee considered, as it seemed to take all his will power to maintain that posture. Lee didn't understand why. Perhaps the soldier had a sidearm and would have grabbed it given the chance. Perhaps all he had was a knife and he mistook the flare gun strapped to Lee's thigh as a pistol and didn't want to force a mismatched confrontation.

The young man clenched his fists. His lips quivered as though he wanted to say something but was holding himself back to keep from saying the wrong thing.

Lee tried to understand how this looked from the perspective of a young North Korean soldier hellbent on destroying the southern devils. He had to know Lee meant Sun-Hee no harm, but his mind must have been running through a myriad of possibilities as to how she had been injured and whether Lee was involved.

Lee had to say something, to explain what had happened.

"The wagon fell into a gully and her leg was broken. I found her like that."

The old man lifted the lantern from the table, and the shadows seemed to come alive. He ignored the soldier sitting there and brought the lantern over to get a better look at Sun-Hee's leg. She was mumbling something, but Lee couldn't make out the words.

"I," Lee continued, stuttering. "I had to help."

The young soldier turned his head slowly to one side, eyeing the rifle out of the corner of his eye. Lee wondered who would get there first. The soldier was closer, but Lee could have got to him before he brought the weapon to bear.

Lee didn't dare make any sudden moves, not wanting to provoke a violent response. He held his hands out in a gesture for the young soldier to stay calm. In the cold, Lee could see sweat beading on the soldier's forehead. He understood the conflict in the young man's mind. The contradiction he saw before him must have shaken his foundation. Everything he'd been told about the southern devils would have been called into question when Lee staggered through that door holding his sister. Now his sister was safe and the devil stood before him, what would he do?

"Don't," Sun-Hee whispered, and her whisper carried through the empty wooden hut. Lee had no doubt Sun-Hee meant well, but he doubted her brother could turn his back on his country.

Lee stepped backwards, inching toward the door. He could feel the wind gusting around his legs, the rain driven against his lower back.

There were voices outside, boisterous and loud, but they weren't behind Lee, they were coming from somewhere beyond the back door of the hut, behind the soldier.

The young man's dark eyes betrayed what was about to happen. Lee understood before the back door opened: this young soldier was not alone. The soldier's trembling fists told Lee he should run, that he should flee while he could, that the brother had to come after him but that he would give Lee a head start.

Deep down, Lee knew there could never be any other outcome. The young soldier could never let him go, but it seemed he would spare his grandfather and sister from seeing Lee killed in cold blood in front of them.

Lee had to run.

Sun-Hee reached out her arm toward Lee, distracting him for a moment. He could see the pity in her eyes, but a woman's pity could not save him, not in North Korea.

The rear door opened and two more soldiers walked into the hut. They must have been outside smoking as one of them stubbed out a cigarette on a metal case, saving the stub. With rifles slung over their shoulders, they joked with each other, smiling and laughing. Their features froze as they locked eyes with him.

Lee wanted to run, but his legs wouldn't move. He thought about running, but the time lag between that thought and the muscular response in his legs felt like an eternity. The soldiers swung their rifles down from their shoulders, dropping their cigarettes and yelling as they brought their guns to bear on him.

Lee's boots scraped on the wooden floor. Turning, he slipped, falling against the door jamb. With his hands, he grasped at the frame, pulling himself out onto the wet porch.

"Halt!"

Lee swung his arms and began pumping his legs as he bolted into the drizzle.

Water splashed beneath his boots as he ran through puddles.

The mud caked on his boots slowed his pace, acting like lead weights tied around his ankles.

He could hear someone behind him, pounding across the porch, their heavy boots thumping on the old wood.

He drove his legs, scrambling across the muddy gravel outside the hut.

The rattle of a diesel engine starting up cut through the quiet of the night. Headlights blinded him.

He turned, darting between two huts.

Voices screamed behind him. Coming around the corner of the rickety old hut, he lost his footing and slipped, falling sideways in the mud.

He looked back.

Several soldiers ran down the alley behind him, their dark silhouettes illuminated by the lights of a military jeep.

Lee scrambled to his feet and ran on, his heart pounding in his chest, his lungs burning in the cold air.

A shot rang out, piercing the night like the crack of thunder.

At first, Lee wasn't sure what had happened. Fire burned in his thigh, tearing through the muscle like a red hot poker.

He fell.

Adrenaline demanded he keep going. He struggled to get back to his feet, but his left leg refused to respond. He grabbed at his thigh and his hand came away covered in blood. Still, he staggered on, turning into another narrow alleyway between the huts of the village, trying to weave his way back to the fields and into the forest.

Voices yelled behind him.

"He is here. Down here."

"Cut him off!"

Lee hobbled, using the rough wooden walls to keep himself upright, falling against the warped panels and pushing off them, dragging himself on.

Dark shapes moved across the alley ahead of him.

Flashlights shone down the narrow, muddy gap between the huts.

Lee could see two soldiers at the end of the alley with rifles raised. He turned. Behind him, three more soldiers stood poised, ready to fire.

Lee fell to his knees in the mud as the rain picked up, soaking him once again.

The huts had been built on raised stumps. Lee realized he could crawl beneath them. He couldn't give up. In his mind, he could still see the US Navy SEAL being savaged by dogs on that lonely, windswept beach. He couldn't die like that. He had to believe he could escape.

Soldiers ran in from both ends of the alleyway.

Lee had begun scrambling beneath one of the huts when a hand grabbed his leg. He kicked, lashing out with his boots, but the soldier was strong, dragging him back into the alley.

Lee clutched at mud and stones on the ground, desperately trying to claw his way beneath the hut.

Another set of hands grabbed at his clothes, wrenching him out and flipping him over on his back.

Flashlights blinded him.

The last thing he remembered was the sickening crunch of a rifle butt being slammed into his forehead.

Professor Lachlan

Jason checked the time on his phone – 11:47.

He rushed up the broad stone stairs leading to the physics hall, holding his paper under his arm.

The campus was deserted.

Normally, the ebb and flow of students gave life to the old buildings, giving them a charm beyond the lifeless red bricks and the white wooden window frames staring back at him. Without students, the physics hall seemed more of a museum than a university.

The main door was locked.

Jason shook both doors, testing them for any give.

"Fuck!"

Why the hell didn't Professor Lachlan allow him to email his paper? How could such a brilliant mind be so backwards in regards to technology? What was wrong with email? What plausible reason could there be for not allowing papers to be submitted electronically? Especially on a holiday! Why did the professor insist on coming into the university on his day off? Professor Lachlan needs to get a life, Jason decided.

Damn, he thought, Lachlan is probably sitting in his office waiting. How the hell am I going to get in there? He peered through the thick glass, trying to see if there was anyone inside the hallway, perhaps a security guard.

Jason took a deep breath, trying not to get frustrated.

Lachlan loved working with paper. He would use three different colored pens to mark his papers: blue for general comments, green for praise, and red for everything in between, showing his disdain for anything out of the ordinary. Jason tended to get a lot of red. Paper was the soapbox upon which Professor Lachlan proclaimed his disdain for change.

"The 1930s called," Jason muttered. "They'd like their slide rules back."

"Sorry," a voice said from behind him. "I didn't catch that?"

"Professor!" he cried, jumping at the sound of Lachlan's voice. Jason's eyes were wide with surprise. He turned to see Professor Lachlan standing behind him smiling.

"Ah, nothing," Jason continued, almost dropping his paper. The loose sheets slid in the manila folder and he grabbed at them, catching them before they fell.

The professor was of Asian descent, and Jason had often wondered how a Scottish surname had entered the mix. There had to be quite a story behind that union. A warm smile lit up a kind face. Well, Jason thought, a kind face if you were doing what you were told. Deviate from the norm and Professor Lachlan could be as tyrannical as Joseph Stalin. Ah, that was an exaggeration, he thought, but Jason did wonder if his various professors knew how intimidating they could be with their vast intellects. It seemed decades of lectures to snotty nosed teens had shortened the fuse of everyone on the faculty. Today, though, the professor seemed delighted to see Jason, greeting him with a hearty handshake as though he were catching up with a student from years past.

Jason stood there awkwardly, not sure how to respond. In the background, a teenaged girl rode by on a bicycle as a young guy chased her playfully on roller blades. They called to each other, laughing and smiling. At least someone was enjoying the holiday.

Lachlan pulled a set of keys from his pocket and fiddled with the lock on the door.

"Come in," he said, stepping into the lobby and punching a key code to disable the alarm. He was holding a cardboard tray with two drinks in Styrofoam cups. White plastic lids hid the content. "Mocha Latte, right?"

"Oh," Jason said, accepting the cup from the professor. "I'm quite fussy, sticking only to high-brow brands like *International Roast*, but … I'm sure I can make an exception."

Lachlan grinned.

They walked along the polished wooden floor, past the staircase and over to the professor's office at the back of the physics lecture hall. Lachlan opened the door and signaled for Jason to step in ahead of him. The office was unusually cramped, being wedged between two lecture halls and was shared with another professor as a prep room.

Jason knew Lachlan had a more luxurious main office on the second floor, one that was spacious, with green palms and brown leather seats, the kind of plush seats with brass buttons pinning the stiff leather in place at regular intervals. He liked that office, it had an air of importance about it, but this room between the lecture halls was little more than a long storage room or a tiny corridor. A mop and bucket wouldn't have been out of place.

The chairs inside the long room had to be pushed into the desks before he could squeeze past. For such a narrow room, the ceiling was absurdly high, reaching up over thirty feet. The ceiling height matched the lecture halls on either side with their raised, theater seating, and made the prep room seem even more claustrophobic than it already was, as though it were modeled after a deep desert canyon from an old western. The dust on the shelves reinforced that notion.

"Grab a seat," Lachlan said warmly.

Jason pulled out a desk chair and rolled it back against the narrow window at the far end of the cramped room. He sat between the internal doors that led out to the lecture halls on either side, feeling the warmth of the sun on his back. The chair squeaked as he rocked slightly, settling into the seat. It was an old wooden framed chair, like something from the 1930s, just like the imaginary slide rule he'd ascribed to Professor Lachlan.

"Einstein taught here, you know," Lachlan continued, taking a seat in a similar chair between the two desks.

The desks were more like waist-high work benches, lacking drawers. The finish was worn and scratched.

"Einstein gave a lecture here in 1948 on how gravity warps space-time. Beforehand, he sat in one of these chairs. No one's sure which, but like some lost Roman Catholic relic, these chairs are destined to be honored forever. Silly, huh, how even scientists can cling to such irrational, meaningless objects as though they could somehow impart a mystical power the man never had?"

He laughed, adding, "I tried to get rid of them. You wouldn't believe the backlash I got from the head of faculty. I should have just thrown them in the dump without telling anyone and been done with it, but the Dean is determined that this tiny back room remains pretty much as Einstein saw it in the 40s. I think Einstein would be horrified to see that this room has become a sort of shrine."

"I think it's pretty cool," Jason said, not afraid to contradict Lachlan. He didn't feel he had to agree with the professor. Lachlan was never one for ass-kissers, Jason thought, and he respected those that had confidence in their own convictions. Jason had picked up on this quite early in his time at the university, and the professor's mature attitude gave him enough leeway to feel he could be himself around the old man. There were no airs or pretenses with Lachlan.

Lachlan smiled.

Jason glanced around the room, trying to imagine Einstein reviewing his notes. The tiles on the ceiling were decaying and probably dated back to well before Einstein's lecture. Pulley ropes were visible on both walls, connecting with moveable blackboards inside the lecture halls. They were whiteboards now, but Jason could imagine Einstein standing in front of dusty chalkboards, his air of confidence unmistakable, with his wild hair tossed carelessly to one side. With a stub of chalk in hand, he would do battle with the blackboard, defining reality in white strokes hastily buffed against the darkness, revealing secrets hidden since the dawn of the universe.

"Maybe it's ..." Jason ventured, but he stopped mid-sentence, doubting himself.

"No," Lachlan said, "Go on."

"I know there are no authority figures in science, but I'd like to think Einstein would see this tiny room for what it is: an attempt to retain the heart of the times, to capture the spirit of theoretical physics reaching beyond the technological limits of the day. He saw more in the scratchings of chalk on a blackboard than anything we could see until we put telescopes in space. Perhaps he would be pleased to see us learning from that."

Lachlan smiled warmly, saying, "You're right, and yet there's more to Einstein than exotic formulas. His genius, his brilliance lay in seeing the obvious. Some eighteen years before he formulated the theory of relativity, two scientists, Michelson and Morley, demonstrated that the speed of light never varied regardless of motion. All the clues were there, plain for all to see for the best part of two decades, but it took Einstein to put it together, and do you know why?"

"No," Jason confessed.

"Because everyone else looked to explain away the result. Everyone else became embarrassed by what looked like an inconsistency, a mistake, but not Einstein. For Einstein, inconsistencies were a red flag, the key to unlocking a greater understanding of the universe. For Einstein, the contradiction was the answer. He realized scientists had been asking the wrong question. Many a good idea has been brought low by observations. Einstein understood reality is not subject to our theories, our whims and desires, it is reality that must define them. He started with the assumption that reality was right, it was our thinking that was wrong, and then it was just a case of figuring out the relationship described by reality. I don't mean to say his reasoning and equations were some blithe, simple step, but the hardest part of formulating his theory was letting go of what he'd previously assumed was true."

Jason was mesmerized. He sat there in awe of the professor. For him, this was the essence of science: an awakening of the mind.

"Don't let anyone ever belittle a good question," Lachlan said softly. "There are no dumb questions, only dumb people afraid to ask good questions."

Jason smiled. This is what he loved about Lachlan. The professor had a way of making him feel like he was part of the family. It was good advice, advice he hoped he wouldn't forget.

"Did you complete your assignment?" Lachlan asked.

"Yes," Jason replied, handing him the folder.

Lachlan reached out for the folder. As often as he'd seen the professor's right hand, Jason never got used to the sight. Lachlan had lost three of his fingers in an accident; his little finger, ring finger and middle finger were barely stubs, leaving just his thumb and index finger on his right hand. The injury was old. The scars were rough and lumpy. Tiny bumps marked stumps where his fingers had once been. Jason could see them twitch as the professor reached for the folder, phantom fingers stretching out where they no longer existed. He tried not to stare.

Lachlan had been Jason's professor for the past four years. Although Lachlan was hard on him, Jason appreciated the rigor and discipline the professor brought to physics. There was nothing mean, nothing unfair. The old man's professionalism carried a sense of regency and respect. The professor had probably never had an impure thought in his life, Jason thought.

Each year Lachlan would tell the class how he lost his fingers, only it was never the same story. Normally, he'd spin his yarn during orientation week to freak out the new students. Those who took his class for only a year never knew quite what to think, but the old timers like Jason understood. One year it was that he lost his fingers trying to stop the lift doors from closing in the biology wing. That made the girls squirm. Another year it was as the result of playing with lasers in his basement laboratory. Of course, there was no such lair for this mad scientist. He later admitted to Jason that he lived in a third floor apartment, so there wasn't even a basement. Jason had heard rumors on campus that the professor had lost his fingers rescuing a young boy from a shark while on vacation in Miami. Mitchell swore it happened while the professor was wrestling a girl free from the jaws of a tiger in Cambodia, as he found an article on the Internet describing the incident. No one really knew, and that was clearly the way the professor liked it.

Lachlan put his glasses on and began looking at Jason's paper.

Jason's phone chimed with an incoming message. He looked at his pocket and then at Lachlan, who had his head down, reading the assignment. Lachlan waved his good hand, and a flutter of fingers signaled that he didn't care if Jason checked his messages. Jason didn't need permission, but he felt his respect for the professor required that tacit permission as a courtesy. He pulled out his phone, entered the password and looked at the message:

From Helena: Lily wants to know if you've heard from her father. She's worried.

Jason typed a quick response into his phone using his two thumbs.

From Jason: At uni with prof. Nothing yet. Tell her not to worry, we'll find him. Or, more likely, he'll find us. I stuck more posters at surrounding intersections. c u guys soon.

Jason sat there quietly, wondering if he should leave and help Lily. He started getting nervous himself, even though he knew there was nothing to be done. He felt as though he ought to be doing something, regardless of how irrelevant it might be. It would take most of an hour for Lachlan to review his work, but the professor appeared to be skimming over the content, so Jason thought it would be best if he waited patiently.

As Lachlan finished each page he placed it face down on the table.

Jason's heart skipped a beat.

The back of each page was covered with his trademark fidgeting scrawl, the calculations that wandered through his curious mind. At first, Lachlan didn't notice, but then he started paying more attention to the back of each page than the printed content on the front.

Jason clenched his lips, waiting for the inevitable scolding. The funny thing was, he had no idea he'd written anything on the blank side of each page. He could have sworn he'd printed out his assignment and headed straight here. Although, thinking about it, he recalled leaving Mario's around nine. He had gone back to his apartment to pick up the paper but hadn't left for the university until just after eleven. He'd been doodling, lost in thought.

By now, Lachlan was completely ignoring the printed side of each page, turning the small stack of paper over and looking intently at the formulas and symbols hurriedly scribbled on the back. He nodded his head thoughtfully.

"I recognize some of the equations," he said, waving his mutilated hand as he held the sheets of paper in his left hand, "but sections of this seem abstract. What is it you're looking to prove in your equations?"

He held up a sheet of paper. Jason cringed as he looked at it.

"Ah, it's just an idea," Jason confessed, wishing he could shrink into obscurity.

"Ideas are good," Lachlan replied, leading him, looking for more.

Jason wondered if he was going to regret what he said next, but he couldn't help himself. He had such respect for the professor. He desperately wanted to hear his thoughts on these calculations.

Lachlan seemed to sense his angst, saying, "Crazy ideas can be some of the best ideas."

"OK," Jason replied. "This is speculative, but speculation is the heart of innovation. You've got to think laterally, right?"

Lachlan nodded.

Jason continued.

"There are eleven dimensions in M-Theory."

With a slight tilt of his head, the professor agreed.

"We've got our regular three spatial dimensions, plus time, and then seven minuscule dimensions looped over each other like the coils of a snake."

The professor listened intently.

"But by our own admission, we're dealing with space-time, yet all we ever talk about is space. Time is taboo. We have all of these extra spatial dimensions, but not a single, extra chronological dimension."

The professor held up a finger as though he were asking for permission to speak, which surprised Jason a little. Jason paused, letting him talk.

"But we can't have more than one dimension in time," Lachlan said. "That would be contradictory, chaotic. It wouldn't make any sense."

"Ah," Jason continued, "but perhaps that's the point. We look at time and wonder why it's not only linear, but ruthlessly sequential, with one second always leading to the next. Cause always precedes effect, but the math works both ways. On paper, time is bidirectional, but in practice, time marches on relentlessly, and yet no other dimension works this way? What's more, we know time dilates just as lengths contract.

Everything about time screams that it is a dimension as plastic and malleable as any other, and yet we treat time with kid gloves, as though it were made of glass and might shatter if we squeeze our theories too hard.

"Why is there an arrow of time? Why is time a one-way street? Maybe it's because time is not a single dimension at all, but instead it's a clash between two or more chronological dimensions, and so time is propelled forward like an ever tightening ratchet."

As Jason spoke, Lachlan continued looking over the young man's notes.

"Interesting," the professor said, not giving anything away in his tone of voice.

"Think about gravity," Jason continued. "For centuries, people ignored gravity, taking it for granted. No one questioned why the Moon didn't fall from the sky, because that seemed silly. Of course the Moon doesn't fall from the sky—it floats!"

Lachlan grinned. Jason could see the professor knew what he was getting at. He continued, saying, "It took Newton to rethink the notion and realize that the Moon was falling just like an apple from a tree. The only difference was, the Moon missed! Newton's apple fell and hit the earth, but the Moon kept on missing. It was an extraordinary insight!"

"Yes," Lachlan said. "Yes it was."

Jason could see the knowing smile on Lachlan's face. None of this was news to him, but like all scientists, he never tired of hearing it re-couched by an inquiring mind.

"In the same way, think about dark energy," Jason added. "We don't know what dark energy is, but we know it drives the expansion of the universe. The problem is, we're again looking at space as though it were a cohesive element in itself. It's not. There's no such thing as space, there's only space-time. You cannot separate space from time. Dark energy is driving the expansion of space-time. The Big Rip affects not only space but time as well.

"What if dark energy is the impeller, the impetus for the arrow of time? What if dark energy is what drives time in a single direction within our hidden quantum dimensions? Sending it forwards instead of backwards."

Professor Lachlan leaned forward on his knees, holding Jason's paper before him, his eyes locked on the hastily scribbled equations.

Jason wasn't finished. He loved how the professor heard him out rather than shooting him down in flames. He appreciated Lachlan's willingness to provide him with the latitude to think broadly. He was probably wrong, and he knew it, but even just having the chance to think out loud helped to solidify more ideas.

"What would you say if I said I could propel a mass the size of Earth to 99% of the speed of light?"

That got the professor to look up from the paper.

"I'd be seriously impressed," the professor admitted. "But the amount of energy required would be astronomical."

"Exactly," Jason replied. "And that's my point, as Earth is already traveling through space at 99% of the speed of light due largely to dark energy."

Lachlan raised an eyebrow, but he let Jason keep speaking.

"We're orbiting the Sun at 67,000 miles per hour. That's like traveling from New York to LA in three minutes.

"And the Sun is orbiting the center of the Milky Way, and our galaxy as a whole is spinning at the dizzying speed of almost half a million miles an hour. That's what? A flight-time of twenty seconds to get to LA?

"You see, the issue is whenever we think of accelerating any mass to a significant fraction of the speed of light, we assume we're starting with some kind of absolute rest, but we're not. Our local group of galaxies is plunging toward the heart of the Virgo cluster at over a million miles an hour. Due to the expansion of the universe, there are distant galaxies receding from us at 99% of the speed of light, but again that assumes we're stationary. We're not. We have no reason to think of ourselves as special, as being at rest relative to the universe. It's equally true to say these other galaxies are stationary and we're the ones that are racing off at 99% of the speed of light."

"Where are you going with this?" the professor asked.

"Ah," Jason replied, trying not to get too excited. "Everyone's obsessed with the speed of light. They want spaceships that can go faster than the speed of light. They look for wormholes and warp drives to bridge the vast distances that surround us, but they're looking for advances in all the wrong areas. The whole notion of traveling faster than the speed of light is bogus. Light is ALWAYS going to travel 299,792 kilometers per second faster than us, regardless of our speed. And so the notion of speed is meaningless when it comes to light. My point is, we've asked the wrong question. We don't need to go faster than the speed of light."

Professor Lachlan smiled. Jason could see he understood where his reasoning was leading.

"Think about the speedometer in a car. Miles per hour," Jason added. "Speed is distance travelled over time taken. Manipulate time and you can go anywhere you like regardless of the distance as it will take you no time at all!"

"Ha!" Lachlan cried. "So these equations are to manipulate dark energy in quantum dimensions, they're ..."

The professor's voice trailed off, lost in thought.

Jason finished his sentence.

"Calculations for time travel!"

Lachlan looked around, his eyes darting from side to side as he spoke, although in the narrow, cramped confines of the anteroom between the lecture halls, there was no way for anyone to be watching them.

"You cannot tell anyone about this, do you understand?"

The intensity in Lachlan's voice took Jason by surprise. Lachlan leaned forward, emphasizing his point.

"I need some time to verify your calculations, to think about the math. You must trust me on this. Not a word of this to anyone."

"OK, sure," Jason replied, not thinking his wacky theory was that big a deal. From his perspective, it was largely conjecture, and the energy requirements to make the concept a practical reality were horrendous. His initial estimates were that a journey of just a few minutes back through time would require the equivalent of the entire output of the Sun over its lifespan of roughly seven billion years! It wasn't like anyone was going to come up with an energizer bunny with enough juice to test his theory anytime soon. He understood there were probably errors in his assumptions, but even so, the energy requirements weren't likely to be fulfilled by anything that could be found on Earth.

"This is important," Lachlan continued. "I need you to keep this between you and me for now. There will come a time when we can go public with this, but for now you can't tell anyone, not even your closest friend."

He wouldn't believe me anyway, Jason thought, then he mentally corrected himself. Actually, Mitchell would believe him. He'd believe anything weird. Jason tried not to smile at the thought and struggled not to grin. Lachlan looked stern, he must have seen the subtle twitches, the telltale signs of Jason suppressing his instinctive reaction.

Jason wondered what Lachlan was thinking. The professor couldn't have known the zany sequence of thoughts that had flashed through his mind. Lachlan probably thought Jason was a little embarrassed.

"What you've done here is important," Lachlan said. "I need some time to verify the logic. I need you to sit on this for the next day or so. Can you do that for me?"

"Yeah, sure. Of course."

Jason's phone beeped as another message flashed on the lock screen.

From Helena: Lily's freaking out! I'm taking her back to your pad.

"I ... ah," Jason began, signaling to his phone.

"Yes, yes," Lachlan replied, flipping back through the papers. "You can go."

Jason stood and the professor rolled his chair to one side. There was just enough room for Jason to squeeze through beside him if he sucked in as he shimmied past. The professor wasn't going anywhere. He'd turned on his computer and had a pen out, numbering the back of each page. Jason observed that he was deliberate in his actions, checking against the numbers printed on the front of each page to ensure he had Jason's calculations in order.

Jason tiptoed as he squeezed past. He turned and looked back at the professor. The old man was engrossed in Jason's scribbles. How bizarre, he thought, Lachlan barely looked at his actual assignment. Up until then, the assignment had been such a big deal, it had been the reason the two of them had come into the university on a holiday, and now it was sidelined. Knowing Lachlan, Jason ruefully expected the professor would commend him for his speculative work and still flunk him on his paper.

He opened the door as Lachlan added, "Tell no one, remember? I'll be in touch over the weekend."

"No problem," Jason replied nodding. He closed the door quietly behind him, feeling like he was in a library, as though any stray sound could destroy a fragile idea.

Out in the corridor, he typed a quick message to Helena on his phone.

From Jason: I'm on my way.

The outer door opened easily as he pushed on it, but he could hear it lock behind him as he stepped out into sunshine. Jason turned and started walking down the steps toward the bus stop a couple of hundred yards away across the open area. Birds flittered through the trees.

"Hey, you! Stop where you are!" a voice boomed from behind him, and Jason felt himself flinch even though he'd done nothing wrong. Instinctively, he raised his hands slightly as he turned, expecting to see one of the campus police officers standing there with his hand resting on his holster. Campus police were notoriously paranoid about after hours access.

"You are such an easy mark," Mitchell said, jogging over to him.

"What the?" Jason replied. "Are you stalking me?"

"A pimp's got to keep track of his bitches," Mitchell replied, and Jason could see he was trying to make light of his comment. "So is Lachlan a happy camper?"

Jason started to speak, but caught himself, not wanting to betray the professor's confidence.

"What?" Mitchell asked, his hands spread wide in a gesture of openness. For a moment, Jason thought Mitchell was going to hug him. "Did he read your paper?"

"Yes."

"I can't believe that grumpy bastard dragged you in here on our nation's birthday. What a douchebag! What's the rush? Why couldn't he wait till Monday?"

Jason shrugged as they walked along the cracked footpath.

"Did he have his way with you?" Mitchell asked, half laughing.

"No," Jason laughed. "What the hell makes you say something like that?"

"I don't know," Mitchell replied. "I just can't figure out why he'd want to get you alone like that,"

Mitchell was fishing. Jason could see he wouldn't be content until he told him something so he said, "He wanted to show me the desk where Einstein sat before some lecture here back in the fifties."

"Oh, yeah," Mitchell replied. "Between the lecture halls, right?"

"Yeah."

"So he took you into the Holy of Holies."

"I guess," Jason replied as they spotted the bus stop through the oak trees lining the walkway.

"And gave you a good spanking."

Jason chuckled.

"Was he wearing leathers?" Mitchell asked in a whisper. "Fluffy handcuffs?"

Jason slapped him on the shoulder. "You wish!"

It being a holiday, they waited for almost an hour before a bus turned up. Mitchell griped about how they could have walked home in that time. When the bus finally came, they took it to within a block of Jason's apartment. As they approached the intersection in front of his building, Jason could see Helena sitting on the far corner with her back against a red brick wall. Lily was there, pacing back and forth. Jason waved and Mitchell called out, but neither of the girls noticed them until they crossed at the lights and headed over toward them. Lily was again looking the wrong way down the one-way street while Helena was engrossed with her smartphone, reading something on the screen.

"Hey," Jason said, walking up to Lily.

Lily smiled, blushing slightly as her eyes darted away for a second before returning to look at him. That must have been some kind of cultural thing, he decided.

"How are you doing?" he asked.

"I am worried about my father."

"I know," he said, taking her hand. Touch seemed like the right response, saying something more than words could convey. "It's going to be OK, we'll find him. Either that, or he'll find us. Try not to worry. Everything will work out. Just give him a little more time."

Lily glanced at the color print out taped to the pole supporting the traffic lights. Her own smiling face looked back with Jason's mobile number written on tiny stubs beneath. A couple of the stubs had been torn off, but that didn't mean anything. The wording beneath her photo read, "Lee, please call me."

"Well, you guys took your time," Helena said, getting to her feet. It was only then Jason noticed what Lily was wearing. When he'd left her in the morning she was wearing a baggy New York Jets t-shirt. Now she had a snug fitting t-shirt tucked into a pair of jeans. It was the wording on the t-shirt that took him off-guard. Lily noticed his attention focusing on the words and stepped back slightly, showing off the clothes she'd borrowed from Helena.

"You like?" Lily asked.

"Ah, yeah. I guess," Jason replied, glancing at Helena. She had a grin a mile wide, while Mitchell was visibly trying not to laugh.

"It's funny, no?" Lily asked. She pulled at the hem of the shirt, pulling it tight over her breasts so Jason could read the wording easily. Jason had no problem making out the large arrow pointing upwards and knew exactly what the wording beneath said: *My eyes are up here.*

"And my eyes *are* up here!" Lily added with innocence in her voice.

Helena lost it, laughing as she put her arm around Lily briefly, hugging her as she said, "They certainly are."

"I don't get it," Lily replied. "This is funny?"

"Hilarious!" Mitchell added.

"I'll explain it to you later," Jason replied, glaring at Helena.

"I knew you'd like it," Helena said, batting her eyelids at Jason. "We girls have had a fun day. Lily is pretty much the same size as my roommate so it was no problem getting her a t-shirt and some jeans."

"Hey," Mitchell said. "Are we going to head off to the fireworks tonight?"

"Ah, yeah," Jason replied, glancing at the time on his phone, surprised to see it was already five o'clock.

"No. We must wait for my father," Lily insisted.

Jason gestured at the quiet streets around them, saying, "Lily, I don't know where your dad is, but I know he wouldn't want you waiting for him on a street corner. Maybe he got the dates wrong. You could be waiting here a long time.

"Honestly, I think we need to get in touch with your family back in South Korea. They must be worried about you. There must be someone there that can help us find your father."

"He's right," Helena said, resting her hand gently on Lily's shoulder. "There's nothing more we can do here than we've already done."

Helena pointed at the poster as she continued, gesturing at several other posters Jason had stuck up on each of the corners. "If your dad turns up tonight, he'll call."

Lily's lower lip quivered. Her eyes cast down at the chewing gum stains on the concrete sidewalk. A tear came to her eye.

"Hey, it's OK," Jason said. "We'll find him, or he'll find us. Either way, we'll get the two of you back together. Everything will work out for the best, you'll see."

Lily nodded.

Mitchell signaled, tipping his head toward the 7-11 further down the road, giving Jason an excuse to leave Lily and give her a bit of space and some time to figure things out for herself. Helena nodded, picking up on Mitchell's signal and indicating she'd stay with Lily.

"Anyone hungry?" Mitchell asked. "Come on, there's got to be something edible around here."

"I'll come with you," Jason said, and the two young men walked off, leaving the girls on the street corner.

As they walked away, Mitchell spoke under his breath, saying, "I'm telling you, dude. It would be better if she were an alien. Less baggage."

"Will you give it up?" Jason replied, wanting him to be serious. Jason understood a little of what Lily must be feeling, lost and alone in a strange city on the other side of the world.

She probably did feel a little alien, although not in the extraterrestrial sense of the word.

Jason remembered how he'd felt when he'd visited Seoul. It was the little things that gave a feeling of dissonance, things you wouldn't normally think twice about. Sure, he figured, there were the obvious cultural differences like the ceramic squat toilets in the rural areas, but even seeing something as benign as a stop sign with both Korean and English written on it had been strangely unsettling. He could speak fragments of Korean, but couldn't read anything, leaving him feeling bewildered. At the time, he felt like he was on another planet.

There had been all the usual fast food restaurants in Seoul: McDonalds, Pizza Hut, Kentucky Fried Chicken. And they carried all the same staple items on their menus, but there were also offerings that catered to local palates: Korean fried chicken with soy sauce, Teriyaki McBurger and sweet potato pizza. Technically, there was nothing wrong with the combinations and flavors, they were just different, and that difference reinforced the sense of alienation for him. Jason supposed Lily was struggling with similar subtleties, things he'd overlook. So many things that seemed natural to him must have been jarring for her.

"Hey," Mitch said as they walked up to the 7-11. "Where the hell's a hot dog stand when you need one?"

"They must have converged on the docks for the fireworks," Jason replied.

The 7-11 had the usual array of junk food, with bags of potato chips and candy bars along with ramen noodles and milk, but there was nothing of any real substance. Mitchell bought some shriveled hot dogs in buns that looked like they were made from compressed cardboard. Jason smothered the hot dogs in ketchup and mustard, vainly hoping to impart some flavor. They walked back to the intersection with sauce dripping on the pavement behind them.

Lily was still pacing.

Jason handed her a hot dog and a can of Pepsi.

"Oh, this smells wonderful," she said, looking at the brilliant reds and yellows drowning the long, thin dog and soaking into the white bread.

"New York's finest," Jason replied, laughing.

Mitchell coughed into a closed fist, blurting out a muffled, "Bullshit."

Helena laughed as well. The four of them sat on the hard concrete, leaning up against the brickwork of an old building as they ate their dinner on the street corner. They could have crossed the road and gone up to his apartment, but sitting there felt right, as though they were providing solidarity in support of Lily.

"Hmm," Lily said between bites. "This is good."

Helena looked at Jason as she said, "No cheap dates, right? Promise me. You have got to take this girl to a real restaurant. Somewhere like Cipriani's or 21 Club. Don't be a tight ass."

"I promise," Jason replied as the setting sun cast long dark shadows down the poorly lit alleyways. Helena had expensive tastes, but she was right. Lily should see the finer side of town. 7-11 didn't cut it.

The streetlights came on, but the dark clouds rolling in overhead looked ominous.

"What's the weather forecast?" Mitchell asked.

"It's supposed to be nice," Helena replied.

"So are we going to the fireworks?" Mitchell asked.

"He's like a little kid," Helena said, talking to Lily. "It helps if you humor him."

Lily smiled, saying, "Fireworks would be fun, wouldn't they?"

"Yes," Jason replied, noticing her smile seemed forced.

"There's a bus due soon," Helena said.

"We could walk," Mitchell replied. "It's only about four blocks."

"You could walk," Helena replied curtly. "Some of us are in heels."

A few minutes later, a bus pulled up at the stop outside the 7-11. Mitchell and Helena climbed the steps, swiping their transport cards and laughing as they moved down the bus to a bunch of empty seats near the back.

Jason swiped his card and fumbled with his wallet.

"Exact change only," the driver stated.

Jason gave up counting quarters and handed the driver a five dollar note, saying, "Keep the change."

He took Lily's hand and led her down the bus. Even though she'd agreed to go to the fireworks, he could tell she longed to stay, and he half felt as though he should respect that and just return to his apartment to wait for her dad. And yet, there was no guarantee her father would show. How long could this go on? Lily had to have family back in South Korea she could call. And what would happen once she found her father, he wondered. At the moment, theirs was a relationship of circumstance, and not even a relationship, really.

Jason knew the stats. He'd been backpacking in Canada and had met people he thought he'd be friends with for the rest of his life. They'd swear they'd stay in contact. They'd exchange addresses, emails and even link up online, but in the end, they drifted away from each other as there was no bond, no common link between them, no basis for their friendship other than a chance meeting. Jason hated to think Lily would be the same, but he knew that was the most likely outcome. Oh, she'd tell her friends and family about her adventures in the Big Apple, she might even chat with him online once or twice, but before much time had passed they'd forget about each other and be strangers again.

The bus pulled away from the curb as he grabbed a handrail to steady himself and headed down the aisle. Lily seemed to fall further behind as the bus lurched on through the lights.

"Hey, guys!" Mitchell cried with his irrepressible smile, drumming his hands on the seat in front of him and signaling for Jason and Lily to sit down. "What do you say we hit a few bars afterwards, maybe a nightclub or two?"

Mitchell was up against the window, with Helena sitting on the aisle. Jason slipped into the seat in front of Mitchell, with Lily sitting beside him, although she didn't move up next to him, keeping one leg in the aisle. She was in two minds about the fireworks, that was obvious, and the idea of partying into the early hours of the morning didn't seem to appeal to her. Helena sensed it too.

"It'll be fun," she said, reaching forward and massaging Lily's shoulders. Jason understood what Helena was trying to do, she was trying to help Lily relax. But Jason had a fair idea unwelcome contact would do more to upset Lily than to help. He felt much the same way about well meaning but uninvited contact. As he expected, Lily pulled away, leaning forward slightly. Helena took the hint and pulled her hands back.

The bus pulled up to another stop and an elderly man sitting across from them got up and left by the rear doors.

Lily mumbled, "I can't do this. I can't leave my father."

A police car raced past with its lights flashing and its siren blaring.

Jason barely realized what was happening next. He was distracted by the police cruiser and the flickering blue and red lights lighting up the neighborhood. Suddenly, he realized Lily was gone. The rear door of the bus closed and the bus pulled away into the street again, leaving Lily standing on the sidewalk.

"No," he cried, jumping out of his seat and running to the door.

The bus continued to accelerate.

"Stop the bus!" he cried, striking the door with his palm.

"Next stop's a hundred yards down the road," the driver called out, making eye contact with him in his rear-view mirror.

"Let me off," Jason yelled, again striking the glass in the door panels with the flat of his hand.

"What are you doing?" Mitchell cried out, still pinned by the window by Helena. "Leave her, dude. If she wants to wait on a street corner, let her do it. You don't owe her anything."

Jason grabbed the emergency release lever and pulled. The door opened, but the bus was speeding along at easily thirty-five miles an hour. The concrete raced by in a blur. The wind howled through the open door, swirling into the foot well.

"Hey!" the driver called out. "What the hell do you think you're doing? Get back in your seat!"

The driver eased off the accelerator and onto the brakes with the kind of precision that had been missing from his driving so far. He slowed the bus, pulling over close to the curb. Jason watched as lampposts and trash cans whipped past, timing his jump.

"Don't you—" the driver called.

"No!" Mitchell yelled.

Jason jumped from the bus, landing on the concrete sidewalk, surprised by his forward momentum. He could have sworn the bus had slowed to a running pace, but it must have been still moving considerably faster than he realized, and he found himself rolling on the pavement with his arms up protecting his head.

"You stupid dumb fuck!" the driver called out. He'd brought the bus to a halt about thirty feet away and had opened the front doors, standing on the bottom step as he shook his fist at Jason. "Damn kids!"

Jason got to his feet, grimacing at the skin torn from his forearms and his bloody elbows. Pain surged, surprising him with how much it hurt.

"What the hell is wrong with you?" Mitchell cried, stepping down out of the rear doors of the bus, followed by Helena.

"Just go on without me," Jason called out, feeling stupid. He waved them away. What was wrong with him? This was unlike him. Jason wasn't one to be impetuous and stupid. As far as stupid went, that stunt was right up there with the dumbest things he'd ever done. If his head had struck the concrete he could have suffered a serious, life threatening concussion. People had died from less, and he knew it.

"What the hell is wrong with me?" he whispered, turning his back on Mitchell and Helena and looking at Lily in the distance.

The driver of the bus closed the doors and the bus pulled back out into the traffic, leaving them on the sidewalk. He could hear Mitchell walking up behind him.

"Oh, my God. Look at your arms!" Helena cried.

Jason could feel blood dripping from his fingers.

"I'm OK," he said, raising a hand and requesting some distance. "Just ... give me some space."

"No problem, dude!" Mitchell said, holding his hands out in a non-threatening gesture, his fingers splayed wide.

Jason ran down toward where he'd last seen Lily a couple of hundred yards away on the next block. He jogged across the street, barely pausing to look for traffic. She'd disappeared down a darkened alley. Rain began falling from the night sky. Twilight was over. Even with streetlights, the night seemed unusually dark.

As he approached the alley, Jason heard a deep, resonant hum like that of a generator. Lights flickered from the narrow alley between the buildings, flashes of blue-white like those from an arc welder cutting through the darkness.

He glanced back at Mitchell and Helena. They were waiting to cross at the lights.

Jason slowed to a walk, wondering what could be causing the flashes between the buildings. Wisps of smoke drifted from the alley. He stepped around the corner and into a gale not dissimilar to what he'd once felt from the downdraft of a landing helicopter. Flecks of dust and dirt whipped through the air. Scraps of paper tore around him.

Lily was no more than thirty feet away in the middle of the alley, bathed in a blinding green light. She was leaning slightly backwards, pitched at an unnatural angle, one that should have caused her to fall to the ground, but somehow she remained upright. Her arms were outstretched, as though she had been crucified on some invisible cross, while her feet drifted a few feet above the ground. White smoke billowed down from above. Bursts of vapor surged out of a series of flickering lights some twenty stories above the alley. The smoke swirled around her body as she slowly gained height.

"No."

Jason's one word was barely audible above the pulsating hum coming down from above.

The white light transformed into a kaleidoscope of color. Tiny, circular rainbows formed in the cold white mist, giving the view a trance-like quality.

Jason fell to his knees just a few feet inside the alley.

"No," he repeated. "This can't be happening."

Lily was being drawn up toward the light, with her arms outstretched and her hands limp. Her body was pulled up into the swirling clouds still churning down from above.

The circle of lights above the building began turning, slowly building in speed as Lily's body rose higher, becoming lost in the mist. From what Jason could tell, the lights were roughly forty to fifty feet across, but their exact width was obscured by the rooftop. Whatever this was, it had to be hovering no more than a few feet above the roof. Jason wanted to run for the stairs, to chase after Lily, but his body felt weak, drained of strength.

The rainbow of colors radiating above him reached a fever pitch, moving so fast the individual lights became indistinguishable.

And then it was gone.

The mist cleared, dissipating and disappearing into the night, leaving a clear view of the clouds thousands of feet above.

There were footsteps behind him.

"Tell me you saw that?" Jason said, his eyes still looking skyward.

"Saw what?" Mitchell asked, coming up beside him.

In the distance, well beyond the rooftop, bursts of light broke through the night. Spectacular splashes of color lit up the grey, moody clouds as fireworks burst in the sky over the river.

"Oh, damn. We missed the show," Mitchell said with a hint of disappointment in his voice.

"We need to get you to a doctor," Helena said, ignoring Mitchell as she reached out her hand and helped Jason to his feet.

Jason was shaking. His fingers were trembling.

"You're in shock," she said, looking into his eyes with compassion. She raised his forearms, taking a good look at the grazes on his arms. "Oh, that's got to hurt. Come on. Let's get you to the emergency room and get you cleaned up. I hope your tetanus shots are up to date."

Jason was in shock, but it wasn't the pain in his arms that had shaken his being. He'd spent the best part of a decade building a rational model of the universe in his thinking, establishing a framework for understanding the cosmos and formulating his theories and calculations, but here, in a matter of seconds, his world had unraveled. What seemed so crazy when Mitchell talked about it now seemed probable. No, he thought, not probable, actual.

Could it be that the anecdotes of UFO sightings were true?

Was Earth being surreptitiously visited by aliens from some other world?

Could his eyes be believed?

Should he discard his scientific training over some fleeting experience that seemed more like a dream than reality?

Could these two views be reconciled?

They couldn't, he decided, and yet he had no plausible alternative explanation for what he'd witnessed. Although he knew eyewitnesses were notoriously unreliable in a court of law, he couldn't bring himself to ignore what he'd seen.

Lily had been taken.

"There has to be another explanation," he mumbled to himself. "There has to be."

Caught

Lee woke bumping around in darkness.

He was in the back of a truck weaving along a rough track. He bounced on the cold metal bed of the truck, sliding as the clumsy diesel engine rattled in his ears. His hands were tied behind him. A shroud covered his head. Dim light seeped in from around his neck. He felt sick. The smell of fumes wafted around him, making it difficult to breathe.

As the truck rounded a corner, Lee fought with his hands to steady himself. His bound fingers grabbed at the corrugation built into the steel deck beneath him, and he tried to avoid bumping into what felt like wooden logs or boulders on either side of him. Lee shifted his knees, trying to get some grip when a boot kicked him in the stomach.

"Lie still!"

Lee grimaced. He hadn't anticipated the blow. He had no way of knowing he was being watched and the boot caught him on the side of the hip, causing a jolt of pain to surge through his body. He groaned in agony, sliding into the closed tailgate as the truck rounded another corner.

It was at that moment he understood the gravity of his situation.

Lee had been part of evade-and-escape drills during his compulsory service in the South Korean air force and understood what was happening. This was the first stage of his imprisonment. No one ever escaped, either from the training exercises or the real thing. Evade and escape was a misnomer. Evade meant prolong and delay, hopefully buying others time. Escape was a false hope, something to help you through the initial interrogation. His heart sank at the realization he'd probably spend the rest of his life in a North Korean labour camp, but he knew even that estimation was overly generous. In reality, his life was probably now measured in terms of days or hours, not years.

Several boots pinned him to the metal bed of the truck, preventing him from swaying with the suspension. What he'd thought were logs were actually the boots of at least a dozen soldiers sitting on either side of him, facing in toward him. They joked among themselves, knowing he was listening.

"We will be rewarded for catching this American dog."

"Ha, not dog. He is a pig."

"Swine!"

"He is a spy. He will be shot."

"Not before Eun-Yong has had this son of a bitch castrated."

"Ha!" another soldier replied, but it wasn't so much a laugh as a forced response to meet peer expectations.

The soldiers were cruel, kicking him without warning as he lay there trying not to move, but that was the role of soldiers from all nations, he understood. They had to dehumanize their enemy. It was the only way to justify their acts. Just yesterday, he was an officer, a title that carried a sense of pride and prestige and now he was a prisoner. One brutally subjugated by an enemy. He already felt his sense of self-esteem slipping away, driven from him by the petty violence being arbitrarily inflicted on him as he lay there blinded by a sack pulled over his head.

"Stupid fool," another voice said, and a boot crushed his little finger against the steel bed of the truck. Lee cried out in pain.

"Be quiet, idiot!" another voice cried out, kicking him in the small of his back with a steel-toed boot.

The truck slowed. Lee could hear muffled voices speaking from the cab. The driver was talking to a sentry. He could hear other vehicles idling nearby. A helicopter flew low overhead. The smell of diesel hung in the air. He was at a checkpoint, possibly at the entrance to a military compound.

Lee tried not to panic, but he couldn't help himself. The sack over his head made it hard to breathe. His arms were pinned behind him in a stress position. His leg hurt. Without being aware of it, he began to hyperventilate.

The butt of a rifle hit him on the head, knocking his forehead against the metal and he screamed in agony.

"Shut up, you suckling pig!"

Again the butt of the rifle struck him, only the wooden stock glanced off his shoulder and onto the floor of the truck, sparing him from the full force of the blow.

Lee whimpered. Blood pooled in his mouth.

The truck continued on, turning to one side. Gravel crunched beneath the wheels, a stark contrast to the squelch of mud and rock he'd heard before. He'd entered a military base, he was sure of it.

The truck came to a halt. Seconds later, he heard a steel tailgate being lowered and felt himself being lifted out of the truck. Several soldiers had him by his upper arms. They dragged him over and dropped him like a sack of coal. He expected to fall to the ground, but landed on the back of the truck. He could feel the edge of the truck fall away beneath one leg. A couple of soldiers on the ground grabbed him, pulling him over the edge. They held him by his shoulders, allowing his feet to swing down on to the gravel.

"Come, you lazy heifer."

The references to farm animals surprised him. He'd expected more vulgarity, but North Korea was an enclave, an isolated country not subject to the Hollywood tropes of verbal abuse. For them, these references must have been insulting comparisons.

His captors pushed him on in front of them as his head hung low.

Lee tried to walk, but could only shuffle. He was still reeling from the blow to his head, and the bullet wound to his right thigh ached. Without being able to look at the wound, he figured the bullet had only grazed the muscle. When he'd fallen in the village, it must have been largely from shock. There was some kind of bandage wrapped around his leg, stopping the bleeding, but had the injury been bad, he wouldn't have been able to walk at all. Small mercies, he thought to himself as he continued on.

The world seemed to spin around him in the darkness. He could see glimpses of mud and rocks out of the bottom of the bag over his head.

Someone grabbed the sack from behind, grabbing a handful of hair along with it and jerked his head back, forcing him on at a faster pace. His feet struggled to respond. That was the point when Lee realized they'd taken his boots. He was still wearing his damp socks, but his boots had been removed, perhaps as a trophy, or perhaps just out of practical necessity by another soldier wanting better boots.

He was pushed into a hut. His feet caught on the step in the doorway, and he struggled not to fall to the floor as he was dragged inside.

A chair scraped across a wooden floor.

Someone untied his hands before pushing him down in the chair and strapping his forearms to the arms of the chair.

Lee tried to be objective and observe the fine nuances around him. This was an endurance trick the South Korean military had taught him during his evade and escape training. As a prisoner, he was powerless over all aspects of his confinement save one, his mind. He had to keep his mind sharp, to look to learn from the subtle nuances of his captivity. Details were important. Details spoke louder than words, and what's more, they were a distraction, a way of removing himself from the emotionally crippling reality that surrounded him. His captors would want to break him, and the truth was, they would, given time. His only hope was to hold out as long as possible and slowly capitulate, to appear more broken than he was. This was a game of deception on both parts, only the North Koreans were working with a stacked deck.

Details. He'd keep his sanity only by focusing on details, and so he drove his mind to be clear and objective.

Previously, Lee's hands had been bound with rope no thicker than his little finger. The rope had been too thick to break, but it wasn't the sort of hand spun rope he'd expect to find in a fishing village, it had to be something the soldiers had carried with them. Now, though, thick leather straps bound his forearms and lower legs to the chair. His hands were free, which seemed strange. Although he was relieved to get some feeling back into his wrists, he was alarmed by the change. He understood that everything he was enduring had a purpose, nothing was accidental or haphazard. More often than not, that purpose would be brutal and cruel. Lee doubted this wooden chair held any relief.

The sack was pulled from his head.

There was no one in front of him or to either side. Whoever it was that pulled the sack from his head remained out of sight behind him. Light peered under the door to his right. From the angle, it couldn't have been more than seven in the morning. Given the angle of the sunlight, he was facing roughly due north. This is good, he thought. Keep focusing on the minutia, work those details.

The wall in front of him was bare of all adornment other than a framed picture of the Supreme Leader Most Glorious. The wooden frame was thin, providing a flimsy border to an image no larger than a sheet of printer paper. The Glorious Leader had been photo-shopped. His features were airbrushed. White teeth radiated from a hollow smile, that of a jackal gloating. His eyes looked upward and to the side, as though he were illuminated by the rising sun. Not a hair on his head was out of place. Each strand had been meticulously pulled into place in a hairstyle that looked like something from the 1950s.

Lee turned to see who was behind him. A rifle butt clipped him on the shoulder, directing his gaze back at the Leader without a word being spoken.

Lee waited. He wasn't sure how much time had elapsed, but it felt like he sat there for hours. The day stretched on. He was hungry, tired, exhausted. If his head began to droop, a rifle butt prodded him awake again.

He noticed that a crude bandage had been wrapped around his leg. Blood soaked through from the bullet wound, but seeing how little blood there was convinced him his initial assessment was correct. Thankfully, it was barely a graze. A couple of inches to the right and a measly hundred and twenty two grams of copper-plated steel would have punched through the bulk of his thigh at a phenomenal speed, covering seven football fields in barely a second and turning his soft tissue into shredded meat. The bullet could have severed his femoral artery or broken his leg, cutting through the muscle like a hot knife through butter.

The chair had no padding and his backside felt numb.

If he moved, trying to shift his weight to gain relief, the guard behind him would strike him with his rifle.

There were dark stains on the floor, blood splatter patterns. A metal toolbox was open on a table to one side, just visible on the periphery of his vision. It could have belonged to a mechanic, but somehow he doubted that.

After an age, the door behind him opened and several soldiers walked in. He could hear the crisp sound of their boots on the wooden floor. The manner in which they strode on the hollow floor conveyed a sense of purpose, and Lee had no doubt as to why they were here: they wanted answers, answers he didn't have. He recalled his training. Be the grey man, he reminded himself, be compliant, be submissive. Avoid eye contact. Appear broken. That won't be hard, he thought.

A North Korean officer walked in front of him with his parade dress hat tucked tightly under one arm. His boots were polished to a brilliant shine, while his shirt and trousers had been pressed with starch. Lee doubted this was his usual dress—he seemed too formal. He was dressed this way to intimidate Lee with his authority, and Lee felt that immediately. Lee understood this man held the power of life and death over him.

"You wear no dog tags," the officer said coldly. "You are a spy."

"I am a civilian pilot," Lee replied, being careful not to contradict him with the word 'but.' He paused before continuing, surprised by the sound of fear in his own voice. "I am Captain John Lee with the South Korean Coast Guard, a civilian organization."

The officer eyed him with suspicion. He paced slowly across the floor, taking measured steps. Lee swallowed the lump in his throat. His hands shook.

"A government organization?" the officer asked after due deliberation, clarifying Lee's comment about the Coast Guard.

Lee nodded. He didn't know where to look. His eyes betrayed him, darting around the room, wanting to settle somewhere but finding no rest.

"Can you prove this?" the officer asked.

His voice was deceptively calm, almost as though he were genuinely trying to be helpful. Lee doubted his response was anything other than a facade. His head hung low, forcing his eyes to look straight ahead.

The wooden floor was rough, lacking the smooth polish he was familiar with in the South. The planks were uneven and slightly irregular in shape, leaving gaps between them. A cold draft drifted up from beneath the hut. The planks had probably been processed in some local lumber mill, perhaps a temporary camp set up to build the military base. Lee found himself trying to focus on anything other than the horror unfolding before him, but reality would not be so easily denied. Try as he might, he couldn't ignore what was happening.

"What identification do you have?" the officer asked when Lee failed to respond. The officer bent slightly, being sure to intercept his gaze.

"Ah," Lee replied, knowing the officer would have already seen everything the soldiers had taken from him: his survival kit, flare gun, knife. He whispered, "We don't carry personal effects while on patrol."

"What was that?" the officer asked. He knew damn well what Lee had said. He was tightening the noose around Lee's neck, getting him to condemn himself with his own words.

Sheepishly, Lee replied, "We leave our wallets in the ready room before going out on patrol."

"So you have no identification?"

The officer took his time, speaking with slow deliberation, pretending to slowly piece together the puzzle.

"You are, by your own admission, from the renegade state of South Korea, having illegally entered the Democratic People's Republic of Korea with the intent of conducting subversive activities against our sovereign nation. You are, by definition, a spy."

Lee shook his head slowly, still looking at the knotted wooden planks that made up the floor.

The officer placed his hat on the table. The only sound in the room was that of his boots squeaking on the wood. Like the European armies of the 1800s, his ceremonial uniform was based on the concept of mounted cavalry, and Lee wondered if horses were still actively used in military operations within North Korea. He doubted that, as horses were too good a source of meat. The soft, supple sound of leather flexed in time with the officer's steps, heightening Lee's sense of fear.

He had to speak. He had to defend himself.

"I am a civilian pilot, captain of a search and rescue helicopter, a Sea King based out of Incheon, South Korea. Call sign Foxtrot Echo Sierra Four Zero. We were fired upon by a North Korean fighter while in international waters."

"Do you know who I am?" the officer asked, his posture impeccable, his arms tucked behind his lower back as he marched slowly in front of Lee.

Lee avoided eye contact.

"Colonel Eun-Yong of the 54th mechanized battalion, commissioned to protect the motherland against western aggression."

He paused, letting his words sink in before adding, "I catch spies."

Eun-Yong turned his back to Lee, straightening the picture of the Supreme Leader Most Glorious. He touched the wooden frame with a deft motion, barely moving the picture as he asked, "What do you know about him?"

"Nothing," Lee replied softly, his voice barely audible.

Without facing Lee, Eun-Yong snapped his fingers.

One of the guards grabbed Lee's right hand, holding it rigid against the wooden arm of the chair, splaying his fingers wide. Another soldier opened the toolbox on the table and pulled out a pair of bolt cutters.

Lee felt his heart race.

Adrenaline surged through his veins. Fear swelled in his mind, causing him to sweat in the cold air. He looked at the soldier holding his hand with such brute force and fought to pull his fingers free. From the way the soldier positioned his arm over Lee's, gripping Lee's arm beneath the wing of his own arm as he grabbed at Lee's fingers, it was clear he had done this before, and that terrified Lee. He shook in the chair, fighting against the leather restraints. The soldier's baby face belied the savagery of the moment. The other soldier exercised the bolt cutters, working the levers back and forth and smiling as he made eye contact with Lee.

"What are you doing?" Lee cried, his voice breaking in a quiver.

"You will answer the question," Eun-Yong replied calmly, turning back toward him, allowing the second soldier to step in front of Lee. "What do you know about him?"

Lee found his mind racing. What did he know? He couldn't think of anything of any significance. He knew the North Koreans were paranoid, but did they really think his intention was to assassinate their leader?

The sight of the bolt cutters caused him to tremble. With his fingers spread, held rigid by the younger soldier, Lee found his mind racing.

"His name is Kim Jong-chol," he blurted out.

"Don't play games with me!" Eun-Yong cried in anger, waving his finger at Lee. "I will not be mocked! I will ask you one more time. What do you know about him?"

"Nothing," Lee cried, on the verge of hyperventilating. "Nothing!"

Eun-Yong gave the slightest of nods, signaling to the soldiers. The first soldier tightened his grip, getting one hand beneath Lee's palm and raising his pinky finger. The other soldier opened the bolt cutters.

"No," Lee cried. "No!"

There was no further warning, no deliberation, no mercy. The soldier before him stepped in and snipped at Lee's hand in an instant, severing his little finger in a single, brutal act.

"ARRRRGGG!" Lee screamed.

He rocked forward as the muscles throughout his body trembled in response to the surge of pain. Lee fought in vain against the leather straps, trying with all his might to tear free from his restraints. Blood gushed from the stump on his hand, pulsing as it sprayed across the floor. The severed finger fell to the floor, rolling to one side away from him.

Lee pursed his lips, breathing in short pants, his mind reeling from the physical shock of the amputation. Every nerve in his body screamed in agony. He couldn't think.

Eun-Yong paced as the soldiers positioned the bolt cutter over Lee's ring finger. Lee was manic, his eyes focused on the steel blades already cutting into his skin. Blood welled from around the blades of the cutter. He fought to wriggle free, but the soldier beside him held him firm. His entire arm throbbed with pain. Waves of agony pulsed through his body.

"WHAT DO YOU KNOW ABOUT HIM?" Eun-Yong yelled.

"NOTHING!" Lee yelled in reply.

Through the haze of pain, he felt the soldier clamp down on the bolt cutters slowly this time, the leverage building till the point the bone leading to his knuckle snapped and pain again surged up his arm, tearing along his forearm, his bicep and into his shoulder.

"AHHHHHHHHHHHHHH!"

Lee shook violently, slamming his torso back and forth, clinching and struggling in vain against the leather restraints. He arched his back, trying to wrestle free, fighting to slip free from the soldier pinning his arm. The legs of the chair scraped across the ground, lifting off the floor and slamming back again as he flexed every muscle in his body trying to wrench himself free. Another soldier came up on his left, grabbing him and anchoring him in place.

"No. No. No," Lee cried, his mind reeling from the pain. He was in shock. His heart raced, thumping in his chest. Blood flowed copiously from the severed stumps on his hand.

Eun-Yong was in a rage. His face was red with anger. Spittle flew through the air as he screamed at Lee.

"TELL ME WHAT I WANT TO KNOW!"

Lee couldn't speak. His head throbbed. He felt like someone had stuck a red hot poker up behind his eye. Spasms of pain shot through his arm and up his neck. He fought like a wild animal caught in a snare, thrashing and roaring in anguish. His vision narrowed. He thought he was blacking out, hoping darkness would come as a relief from the torture, but Eun-Yong was no amateur. Through the sweat and tears clouding his vision, against the flexing and trembling of his body, Lee caught the subtlest of nods from Eun-Yong to the soldiers.

"NOOOOOOOO!"

The pain of having a third finger amputated caused Lee to convulse. Having his middle finger severed struck him like a bolt of lightning, as though an explosion had gone off in that instant, blinding him for a second. The pain seemed unbearable, as though there were no more he could endure, and yet each time he lost a finger the pain surged higher again. Eun-Yong knew what he was doing, he seemed to understand how each cut increased the agony Lee was suffering.

Lee's head whipped back. He was shaking involuntarily, struggling for breath. Urine ran from his bladder, pooling on the seat of the chair and running down the back of his legs. His world shrank. His eyes focused on the stumps on his right hand, staring at the blood flowing from the wounds. He was in shock, swept up in disbelief, but the pain was very real. He pursed his lips, hyperventilating as he fought to control the pain, but it was overwhelming.

The soldier pinning his arm to the chair pressed a dirty cloth hard against the bloody stumps. Lee could see two of his three severed fingers lying on the bloodstained floor before him, the third lay out of sight. He could barely breathe. His eyes were wide with fear, watching as the soldier in front of him positioned the bolt cutter over his index finger.

He fought, trying to wiggle free, but the soldier beside him held him forcibly in place. Again, Lee felt the steel biting into his finger, already the pressure was building.

"No," he whimpered, helpless, the anticipation of pain already shooting through his arm.

Eun-Yong composed himself, speaking in an even tone. "You don't need to go through this. Just tell me what I want to know."

"I don't know anything," Lee pleaded, sobbing. "Please, I don't know."

"Three down," Eun-Yong said coldly. "There are seventeen more. Are you sure there is nothing you want to tell me about him? Why did you come for him?"

"For him?" Lee cried, finally understanding. In that moment, he froze, his mind reeling from all that had happened, from the realization they were after the girl from the stars. He had to tell them. He couldn't put up a facade. He hated himself for betraying her, but he knew nothing of this child.

"Not him," he said. "Her. We were sent to rescue a girl."

The soldier with the bolt cutters flexed as the soldier looked to Eun-Yong for the signal, but the colonel raised his hand.

"You really don't know, do you?"

Lee shook his head. He couldn't reply. His mouth was dry. Words failed him.

Eun-Yong raised his hand, flicking his fingers. He gestured toward a soldier standing behind Lee. "Bring in the American child."

A young boy was thrust in front of Lee as the soldier beside him applied pressure to his wounded hand. The boy looked Korean. He couldn't have been more than three or four years old. His long hair was matted and unkempt. He was wearing an oversized Nike T-shirt that looked like a dress on his small frame.

Lee stared at the boy with disbelief as the soldier before him with the bolt cutters held steady pressure on his index finger, cutting into the skin.

Blood dripped from his mutilated hand.

The child should have been horrified, but it was almost as though the young boy expected this, as if he had anticipated what was happening before he was dragged into the room. Perhaps he'd heard the screams. His head tilted to one side as he took a good look at Lee's trembling hand still held forcibly in place by a kneeling soldier. Lee's index finger was poised between a pair of bolt cutters. The boy seemed strangely detached, as though he were carefully examining the dynamics of the situation. There was no pity in his eyes, just acceptance.

"This dog knows nothing!" Eun-Yong cried. "He is no better than the others."

The soldier with the bolt cutter eased the tension on his index finger.

"Take him away," the colonel ordered.

The soldiers released the straps around Lee's arms and legs, pushing a bloodied rag into his left hand so he could tend to his wound. Still fighting the pain, Lee pushed the rag hard up against the three stumps on his right hand, trying to stop the bleeding. He felt weak, drained of any strength.

As the soldiers dragged him from the interrogation room his eyes locked with those of the child.

"I remember you," the child said, speaking in American English. "I remember how you died."

Lee was stunned. Up until that point, the torture had been conducted in Korean. The soft, docile tones of English being spoken by a child sent a chill down his spine, leaving him speechless. To have this child speak of his death in the past tense terrified him.

Blood dripped from the rag he held over his hand. It hurt to apply pressure to his wounds, but he had no choice. Gritting his teeth, he fought through the pain, watching as the soldiers led the child away, laughing among themselves.

Lee couldn't walk. The soldiers didn't care. They dragged him across the gravel outside, carrying him between them. Another soldier opened a steel bolt barring a heavy wooden door and the soldiers dragged him down several concrete steps before throwing him in a darkened half-cellar. Leaving him in the shadows as the sunset shone through the trees behind them.

Lee whimpered, curling into a ball on the loose straw covering the floor. He felt physically sick, still struggling to comprehend what had happened.

In the darkness, a hand reached out for him.

Reality

"Are you sure you're going to be OK?" Helena asked as Jason struggled to steady his shaking hand and insert the key into the lock of his door.

"I'll be fine," he insisted, finally feeling the brass key slip into the lock and click in place. He turned the key, turning the handle of his door at the same time and opening the door to his darkened apartment. A window had been left open. The curtains fluttered as rain blew in.

"You should stay with him," Helena said, turning to Mitchell.

"I'm happy to stay with you," Mitchell said.

Jason turned back toward them. "I'll be OK. I just need to get some sleep."

Mitchell pursed his lips, nodding. He didn't seem convinced.

Helena's phone beeped with an incoming message. She turned away to pull a pair of reading glasses from her purse, leaving the two men for a moment.

"Dude," Mitchell said. "Is this about Lily?"

"No," Jason replied, shaking his head. Lying didn't come easy, and he looked down at his shoes.

"I told you, man. She was never going to be more than a one night stand. She probably found her dad and is already on her way upstate or heading over to Jersey ... You'll hear from her again, I'm sure. She'll send you a postcard or something. She's a nice kid. She'll be in touch, but you know nothing will ever come of it, right?"

"Right," Jason replied reluctantly.

He stood there in the doorway, nodding his head softly, his eyes still cast down. Part of him wanted to tell Mitchell what had happened, but another part of him felt he'd be ridiculed by his friend, and right now that was more than he could handle.

It had been a long night. After a couple of hours spent watching reruns of Seinfeld in the emergency waiting room, a nurse had patched him up, cleaning the specks of gravel out of his graze and bandaging his arms. He hadn't needed stitches. A squirt of plastic skin covered the worst spots, and the compression bandage on his arms was more precautionary than anything else, to help reduce swelling and bruising.

Jason felt stupid.

He felt stupid for jumping out of the bus. He felt stupid for falling for Lily. He felt stupid seeing Lily levitating and disappearing into the belly of a UFO. He felt stupid thinking about the paper he'd given Professor Lachlan. In that moment, it was as though nothing in his life made any sense. If he had kept whiskey or beer in his apartment he would have drunk himself silly.

It was well after midnight and Jason just wanted to collapse on his bed and go to sleep and forget about the day. Maybe in the morning he'd be able to think straight and make sense of things. Right now, he was confused and hurt. Although his pain was more than physical and far more than the result of some emotional attachment to Lily. Seeing the UFO had left him feeling gutted, empty, stripped of the intellectual clothing with which he'd trusted his life.

Jason started closing the door, positioning himself behind it with only his head visible.

"Are you going to be OK?" Mitchell asked.

"I'll be fine."

"Breakfast. Mario's. 9am. OK?"

"Make it ten," Jason replied.

"Done. See you then, bro."

Jason closed the door softly, pushing gently until the lock clicked into place. He could hear Helena talking to Mitchell outside.

"Someone should stay with him."

"He's a big boy," Mitchell replied, as their voices disappeared down the stairs. "He'll be fine."

Inside his apartment, Jason slumped to the worn carpet, leaning against the door. A cool wind blew in through the window, but already the humidity was building again.

Several of Jason's posters had come away from the walls. The Blue Marble had peeled away and twisted, falling forward, still held on by tape at the base, but it was no longer a thing of wonder. It was just a poster. Looking at the glossy white backing, it could have been a poster for some rock band. All the meaning was lost, which was quite ironic, he thought.

Jason felt his heart sink. Words failed him. He'd done his best. He'd tried hard to stay objective, to think rationally, to look at life through the prism of science, and yet he couldn't explain what he'd seen a few hours earlier. If Mitchell had described a similar scene, Jason would have ridiculed him, asking him what he'd been smoking. Jason never would have believed him, regardless of any details Mitchell could have recalled. Alien abduction was an absurd notion, and yet he'd seen one. Could his eyes be believed? Was he in denial by not believing?

Jason would have stayed seated there against the door for hours had his bladder not insisted otherwise. Yawning, he resolved to put the idiocy and inconsistencies of the day behind him. Perhaps things would look different in the light of a new morning. He doubted it, but the rhythm of life demanded rest, and he hoped sleep would bring respite.

There was enough ambient light in the room to move around without bumping into furniture, so Jason left the lights off. He closed the window and then wandered into the bathroom, scratching at the patchy stubble on his cheek. Out of habit, he closed the door behind him. He could have stood in front of the toilet to relieve himself, but he was tired so he plonked down on the plastic seat.

Sitting there in the darkness, he noticed a faint glow on the glass shower door. Slowly, the outline of a woman holding a sign appeared. His eyes darted up, looking at the drop light directly above his head. The darkened light bulb flickered. Someone had hidden a tiny projector behind the light fitting, aiming the projector at the shower.

"What the?"

Shush.

That one word was written in thick, black letters. The woman's fingers clutched at a marker, a Sharpie from what he could tell. As the image became more distinct, Jason could see Lily standing there holding a stack of cards facing him. She peeled the front card away, tossing it carelessly to one side, out of camera view.

Don't speak.

Jason dropped his hands instinctively in front of his crotch, even though his baggy t-shirt covered his lap. He felt embarrassed regardless of the low light making any details around him a hazy, grey blur.

From his perspective, it seemed as though Lily could see him, as though she were responding to his motions. She flicked quickly through several more cards, tossing them carelessly to her left.

I'm sorry.

Confusing, I know.

I can explain.

So much you need to know.

Please, forgive me.

I meant no harm.

Trust me.

She had tears in her eyes.

"I don't understand," he said, and she held her finger to her lips, signaling for him to be quiet.

The next series of cards made his blood run cold.

You are in danger.

You must leave.

Not safe.

Please, trust me.

Without saying anything, he mouthed the word, "OK."

Wherever she was, she was watching him in real time as she smiled in response. Tears rolled down her cheeks as she turned over four more cards.

Count back from 60.

Be out front on one.

No sooner.

No later.

As she discarded the last cue card, her image faded, being replaced with a series of numbers counting down.

59, 58, 57, 56, 55...

Jason sat there on the toilet stunned with his pants still around his ankles. Did he trust her? Could he forgive her? What was going on? Why the mind games?

46, 45, 44, 43...

Time was slipping away.

Jason hated being backed into a corner, being forced to make a snap decision. He needed the opportunity to assimilate what was happening.

Lily must have hidden the projector while she was having a shower the night before, but why the charade? She had to be nearby. Jason stood up, partially blocking the numbers as he pulled up his pants.

31, 30, 29, 28, 27...

He closed the seat on the toilet, flushed, and stood on the lid. His fingers pulled at the projector. It was tiny, no larger than a quarter, and had been wedged between the steel rim of the light fitting and the drywall that made up the ceiling. A long straggly wire acted as an aerial. He turned the device over in his hand. He'd never seen anything this complex in such miniature form before. There had to be a self contained power supply, a radio receiver, not to mention the projector with its bulb and lens.

18, 17, 16, 15...

Was there a microphone embedded in it as well? Was there a camera as well as a projector? She'd seen him. Was there some other device hidden somewhere else inside the bathroom?

10, 9, 8...

He couldn't see anything over the sink, but in the darkness he could easily overlook a pinhole camera. He reached for the light switch but paused as he realized the countdown was coming to an end.

6, 5, 4...

Shit!

In a panic, he tossed the projector on the ground and threw the bathroom door open. With his heart pounding in his chest, he leaped onto his bed, scrambling across toward the door. Both of his hands worked with superb synchronicity, turning the lock and handle in unison and allowing him to fly through the door and out into the hallway with barely a thought to what he was doing, abandoning his apartment and leaving the door wide open.

Mentally, he had already reached the number one and there was still a flight of stairs ahead of him leading down to the building foyer.

Fuck!

A motorcycle pulled up outside. The exhaust was rough, coughing and spluttering as though the fuel/air mix was too rich. Jason took the stairs three at a time, reacting, not thinking.

There was something deeply intriguing, perhaps even fascinating and satisfying in the heart-thumping sense of embarking on a mysterious, forbidden adventure.

Lily's tiny frame looked out of place on the motorbike as it waited there idling. Had he stopped to think, even for a moment, there was no way he would have climbed on the back of a motorbike, but there she was, waving for him to hurry.

He ran across the lobby, almost crashing into the doors as he pressed the exit button. Ordinarily, the door opened almost instantly, but that night the electronics seemed to pause for an eternity. Deep inside the door, the lock clicked, indicating the door could be pushed open, but he didn't have either the keys to his apartment or the keycard for the main door to get back into the building. Too bad.

"This is crazy!" he said, unable to suppress the grin stretching across his face at the sight of Lily on the back of a dirt bike modified for riding over the rough countryside well beyond New York City.

The motorbike was a contradiction of clashing colors. Large red coils at the front provided stiff suspension for the handlebars, while the seat at the rear was bright green. The seat was set surprisingly high, exposing the off-road tire. Fumes drifted from the chrome exhaust. There was no license plate.

"You're late," Lily cried as he rushed outside into the night. She handed him a helmet. Lily was wearing blue jeans and a black leather jacket, and not a formal dress kind of jacket, one custom made for motorcycle riders. The thick leather and padded sections on the shoulders made her tiny frame look bulky, almost butch, as though she had muscles bigger than his.

Jason smiled, looking at the helmet she handed him as he said, "What's going on?" He almost laughed. He found it preposterous to see her fragile frame on such a large, powerful motorbike.

Lily revved the engine, keeping the bike from idling.

"No time to explain. Get on!"

"Now, wait a minute," Jason replied, but Lily grabbed him by the scruff of his shirt, pulling him close and kissing him briskly on the lips. She pulled back from him just as abruptly, looking deep into his eyes as she spoke.

"I know this is difficult. But we have to leave."

Jason turned. There were a dozen or so men and women running down the street toward them.

In the distance, easily a quarter of mile away, several police cars turned into the street with their lights flashing and their sirens blaring.

"Now!" Lily cried.

What had started out somewhat playfully, suddenly made his blood run cold.

Gun shots rang out.

Although Jason had been intrigued by Lily's sudden appearance and what seemed to be a transformation from her shy and quiet demeanor to an overtly aggressive and assertive persona, this was no joke. Something had gone horribly wrong. A state of panic swept through him, paralyzing him.

"Please," she pleaded. "You've got to trust me. Your life is in danger!"

There was something in her voice, in the look in her eyes and the desperation in her actions that cried out louder than the gunshots.

Jason jumped on the back of the bike and grabbed onto her waist. In his rush, he dropped the helmet. But why would she give him a helmet when she wasn't wearing one? Before he could consider that thought, Lily popped the clutch and the bike roared away, accelerating sharply. Jason tightened his grip and held on.

The engine roared as the bike cut up over the curb and onto the side street crossing Columbus Avenue.

Jason found himself holding on with desperation, fighting not to be thrown from the bike. He kept one hand around Lily's waist, gripping the belt running through her jeans, while his other hand held a handle on the back of the seat.

The wind cut through Lily's hair, causing the long strands to whip painfully across his face.

The high pitched whine of the engine sounded absurdly strained, as though she had long forgotten to change gears as she continued to accelerate. When the gear change finally came, though, it was smooth, and the bike shot forward at breakneck speed as they raced toward Central Park.

A police car skidded around the corner ahead of them, sliding sideways and blocking half the road. The officer leaped from his car and threw a spike strip across the remainder of the road. What the hell is going on, he wondered? Jason had gone from being half asleep to his heart pounding in his throat in barely a minute. How had he ended up on the back of a motorcycle? His mind was struggling to keep pace with events.

"Hold on," Lily cried, and he could see she had no intention of stopping for either the police officer or the red light in the distance.

Lily timed her ride, cutting up onto the footpath at a low ramp designed for wheelchairs, but the angle she crossed the ramp on was acute, still catching part of the curb and Jason found himself launched airborne on the back of the dirt bike. He had to pull himself back down onto the seat by the handle as Lily raced past lampposts, trash cans and bus stop seats mounted on the sidewalk. His feet struggled to find the passenger footrests that were mounted absurdly high as the bike was designed for riding through creeks and streams.

They shot past the police officer and flew off the edge of the footpath and out across Central Park West. Police cars continued to race along the streets toward them, but Lily cut across into the park. She was working hard with the handlebars, making numerous small corrections as they continued to gain speed. Jason was very aware of his own center of gravity and how his motion affected their overall balance. The slightest movement, turning to look at the police or even looking over her shoulder caused the dynamic of the bike's balance to shift.

Lily's body felt taut and stiff, every muscle seemed tense. The bike's engine screamed like a swarm of angry hornets as they cut through the darkened park.

"What are you doing?" he yelled over the noise. "You're heading toward the lake!"

At the speed they were traveling, they bounced across thousands of tiny bumps on the gravel walkway. The undulations in the ground caused the bike to shudder and shake. Lily kept the throttle wide open, gunning the bike as they raced down a grassy slope toward the water.

"Ninety miles an hour," she cried, yelling into the wind. "At ninety miles an hour we'll make it three hundred and twenty feet!"

The bike skipped, its knobby tires eating up the grass and bouncing from one mound to another, tearing across the park at breakneck speed.

"You're a scientist," she added, not taking her eyes off the shoreline rapidly approaching in the moonlight. "This is physics in action!"

Jason tightened his grip on her waist, trying not to bounce off the seat behind her as the bike flew toward the edge of the lake. He yelled out, "You're mad! Crazy!"

"I know!" she screamed as they hit the water.

The bike roared across the surface of the lake.

He understood that as long as they had forward momentum they'd avoid sinking, glancing across the pond like a skipping stone, but their momentum began to wane ever so slightly. White spray lashed out to either side of the dirt bike as they skimmed across the waves. Water splashed fifteen to twenty feet on either side of them.

"Come on, you son of a bitch!" Lily yelled over the roar of the engine.

The cycle screamed as the wheels threw water out to either side of the bike. Jason was so petrified he could have laughed. This was preposterous, but Lily was right, this was physics in action! They were a skimming stone on a pond, moving so fast they were being buffeted by the water beneath them. Just like a water skier, as long as they kept their speed up they wouldn't sink. They were skipping over the water, moving so fast they were bouncing off the surface of the lake, but they were losing momentum with each passing second.

Jason could feel the bike sinking as the water slowed their forward momentum. Red and blue lights flashed on the shore, blocking the path on land, but the police car was slightly behind them.

Jason had no idea how fast they were going when they hit the water, but it seemed as though they had carved their way across the pond for three or four seconds. The far shore approached as the bike sank, but they were close enough that the water near the edge was barely knee deep.

Lily worked with the gears, revving the engine as they settled on the muddy bottom. Water sprayed out behind them as the rear wheel struggled to gain traction.

Gun shots rang out through the night.

"Come on!" Lily yelled. The rear wheel bit beneath the water, and the bike lurched forward.

Lily had the front wheel up on the bank and her legs out to either side, steadying the bike as the rear wheel fought to free itself from the pond, slipping and sliding as water shot out some thirty feet behind them in an arc of fine spray.

After what seemed like minutes, but must have only been a second or two, they were free and the bike rode up out of the pond, across the rocks and back onto the grass. The engine roared in fury. Steam rose from the engine block and exhaust pipe. Dirt sprayed behind them and Jason felt himself being catapulted back to an absurd speed as they sped off through the trees, following a gravel path winding through the park.

They whipped across a concrete path and screamed up a low grassy field, becoming airborne as they crossed the brow of the hill. Again, Jason found himself floating in mid air holding onto the seat with one hand and Lily with the other. They hit the ground with a thud and Jason figured they must have flown a good fifteen to twenty feet. Clods of grass flew from beneath the wheels of the motocross bike as they bounced on the landing. It felt as though they were losing their balance.

Jason was terrified. All he could think about was the kinetic energy they had gained and how a collision with one of the trees would break just about every bone in his body.

Lily hunched over the handle bars with her head down. As they raced through a thicket Jason quickly realized why as twigs and branches slapped at him in anger.

Lily seemed to be able to anticipate the gaps in the trees before they appeared. It was as though she had memorized the route, knowing every single bump and depression, understanding precisely how the motorcycle would respond. She shifted her weight, working with the handlebars and lining up the bike as they roared through the trees and out into an open field.

Several police cars were still in pursuit, but they had fallen a considerable way behind them. Lily's hair no longer whipped through the air regardless of their speed, and it took Jason a second to realize why: they were both dripping wet.

Lily wasn't stopping for anyone, of that Jason was sure, and that scared him, but there was nothing he could do other than hold on for dear life.

"Stop!" Jason pleaded. "You've got to stop."

Lily ignored him.

The motorcycle shot out of the park and across Fifth Avenue, getting airborne again as they flew off the curb. They cut off a taxi and darted away as the driver honked his horn at the empty air.

Lily accelerated along East 72nd Street, flying across Madison and Park Avenue.

Jason wasn't sure how he knew, perhaps it was merely instinctive, but as Lily raced along she brought the bike hard up against the curb on the left hand side of the road and he knew she was going to swing hard to the right. Had there been any oncoming traffic they would have run headlong into them, but she didn't seem to care.

Hadn't she heard of brakes?

As absurd and comical as it seemed, he felt like pointing out to her that slowing for a corner was the norm. Racing around a corner at the same speed as you travelled in a straight line was not advisable. The law of the conservation of angular momentum meant there would be an illusion of centrifugal force causing understeer and they'd hit the building on the far corner. How his mind arrived at such a conclusion in that fraction of a second was something even he didn't fully understand, but it did. She was pushing physics too far!

The motorcycle raced along barely half a foot from the curb as Lexington Avenue raced toward them. The streets were slick, with pools of water still sitting on the surface after the rain. Oil floated on the road, giving the concrete a glossy sheen. This was suicide. Jason clenched, expecting to be hurtled from the bike as Lily cut in across the apex of the corner.

The motorcycle slid on the oily surface water.

The rear tire slipped out from beneath them.

Lily had her right foot down. She was standing on the road with one foot, or she would have been standing if she'd been stationary. Instead, her thick riding boots acted as a foil, skimming across the concrete, stabilizing them as they skidded around the corner, gliding across the slick road. She was standing, with her weight split between the bike and her right leg as they drifted through the corner. The bike lay sideways, almost parallel to the concrete. Jason found himself shifting his weight, trying to stay on the bike.

For a moment, he thought his leg was going to be pinned beneath the bike, but the exhaust took the brunt of the slide, scraping on the ground and kicking up sparks.

Lily gunned the throttle, dropping down a gear and accelerating through the corner. The motorcycle responded like a demon possessed, howling at the night as she straightened up.

Police cars poured into East 72nd almost two blocks behind them, but they'd made the corner into Lexington Avenue at speed.

Jason was shaking, his hands trembled as he struggled to hold on to the bike. Shock was setting in.

"Please," he cried. "Please, let me off."

Lily raced south along Lexington Avenue, coming up rapidly behind a semi-trailer trundling down the road before them at a leisurely pace. To Jason's surprise, the back of the semi opened, with its door lowering and becoming a ramp. Without either the bike or the truck stopping, Lily raced up into the back of the darkened truck, slamming on the brakes at the last minute.

Lights came on inside the trailer as the ramp raised, closing behind them, and the truck turned off Lexington.

Standing there at the rear of the truck, holding onto a set of ropes, was Professor Lachlan.

"Hello Jason," he said, smiling as Lily cut the engine on the bike. "I told you I'd be in touch."

Kindness

"Give me your hand," a voice said from the darkness.

Lee turned, looking around his cramped prison. He could see a dark silhouette in the adjacent cell. Terrified, he scuttled to the opposite corner, cradling his injured hand, nursing himself through the pain. He couldn't speak, all that passed from his lips was a whimper.

Over the following hour, the prisoner in the next cell kept calling for him, pleading with him to come over to the bars, but Lee couldn't move. His mind was still reeling with shock.

Moonlight fought its way through the bars set into the window. Broken glass lay on the cold concrete floor, mixed in with loose straw and clumps of dried mud.

Again, a hand reached out for him through the bars of the adjacent cell. Lee pushed his back up hard against the cold, iron bars of the far cell, desperate to stay away. His reaction was instinctive, unthinking, born of the desire to protect his wounded hand. Fingers grabbed at him through the darkness.

"It's OK. I can help," the stranger said softly. "Let me see your hand."

The voice was American. In the haze of agony he felt following the torture, he hadn't realized that before, but like the young boy, this prisoner was speaking English.

Lee felt his head spinning. There was too much to take in, too much to process. Time seemed to compress, blurring reality, and he struggled to comprehend where he was and what was happening to him. He wanted to run. An impulsive desire swept over him, a longing to flee from danger. The outstretched, dirty arm of the other prisoner intruded into what little sanctuary he had.

Lee's cell was no more than four feet wide, but was at least ten feet long, stretching to the back of the barracks above.

Lee pushed his back against the bars of the far cell, trying to get as far away as he could from the hand reaching out for him. Terror swept through him. In the darkness, there could have been more hands reaching for him, dozens of them grabbing him from behind. That thought shook him.

"Please," he pleaded. "Leave me alone."

He cowered, struggling with his throbbing right hand. Blood oozed from beneath the soaked rag pressed hard up against the raw stumps on his hand.

"What have those bastards done to you?" the voice asked.

Lee felt his heart jump. This had to be one of the Navy SEALs.

He tried to speak, but his trembling lips wouldn't respond. His cheeks quivered. Tears rolled from his eyes.

"Let me look at your hand. I can help."

Help. The concept was foreign to Lee, sounding as though it were spoken in strange, inhospitable language rather than English. With what he'd gone through, Lee couldn't imagine what it meant for one human to help another. A knot formed in his throat. Help? What help could he be?

"Trust me," the man said. "You've lost a lot of blood. Look at the floor. You're still bleeding. We have to stop the bleeding."

Lee could barely make out the man's pale features in the half light. Mud and grime covered his face. His hair was matted and tangled, wild like the trees of the windswept coast. His drab olive clothing was torn and dirty. His boots were scuffed and worn.

Lee kicked against the concrete floor, his socks sliding on the straw as he pushed himself over toward the stranger. What could the American do? How could he help? It didn't matter. Lee needed help, any kind of help. Just to hear a kind voice filled him with a glimmer of hope.

The man moved to the front of the cell, where the moonlight fell on the bars that separated them. He was squatting. It was only then Lee realized the cell was no more than three feet in height.

"Show me your hand."

Lee shook his head. He dared not release his grip on the bloody rag covering his hand.

"I'm a medic. I can help."

In the dim light, Lee could make out a needle and thread held in the man's right hand.

"You're lucky. They worked over Andrews too, but they took all of his fingers, even the thumbs. I managed to get a sewing kit from one of the guards, but there was nothing I could do. He'd lost too much blood."

"He's ..." Lee asked, the word sticking in his throat.

In the darkness, the stranger nodded, his lips pulled taut with anguish.

Lee dragged himself up against the bars, wriggling against them with his shoulders, pushing along the ground with his feet. His left hand was still fiercely protective of his right hand and he felt he couldn't let go.

"Keep the pressure on," the medic said, with both hands reaching through the bars. He held the needle between his teeth as he spoke, saying. "I'm going to peel the bandage back slowly and close up your wounds one by one."

Lee nodded, watching as the Navy SEAL pried the bloody cloth back just enough to reveal the bloody stump where once his little finger had been.

"I'm sorry," he added. "But I'm going to need to close off the severed veins. I'm so sorry, but this is going to hurt."

The medic handed Lee a small lump of wood, saying, "Bite on this. The last thing you need is to crack a tooth."

Lee pushed his wrist and forearm hard against the bars, trying to hold them still as the medic pulled the needle from his mouth and began stitching up the bleeding stump on the edge of his hand. Lee couldn't look. He bit on the wood and concentrated on his breathing, trying to take steady breaths as the needle passed in and out of the skin and flesh on his hand. Each jab felt like a burning hot knife searing through his skin. He kept his eyes focused on the window, looking out beyond the bars to the trees in the distance, watching as bats flittered among the branches.

The pain came in waves and felt as though it would never end. Every muscle in his body tensed. Slowly, the medic repositioned the bloody rag, working in silence, moving the cloth back and revealing what had been Lee's ring finger and then his middle finger.

Lee tried to distract himself. As best he understood the layout of the camp, he was looking roughly west, out toward where he had flown over the Yellow Sea in his rescue helicopter. Lee had no idea how far inland he was, but in his mind he imagined hills rolling gently down to the coast. Mentally, he was trying to escape this prison and the pain surging through his hand.

The medic was rough, pulling at his hand from time to time and repositioning his arm, pushing and pinching and prodding. He had his face pressed hard up against the bars, with both forearms protruding through and anchoring Lee's forearm as he worked on his hand.

"Done," he finally said, relaxing his grip. "I'm sorry I couldn't have helped more, but at least we've stopped the bleeding and closed off the wounds."

Lee turned and looked at his hand for what felt like the first time. Coarse black stitches, irregular and chaotic weaved across the bloody stumps set hard against his hand. The skin had been pulled taut. A semi-clear fluid seeped from around one of the stumps. The other stumps were bloody and bruised.

"Thank you," Lee said, his voice shaking. He held his right hand by the wrist, afraid to touch the hand itself, unsure how much of the surging pain would return.

The medic slumped away from him, exhausted by the effort. He pushed his back against the bars on the far side of his cage. Cell was too nice a term for the filth they squatted in, Lee decided. These were animal cages.

Already, his head was clearing. He was still in agony and his hand throbbed, but just that tiny sliver of compassion and help from the medic lifted his spirits and helped him focus.

"What a cluster fuck, huh?" the medic said. Above his head, boots marched by, crunching on the gravel.

"Will we ever get out of here?" Lee asked.

"Do you mean here?" the medic replied, pointing at the ground, "Or here." He circled his hand, indicating all around them, which Lee supposed was representative of North Korea as a country.

"Either," Lee replied. "Both."

"I don't think they'll keep us here long, as in, here in these cells. These are holding cells at best. I think they're normally used to shelter animals during winter. As for here in this camp, I suspect we'll be taken to Pyongyang before too long. There's nothing the US public hates more than seeing its soldiers dragged through the streets of some foreign capital. They'll keep us alive till then, at least. It's too good a PR opportunity to miss. From there, who knows? Maybe we'll spend a decade as pawns on a chessboard until some kind of trade can be arranged."

Lee was silent. He doubted the North Koreans would be so hospitable to someone from South Korea. More than likely, they'd kill him to avoid any complications. As far as anyone from the south would ever know, he died in the helicopter crash and his body was never recovered. In some ways, that might be the better option for his parents, as it would avoid putting them through a living hell for the next decade, giving them a chance to grieve once and not for years on end.

"And as for your hand," the medic continued. "That'll be a wound sustained in the crash, or they'll offer some other plausible scenario."

Lee nodded.

"As far as getting out of North Korea," the medic said, "I don't care how we leave, so long as it's not in a body bag."

Lee's head dropped. There was silence for a few moments.

"You were the pilot, right?" the medic asked.

"Yes."

"What have they figured out?"

"Uh," Lee began, not sure where to begin. "I don't know. What a nightmare! This should have been a textbook run up the coast, drop you guys offshore and then back to Incheon for breakfast."

He laughed, lost in thought as he spoke, "I was supposed to be playing golf today. Oh, to walk on a carefully manicured lawn taking my frustrations out on a small white ball. What bliss that would be!"

Lee held up his mutilated hand, saying, "Bit of a handicap, wouldn't you say?"

The medic grinned.

"I thought they were after a young girl," Lee continued. "Took three bloody fingers to convince them I was as stupid as I am."

Lee turned to face the medic as the temperature outside plummeted and a chill crept into their prison.

"I hope that boy is worth it, or a lot of good men died for nothing."

The medic was silent, nodding in response, letting Lee talk.

"He recognized me," Lee said. "I don't know how or why, but he did. Freaked me out!"

"Did you see anyone else on the run out there?" the medic asked. "Did anyone else make it to shore?"

"No. No one," Lee replied. "Wait, there was someone, but they caught him. A pack of dogs ravaged him on the beach. I washed up on the rocks, just north of him. I saw him die."

The medic nodded. He turned and crawled to the cell door and struck at the bars with a clump of wood, calling out in Korean, saying, "Open up. I'm finished here."

Lee was confused. He didn't understand what was going on. He scrambled over by the medic, reaching through the bars with his one good hand.

"What are you doing?" he asked quietly.

Suddenly, the realization that he had been betrayed swept over him, chilling him more than the cold of night. The Navy SEALs had all been wearing black wetsuits, not army fatigues. The medic's eyes had the classic epicanthal fold characteristic of people throughout Asia, but his accent was from the American Midwest, Lee was sure of it. And he was wearing boots! Lee had been stripped of his boots. All the clues were there, but he'd missed them.

A guard stepped down and opened the adjacent cell door. His keys rattled as he fought with the old, rusted lock.

"I don't understand," Lee called out, still reeling mentally from all that had transpired. He trusted this man. "Why?"

The medic turned, speaking in English as he said, "We had to know if you were telling the truth."

The door opened and the medic crawled through, getting to his feet and dusting himself off.

"But ..."

"Oh," the medic replied, stepping in front of Lee's cell. He crouched in front of Lee, smiling and pointing across the courtyard as he added. "You thought that was the interrogation over there? No, that was the prelude. This was the interrogation, and you did admirably. You told me what little you knew."

Lee sunk to his elbows.

The medic left, laughing with the guard as they walked off, their boots crunching on the gravel as they crossed the driveway.

Lee was devastated.

He looked at the weeping stumps on his right hand and sobbed, feeling worse than when he was thrown in the cell. As much as the physical pain had crippled him, he'd somehow endured that, perhaps only by holding onto the moment, waiting for the passage of time to provide relief, but the cruelty of those last few words from the medic cut deeper than the loss of his fingers. That laugh, the ignominy of knowing he'd freely given up what little information he had, and the humiliation of his trust being betrayed broke his heart. Lee felt a pain like no other eating away within his chest. His hand throbbed, his muscles ached, but it was the mental anguish that crushed his soul.

He lay there in a fetal position for the next hour, rocking gently, trying to stay warm on what little straw covered the concrete floor. Outside, the routine crunch of boots passed every fifteen minutes. A sentry was walking a set path, walking along the gravel road at regular intervals.

Shortly after the sentry passed, another set of boots crunched on the gravel, only these were more hurried. They stopped outside his cell. The abrupt silence seized his attention and he turned to see nothing more than a set of legs beyond the bars.

Moonlight lit the courtyard, highlighting the soldier's legs in silhouette. Something dropped on the ground and was kicked through the bars, landing not more than a few feet from him.

Lee didn't move.

He lay there looking at the small box no larger than a pack of cigarettes. When he looked up, the legs were gone. He hadn't noticed the sound of boots on the gravel, so whoever it was had approached from across the courtyard but then exited along the side of the building on the grass, before disappearing god knows where.

Slowly, cautiously, Lee picked up the cardboard packet, examining it in the soft light flooding in from outside. He didn't recognize the label on the front, and the writing on the back was too small to make out in the faint light, but one Korean word caught his eye: painkiller.

Frantically, he ripped open the cardboard with his teeth. There were two strips of ten tablets sealed in plastic. It could have been poison. It could have been yet another cruel hoax by the North Koreans, but Lee couldn't help himself. He tore open one of the strips and tossed four or five white tablets in his mouth, crunching them beneath his teeth.

The tablets tasted disgusting. They were bitter and dry, breaking up into a powder in his mouth, making them hard to swallow without water.

As nearly as he could tell, they must have been the North Korean equivalent of ibuprofen.

Lee was surprised by how the sense of taste engaged his mind, drawing it away from the aches and pains, refocusing his world.

Who had given him these tablets?

Had the medic been merciful?

Lee was tempted to take more tablets, but decided it was better to let these take effect and save the rest for later. He'd need them, and he knew it.

Lee stashed the remaining tablets in his socks on the inside of his ankle, feeling paranoid about being searched and losing the painkillers. They were still in their plastic case, so he folded his socks inward, tucking the hem over the tablets, knowing they wouldn't be seen and feeling as though he'd won a small victory over his captors. That he had something hidden returned a sense of power to him. He took the cardboard packet and forced it between the grates of a drain, getting rid of any evidence.

Lee wasn't sure how effective the painkillers actually were and how much of a placebo bounce he was getting out of suddenly having a sense of purpose, but the pain subsided.

As he moved back by the door he noticed a scrap of paper lying on the straw. It must have fallen out of the packet as he'd ripped it open with his teeth. He unfolded the paper and read one word scrawled hurriedly in pencil: *Midnight.*

Questions

"I don't understand," Jason said, getting off the motorcycle inside the back of the semi-trailer, surprised by how much his legs were shaking. For a moment, he thought his legs were going to give out beneath him. With the swaying of the truck, Jason felt clumsy, and had to reach out for the inside of the trailer to steady himself.

Lily put the motorcycle on its kickstand and hopped off of it.

"Jason," she said, gesturing toward the professor. "This is my father, Captain John Lee of the South Korean National Intelligence Service."

"Am I dreaming?" Jason asked. "Tell me this isn't real. None of this. None of this can be real."

"Please," Professor Lachlan said, pulling a thick folder from under his arm and gesturing at a crate loaded against the wall of the trailer. "Have a seat. There is a great deal we need to tell you."

"I ..." Jason was speechless.

Lily scooted up onto the crate, leaving room for him beside her. She patted the wooden surface, signaling for Jason to sit next to her.

"It's OK. I don't bite," she said. "Well, at least, not on good days."

Given all they'd just been through, her small joke seemed almost normal, bringing a smile to his face.

The truck swayed and Jason lurched. He widened his stance, fighting to keep his balance as the truck rounded a corner. He reached out and grabbed the edge of the crate, pulling himself closer.

"We have a ways to go," the professor said. "We need to get well clear of the city before they have time to analyze the video footage and realize where we've gone. We chose Lexington for the switch because there are no traffic cameras in that block, only a few surveillance cameras mounted on ATMs. That should buy us a few hours."

"What's going on?" Jason asked, raising himself up on the crate and leaning against the thin sheet metal wall of the semi-trailer.

Lachlan held up his mutilated hand, displaying the stumps of three fingers, saying, "You don't remember, do you? No, you wouldn't. You were young, too young, and so much has happened since then."

Jason pursed his lips. For him, the strangest thing that had happened so far was not the insane motorcycle ride flying across a lake, or riding up into the back of a moving truck, or even running into his physics professor in the middle of the night in the back of a semi, it was the sense of calm that swept over him as Lachlan spoke. There was something familiar about the professor's words, as though he'd heard them before. The professor had always had a calming effect on him, and now more so than ever. Jason didn't understand why, but he trusted Lachlan implicitly.

"None of this was our doing," the professor continued. "For decades, we lobbied against the subterfuge, but DARPA insisted. They felt the best way to get information from you was to allow you to be free. Your subconscious seemed to be providing them with the answers they wanted, so they allowed you to live a normal life while they collected the data they needed, but progress has been slow. In the last few weeks, there's been a change of administration. The presiding general decided it's time to bring you in and extract the knowledge that's buried in your mind. They're tired of waiting and they don't care if they break you."

"I don't understand," Jason said. "None of this makes any sense."

"They were coming for you," Lily said, cutting through the explanations and going straight to the heart of the issue.

"Me? Why me?" he asked.

Lachlan raised his hand, scratching at his forehead. Jason could see he was struggling to decide where to begin and what to explain. Jason had never seen the professor flustered before.

"What about the UFO?" Jason asked, turning to Lily.

"You fell for that?" Lily asked, punching him playfully on the arm. "I can't believe you fell for that. I thought it was too corny."

"Smoke machines and wires," Lachlan replied. "A disco ball and strobe lights, nothing more. Just like Hollywood."

"And the projector in my bathroom?" Jason asked incredulously, nonplussed at hearing these revelations about a murky world that existed in parallel with what he perceived as reality.

"It's the only place inside your apartment that's not under constant surveillance."

"What? But why?" Jason protested. "Why me?"

Professor Lachlan held up Jason's research paper, but he was holding up the reverse side covered in Jason's doodles and speculative calculations.

"Because ever since you were a child, you've been drawing these equations."

Jason went silent. Lily held his hand, squeezing his fingers. Initially, he wasn't sure what to make of her touch. On one hand, her support was welcome. On the other, this wasn't the Lily he knew. The Lily he'd known had never existed. She'd never been more than an actor on a stage playing a role for the crowd. Yet there must have been a genuine connection between them, as she seemed to feel something for him. He squeezed her fingers gently in reply, letting her know he was doing OK.

Lily turned to him, saying, "You don't know just how special and unique you are."

Her comment took him off guard. She wasn't trying to flatter him or appeal to his vanity. He could tell that from the sincerity in her voice. She was speaking as though this was something he didn't understand about himself.

Rain lashed the outside of the truck, pelting the trailer with what sounded like hail. It probably wasn't hail, but the thin sheet metal magnified the sound of the torrential downpour that had begun to fall.

Jason felt as though the night were a dream. He looked into Lily's eyes and saw her compassion for him. To her, this whole scenario apparently seemed quite ordinary, and as bizarre as that was, he was drawn to accepting her position. Her demeanor was relaxed, as though her blistering bike ride was nothing, as though sweet, little, lost Lily had returned to sit beside him. In his mind's eye, he saw her again asking something quirky about the torn, tatty posters in his rundown apartment. She may have been acting for the past few days, he thought, but even knowing that, he felt he understood those points at which the real Lily had shone through.

Between the demeanor of Lily and the familiarity of Lachlan, Jason felt accepted, as though this twisted reality that had caught up with him was the norm. While he was tempted to freak out, they set him at ease with their matter of fact handling of the bizarre tempest breaking around him.

Lily was Lachlan's daughter! As strange as that was, that was perhaps the easiest thing to believe so far. In the back of his mind the notion that someone had been shooting at him was disturbing.

Lachlan must have sensed his distraction. He flipped through a thick folder as he spoke.

"The NSA has been working with DARPA for decades, trying to figure out what these equations mean," Lachlan continued. Jason wondered if he should think of him as Captain John Lee? But that name meant nothing to Jason. To him, this was Professor Lachlan. As surreal as his world had become, the professor was a link with reality, with sanity.

"Do you remember these?" the professor asked. He held an old piece of crumpled paper marked with crayon. The formulas weren't as advanced and the handwriting was childish, but Jason remembered them. Somewhere in the back of his mind, that sheet of old, brittle paper looked strangely familiar. "You've been drawing these equations ever since you were a child. Haven't you ever wondered why?"

Why?

No, he hadn't ever stopped to think about why he scribbled.

For Jason, abstract thinking was as unconscious as humming a tune or chewing on gum. He'd never wondered why he doodled, he just did, in the same way some people chewed their nails when lost in thought. It was more than being absentminded, he knew that. Time would drift. Hours would pass, but he was content, at peace. Nothing else mattered, nothing other than those equations. Slowly, they'd take different forms. Each time, his perceptual awareness enlarged, and he found himself with a deeper appreciation of the universe.

Most of the equations were common, having been derived by others like Bohr or Schrödinger, but Jason had arrived at them himself, having reasoned through the math alone, and he found that intensely satisfying.

Why did he scribble physics equations? Was there a reason beyond his own simple whim and want? He could see

Lachlan was giving him time to think this through for himself. He thought he knew, but clearly there was more for him to learn. He pursed his lips, leaning forward intently, listening carefully as Lachlan explained.

"Twenty years ago, a meteor streaked across the Russian Federation, entering the atmosphere over the region of Krasnoyarsk. US EarthSat picked it up over Lake Baikal. It should have struck somewhere in Mongolia, but the meteor conducted a course correction."

Jason felt his mouth dry out at the implications of Lachlan's matter of fact recounting of this distant, historical event. He had no reason to doubt the professor. This wasn't Mitchell sitting next to him in a diner with some trashy online tabloid, bullshitting his way through some crackpot conspiracy theory. This was a senior college professor with a mastery of physics.

"The object crossed the northern plains of China, passing over the Gulf of Chihli before ditching in the Yellow Sea, off the coast of North Korea."

"Ditching?" Jason asked.

Lachlan nodded, adding "The USS Winterhalter was on exercise out of Seoul. She picked up the craft doing Mach 2 and observed it decelerate before ditching roughly fifty nautical miles north of her position. The Winterhalter then launched a helicopter, assuming she was searching for survivors from a downed military jet."

Lachlan handed Jason a couple of photos. Although they were in color, they were grainy, highlighting the distance at which they'd been taken. The first image showed what looked like a whale or a submarine sitting heavy in the water, with just a small, broad, flat expanse above the waves. The object was circular rather than elongated, though, and looked out of place beneath the sea. A North Korean fishing boat floated just off to one side of the submerged object, providing a sense of scale. The dark object was roughly a hundred feet in diameter, with faint lights glowing around its circumference.

The second image was one Jason had seen before. This was the picture Mitchell had shown him in the Weekly World News article, only this image was grainy, with features like the mast and sails on the fishing boat barely visible. Jason looked up at Lachlan who seemed to know what he was thinking.

"These are the originals," Lachlan explained. "Taken from the raw footage before any digital enhancements were applied."

As in the crisp, clear version he'd seen in the Weekly World News, a North Korean fisherman was leaning over the side of his boat pulling a young child from the water. The UFO was completely beneath the waves in this shot, drifting slowly below the fishing boat.

"So this is real?" Jason asked, already knowing the answer. "This actually happened?"

Lachlan must have recognized the rhetorical nature of Jason's comment as he didn't respond directly, he simply said, "Two days later, I flew in with a SEAL team to rescue you."

"Me?" Jason replied, still struggling to accept everything that had happened since he'd returned to his apartment. His hand brushed against the bandages on his arms, marking where he'd rolled on the ground after jumping from a bus earlier that evening in what seemed like another lifetime.

Had he hit his head and been concussed?

Was this some kind of trauma induced hallucination?

Blood seeped through from around one of the plastic bandages sticking to his arm like a second skin. His left forearm was tender. The throb of pain after so much exertion holding on to the back of the bike convinced him this was real. This was no illusion. This was reality.

"I know it's hard to believe," Lachlan said, crouching before him. "But I was originally a search and rescue pilot, and look at me now, teaching physics in New York, and all because of you, all to try to unravel the mystery surrounding your life."

Jason was shaking.

"It's OK," Lily said, squeezing his hand. "We're here to help."

"Me," Jason repeated, only this time not as a question uttered in disbelief, but rather in sullen acceptance.

"I'm sorry," Lachlan said, standing up. "Your life has been an elaborate ruse to try to unlock the secrets buried deep within your brain."

"And my parents?" Jason asked.

"They never knew," Lachlan replied. "They only ever saw a beautiful young boy abandoned in an orphanage, but you were never out of sight. DARPA, the South Korean Intelligence Service, the US Secret Service, they've never been more than a heartbeat away."

"But you're saying—"

Jason was cut off by a radio squawking on the professor's hip. Lachlan raised the radio to his lips, depressed the transmit button and said, "Are we close?"

"Thirty seconds out," a disembodied voice replied.

"Quick," the professor said, gesturing to the back of the truck. "Time to go!"

Lily hopped off the crate, still holding Jason's hand, gently leading him along with her. Jason followed her, dazed.

The truck swayed and he reached out with his hand, steadying himself against the wall.

"We need to switch vehicles," Lachlan said, gesturing for him to follow. "We'll continue this conversation in our next ride."

Lily let go of his hand and grabbed the motorcycle.

She pulled the bike up, standing beside it as she flipped the kickstand back beneath the exhaust pipe. Lily began wheeling the bike to one side, walking it in a three point turn as the truck began to decelerate slightly.

Professor Lachlan stood by the door. He had an industrial control panel in his hand, a thick, long rubber-coated panel with only a couple of buttons. As he held his thumb on one of the thick buttons, the door began lowering back down as a ramp again. Hydraulic pistons eased the ramp down until it was level with the scuffed wooden floor of the truck.

Jason came up behind the professor.

Wind swirled into the back of the trailer, drawing in the spray and rain. The freeway behind them was devoid of cars. Streetlights stood at regular intervals, lighting up the lanes of the freeway as they receded behind the truck.

The rain stopped, swiftly and abruptly, and Jason realized they were driving under an overpass as they slowed. No sooner had the rain stopped than Lily rushed past Lachlan and Jason, wheeling the motorcycle out of the truck and onto the ramp. She let go and the motorcycle freewheeled over the edge of the ramp, crashing onto the road and skidding into the dust and mud on the shoulder of the freeway.

The truck didn't stop.

"Come on," Lachlan said, jumping down from the moving truck and breaking into a run beneath the overpass. Lily waited for Jason.

Rather than hesitate and talk himself out of jumping, Jason sprang out, surprising himself with how confidently he could move when he really wanted to. He gripped the side of the ramp, swinging his legs over and dropping to the ground. The concrete was further away than he anticipated, and he stumbled, almost falling, but Lachlan grabbed him, jogging alongside as Jason broke into a clumsy trot to keep from keeling over. Lily jumped from the moving truck as Jason came to a halt on the side of the road. She moved gracefully, with the tone and precision of an athlete.

The back of the truck was already rising into place as the truck accelerated out from beneath the overpass. The driver worked through the gears rapidly, racing the engine and picking up speed again as he cut back into the storm.

Standing there beneath the overpass, with the truck already just a set of red lights disappearing into the rain, Jason felt vulnerable, but Lachlan and Lily looked relaxed.

"So," Jason said to Lily, trying to hide his discomfort with humor. "Do you come here often?"

She smiled. Her face radiated warmth in the cold of night. She had a beautiful smile, but it seemed out of place beneath a decrepit overpass in the midst of a storm.

Lachlan was talking intently on the radio. He walked off beneath the overpass and Jason couldn't hear what he was saying over the sound of the rain falling on either side of them.

The motorcycle lay in a heap on the side of the freeway. Its handlebars had twisted awkwardly as it fell and green fluid leaked from beneath the front struts. Whether it was antifreeze or brake fluid, Jason wasn't sure, but another clear liquid soaked into the dust from beneath the seat. That had to be gasoline. Lily didn't seem to care that her bike had been wrecked.

"I don't get it," Jason asked, gesturing toward the expensive dirt bike. "Why go to such elaborate lengths and then dump your motorcycle on the side of the road?"

"We can't leave any evidence." Lily replied. "Sooner or later, they'll match the truck and search the trailer. We need to make the trail as difficult as possible to follow."

"And that's going to help?" Jason asked, walking around the bike.

"Oh, it'll be gone by dawn," she replied casually, pointing across the freeway, out over the river beside them. "Someone from the Bronx will nab it, someone not related to us, and that will lead DARPA on a wild goose chase into a dead end."

"But look at it," he said, gesturing to the cracked plastic and dented muffler. When Lily had first pulled up in front of his building, the motorcycle looked brand new. Now it was a dusty, muddy wreck.

"You'd be surprised," she replied. "This makes it more attractive. If the bike looked too good, they wouldn't touch it, expecting a set up. It's got to look like something they can fence with no questions asked. Nah, this is just about right. It's a diamond in the rough."

Lily stood there walking slowly around the motorcycle, admiring her handiwork. She pulled out a smartphone and took a picture of the bike as it lay there on the shoulder of the road.

Rain continued to pour down beyond the overpass. A cold wind blew around them, peppering them with spit and spray.

This was the first opportunity Jason had to stop and think since he'd seen Lily flipping through her cue cards in his bathroom. Lachlan was still talking on the radio. Lily was checking something on her phone. She didn't have that with her yesterday, he knew. Yesterday, he thought she was sweet and innocent, now he wasn't so sure.

Jason found himself wondering which side of this battle he'd inadvertently joined by jumping on that motorcycle with her. Something dark was going on, that much was obvious, but what it was still eluded him. He trusted Lily and Lachlan, but he was also aware his trust was without cause. He could be trusting the wrong people! Yes, someone had been shooting at him. But was it him they were aiming for? Or were they warning shots, trying to intimidate the two of them into stopping? He didn't know.

The rain was somewhat hypnotic, causing him to feel numb.

"Upsetting, huh?" Lily said, coming up behind him and snapping him out of his lethargy.

As if reading his mind, she added, "If it's any consolation, those guys back there were firing rubber bullets.

Body shots sting, but even a rubber round can be lethal if you take one to the head."

"Ah," he replied. "That's why you gave me the helmet."

"Well, it wasn't to compensate for my riding," Lily added, grinning.

"Here they come," Lachlan said, joining Jason and Lily as he clipped the radio on his belt.

White lights appeared through the night, breaking up in the rain.

"Professor," Jason began. "I have to say, all of this is freaking me out a little, and a little is an understatement. I'm having a hard time buying what's going on here. This is crazy! Nothing you've told me makes any sense."

"I know," Lachlan replied in a soft, kind voice.

"Please be patient," Lily added, but her words weren't reassuring. Jason wanted answers. He wanted an explanation that was coherent and complete. So far, all he had were fragments of a puzzle.

"I will tell you anything you want to know," Lachlan promised, resting his hand on Jason's shoulder with fatherly care. "There is nothing I will keep from you, Jason. You have to believe me."

Jason appreciated his honesty, but he was aware that Lachlan was only now offering this promise to him. He'd known Lachlan for years. For at least four years, Lachlan had maintained a facade, a charade.

A handful of grainy pictures seemed flimsy as far as explanations went, Jason thought. They were hardly credible as evidence. Jason didn't want Lachlan to tell him anything he wanted to know, he wanted Lachlan to tell him everything, regardless of whether Jason wanted to know about it or not. Somehow, Lachlan's promise felt contrived, murky. The trust Jason had felt in the truck was eroding, washing away like the mud in the rain.

Within a minute or so, a recreational vehicle pulled up beneath the overpass, but it didn't stop either, slowing just enough for them to hop in as they jogged beside the side door.

The RV was nondescript. Dents and scrapes spoke of careless driving. The top rear of the vehicle had crumpled slightly where someone had tried to back up under a low ledge. They probably had to let the pressure out of the tires to free the jammed RV, Jason thought, looking at the crushed, accordion like metal, his mind running faster than his body as the three of them ran to keep up with the vehicle.

The side door was open, it had been clipped back in place. Rain had soaked the carpet in the stairwell. Lachlan got in first, followed by Jason, while Lily brought up the rear again. The RV was already beyond the overpass when Lily finally got on board. Torrential rain broke as she shut the door of the RV behind her.

The RV was spacious.

Fake wooden veneer lined a kitchen on one side. There must have been a bedroom beyond the kitchen, but the door leading to the rear of the RV was closed. Jason could hear voices from back there.

Lachlan moved up next to the driver, talking with him as he sat down in a plush leather seat while windshield wipers swished back and forth across the vast glass window. The driver signaled as he pulled back onto the highway. Lachlan scolded him for that, hurriedly getting him to switch off the turn signal as he said something about aerial surveillance.

Lily squeezed past Jason, resting her hands gently on his hips as she stepped around him and perched on a couch covered in a floral pattern. Jason hated being touched. Most of the time, he'd flinch if someone came up and grabbed his waist like that, but with Lily he had no such reaction. Funny, he thought. Subconsciously, he was more at ease with her than he would have consciously admitted.

"Here," she said, patting the soft, dry, cushioned seat beside her.

Jason sat down next to her. Lily pulled out a couple of plastic water bottles from beneath the coffee table in front of them and handed a bottle to Jason.

They were seated facing forward, with the kitchen behind them. A pair of matching seats faced them. Beyond those seats lay the open cabin of the RV, with Lachlan sitting beside the driver. His radio hissed and he pulled it from his hip and began talking into it. Jason would have loved to listen in, but he wasn't close enough to distinguish the words being spoken.

Lily sipped at her water.

"Well, this is nice," Jason said, relaxing for the first time, allowing his body to sink into the soft cushions.

"Much nicer than the truck," Lily agreed.

That they could make small talk was surreal after everything else that had happened that evening. In any other context, their conversation would have been banal, just courteous pleasantries being exchanged. Now, though, they both seemed to be grasping for normalcy, clinging to the fleeting illusion that reality would correct itself. What happened had to be a dream, Jason thought. Please let it have been a dream. Let me wake up in the morning to the sound of traffic and pigeons cooing on my windowsill. He sighed, letting out his breath in resignation, knowing that there would be no such awakening.

Beads of rain streaked at an angle along the side window, the angle corresponding to their speed on the highway. The storm outside was getting worse. Lightning lit up the cloud bank overhead.

The folding door concealing the bedroom behind them opened.

Jason turned, startled to see a woman walk out followed by two men. One of the men was carrying what looked like a television quality video camera. Lachlan ended his exchange on the radio, and rose to join them.

"Jason," he began. "This is April Stegmeyer of the Washington Post, John Vacili, a cameraman from PBS, and Special Agent Jim Bellum from the FBI."

Jason stood, shaking three surprisingly warm and friendly hands. Bellum and Stegmeyer sat in the chairs opposite Jason and Lily, while Vacili lifted his camera onto his shoulder and peered through the viewfinder. An obligatory red LED lit up, indicating the camera was recording their conversation.

"The FBI!" Jason said. "This is wonderful! This is just what we need. We don't have to run anymore."

234

"It's not quite that simple," Bellum replied. He had chiseled features. The angles of his jaw and cheekbones could have been carved from stone, and his gruff voice had a ring of authority. "I'm here to protect you, but you won't be safe until we've gone public with your story."

"My story?"

To Jason, there was no story. As far as he knew, his story had only started earlier that evening when he'd foolishly jumped on the back of a motorcycle. At least he thought it was foolish. He seemed to be running from something but he didn't know what. As far as he knew, he had nothing to run from.

"It's wonderful to finally meet you," April Stegmeyer said, pulling a handheld voice recorder from her pocket and clicking record. Another red LED glowed. Stegmeyer and Vacili, it seemed, weren't taking any chances on missing anything that was said.

Stegmeyer put the voice recorder on the table, but to Jason's surprise, she didn't put it in the center of the coffee table. She placed it to one side, next to a small vase with fake silk flowers. Jason had noticed them when he'd first sat down. It was one thing to have fake flowers, it was another level of cheap to have fake silk fake flowers, and in his opinion defeated the purpose of even having flowers at all. The recorder, though, was now slightly below the rim of the small vase and Jason understood what Stegmeyer was doing. She wanted to obscure the intrusion, to lessen the appearance of an interrogation. She must have wanted him to relax and forget about the recorder, but placing it the way she did had the opposite effect on him. Overt would not become covert. His analytical mind would not allow such deception to slip by, regardless of intent. That just wasn't the way his mind worked.

Jason had never seen Stegmeyer before, but he knew of her, having occasionally come across articles she had written on the Internet.

April looked to be in her mid-fifties, perhaps early sixties. She had certainly aged gracefully. Curly grey hair brushed against her shoulders and her makeup was tastefully done. She had a warm and inviting smile. He wanted to believe she was sincere, but warm smile or not, she was acutely aware of his every move. Every facial expression and choice of words was being captured on video and audio for later analysis. But why? And for whom? Who would care about a college grad student struggling with his masters?

Jason wondered if this was how the media twisted people's words? Record enough footage and you're bound to catch a smirk here, a poorly chosen phrase there. String them together and you can make any story you want. Take a couple of hours of footage and splice it down to a minute or two, and you can make someone out to be anything you want, monster or hero.

"It's OK," Stegmeyer said, apparently reading his thoughts. "You can trust us. We're all here to help."

Jason nodded in reply. Against his better judgement, he wanted to give her the benefit of the doubt, but he wasn't sure quite what was expected of him.

"What can you tell me about the alien craft?" she asked.

Jason looked at Lily.

Lachlan spoke, saying, "His memory is hazy."

"Let the man speak," Stegmeyer replied gently. "We need to get as much of this as possible from him, in his words."

Jason was acutely aware of the video camera focusing on him.

"I ... ah," he began. "I'm sorry. I don't know what you're talking about. This is all new to me."

Stegmeyer looked over her shoulder at Lachlan as he got out of the front seat and moved back into the RV.

"His memory is incomplete," the professor said. "Given time, he'll remember the details."

"You told me he would remember by now."

"Look," Jason offered. "Maybe there's been some kind of mistake."

Lachlan ignored him, speaking to Stegmeyer as he said, "Even without the spacecraft, we still have him. Jason carries the proof of his origin in his body."

Jason was horrified by what he heard. He leaned back in the chair, pushing himself into the cushion. Lily must have felt his muscles stiffen. She rested her hand on his knee, and whispered, "It's going to be all right."

Lachlan crouched down beside Stegmeyer, looking Jason in the eye.

"I know this is a lot to take in," he said. "But your body is remarkable. You're a miracle of biology."

"Me?" Jason replied. "But I have Cander's Syndrome. A genetic defect that causes blood anemia."

"There's no such thing," Lachlan said smiling. "They made that up as an excuse to keep you under close medical supervision. Your medication is nothing more than sugar pills. Oh, occasionally they'll slip something in there to make you feel sick and get you back in for MRI and blood tests, but it's all just a cover."

"It's true," Lily added. "They even faked the PubMed papers on Cander's, faked the research results and peer reviews, all so they could get a credible entry in Wikipedia in case you ever looked it up."

"But why?" Jason asked.

Lachlan opened his folder and tossed a couple of scan results on the table.

"Your heart is the size of a newborn infant's, and yet it pumps almost four thousand gallons a day, well over a million gallons a year. That's twice the volume of an Olympic sprinter."

"No," Jason said, shaking his head, looking at a chest scan showing a tiny heart. "I have a weak heart. I have annual ECG scans."

"You see the results they want you to see," Lachlan continued. "The average lung capacity of an adult male is just under two gallons, yours is over three. Your kidneys, liver and spleen are all enlarged. They're roughly the same size as someone that's twice your weight. What's more, your elastic muscle strength and peak force strength are off the charts. Your muscle tissue is denser and heavier than anything we've ever observed."

Jason laughed, saying, "This is absurd! Next you're going to tell me, Jor-El's my father and I've got to steer clear of Kryptonite."

"Not quite," Lachlan replied, smiling. "But close."

"Perhaps a demonstration would help." Lachlan turned to the FBI agent, saying, "Agent Bellum, you look buff. How much can you bench press?"

"I'll warm up with two hundred pounds and work up to three fifty, maybe four hundred on a good day."

"Would you mind demonstrating your strength by arm wrestling Jason?"

"What?" Jason asked, watching as Agent Bellum removed his jacket. He was a huge man with a barrel chest and muscles like an ox. Agent Bellum grinned, rolling up his sleeve and revealing the thick muscles of his forearm. His biceps were hidden by his business shirt, but only just. There wasn't a lot of extra room in those sleeves.

Jason looked to Lachlan for an explanation.

"Did you ever wonder why you were discouraged from sports? You were a natural. The problem was, you were too natural. You'd outrun your classmates and wonder why they were out of breath when they caught up to you, right?"

"I was never any good at sports," Jason replied. "Sports made me sick."

"Not quite," Lachlan said. "Your meds made you sick. Your handlers would see you starting to assert yourself physically and they would switch your meds to make it unpleasant for you. Think about it. All those times you felt sick, it was never on the same day. It was always the next day, wasn't it?"

Jason nodded as Lachlan continued.

"You'd kick a football half the length of a field without really trying. The people assigned to you did all they could to steer you away from anything physical, but they couldn't stop you from throwing a basketball the length of a court in the fourth grade for an impossible three-pointer!"

Jason smiled at that. He remembered that day well. He remembered the awe and amazement he got from the other kids in the gym, and he remembered being sick for almost a week afterwards. Had he been punished? Was that it? Could anyone be that cruel to a child?

Agent Bellum knelt down, resting his elbow on the coffee table. He flexed his fingers, smiling at Jason.

"Go on," Lily said, encouraging him.

Jason felt stupid.

He wasn't going to roll up his sleeve. His arms were embarrassingly thin compared to Bellum's.

Agent Bellum had to be in his late twenties, early thirties. He was in his physical prime. His arm was massive compared to Jason's. There was a compression bandage just visible beneath Jason's shirt. His fingers touched at the bandage beneath the cotton.

"It won't matter," Lachlan said confidently, observing Jason's reluctance. "You won't break a sweat."

Getting down on one knee, Jason offered his hand. He rested his elbow on the table across from Bellum.

The FBI Agent grinned. He'd clearly done this before. From the way he positioned his hand, arching his wrist over Jason's, it was obvious he knew what he was doing. He was relishing this.

Jason felt his hand swallowed up by Bellum's paw.

"OK," Lachlan said. "Ready?"

Jason felt the big man beginning to apply pressure, trying to force Jason's hand backwards onto the table.

"Go!" Lachlan cried.

Bellum surged, applying a massive wave of strength that took Jason by surprise, bending his hand back to within an inch or so of the stained wooden veneer.

Bellum leaned over the coffee table. The veins in his neck bulged and his face started turning red. Jason's forearm was trembling under the strain, but he found he could hold onto those last few inches. The bigger man shifted his weight, trying to get more leverage, but to Jason's surprise, the added pressure didn't bother him. He had plenty of strength in reserve. It was quite fascinating to observe, he thought, mentally detaching himself from the action. Across from him was this huge man on the verge of pinning his arm to the table, but only if Jason let him. Here was an FBI agent struggling with someone half his size.

Jason looked over at Lachlan and Stegmeyer. Lachlan looked relaxed, as though he had no doubts about what would happen next, whereas Stegmeyer looked nervous. She didn't want Jason to lose, much to his surprise. The contrast in their visages was stark. Stegmeyer never expected him to win.

With a little upward pressure, Jason straightened his arm, easily bringing Bellum back to their starting point.

Bellum's face flushed. Veins appeared on his forehead. His right arm trembled under the strain.

"Finish him," Lachlan said. Stegmeyer may have doubted Jason, but Lachlan didn't. Jason took pride in the confidence of his mentor.

In one fluid motion, Jason rolled Bellum's arm backwards, watching the big man fight with all his might not to lose. Rather than slamming Bellum's hand into the table, Jason touched it gently against the veneer, and Bellum released his grip, gasping for breath.

"Damn!" Bellum cried, shaking his fingers. Jason hadn't even thought about how hard he'd been holding Bellum's hand, but Bellum flexed his fingers, apparently trying to get some feeling back into them.

"Did you catch that?" Stegmeyer said to her cameraman.

"Oh, yeah."

"Amazing," the Washington Post reporter said. "So, he's an alien?"

"No," Lachlan said swiftly, cutting her off. From the tone of his voice, it was clear the professor was defending Jason, and Jason appreciated that. With everything that had happened, Jason felt almost a sense of vertigo. He wasn't physically dizzy, but mentally he was struggling to come to terms with the pace of events unfolding around him. To have Lachlan staunchly defending him was reassuring.

"He's unique," Lachlan added.

"Look at him," Bellum protested, getting up and sitting in his seat. "There's no way he's human."

"I've heard the rumors," Stegmeyer said. "Either he's an alien or he's some alien hybrid experiment."

Lachlan was visibly annoyed with both Stegmeyer and Bellum. Jason could see him going red in the face, but somehow he retained his composure and spoke with deliberation.

"You have no idea what we're dealing with here. Wild and fanciful guesses will not help."

"So what is he?" Stegmeyer asked. She was abrupt, and Jason got the feeling he was seeing the real April Stegmeyer, the cold, calculating reporter behind the warm smile.

"Human," Lachlan said, with a note of triumph as though that one word required no more explanation.

"Nah," Bellum replied. "Not with strength like that!"

"You don't understand," Lachlan continued. "You've heard the old mantra so many times you've come to believe it, that all men are created equal. They're not. No two men are physically alike. This is something Charles Darwin understood, but lately we seem to have forgotten it.

"Not only is your fingerprint unique among over seven billion of us walking around on this planet, so too is your nervous system, the attenuation of your muscle shape, size and tendons, your skeletal structure, and your cardiovascular and lymphatic system. They're similar and yet distinctly different."

"But he's too different," Stegmeyer stated bluntly.

"Is he?" Lachlan asked. "Usain Bolt can run a hundred meters in less than ten seconds. Does that make him an alien? Or does it make him exceptional in both his physical capabilities and discipline?"

Jason was fascinated by the professor's perspective, and somewhat relieved to know he was counted in the ranks of humanity.

"But ... But there's no discipline here," Bellum countered, gesturing with his hands toward Jason.

"No, there's not," the professor replied. "But Jason is human. I assure you, the scientists at DARPA are wrong in their assessment of his physical origins."

"How can you know that?" Stegmeyer demanded.

"Because science is founded on the principle that you don't jump to conclusions. Honestly, what's more likely? That Jason's an alien? Or that Jason has exceptional physical characteristics for some entirely valid reason we've yet to discover?"

"And that's enough for you?" Stegmeyer asked. Jason noticed she didn't answer Lachlan's question.

"It is," Lachlan replied. Jason's admiration for the professor grew in that instant. Lachlan wasn't going to abandon him. Jason might only just now be grasping at the threads of all that was happening, but he was confident he was in the right place, with the right people, with Lachlan and Lily by his side.

Midnight

Lee peered through the bars of his sunken cage.

After hearing that these narrow, low confines were used to house animals during winter, he couldn't think of his confinement as a jail. They'd imprisoned him in a stock holding pen, a stall.

The moon fought to break through the low clouds. The bars covering the window of his cage were level with the ground, allowing him to see out across the courtyard. In the darkness, he could make out the main gate roughly two hundred yards away. A dim light hung from a high pole, illuminating the barrier by the guardhouse. There must have been fences stretching to either side, but in the dark of night he couldn't see them.

Somewhere to his right, a yellow light bulb flickered slowly above a door, stuttering as it struggled to produce light from the irregular surges of electricity. Every now and then, the clouds would part and allow the full moon to shine through, highlighting the feeble effort of the artificial lights.

Lee cradled his wounded hand, trying not to feel sorry for himself. With spasms of pain shooting up his arm from time to time, he struggled not to let the weight of hopelessness bear down upon him.

"I'm going to make it," he muttered to himself, reminding himself of the note, trying to convince himself this wasn't the end.

Lee felt useless. It was an irrational feeling, he knew that, but knowing didn't help. An impending sense of dread swept over him.

"Don't feel sorry for yourself," he whispered, trying to buoy his spirits. "Don't go there, you dumb son of a bitch! You're alive, that's all that matters. Now, get yourself the hell out of here!"

Lee steeled himself, trying to remain grounded in the present.

A series of huts lined three sides of the yard outside his low cage, with the road to the main gate passing where the fourth side of the square should have been. What he'd thought of as a courtyard was little more than a muddy parade ground surrounded by a gravel road that ran past each of the old wooden buildings. A truck was parked to one side, but in the dark he couldn't make out what kind of truck it was, only that it looked old, like something from the Korean War in the 1950s. Surely, they couldn't have nursed their aging technology that long, he thought. Perhaps it was just that they had no need for new models and considered the old style trucks perfectly adequate.

There was a car on the far side of the truck, but all Lee could make out was the hood and the front wheel guard. Small flags were proudly displayed on either side of the curved hood. He hadn't noticed the car before, but then he hadn't noticed much of anything before now. Only now was his mind starting to think tactically, trying to glean any information that might help with his bid for freedom.

Who was helping him?

Had one of the Navy SEALs somehow escaped?

Or perhaps the SEALs had evaded capture in the first place?

Why would they come for him?

How did they know where he'd been taken?

Why would they risk exposing themselves by sneaking into a military base to free him?

He didn't know the answers to these questions, but he was glad they had.

Lee could see the hut where he had been tortured directly opposite his sunken cage, on the far side of the yard. It didn't look that different from any of the other old wooden huts, with their warped weatherboards and peeling paint. Lee could pick out that building only by remembering what direction he'd been dragged in as he staggered across the gravel road.

Even back then, through the haze of pain, he'd fought to retain at least a vague notion of distance and direction. His mind was all he had left. Physically, they had taken away his freedom. He had to fight to ensure they didn't win the mental battle.

His hand still throbbed but the tablets had taken the edge off the pain.

Trying to think objectively about where he was distracted him from the physical torment of his injuries. Focusing his mind brought relief, restoring his confidence.

Lee watched the guards, observing their routines, noting how they switched routes over by a darkened building he assumed was used for administration. They would retrace each other's steps to the barracks where he was located before marching past. The camp must have extended further to his right, as they marched out of sight for roughly ten minutes. He knew his helper had come from that direction with the painkillers, creeping up silently behind the guards as they marched on, and that seemed to validate that this wasn't another ruse by the North Koreans. Whoever it was that brought the painkillers, they had to be watching the camp, observing the same routine, and that thought gave Lee hope.

He reasoned that it couldn't just be one person. It might have been a single person who came in and made the drop, but there had to be several people working together. Lee was buoyed by that thought.

There was another window at the back of his cell, but it was boarded up. Perhaps that would show where the sentries went, he thought, and with some difficulty, he crawled to the far end of his basement cage, protecting his right hand by holding his arm across his chest, keeping his wrist to his sternum.

There were cracks in between the boards nailed over the outside of the window.

One of the bars was missing and another had come loose.

Lee could feel the crumbling concrete crunching in the window frame as he wriggled the bar around. He lifted the loose bar a little and got a feel for how shallowly it had been set into the concrete. With a bit of work, he could probably pull it out, and that brought a smile to his face, his first smile in days. Knowing why the soldiers had boarded up the window made him feel as though he was gaining some small advantage over them. They'd been lazy. Laziness was easily exploited.

Lee worked at twisting and tugging at the iron bar until it came free, knowing he could use the bar as a club. Having a weapon lifted his spirits, even if it was a poor match for a gun or a knife. Being armed felt good. Slowly, he was reclaiming the confidence that had been stripped from him.

Lee sat there for a few minutes, feeling the weight of the rusted iron bar in his left hand, thinking about how he'd have to swing it as a southpaw. He got used to the feel of it, of the leverage it would give, imagining how he could wield the bar in a fight. A blow to a raised forearm would break the ulna and possibly the radius as well if he could muster enough force. He pictured a blow to the windpipe of an assailant, incapacitating and silencing his attacker at the same time. Sitting there in the darkness, he paced himself slowly through the motion. The inbound swing would be at the windpipe, while the backlash would be directed at the temples.

"Nice," he whispered to himself. It wasn't the thought of violence he relished, rather the ability to defend himself, to wrest back the power stripped from him.

He pushed on the wooden boards, testing the nails that held them fast. There was a little flex, but he'd need some leverage to pry them away from the outer frame. The bar he'd pulled free was too thick to wedge between the boards as a crowbar, but he could use it against the other bars, jamming it between the bars and the planks of wood. Quietly, he forced one of the boards loose. It felt good to be taking the initiative. Lee peered through the crack he'd made between the boards, squeezing the bar through to stress the wood and nails, further widening the gap.

The rear of the camp was some kind of motor pool. Rows of cars and trucks obscured his view, but he caught the distinct edge of a helicopter rotor sagging under its own weight. Moonlight gleamed off the canopy of the helicopter, barely visible between the rows of vehicles. It wasn't one of the old Soviet Hinds. This helicopter was smaller than the ones he'd seen by the coast. It was closer to the bubble shaped Bell helicopters he'd done his flight training in.

Suddenly, the ambient light in his cage dropped, and Lee felt his heart race. He turned and saw something leaning up against the bars behind him, blocking the moonlight. He scurried over to the window and pulled a pair of boots and a heavy overcoat through the bars and into his cell as boots crunched on the gravel outside, walking away from him.

"Now you're talking," he whispered, allowing himself the luxury of excitement.

The coat was army issue and had an insignia on the shoulder, but the moon was behind the clouds so he couldn't make it out in any detail. He put on the boots but was unable to tie the laces. Just the thought of using his right hand caused pain to surge from the bloody stumps.

Lee pulled at the laces with one hand, working them tight and looping them around before tucking them into the top of the boots. That would have to do, he thought. If he had to run, he'd make it maybe fifty yards before the laces worked loose and then he'd flounder like a goose and probably have to kick them off.

Lee sat waiting with his back against the low wall. He didn't put the coat on, as much as he wanted to ward off the cold. He realized it was important not to get mud and dirt on the coat. If someone looked at him while he was wearing it, he had to pass for a guard or a soldier, and that wasn't going to happen if he looked like he'd been crawling around in a pigsty.

With his left hand, he ran his fingers continually through his hair, trying to pat down the loose strands.

Dew had begun forming on the grass beyond the bars.

Lee reached out and rubbed his left hand on the wet grass and then rubbed his fingers over his face, desperately trying to clean up his appearance. He had no mirror, but he felt he needed to look as normal as possible during the escape so he worked fastidiously, somewhat manically rubbing at his face, his neck and hair. A wave of paranoia swept over him at the realization that his bid for freedom could come undone because he looked like a hobo.

"Got to get dolled up for the ball," he muttered to himself, methodically rubbing his damp fingers on his forehead, trying to clean every inch of his unseen face.

"A mirror would have been nice," he mumbled.

Lee rubbed softly at his cheeks, licking his hand in the hope of tasting dirt to get an idea of how clean or otherwise he appeared, but he couldn't make out any difference. He was careful not to rub so hard as to be abrasive, gently cleaning under his eyes, across his chin and around his nose. He could only guess what he looked like. After a few minutes, he decided he must look semi-presentable, but he probably wouldn't win a beauty pageant. In the low light he hoped he could fool a guard.

Lee ran his fingers through his hair again and again, using what little dew there was to stick down his hair, slicking it back so hopefully it looked natural. Preparation is good, he thought to himself, preparation gives purpose.

He was ready.

No one came.

Minutes seemed like hours.

Lee got worried.

What if something had gone wrong? What if they changed their plans?

As nearly as he could tell, the painkillers had been kicked in his cage almost two hours ago. The jacket and boots had come over an hour later. What was the delay? He just wanted to get moving, to get out of his squalid, cramped prison. He was bouncing between emotional extremes, feeling a high when he pried the bar free, and a low when time dragged. Like a pendulum swinging back and forth, his emotions swung between extremes.

Lee had no way of knowing the time, and he began to get nervous. He couldn't see the moon from where he was as it had moved high in the sky, casting short shadows. At the point it reached its zenith, it would be midnight. If only he could see the moon. That one, small consolation of being able to tell the time, even if only as an approximate, would have lifted his spirits, but there was no such mercy. From where he was, it was impossible to estimate shadow lengths. It could be barely 11pm or already after midnight for all he could tell.

Rats scurried along the far wall, keeping to the shadows. Oh, how he envied those creatures, able to pass through the bars with ease, eking out an existence regardless of ideology. Life was simple, uncomplicated. They could forage or flee, mocking him with their freedom, sniffing as they crept through his cage. They could smell the blood, his blood. The thought of his fingers lying severed and cold in some garbage can, discarded like offal, caused him to gag.

"Get out of here," he yelled. With his left hand, he threw a handful of dirt and straw. Tiny bits of debris scattered across the floor. One of the rats darted away while the other turned and stared, its beady eyes locked with his, its whiskers twitching in the moonlight.

"Leave me alone," he cried again, kicking at the loose straw with his feet and flinging another handful of debris at the rat.

Lee kept his wounded hand close to his chest. The muscles in his forearm shook as he sought in vain to protect his bloodied hand. His actions were a pathetic attempt at keeping the wound clean and he knew it. He could no more protect his hand than he could demand that the sun rise. Regardless of whether it was Eun-Yong or the revolutions of the planet beneath him, the cruelty of his captors or the rhythms of Earth, Lee came to realize he had no control over his own life, and that realization hurt. For a captain, someone who was in charge of a flight crew and a multi-million dollar helicopter, this was a sobering thought, bringing tears to his eyes. His heart sank in despair. This ache was a pain no other could ever inflict on him: it came from his own realization of helplessness.

"Please," Lee said, pleading with the rat.

As a pilot, he had exquisitely tuned control over his world with just the slightest twist of his wrist. Rocking to the left as he sat there in the cockpit of his Sea King helicopter would cause reality to obey his slightest whim. Eight tons of steel would sway gently through the air in response to his touch, following his fleeting thoughts as though the craft were an extension of his body. Just the lightest of touches on the pedals would cause corrections, minute or sweeping, allowing him to perform aerial ballet. He'd been a god in the sky. Here in this prison, he had been cast down out of heaven, a mere mortal, naked and bleeding.

"Please," he said again, his voice breaking, barely a whisper in the night. The rat seemed to understand. It turned and crawled away, its tail dragging on the ground as it disappeared silently into the shadows.

The guards continued their routine outside, and each time they marched past on the gravel Lee listened for an extra set of footsteps, but there was only the soft rustle of the breeze through the trees looming over the barracks.

Had something happened?

Had one of his rescuers been caught?

His mind raced in panic. They couldn't have been caught, he reasoned, as there would have been a flurry of activity from the other soldiers in the camp. Instead, a few lonely guards trudged through the night. They were still coming, he told himself.

What was keeping them?

Peering out through the bars, Lee could see rain beginning to fall. The soft patter was soothing, filling the quiet of the night with a gentle rhythm.

One of the guards marched along the gravel, right on time, but this time he stopped beside the cell. In the dim light, Lee could see the man looking around as he stood there silently in the rain with an old carbine rifle slung over his right shoulder. Casually, the guard stepped off the gravel path and down the concrete steps leading to Lee's holding cell.

Lee felt his heart pounding in his chest. His hand throbbed. The sound of the key in the lock teased him. He wanted to spring forward and out of the door, but he held his nerve, waiting for the guard to open the rusted lock.

"Come," a voice said softly in Korean.

Lee crept out of the sunken basement, slipping the heavy overcoat across his shoulders as he stepped out into the rain. Although his left arm was in the coat, he struggled to get his right hand down through the sleeve. Just the slightest of touches against the rough wool sent pain shooting up his arm. He fought to curl his wrist and jimmy the coat on, trying not to let his wounded hand scrape against the inside of the sleeve.

Lee looked at his rescuer.

At first, he didn't recognize him. The young man's baby face looked slightly rounded and plain. His hair was hidden beneath a cap, warding off the rain. He didn't smile. He barely acknowledged Lee at all, treating him with what seemed like disdain.

"I ..." Lee began, not sure what he was going to say, but feeling an overwhelming sense of gratitude. Freedom lay a long way off, but to stand on the other side of those bars, no longer humbled by the filthy straw and the low wooden ceiling, made him euphoric, if only for a moment.

"We must hurry," the soldier said softly.

As the moonlight lit the side of his face, Lee caught a glimmer in his eye, a glimmer he had seen briefly the night before in the light of a fire burning inside an old wooden cabin. This was Sun-Hee's brother.

"We will help you, but you must help us."

Lee nodded, walking alongside the young man.

Clouds passed in front of the moon and the ambient light faded.

Rain fell in a light drizzle.

Gravel crunched underfoot, revealing the distinct sound of two men walking slightly out of sync.

Lee stepped to one side and walked on the muddy grass to hide his presence from anyone sleeping in the rude buildings. He kept to the shadows that were cast by the huts, afraid of prying eyes peering out from behind their darkened windows.

"Sun-Hee and my grandfather are waiting by the coast. I will take you there. From there, you must take all of us to the south."

"Won't they stop us?" Lee whispered, gesturing at the gate, more concerned about getting out of the camp than getting back to South Korea. To Lee, Seoul seemed as unreachable as Mars or Jupiter. All he could focus on was the next step. Beyond that, chance would play its hand, but until then he wanted to take control of anything he could.

"Ha," the young man laughed under his breath. "This is a North Korean army camp. We have rice, maize, fish and eggs. We keep peasants out, we don't keep them in."

"What about the boy?"

The soldier stopped in his tracks and turned to face Lee as he spoke. "We leave him."

"No!" Lee replied, surprising himself with the vehemence of his response. "We have to take him with us."

"He fell from the stars," the guard replied, his eyes looking up at the clouds billowing across the sky. "If he can travel through space, he can care for himself."

"He's just a child," Lee insisted, trying to keep his voice low. His mind brought back the eerie words the boy had spoken after his torture, speaking of his death. How could the child possibly know anything about Lee, let alone how he would die?

Perhaps he should leave him.

Perhaps he should run from such a dire prophecy?

Perhaps by running he could avert disaster?

There was something about the boy's face, some innocence that demanded justice.

"He is under guard," the soldier said, turning and walking on in the rain. "General Gil-Su arrived earlier this evening. Tomorrow, he will take the boy to Pyongyang to see the Great Leader. There is nothing to be done."

"No," Lee repeated, keeping his voice low but speaking with determination. He continued on beside the guard, his boots squelching on the sodden grass. "We cannot let that happen."

"Why would you rescue him?" the soldier asked.

"Why would you rescue me?" Lee asked in reply. "For the same reason I rescued Sun-Hee. Because it is the right thing to do."

"But if we are caught."

Lee held up the bloody stumps on his right hand, saying, "Too many people have died, too many people have suffered for all this to be in vain. I'm not sure I buy the whole star-child thing, but that child is in the eye of the hurricane. I can't leave him to the storm. If they did this to me, what will they do to him?"

"He is in there," Sun-Hee's brother said, pointing at a nearby building.

A dim electrical light hung over the door, barely lighting the wooden steps leading to the entrance.

They walked cautiously up to the administration block. Lee wasn't sure what Sun-Hee's brother was thinking, but for all his bravado, it was clear he dreaded being caught.

Lee struggled to keep his nerve. At any second, guards could burst around the corner, yelling and chasing him as they had in the village. He imagined spotlights blinding him as dogs were unleashed. Doubt swept across his mind. Each step seemed to be a step too far, a step that could never be undone or retraced in a slightly different manner to reach an alternate end. He was committed, regardless, and he knew it. If they caught him trying to escape, they'd kill him, but he knew he had to rescue the boy.

The fingers of his left hand trembled, betraying the fear welling up inside him.

Lee peered through a window beside the door to the administration block.

A light flickered from somewhere at the end of the hallway, casting a dirty yellow hue across the rough wooden floor. The step beneath him creaked as he moved to get a better look. There was a guard on a chair at the end of the hallway, his head propped up in the corner, asleep. He was slouching, slumping to the point that he had almost slipped off the chair. A rifle leaned against the wall next to him.

"What's the layout?" Lee asked. He was trying to be brave, but the tremor in his voice betrayed his nerves.

Sun-Hee's brother pointed to an open door just inside the hallway, saying, "That's the reception area for the camp commander. His office is through there. The next two doors are storage and filing. The guard is outside the secretary pool. That is where they are keeping the boy, on a cot in the corner."

Lee tested the door knob with his left hand. The handle turned.

"No," the brother said, resting his hand on Lee's shoulder.

Lee opened the door anyway. His eyes were glued on the sleeping guard in the distance. He pulled the door ajar, just wide enough to slip through and crept inside. The hinges on the door groaned briefly as he closed the door behind him, all the while keeping his eyes locked on the guard.

A floorboard creaked softly beneath his shifting weight. The guard stirred at the sound but didn't open his eyes. He rocked slightly to one side as he fought to get comfortable and drifted back to sleep.

Lee cursed himself.

If he'd thought about his predicament logically, he would have backed out of the door and fled with Sun-Hee's brother while he still could. If that guard woke, his bid for freedom was over. Even if he had a gun, he couldn't use it. The sound of gunfire would have brought soldiers running from all over the camp. Lee wasn't sure what he could do, but he felt compelled to do something. Two decades of rescuing drowning people from raging seas had given him steely determination in spite of the odds. He'd seen plenty of people survive when they should have died, and that same reverence for life drove him on to rescue the star-child. He'd risked his life before. This night was no different.

His fingers tightened around the rusted iron bar in the pocket of his coat.

Lee crept into the reception area, slipping quietly into the shadows.

Scattered clouds drifted by outside, allowing moonlight to brighten the room.

The furniture was austere. A plain wooden desk blocked the approach to the back office. There was something wrong with the desk, something out of place. It took Lee a second to realize he automatically expected a computer or a typewriter on the desk, but the polished wooden surface was bare. A couple of empty filing trays sat to one side of the desk, along with a cup holding a few pencils. Any unfinished paperwork had been cleared away.

Beside the desk, a coat and hat were perched on a rack. Gold trim wound its way around shoulder boards on the heavy woolen overcoat, while the broad military hat looked new. Lee was surprised by the hat, as nothing else he'd seen in North Korea looked new. Everything he'd observed within the camp looked tired and worn. Even the neatly pressed uniform of Colonel Un-Yong had shown signs of wear, as though it had been handed down over generations. This had to be the general's coat.

Lee slipped off his own coat, placing it carefully on the coat rack, taking care not to make any noise as he slipped the general's coat on. With a rush of adrenaline surging through his veins he barely felt the coat brush against his injured hand. He tried the hat. It was a tight fit, but he could pull it down low over his brow.

Lee peered into the night, looking for Sun-Hee's brother outside. The distraught young man paced back and forth on the wet grass, clearly agitated, mumbling to himself, his head darting from side to side, evidently expecting to get caught at any second.

With only one good hand, Lee struggled to do up the belt on the coat. He slipped his wounded right hand into the pocket, hiding his bloody stumps from view and whispered to himself, saying, "No point in waiting. It's now or never."

He took a deep breath and marched out into the hallway, deliberately stomping on the wooden floor as he charged up to the sleeping guard in a rushed march. The rational portion of his mind screamed at him, telling him he was insane, that this would never work, but he had to try something. He had no time. There was no other way to get to the child. If he was going to free the boy, he had to have the audacity to try something insane. Would his bluff work? He was about to find out.

The laces on his boots worked loose as he stomped down the corridor, causing his boots to clump awkwardly as he thundered on.

The guard jumped out of his seat, knocking his rifle to the ground.

"Wake up, you drunken fool!" Lee ordered, his voice full of bluster.

He was shaking, and in his attempt to mask his fear he found he was yelling when he'd intended only to sound decisive. "I will have you court-martialed for dereliction of duty!"

The soldier was flustered. His cheeks were rosy, revealing the turmoil of emotions going through his mind. Lee could see he was struggling to decide whether he should stand at attention and salute or bend down and pick up his rifle. He struggled awkwardly between the two motions, stuttering in abortive attempts to do both. Lee knew he had him on the ropes.

"Pick that up," Lee commanded, pointing at the rifle. "You are a disgrace!"

The soldier scrambled to pick up his rifle, knocking the chair to one side with his boot. He tried to stand at attention beside the door, but he was clumsy. His eyes looked down at the knots of wood in the floorboards, avoiding eye contact with the general.

The soldier's jacket was twisted half off his shoulder from where he'd slept leaning against the wall. Lee reached out and pulled at one of the lapels, roughly tugging it into place, deliberately intimidating the young man with brute physical contact.

"I'm–"

"Silence!" Lee cried, cutting him off. He had to concentrate carefully on his pronunciation as he mimicked the North Korean slur. The guard kept his eyes low. "I've sent men to the mines for less than this."

He was bluffing. Mines sounded good. He hoped the North Koreans had coal mines or some such equivalent as a labor camp for prisoners. A coal mine was the worst place he could think of, and he cringed at the possibility that they didn't and he'd said something so obviously stupid that it would give him away. If the guard realized what was happening and reacted, he could easily overpower Lee. With his wounded hand, all Lee had was bluster, and he hoped his bluff was good enough.

In his haste, Lee had left the iron bar in his jacket pocket back in the reception area. He was defenseless.

"You are relieved of your post," Lee said forcibly, pinning his shoulders back and trying to make himself appear bigger than he was.

The guard stood there stunned. His eyes began to rise, drifting across Lee's overcoat. Had he spotted Lee's bloodstained uniform beneath? No matter how Lee had wrapped himself, the cut of the coat made it impossible to hide his clothing beneath.

Lee stamped his foot, signaling his disapproval of the guard's fleeting glimpse. Living in a totalitarian state, Lee hoped the man's inherent fear of authority was sufficient to paralyze him with inaction. If their eyes met, the game would be up.

In that fraction of a second, the soldier's nostrils flared, his jaw clenched, and his head dropped in begrudging submission.

"Be gone!" Lee added, not sure what else to say, knowing there was nothing more he could say, and wondering how else he could dismiss the soldier. His choice of words was clumsy, but he hoped the anger in his voice would carry the moment. It was now that his poker face would either win the hand or cause his bluff to fail. He held his lips tight, pursing them in anger, refusing to allow the slightest tremor of fear to creep through. "I never want to see you again."

Well, Lee thought, that much at least was true.

The soldier nodded without saying anything. He stepped to one side and slunk down the hallway with his rifle shouldered and his head hanging low.

Lee turned to watch the guard depart, his heart exploding within his chest. Whispering to himself, he mumbled, "Don't look back. Don't look back."

The soldier opened the door and walked out into the night, closing the door behind him without looking at Lee. His sunken features were submissive, and Lee understood the man was doing all he could to avoid incurring more wrath from what he perceived to be a brutish general. In his mind, he was probably already dreading a dressing down by the camp commander in the morning and packing his bags for a prison labor camp. Well, thought Lee, that was probably going to happen anyway, but for an entirely different reason once they realized the con.

Outside, Sun-Hee's brother jumped out of the way. Lee could see he was visibly shaken as the guard emerged from the building, but the guard didn't pay any attention to him. He kept his head down and hurried into the darkness.

Lee's shoulders dropped as he took a deep breath. He felt like he'd just swum under water for the length of the indoor pool at the Olympic complex in Seoul. His hand was still shaking as he reached for the door to the secretarial pool. The sudden thought that it might be locked terrified him. If so, the guard probably had the key. He tested the handle. The knob turned, allowing him to push the flimsy wooden door open.

The door squeaked on its hinges.

A child stood inside the darkened room, barely five feet from him. Behind the child was a freshly made cot. White sheets had been pulled down over the dark woolen blanket, ready for the child to slip into the bed, but it was clear the cot was undisturbed. The child must have been standing there waiting for him for hours.

"I knew you would come," the young boy said. "You always do."

Instead of a teddy bear or some other form of comfort, the boy was holding a crayon in one hand and a scrap of paper in the other. Lee expected to see some crude drawing of a house or trees, some depiction of the world around them lacking any perspective or depth. Perhaps with stick figures or an oversimplified image of the sun shining brightly in a clear blue sky, but the sheet of paper was covered in scientific formulae, all hurriedly drawn at various angles.

"This is what you want," the child said, handing Lee the paper. "Only you don't know it yet."

Lee glanced at the curious scrap of paper briefly, not sure what he should do with it before handing it back to the boy. He crouched down, making eye contact as he spoke.

"We're in a dangerous place. Do you understand that?"

The boy nodded.

"I need you to come with me," Lee said, and the boy held out his hand in response. His fingers were warm. Lee hated to think how cold they might become before the night was through.

Together, they crept back down the hallway, out of the door and out into the darkness.

Lost

"So what's the plan from here?" Stegmeyer asked, sitting back and sinking into one of the plush chairs in the back of the RV.

Rain battered the windows.

The RV swayed as it was buffeted by the wind.

"We take him to the craft," Lachlan replied as the RV continued on down the interstate highway in the darkness.

"Are you crazy?" Bellum snapped. "DARPA and the NSA are going to tear the East Coast apart looking for him. You think they're going to let you waltz in and take him to see the craft? There's a reason they've kept him away from the UFO for all these years."

"I know," Lachlan replied.

"But you don't even know where it is!" Stegmeyer said. "No one I've spoken to has any idea where they've hidden it."

"It's over a hundred yards in diameter," Lachlan replied. "Where do you hide a gigantic spaceship? Where would you store a spaceship for decades without anyone noticing?"

Lachlan pulled a folder out of one of the drawers in the RV and began flipping through dozens of typed pages and photographs.

"In plain sight," Jason offered.

Lachlan smiled, "Exactly."

He sorted through the loose sheets of paper before shuffling a few pages and tossing them onto the coffee table.

"What do you make of these?" he asked.

There were dozens of pages. Stegmeyer picked up a sheet, as did Bellum. Lily grabbed a sheet and shared it with Jason. She pointed at the title at the top of the page: *Energy Output - US Nuclear Power Plants.*

A table had been printed on the paper, with the names of each nuclear installation down one side. Years were listed across the top to allow for comparisons over time. Several of the locations had multiple reactors, with the output of each reactor shown in the table.

"I don't get it," Bellum said. "What am I looking for?"

"Anything out of the ordinary," Jason replied, his mind in sync with Lachlan's. He was already skimming over the output results, thinking about where the nuclear power plants were located, how much energy they were producing and which electrical grid they contributed towards.

"You think they've hidden the craft in a nuclear power plant?" Stegmeyer asked.

"Makes sense," Lachlan replied as Jason continued scanning the figures. "They need somewhere big enough to house this thing, somewhere they can limit access and ensure tight security."

"So, not out at Area 51?" Bellum asked in his gruff voice.

"No," Lachlan replied with a soft laugh.

"I think I've got it," Jason said confidently. "North Bend, Oregon. My guess would be that it's in reactor one."

Stegmeyer dropped the sheet of paper to her lap, slapping it on her thigh. She turned slightly, looking to Lachlan for confirmation. Lachlan smiled.

"How did you know?" Stegmeyer asked, sitting forward and looking at Jason.

Jason kept his finger on the page, saying, "There are three reactors. The original reactor with a capacity of two hundred megawatts, the other two are newer and capable of almost nine hundred megawatts each."

"And?" Lachlan asked. His pride in Jason was unmistakable.

"Well," Jason said. "According to these tables, all three reactors are on line, but reactors two and three are consistently low over the past two decades, only ever producing between five and six hundred megawatts each. All the other reactors around the country are hitting around 90% efficiency, but these reactors are at around 60%."

No one said anything.

Jason continued.

"They're covering for the lack of power coming from reactor one. Lowering their output so it looks like all three reactors are running when in reality, reactor one is offline. Reactor one may not even be there anymore. They're faking it."

Lachlan nodded, smiling as he said, "That's what we thought too, so we conducted some aerial surveillance."

He handed around some more photos.

Jason looked at the color images of the nuclear power plant from a variety of angles. Unlike the archetype nuclear plant with large cooling towers, North Bend was surrounded by cooling lakes. Large, artificial ponds dominated the landscape to the east, with roads running between them on raised embankments. A series of canals ran between the ponds and the power station.

"It's situated on the banks of the Coos river," Lachlan said. "We think that's how they got the craft there. It's an estuary system, with large mud flats. They must have floated the UFO in under wraps at high tide. Probably on a barge."

"I thought the craft crashed in the sea off North Korea?" Jason asked.

"It did," Lachlan said. "They spent twenty-two months raising the craft with submersibles, inching it away from North Korea while keeping it underwater. It took another year to tow the craft across the Pacific, all under the guise of ostensibly conducting naval training exercises. I've spoken to sailors on those exercises. They thought they were towing a crippled Chinese submarine. We think the sub was the cover story for the craft.

"From what we can tell, they towed the craft starting in late spring and went through most of the summer. There are public records of naval exercises off the coast of Washington and Oregon that coincide with power outages blanketing the North Bend area."

"They wanted to move under cover of darkness," Bellum said.

"Exactly," Lachlan said. "And get this, the training exercises coincided with a new moon, and culminated with a Marine landing at Cape Arago, not more than 10 miles from North Bend."

"So," Stegmeyer said, "there's no question that there were Navy ships in the area."

"And look at this," Lachlan added, holding up a photo of a barge. "They spent three months dredging the channel prior to the exercises. By this time, we think the craft was out of the water. They must have brought it in on barges similar to this one.

Lachlan held up another photograph, saying, "See that large, elongated building right here in the complex? That's roughly twenty stories high and it houses reactors two and three. But it's this one over here, with the old circular dome that houses reactor one. That's where we think the craft is located."

Stegmeyer interjected, saying, "It all sounds convincing, but you've got to have more than some fishy power readings to go on."

Lachlan cleared his throat, saying, "That dome is over two hundred feet high. It's within a few hundred yards of the river, but it's part of a separate annex inside the complex. We've been watching the area for months. See that nearby parking lot? The cars there never move. They're window dressing, just props. All the deliveries go to the administration buildings at the front, or the main reactors inland. No deliveries to the dome, and no external traffic. At least, none that we can see. There must be personnel moving around, but they're doing so via internal walkways."

"I don't buy it," Bellum said. "We need more to go on than a hunch. What are you proposing we do? Storm the place? What if the UFO isn't there? We'll have played our hand."

"Everything we've observed," Lachlan countered, "has revolved around Seattle, but even that seems to be a feint. Intercepted communiques, travel itineraries, credit card records. And it's not just that Seattle is a hub for the Northwest, we think it's more than that. They've got to have this thing nearby, and North Bend is the perfect location."

"Why not New York?" Bellum countered.

"It would be too difficult to get the craft into the Atlantic," Lachlan said.

"What about LA?" Stegmeyer asked.

"Too obvious. Too many people coming and going," Lachlan replied. "No, they need to keep this some place sleepy, some place no one would suspect. Don't forget, this thing has been causing international tension for decades. Oregon provides DARPA perfect cover: no one would take rumors from there seriously."

"No one but you," Stegmeyer replied.

Lachlan laughed.

The RV swerved suddenly, causing Lily to crash into Jason. Lachlan braced himself against the ceiling. Stegmeyer fought not to fall out of her chair.

"Shit!" came the cry from the driver.

The RV lurched, riding up over something on the road. The sound of breaking branches and wooden logs slamming beneath the chassis caused Jason to grimace, anticipating a sudden impact. The RV braked, sliding slightly, but the driver kept the bulky vehicle under control.

"What the hell happened?" Lachlan exclaimed as the driver pulled over to the side of the road. In the panicked confusion of those few seconds, Lachlan had dropped his folder, scattering photographs across the floor of the RV.

"There were fallen tree branches all over the road," the driver replied. "I think we may have lost a tire."

As he heard those words, Jason recognized the familiar thump of a lazy, flat tire. The RV leaned slightly to one side as the driver pulled onto the shoulder of the road.

"Stay here," Bellum said, pulling out a revolver and stepping down into the foot well of the RV.

"Could it be a trap?" Lachlan asked.

"Not likely," the driver said. "I doubt they've traced our movements yet. They won't have picked up our trail."

Bellum, Lachlan and Stegmeyer got out of the RV. Only Stegmeyer had the foresight to don a jacket against the rain. The other two seemed oblivious to the weather. Jason could see them standing outside, talking. Bellum moved out of sight. A few seconds later, Jason saw him moving through the trees, barely visible at the edge of the headlights as he crept in front of the RV.

"He's moving into a covering position," Lily said as though that was somehow supposed to make Jason feel better.

A few minutes passed, a cold draft coming in from the open door.

Spitting rain peppered the cabin, swirling in through the opening.

Jason looked at the photos lying scattered on the floor and thought he should pick them up before they got water damaged. He got to his feet. Lily seemed content to watch, which was nice. If she'd jumped up beside him he would have felt like a prisoner under her watch.

As he stepped out from between the chairs, Jason glanced at the photos.

284

Several of the pictures had fallen overlapping each other. Most of the photos were of scientific calculations, similar to those he loved to sketch on his notepads, only these formulas looked like they'd been carved into the hide of some dark animal. There were fine scratches crisscrossing a black hide with rough calculations carved into what looked like leather.

Jason started to pick one of the images up when he realized they had fallen in such a way as to spell out a word. Each of the overlapping images formed part of a single word, a word that would only be visible if they fell in this exact manner.

fe ED b A ck

Ordinarily, Jason wouldn't have thought of this as anything other than an unusual coincidence. He was well aware of the human tendency to read more into shapes and figures than was there. The overactive imagination of *Homo sapiens* has given us the Virgin Mary on a slice of toast, he thought, along with Elvis on a burnt cheese sandwich.

Jason wasn't one to fall for such mental tricks, except that another bunch of pages had fallen to form another word.

d E st R oY

What were the odds?

He wondered just how much of a freak chance it was to see two English words being spelled out from a scattering of loose papers.

It was nothing, he reassured himself. This was no omen.

Jason never allowed his mind to run to such nonsense.

The term *feedback* did get his attention, though, and he picked up a couple of the photos, looking at the calculations on them, thinking about their relationship to the concept of time travel.

"Like a message in a bottle," Lily said, picking up the photos that had comprised the word "destroy." Jason noticed how the simple act of moving the photos snapped the illusion, allowing any meaning to dissolve back into random, chaotic letters.

"What's the significance?" Jason asked absentmindedly, looking at one of the photos.

A formula had been carved into the surface of the UFO like love letters might be carved into the trunk of an oak tree. But in addition to the formula, a trail of *d's* ran in an arc, leading to the corner of the photo where the *d* had been in *d E st R oY*.

Jason counted the *d's*. There were five of them. They caught his eye because they clearly held some meaning, but whatever their significance was wasn't apparent. As unusual as it was to see scientific formulas scratched into a leathery hide, at least they had a purpose. However, the curved row of *d's* looked meaningless. Why would anyone bother?

Lily didn't reply to his question. She seemed as lost in thought as he was. She flipped through a few photos, pointing at a similar pattern with several other letter combinations that had gone into making up that cryptic phrase: *feedback destroy*.

"It's nothing," she finally said. "It is the equations that are important."

Lachlan poked his head back in the door of the RV. Water dripped from his face.

"We've blown two tires," he said. "It's going to take us a while to change these."

Jason yawned.

"Listen," Lachlan added, pointing toward the bedroom at the back of the RV. "It's going to be a long drive. Why don't you get some shuteye?"

With that, Lachlan was gone, disappearing back into the darkness and the drizzling rain.

Lily gathered the photos, stacking them neatly on a bench beside the kitchen.

Lachlan was right. Jason had had no idea how exhausted he was until they'd stopped. The shift of attention had allowed fatigue to catch up with him. He left Lily in the main cabin and slipped into the darkened bedroom.

Jason decided he'd rest for a moment, perhaps just close his eyes for a few minutes before they got underway again. He kicked off his shoes and flopped facedown on the bed with his feet dangling over the edge. Burying his face in a pillow, Jason was asleep in seconds.

He woke to the sound of birds outside. For an instant, he thought he was lying in bed in his apartment, but those weren't pigeons cooing. He could hear half a dozen different birds calling, and as he opened his eyes, at first he thought he was in a darkened forest. How could he be in a forest?

A hand slid around his waist. As he moved, the soft, gentle arm pulled him tighter, snuggling against him beneath a warm blanket.

Jason turned slightly and saw Lily lying on the pillow next to him. She let go, allowing him to turn and face her.

"Good morning," she said, brushing her hair from her eyes.

The RV rocked gently as someone climbed back into the vehicle. The engine started and Jason felt the vehicle pull back out onto the freeway.

Light filtered in through gaps in the blinds.

Jason lay on his back with his hands behind his head. Lily rested her hand on his chest, sliding her fingers up under his shirt. He sighed, wishing life could be as simple as it seemed right then, but he knew the nightmare would continue today.

"Sleep well?"

"Like a rock," Jason replied as Lily ran her nails across his chest. Damn, that felt good, he thought. He rolled sideways, resting his head on his elbow as he faced her.

"I don't understand," he confided, speaking in soft tones. "Up until yesterday, I was just an ordinary guy going to college. What changed?"

"You were never ordinary," Lily said. She pulled her hand back. Her fingers rested on his forearm. "They needed you to think you were just like everyone else because it's only when you're relaxed that you doodle."

Jason was silent.

"You've been doing them for years. Every time you scribble something on a scrap of paper and throw it in the garbage, someone hunts through the trash and matches the sketch with one of the formulas on the UFO. For you, it's nothing. For them, it's like pieces of a jigsaw puzzle slowly coming together."

Jason looked deep into her dark brown eyes. Her voice was soft. There was compassion in her tone. Perhaps he was reading too much into her manner, but he felt like she cared deeply about him. The connection between them seemed like one forged over years, or perhaps decades, and not just a few days.

"They learned a long time ago that under stress you stop drawing, so they left you in the community."

"What about Mitch and Helena?" he asked.

"I know they're your friends," Lily replied, squeezing his arm gently. "But they aren't, not really. They're NSA agents. They're on a long term assignment."

Jason was stunned. His mind was spinning with disbelief, but then he realized Mitchell was one of the people that had run down the street toward him when he jumped on the bike with Lily. So somehow, Mitch was mixed up in this, too. As much as Jason didn't want to believe Lily, there was a nagging persistence to that statement in his mind. It was the little things. Mitch was always there. Whether it was calling him when he was doodling or catching up with him on the steps of the university after the meeting with Lachlan. Mitchell was always a little too close.

"And you?" he asked, stiffening.

"Me?" Lily replied, touching her hand to her throat and gesturing at herself. It seemed to be a question she hadn't considered before then. "I'm no actor. I didn't come because I had to or because I was ordered to. I came because I wanted to be with you. My father has told me so much about you, about how he rescued you, but it wasn't just you he saved from North Korea. He rescued my great grandfather, my uncle and my mother. He saved all of us."

Jason watched as Lily swallowed a lump in her throat. She struggled to keep eye contact with him as she spoke.

"He told me that what they were doing to you was cruel. He told the NSA team they should be honest with you. They said they were making progress, but DARPA wanted more. My father tried to get permission to try another angle, to get you to relive that moment in the sea so many years ago. They told us this was the final attempt, that after this they would institutionalize you."

She sighed, adding, "They wanted to treat you like a lab rat. That's when my father knew it was time to make a move."

Tears ran down her cheeks. Lily tried to hide the tears, turning away and bringing her hand to her face.

"Hey, it's OK," Jason said, pulling her hand back.

Lily sniffed, wiping her nose with the back of her hand.

"My father has spent two decades trying to unravel the mystery of the young boy from the sea. Some have said you're not human. Others say you're an alien experiment."

"What do you think?" Jason asked.

"I think you are human. I don't know how or why, but somehow you're mixed up in something none of us fully understand."

"And your dad," Jason said, slowly getting used to referring to Professor Lachlan in that manner. "He thinks if I see this craft I'll somehow remember?"

"When the UFO first came to America, they brought you to it. You touched the skin and the craft glowed as if it was radiating energy. It scared them. There was no explanation as to why the UFO should react like that, so they made a decision to separate you from the craft."

"And the pictures?" Jason asked.

"My father has worked hard to get them. I don't think he's seen the craft, but he's talked to people who have."

The door to the bedroom opened and Professor Lachlan poked his head through.

"Good to see you kids are awake. Are you hungry?"

"Sure," Jason replied, feeling awkward lying there with the professor's daughter. He sat up on the bed. Lily sat up beside him, still wrapped in a blanket.

"Well, get dressed and come on out. Bellum's rustled up some bacon and eggs."

The latch clicked as the door was pulled shut again, leaving Jason and Lily lying there in the double bed.

"I'm going back to sleep," Lily announced, flopping on the pillow.

"Oh, you are, are you?" Jason retorted. He reached beneath the covers and grabbed at her waist, tickling her.

"Ah, no! Stop!"

Lily writhed beneath the blanket, kicking feebly with her legs and pushing at him with her hands.

"Drag me into a conspiracy, will you?" Jason cried as he continued to tickle her. "Stand out in the rain like a lost puppy, will you?"

"Not fair," Lily cried, laughing helplessly. She was trying to fight back, trying to tickle him, but she was far more ticklish than he was.

"OK, OK," she called out. "Truce!"

Jason paused, his hands still resting on her hips as she lay there facing him with the blankets and sheets scrunched up around her. She had tears of laughter in her eyes as she added, "I promise, no more standing in the rain!"

"No more puppy dog eyes?" he cried, giving her a little tickle.

"I promise, I promise," she replied, struggling to breathe, no longer trying to defend herself. She had her hands up in surrender. "Please, no more."

Jason sat back on the bed and took a good look at her. Lily was beautiful. Maybe not by the standards of Vogue magazine or Sports Illustrated, but to him she was radiant.

"You did look rather stunning out there on the street corner," Jason said.

"Standing there in the rain?" Lily asked in surprise. "I'm not sure I'd win a wet t-shirt contest."

"Oh, no," Jason replied, wondering how he'd ended up on the defensive. "I didn't mean it like that. I meant, you looked pretty throughout the day."

"Sweating in a hundred and five degrees? Standing there under the blazing sun without any shade?"

Jason was digging a hole for himself. "Ah, I meant—"

"I know what you meant," she said, leaning forward briskly and kissing him on the cheek. "God, I thought you were never going to come down."

"I, ah," Jason spluttered.

"Dad said you would. He said you were a gentleman. But I thought you were going to leave me out there all night."

Jason laughed.

A smile lit up Lily's face as she laughed as well. Even with her tousled hair, she looked like something from his dreams. Strands of black hair fell across her face as she slumped back on her pillow.

"No sleeping in," he said playfully.

Actually, he didn't mind if she went back to sleep, he was just feeling mischievous. She had come to him in the night, and he felt he had to reciprocate in some way, to show her in a playful manner that he was taken by her presence.

"Well," she said, leaning over and resting her hand on his thigh. "Then I get the first shower."

Lily jumped out of bed with a zest for life he found intoxicating. The shower was located with the toilet in a small cubicle to one side at the back of the RV. Lily grabbed a change of clothes out of the built in dresser and slipped into the cubicle. As she slid the door closed behind her, she added, "No peeking."

Jason held up three fingers saying, "Scout's honor," with mock solemnity.

The shower started and it reminded Jason of the rain last night. It wasn't raining outside anymore. He peeked out from behind the blinds at the farmland rushing by. They were on an interstate. The occasional red barn was visible from the road, nestled in with clumps of trees and seemingly endless rows of corn whipping past the window. The Sun was well up. It must have been nine or ten in the morning, he thought. He pulled the blinds up and leaned there gazing out at the world rushing by.

Lily was singing in the shower. Jason smiled. He couldn't have asked for a more perfect distraction after everything he'd been through. Although he couldn't make out the words, he could tell she could carry a tune. The shower stopped after a few minutes, but it was the fact that Lily had stopped singing that got his attention. He could hear her getting dressed, bumping against the closed confines of the tiny room. She stepped out of the shower cubicle still wringing out her hair with a towel.

"There's some spare clothes in the top drawer," she said, squeezing past him. As she brushed against him, he could smell the scent of jasmine in her hair. Lily walked out into the main cabin as Jason hopped in the shower. The cubicle was cramped, and the pressure coming from the shower head was weak, but the water was warm. It felt good to run some shampoo through his hair and rinse off the dust and grime of the city.

Jason dried off and grabbed some clothes from the drawer. There were boxer shorts, cargo pants and an old concert T shirt from some band he'd never heard of before.

As he stepped out into the main cabin, he smelled eggs cooking and heard the crackle of bacon sizzling in a pan.

Lily was already eating.

Lachlan handed him a plate of bacon and eggs and he squeezed in next to Lily at the cramped dining table.

"Where are we?" he asked.

"Ohio," came the reply from the front. "On the outskirts of Columbus."

The RV slowed, turning off the highway and onto a side road. Jason could see a small, rural airport. Several hangars lined one end of a maze of concrete runways. A red crop duster sat to one side, rusting in a field while a white Learjet took center stage.

"So what's the plan?" Jason asked.

"We're going to fly that Learjet into the side of a nuclear power plant," Stegmeyer replied, and with that pronouncement, a perfect morning was ruined.

Dead End

Lee took the child by the hand, saying, "Come."

The boy's eyes looked down as the two of them walked out the door of the administration building. The night air was brisk, much cooler than just minutes before. The temperature was dropping. The rain had stopped. The night was quiet. Lee ushered the young child down the creaking, wooden steps to where Sun-Hee's brother paced nervously on the gravel.

"This is bad," the brother mumbled under his breath. "We should be gone by now. The guard will change soon. We should have left him and run while we could."

The boy looked up at the North Korean soldier, but not with fear. He appeared to be curious, perhaps amused.

The soldier was smoking a cigarette, his rifle slung over his shoulder. Sucking in hard, the hand-rolled paper of the cigarette flared slightly. Bits of smoldering tobacco fell from the tip, drifting lazily to the muddy gravel.

"It's going to be OK," the boy said in English, reaching out and taking the soldier's hand.

Sun-Hee's brother jumped, jerking away from the child as though he'd received a jolt of electricity. Lee doubted he

understood English. Was it that those words sounded so
strange in another language that alarmed him? Or did he fear
the boy? The man looked panicked, like a wild animal caught
in a snare. His hands were shaking, his eyes wide with terror.

"Come," the soldier said with a tremor in his voice,
marching off on the gravel. With his good hand, Lee took the
child's tiny one and followed after the jittery soldier.

They crept along the side of the wooden administration
building, staying in the shadows. As they approached the
motor pool at the back of the camp, Sun-Hee's brother held up
his hand, signaling for them to stop.

He peered around the corner.

Through the quiet of the night, Lee could hear the soft
crunch of boots on gravel.

Another guard was approaching from the far side of the
hut.

Sun-Hee's brother waved, batting at the air behind him
with his hand, signaling for them to slip beneath the
crawlspace below the admin building.

He was still wearing the general's coat and Lee thought
about trying to bluff his way past the guard, but the child
would raise too many questions. This wasn't some soldier

half-asleep on a chair. If the guard looked too closely at him, they were finished.

Lee crouched and began to crawl under the wooden floor, but with his injured hand he was moving too slowly. He'd barely clear the edge of the building before the guard was on them, and the boy would still be in the open.

Sun-Hee's brother straightened. Out of the corner of his eye, Lee could see he was trying to look natural. He tossed his cigarette on the ground, crushing it beneath his boot.

There was nothing else Lee could do. He had to drop and roll regardless of his injured hand.

"Quick," he whispered, tucking his right hand up against his chest as he fell on his shoulder and rolled into the mud and dirt. Being smaller, the boy was able to scoot in beside him.

Pain flared through his hand.

Lee crawled forward on his elbows, moving between the concrete support pillars keeping the raised building off the ground. The boy stayed beside him. Lee's eyes never strayed from the legs of the guard walking up to Sun-Hee's brother.

"Where have you been?" the guard barked.

"Taking a shit!"

"Ha," the guard said. "You were gone too long. What were you doing? Laying an egg?"

"Yeah," Sun-Hee's brother replied, relaxing and laughing with the guard.

"Don't leave your route, you big fat hen!" the guard said, extending his metaphor. He laughed at his own wit, adding, "Un-Yong will have you cleaning the latrine if he catches you slacking off."

"I know," the brother replied as the guard continued past him, his boots falling with an almost hypnotic rhythm on the gravel, grinding and crunching at a leisurely pace.

Lee crept forward beneath the building, working with his elbows and his knees. He could see the motor-pool across the driveway.

Sun-Hee's brother rounded the corner. He crouched beside them as Lee wriggled out of the shadows.

"Stay here."

"No," Lee whispered under his breath. "This isn't going to work. If that guy sees the guard inside the admin building is gone, he's going to investigate and raise hell. Besides, as soon as you start one of these vehicles, you're going to wake the camp."

"Stay," the brother repeated, thrusting out his hand.

"But—" Lee began as the brother ignored him, jogging away on the noisy gravel.

"*Fuck! Fuck! Fuck!*" Lee swore under his breath.

Memories of being caught and savagely beaten in the village haunted him. The concrete support pillars and wooden floor above felt claustrophobic around him, as though they were closing in on him, forcing him out into the night. He wanted to crawl out and run, even though he knew he wouldn't get far on foot.

There had to be a perimeter fence out there somewhere hidden in the darkness.

Lee wouldn't put it past the North Koreans to have lined the perimeter with mines, they had certainly built plenty and were paranoid about being attacked.

The front gate was the only way in or out, but getting out in a car or a truck was suicide. They'd be cut down by machine gun fire. Hollywood might make cars out to be bulletproof, but Lee knew better. Rounds from an AK-47 would punch through sheet metal without losing any of their lethal momentum. They'd pass through a car door like a scrap of paper.

"*Shit!*" he swore, louder this time, no longer talking in a whisper.

"It's OK," the boy said, resting his hand on Lee's shoulder. "You make it! You escape from here, I know you do."

Lee took a deep breath, drawing in the cold, damp air. The child's description of the future was creepy. How could a boy of three or four know that for sure? He couldn't.

"Who are you? Where are you from?"

"It's me, professor," the boy said. "It's me, Jason!"

"Professor?"

Lee was perturbed. He was sure Jason had confused him with someone else. Lying there with the cold, wet mud soaking through his clothes, Lee couldn't help but wish he was caught in a dream. For him, it was a nightmare, but for this young boy, the night seemed to hold a mythical, magical quality. The boy should have been afraid, terrified, but his eyes were peaceful, his voice was calm.

"My name is John Lee, Captain John Lee of the South Korean Coast Guard. I'm going to get you out of here, but I need you to work with me, OK? I need you to do exactly what I say, OK?"

The boy nodded. And what exactly is it you are going to do? Lee wondered, keeping that thought to himself.

"I trust you, professor."

"I'm not," Lee began, but the innocence of childhood in Jason's eyes made him pause. If a case of mistaken identity could help the young boy through this without freaking out, then so be it. What the hell did the Americans and the North Koreans want with such a young child anyway? Lee noticed the child still had his crayon and paper, clutching it to his chest like a talisman.

The boy spoke as though he were talking to another child, saying, "You're Professor Lachlan. I remember you."

Lachlan. That was his mother's maiden name. His mother was a Korean-American. She had been a lieutenant in the US Army, working as a triage nurse in Seoul. She'd met his father while on joint exercises and they'd settled in South Korea after they married. Like most married women, his mother had taken his father's surname, Lee. Why was this child calling him by his mother's maiden name?

Curious, Lee asked, "How old are you, Jason?"

"I don't know."

"We're in danger. You need to understand that."

The boy nodded, saying, "But you will find a way out. You always do."

Lee was tired. He was cold and he was hungry. He was exasperated. Nothing was as simple as this boy assumed. He knew the boy meant well, but Lee was frustrated. Life had stopped being kind to him. Life was cruel. His injured hand throbbed. Deep down, he wanted nothing more than to scream in anguish.

If only life could be relived with different choices.

If only life came with several options available in advance, or allowed for mistakes to be undone.

What would he have done differently?

Should he have pulled out of the mission earlier?

Would the North Korean aircraft have stood down if they'd responded immediately instead of trying to sneak closer?

Should he have broken left instead of right in the Sea King?

And what about Sun-Hee? Should he have left her there?

Someone would have found her in the morning. She might have survived until then. Perhaps someone else would have rescued her and he could have slipped away in the dark of night.

And what if they were caught now?

Would he regret freeing the child? Freeing? Hah, he thought, some freedom. Free to wallow in the mud like an animal. Pig! Swine! That's what the North Korean soldiers had called him as they kicked him in the back of the truck. Irony, he chuckled mirthlessly.

Lying there shivering, he looked at the boy. The trust in Jason's eyes radiated absolute confidence. He shouldn't trust me, Lee thought. I'm going to get us both killed.

"You will think of something," the boy said softly, perhaps reading the heartache and anguish written on Lee's face.

Tears came to Lee's eyes. He reached out to touch the child's hair only to realize he was reaching with his wounded hand. Blood had soaked through the bandages. Jolts of pain shrieked through the torn nerve endings, but he couldn't pull back.

With his index finger and thumb, he touched gently at the boy's forehead, brushing loose strands of hair to one side. He expected the boy to be repelled by the grotesque bloody ball of rags wrapped around his hand, but the boy smiled. It was almost as though he knew what would happen all along, and somehow already knew about Lee's brutal wound.

Tears rolled down Lee's cheeks as he whispered. "I wish I could believe you. I wish I deserved your faith, your confidence."

They were never going to escape, Lee knew that. As soon as Sun-Hee's brother found a vehicle he could start, the noise of a diesel engine turning over would shatter the silence like an air raid siren. Within minutes, the camp would be crawling with soldiers.

Sniffing, Lee added, "If only I had wings to fly, I'd take you away from here. I'd take you somewhere you could be safe."

Lying there, Lee felt helpless.

The pain surging through his hand was too much. He cradled his arm.

After all he'd been through, this was the lowest he'd fallen. Being captured, beaten, tortured, humiliated and deceived had been heartbreaking, but he'd never given up hope. Now, though, he felt defeated.

Being free from his cage beneath the barracks had raised his spirits, but now the impossibility of escaping the camp struck him like a physical blow. What could he do? There was nothing he could do to escape this military base, let alone North Korea. With all he'd endured, the sudden, overwhelming realization of his helplessness was crippling. Lee wanted to curl up into a ball and die quietly in his sleep, but there was the boy. The boy demanded that he be brave.

A moth flew past, fluttering on the breeze. Its wings beat at the air, allowing it to defy gravity as the tiny insect danced among the moonbeams just a few feet away from where they lay.

Lee watched as the moth settled on one of the outer support pillars for a few seconds before darting back into the air and flittering out of sight.

Moonlight glistened on the cars and trucks in the motor pool.

Ropes led from the rotor blades of the imitation Bell helicopter beyond the trucks, holding the blades in place so they wouldn't turn with the wind.

Lee was about to crawl out of hiding when the soft crunch of boots on pebbles marked the return of Sun-Hee's brother. He and Jason pulled themselves out from beneath the administration hut as the brother came over. He had his rifle slung over his shoulder and his head bowed as if in defeat.

"The quartermaster's office is locked," the brother began. "It was unlocked when I last checked not more than an hour ago. We are trapped. We have no way to escape. One of the other guards must have checked the door and locked it behind me."

"And he may have just saved our lives," Lee replied, getting to his feet. "We were never going to be able to drive out of here. They'd catch us before we'd gone a quarter of a mile. But we just might be able to fly out of here."

Lee pointed at the dark outline of the Bell helicopter beyond the trucks. Sun-Hee's brother followed his gaze.

"Are you mad?"

"Aren't you?" Lee replied, taking Jason's hand and creeping across the gravel road. They slipped into the shadow of a truck as Sun-Hee's brother came up behind them.

"You can fly a helicopter?"

"Yes. I'm a pilot."

The three of them jogged lightly down between a row of trucks and halftracks, rusting howitzers and broken trailers. Most of the trucks had flat tires. From what Lee could see, they'd been stationary so long the air must have long since leaked away, leaving them stranded on their rims. Several of the trucks had been cannibalized for parts.

The chopper was a two seater Bell helicopter. Lee hoped it was in better condition than the trucks or they weren't going anywhere.

"Get the ropes," he said to the soldier.

Lee crept up to the cockpit, staying in the shadows of the helicopter. He pulled on the stiff handle and opened the Plexiglas door.

Jason clambered in.

Lee left him there, turning and pulling the covers off the engine seated behind the bubble shaped cockpit.

Oil had dripped on the ground directly beneath the engine. Fresh grease was visible on the metal nipples of the flywheel. That was a good sign. Someone had been maintaining the helicopter.

With his good hand, Lee ran his fingers over the copper piping and steel tubes, tracing the fuel line, pushing his mind to remember his training flights a decade before. He twisted a small butterfly valve below the fuel tank and primed the engine, wondering how much fuel there was in the thin sheet metal tank.

Sun-Hee's brother ran to the other side of the helicopter, pulling the ropes and releasing another rotor blade.

Lee hopped into the pilot's seat and familiarized himself with the controls, quickly identifying the various toggle switches and warning lights. He worked the pedals, feeling how stiff and sluggish they were. As he expected, there was no ignition key, just a master switch. He pumped the throttle to get fuel flowing and flicked the master switch. The hum of an electric pump was a good sign, bringing a smile to his face.

"Jump over the back," Lee said to Jason as Sun-Hee's brother ran over to the cockpit. There wasn't much room behind the seats, but there was enough space for Jason to crouch down, sitting on a toolkit.

Lee flicked several toggle switches and brought the engine slowly to life. The exhaust spluttered and coughed. He kept the clutch engaged, disabling the rotors while the engine came up to speed.

"Halt!" came a cry from the motor pool.

One of the guards had a rifle leveled at them.

Lee worked with the cyclical control, revving the engine. He engaged the rotors. Slowly, reluctantly, the rotor blades began to turn.

A shot rang out.

Sun-Hee's brother had his door open, with one foot resting on the chopper skids. He fired his rifle in response. The guard took cover behind one of the trucks.

"Shoot through the metal," Lee cried and Sun-Hee's brother responded, firing at the wheel arch. A body slumped to the ground, sprawling on the gravel.

Several other guards came running over from the barracks.

The rotor blades wound up to speed and began thrashing at the air.

White cracks appeared in the plastic dome of the chopper. It took Lee a moment to realize they were bullet holes. With the deafening roar of the engine, he couldn't hear the shots being fired.

He pulled back on the cyclic control stick with his injured right hand and his face contorted in agony. With his left hand, Lee worked the collective, adjusting the pitch of the blades as he increased the throttle. His heart leaped with joy as the chopper lifted off from the motor pool. A soft touch on the right foot pedal corrected some yaw, while a nudge of the cyclic counteracted a slight pitch to the right. For a moment, he was back in basic training. The sensation of hanging in the air, even if only a foot above the ground, had never felt so good. The artificial cyclone thrown out by the helicopter forced the soldiers back, kicking fine stones and debris into their eyes. Several kept firing, but Lee could see they were firing wide.

The helicopter gained height, clearing the huts and then the trees as they raced away from the camp heading due north.

"You are going the wrong way," Sun-Hee's brother yelled over the noise as he fought to close his door. He pointed behind them, back to one side at the gates of the camp slowly receding into the darkness.

"I know," Lee cried over the sound of the rotor blades beating at the air. "Believe me, I know!"

Learjet

"Am I the only one that thinks irradiating the West Coast is a really bad idea?" Jason asked as the RV pulled up roughly fifty feet from the Learjet. He wondered how much sway he could have over a decision that had clearly already been made. "We're talking about millions of people being exposed to radioactive fallout!"

"Ah," Lachlan said, getting up from opposite them at the table. "What we're proposing is more theatrical than actual. The jet has been modified so it can be piloted by remote control using the same technology found in drones. Think — Hollywood special effects! Big bang! Lots of flames! No actual damage."

Bellum opened the RV door and stepped outside. Immediately, Jason could hear the high-pitched whine of the jet engines on the Learjet warming up. Lachlan and Stegmeyer were quick to follow, as was the driver.

Against his better judgement, Jason followed Lily out the door, making him the last person to leave the RV.

There was no hint of compulsion, no pressure on him to follow. The others walked away from him as though there weren't a doubt in the world that he'd join them. If it's reverse psychology, it's working, he thought. Whether he liked it or not, he was in too deep to back out now. Perhaps by going with them he could steer things in a more rational direction. And if this was all true, he had to see it. The chance to lay eyes on a craft from another world was a prize beyond compare. The implications were profound: there was another intelligent species in outer space, and it had made contact with Earth. Granted, this wasn't the First Contact he'd ever hoped for, but if they were right, it was First Contact nonetheless, and that was overwhelming to contemplate. First Contact represented a seismic shift for humanity. First Contact was a significant turning point in the 3.8 billion years life had existed on Earth.

Jason jogged over behind Lily and Lachlan, catching up to them. Bellum was already on board. Jason climbed the stairs of the Learjet with a mixture of trepidation and excitement. He'd never been on a private jet before and was intrigued by the lavish appointments in the small cabin. There was plenty of room for the six of them.

Jason and Lily sat in plush leather seats facing each other on the same side of the aisle. There was a small, low table between them. Lachlan sat across from them, clipping his seatbelt in place as the pilot closed the cabin door. Bellum went to the cockpit with the pilot.

As they began taxiing for takeoff, Lachlan said, "This plane makes the run to Portland twice a week for a mining corporation executive operating out of Albany. It's important that we blend in with routine activities. The NSA will be trawling public records for any anomalies that might tip our hand, so it's critical we stay in the shadows."

The Learjet accelerated down the runway, lifting smoothly into the air.

Once they reached cruising altitude, Lachlan made some coffee in the galley as Jason and Lily talked idly. Jason found it strange to talk about mundane things, like the shape of a cloud or the small farming communities dotted across the countryside beneath them, but Lily was chatty.

"Latte?" Lachlan said, holding two cups and offering them to Jason and Lily.

"Thanks," Jason said, taking the cup and sipping at the coffee.

Lachlan returned with a cup of coffee for himself and Stegmeyer, sitting down across the aisle from Jason and Lily.

Jason wanted to say something, but he waited as Lachlan sipped some coffee. Lachlan picked up on his anguish, and continued the conversation they'd started in the RV. Jason smiled. Lachlan picked up almost exactly where he'd left off, with little or nothing in the way of segue, as if there had been no interruption.

"Don't worry about the reactor complex. The main building is designed to withstand precisely this kind of attack. We'll be flying an unmanned Learjet into a twelve foot thick wall built out of reinforced concrete and steel. Nothing short of a fully laden 747 is going to make anything more than a scratch on the outside of that thing. That structure will outlast the pyramids!

"Now, if we were to hit the old dome that would be a different story. We'd punch straight through the shell, but the main building has been hardened on three separate occasions over the past fifteen years. We'll leave a nasty, ugly black scar, but not much else.

"The plane is carrying 1500 gallons of avgas in addition to the 900 gallons in the fuel pods. It's going to create a fireball a thousand feet high and bring emergency services pouring in from all across the city, and that's what we want. We want the world's attention on North Bend. We want federal investigators crawling all over that site, asking all kinds of uncomfortable questions."

Bellum wandered out of the cockpit, clearly wanting to join the conversation.

"But," Jason countered. "What about the law of unintended consequences? What if something goes wrong? What if the wall collapses? What if the fire spreads?"

"She's a class four reactor," Lachlan replied. "The core is built on a gravity failsafe. If there's no power, the uranium rods sink back into their lead shell and the reaction is over. This isn't Fukushima or Three Mile Island. There's no chance of a meltdown."

Jason didn't like it.

"Is this really necessary?"

"North Bend is a private nuclear power plant," Lachlan replied. "They're answerable to the Nuclear Regulatory Commission and no one else. It's the perfect cover for DARPA. The image of a glowing mushroom cloud billowing above a nuclear power plant will ensure there's no room to hide. They're going to have to open the gates to local fire crews, and that will allow us to drive straight through to the dome."

As a reporter, April Stegmeyer added her perspective. "The media focus will cripple them. It will take weeks, maybe even months to convince the public the explosion was superficial and didn't damage any of the critical infrastructure."

"Then after that," Bellum added, "they're going to have to deal with every conspiracy nut in the country alleging that they're hiding the truth."

"And they are," Lachlan said. "Only the truth is more bizarre than anyone could ever imagine."

"We'll leak the footage of our investigation," Stegmeyer said. "Once we get inside that dome and get shots of you interacting with the craft, they'll have no way to hide. We're going to force their hand, force them to admit this to the public."

"I hate to throw a wet towel over all this," Jason said, resting his coffee spoon on the table in front of him. "But I don't know what you think I can do with this thing. I'm not even sure I believe you guys. Hell, for all I know, you're all crazy and this is some delusional group construct."

No one answered him.

"No offense," Jason added. "But look at this from my perspective. None of this makes any sense. Yesterday, I was just an average guy just trying to work his way through college. Today, you want me to believe I'm the key part of some international — no, interplanetary, or is it interstellar conspiracy?

"You're talking about committing a criminal act, a terrorist act! I don't see how you can justify this. Even if you're right and we get inside that dome and find a spacecraft from another star system, what the hell makes you think I can do anything about it?"

Jason looked around at Bellum, Stegmeyer and Lachlan. No one said what they were thinking, but he could see it in their eyes. They knew something he didn't, something they weren't prepared to tell him.

"I can't do this," Jason said. "Listen, I've got family in Seattle. I'll head up there from Portland. I'll hitchhike back to New York. Or I'll call Mitch. He's always up for an insane road trip."

"This isn't a game," Lachlan said softly.

"You've got to tell him," Stegmeyer added. Her voice was blunt, hinting of tragedy and heartache. Even before Bellum turned on the television mounted by the door to the cockpit, Jason understood the ominous tone of Stegmeyer's voice. Her few words resounded like the rumble of an oncoming storm. In that instant, he knew. His heart sank. Jason didn't know the particulars, but he understood enough to know something terrible had happened.

Lachlan nodded his consent and Bellum inserted a flash drive into the side of the TV.

The FBI agent picked up a remote and switched on the television. He scrolled through the stored memory, rewinding to a news broadcast they must have recorded earlier that morning. Lily rested her hand on Jason's knee.

Jason bit his lip.

"The manhunt continues," a young, petite news reporter began. She was standing outside his apartment building, fighting to keep her blond hair from blowing in front of her face as she spoke. "Police have released photos of the suspects. They are considered armed and dangerous, and should not be approached by the public."

Jason's driver's license photo appeared on the screen, along with equally bland and impersonal photos of Professor Lachlan and Lily.

"Investigators have told CNN that a large quantity of homemade C4 was recovered from a storage unit rented by one of the fugitives. It appears that there was some kind of falling out with co-conspirators Mitchell Jones and Helena Young that caused infighting among the terror cell members. During a heated argument that spilled out into the street, witnesses say that Jason Noh gunned down both Jones and Young. Jones died at the scene, while Young is undergoing surgery for a gunshot wound to the head."

Bellum froze the image. A body was being wheeled away on a gurney into the back of an ambulance. The body had been zipped into a black bag, but scarlet blood ran down one of the aluminum legs of the stretcher.

"I'm sorry," Lachlan said.

"Why?" Jason asked. His voice was barely audible over the hum of the jet engine. He ran his hands up through his hair, grabbing at the strands and pulling at the roots in anguish.

"Why them?" he asked again looking up at Lachlan with tears in his eyes. He held out his hands in a plea for mercy. "I don't understand. I thought you said they were working for those guys. Why would they kill them?"

"I'm sorry, son," Bellum said, resting his hand on Jason's shoulder. "This is the major league. This goes beyond anything DARPA has ever done before. They won't hesitate to sacrifice anyone or anything to get what they need from you."

"DARPA is sending a message," Lachlan said softly. "That they're coming after us, and nothing will stand in their way."

Lily unfastened her seatbelt. She sat forward on the edge of her seat, taking his hand. She didn't say anything. She didn't have to. He knew what she was thinking. A soft squeeze told him all he needed to know. She hated this, he was sure of it. She was grieving with him.

Jason's head spun with the knowledge that his closest friends were dead, had been murdered because of him. Would he ever wake from this nightmare? He felt sick. Vertigo swept over him. He felt as if he were standing at the edge of a skyscraper, leaning over. A tingling sensation ran through his hands and feet. He wanted to get up, to get out of the plane, to be anywhere else. Sitting there trembling, he flexed his muscles trying to shake off the anguish washing over him.

Lily stroked his hand gently. She must have felt him shaking. Out of the corner of his eye, he could see her downturned mouth. She too felt the grief that had been omitted from the sterile news report.

A thin, black bag hid the heartache on that stretcher.

Hearing the tone of her voice, the reporter could have been talking about a lost puppy or an approaching storm, but not an entire life, Jason thought. He wanted to shout at the screen, to cry out for compassion.

Bellum turned off the television. The screen went black, but in his mind, Jason could still see the lumpy outline of Mitchell's body being wheeled away.

Tears rolled down his cheeks.

"I'm sorry," Lachlan said, crouching down beside him and looking him in the eye. "You don't deserve this. You don't deserve any of this. You're caught up in something that's bigger than any of us."

The professor got back to his feet. He was staring absentmindedly at his mutilated right hand. He seemed to be flexing three phantom fingers. The scarred stubs on his hand twitched and moved.

"They're afraid," he added. "They've covered this up for decades now. The longer this goes on, the deeper the hole they dig for themselves. They're entrenched. They think they're protecting humanity."

Jason wiped the tears from his cheeks, surprised by his trembling hands.

"In their minds," Lachlan continued, "they think there's danger in this knowledge getting out. They're fighting to maintain the status quo while they try to figure out what the hell to do next. They're afraid one of these UFOs will materialize in Washington D.C. and they'll be defenseless. They're afraid of panic if the public finds out. DARPA is convinced this is a threat to our national security."

"And you?" Jason asked, looking at his mentor with a heavy heart.

"I've always believed in you." Lachlan spoke softly, adding, "You may not have been aware of me, but I've always been there in the background, fighting for you, and for what I believe is in your best interests."

Jason watched as the old man swallowed hard before continuing.

Page 326

"I never wanted it to come to this. I didn't want to endanger you, but I had no choice."

"We're all in this together," Stegmeyer added.

"We're doing this because we believe there's another way," Lachlan said. "We believe the public will embrace this knowledge. We don't think there's anything to fear from the knowledge that we are not alone in the universe."

Jason nodded.

Stegmeyer said, "They hold all but one of the cards in this deck."

"You're our ace in the hole," Bellum added.

"I know this is a lot to take in," Lachlan said, placing a thick folder on the table in front of Jason. "This is everything we know. You're welcome to look at everything."

Lachlan signaled with his head and both Stegmeyer and Bellum followed him to the cockpit, leaving Jason and Lily sitting at the table.

Bellum sat down in the cockpit while Lachlan and Stegmeyer stood beside the door talking. They chatted softly with each other, but their conversation sounded forced, as though neither felt at ease. They were being polite, giving him some distance.

Jason stared at the folder.

"I'll go too," Lily said.

"No," Jason replied softly, opening the folder and looking at the first page. "Please, don't."

Lily leaned over and kissed him on the cheek, smiling, "OK, then let me get you a fresh cup of coffee."

"That would be nice. Thanks."

Within minutes, Jason was engrossed.

Time seemed to come to a standstill.

Lily handed him a pad and pen. Jason arranged the photos across the table, shifting them around and linking them together. Photos were laid out on the floor, but not randomly. He was looking for patterns.

In among the formulas he saw the occasional word hastily scratched into the surface of the dark craft.

As he looked through the photos, he realized a number of terms had been repeated, so he tallied them. But whoever had taken the photos had been concerned with the formulas, catching only passing glimpses of whatever had been written elsewhere. It was stupid, Jason thought. He wanted to see everything written on the UFO, not just the scientific notations.

The writing was in English. That alone should have caught the attention of whoever took these pictures, he thought. They should have been trying to record everything, but they seemed to be interested only by the calculations, with some of the formulas being photographed several times from a variety of angles.

You're Damned x 14

Doomed x 3

Forsaken x 2

Pointless x 8

Death or Dead x 7

Cursed x 12

Fate x 4

Inescapable x 3

"What do you think this means?" Lachlan asked. He had returned from the cockpit some time ago. Stegmeyer was seated across from Jason, but he hadn't even noticed her sit down. He was startled by the professor's voice. He had lost track of time. The Learjet was beginning its descent. Jason glanced at his coffee. A thin film of milk had left a skin on the surface. Touching the cup, he felt how cold the drink was and resisted the temptation to take a sip.

"I think you've missed the real story here," Jason said to Lachlan. "The formulas only paint part of the picture. Look at these words. Why are they here? What's their purpose?"

Lachlan picked up one of the images, the word "*Condemned*" was visible on the edge of the picture, with only the lower half of the last three letters in the frame.

"What do you think it means?" asked Jason.

"I don't know," Lachlan replied.

"If you're right, and this is a craft of extraterrestrial origin, then a number of questions spring to mind. Where's the pilot? Where's the crew? Why is the craft covered in scientific formulae and English notation?"

"I'm not sure," Lachlan said. "DARPA are playing a long game with this thing. Rather than being invasive, they've gone for passive investigation, using sonics, x-rays, spectrographic analysis, even going so far as to build a massive scanner in place. They're convinced the alien technology is recoverable, but it's so advanced, so far beyond anything we can achieve they're scared of breaking things without realizing it. Imagine Socrates examining an iPad and you get an idea of what they're dealing with."

"Do they have any thoughts on why the craft was defaced? Or who could have done this?" Jason asked.

"No," Lachlan replied. "But some of those etchings are tens of thousands of years old."

"That's impossible!" Jason said. "The English language is barely a thousand years old. How can they …"

Jason's voice trailed off. He could see the knowing half-smile on Lachlan's face.

"Time travel," he said.

"Precisely," Lachlan replied. "And on a scale that is unimaginable to us. We're not talking a few decades or even a century or a millennium. This craft can traverse tens of thousands of years in the blink of an eye. Now can you see why they're willing to kill to keep this secret?"

"So," Jason continued. "It's not so much a question of where this craft has been up till now, but when."

Lachlan broke into a full smile, adding, "English may only be a thousand years old, but given what we're witnessing with the stability of existing languages on the Internet, radical changes are going to be the exception. Languages will continue to evolve, but they won't drift and languish as they once did. English could last in pretty much its current form for the next ten thousand years!"

"And me?" Jason asked. "Does that mean I'm from the future?"

Lachlan couldn't keep the smile from his face. He tried to, but he was clearly excited. He restrained himself, saying, "That's one theory, my theory."

"But why send a child back in time?" Jason asked. "What happened to the craft? What caused it to crash?"

"I don't know."

They were three simple words, but they were not the words Jason wanted to hear.

"We've struggled with this for decades," Lachlan continued.

Jason saw Vacili's camera was running, catching their impromptu conversation in electronic format.

"There's a problem with your theory," Jason said, gesturing at the camera. "If this craft is from the future, they'd know. They'd see this recording and could replay this conversation. They'd know something went wrong. They'd be able to reconstruct what was about to happen from their perspective, but what had already happened from ours. This should have never happened."

"Unless?" Lachlan said.

"Unless somehow that knowledge is lost. But that's fatalistic. It implies all our efforts are in vain, that everything we do becomes buried in time."

Stegmeyer piped up, saying, "Now you see why we're flying a bird into that power station? We need this to register on their radar."

"But you don't understand," Jason said. "If the developers of this craft haven't already seen that recording you're making right now, they never will."

"We could be wrong," Lachlan offered.

"We could," Jason conceded. "But then, what other explanation is there?"

"The future isn't fixed," Lachlan said. "Neither is the past. From our perspective, the past looks settled, but it's not. Time is like a river. Water flows from the hills to the sea, but even a river is not a closed system. There's evaporation, condensation and precipitation constantly renewing the river. In the same way, time looks like a closed system to us, but it's not. Quantum probability waves move backwards in time changing the outcomes in the double-slit experiment. It's a gross oversimplification to see time as fixed."

Jason was quiet. He tapped the photos in front of him, thinking carefully before speaking.

"These equations," he said. "They're not related to time travel. They're field strength calculations. They're looking at the consequences of time travel, the causal relationships between matter and energy. Whoever wrote these wasn't trying to figure out how to travel in time, they were trying to figure out the effect time travel would have on multidimensional space."

A voice came over the intercom. "We'll be landing in approximately five minutes."

Jason looked out the window. They were flying along a valley, dipping below the lush, green hills on either side. They touched down and came to a stop in sight of a sign that read:

Welcome to Portland, Oregon

Alis volat propriis

She flies with her own wings.

Flight

Being airborne had never felt better to Lee. Even in the darkness above a hostile country, he felt at home in the cockpit of a helicopter.

Sun-Hee's brother looked scared senseless. The whites of his eyes were evident as he yelled over the sound of the rotor blades.

"You are heading toward Pyongyang!"

"I can explain," Lee replied, struggling to be heard over the sound of the helicopter. "Look for some headphones in the back and we can talk."

Once they were well clear of the camp, Lee took the helicopter up a couple of hundred feet so he could get a feel for the lay of the land.

Broken clouds drifted across the sky. Patches of moonlight revealed dark shadows where the hills below gave way to gullies and valleys. Occasionally, a small village or a farm appeared. Lee adjusted his course, heading north-northeast in the general direction of Pyongyang.

Sun-Hee's brother rummaged around behind the seat for a while before emerging with several sets of headphones. He tried to hand a pair to Lee, but Lee yelled above the noise, saying, "You're going to have to put them on for me. With this hand, I can't put them on and fly at the same time."

Sun-Hee's brother leaned across the cockpit and slipped the headphones over Lee's head, catching his ears awkwardly and twisting the cartilage. Lee plugged the loose cord into a phone jack and Sun-Hee's brother copied him. Jason had a pair of headphones on as well, but his weren't plugged in. Glancing over his shoulder, Lee could see the young boy was fascinated by their flight. He peered down at the landscape rushing by beneath them.

Lee held the control stick between his legs and adjusted the microphone on the side of his headphones before explaining his thinking.

"At night, a helicopter can be heard for anywhere from two to five miles, depending on altitude and wind conditions. By heading North, we're misleading them. Hopefully, it will take them some time to respond, and when they do start looking for us, we want them to look in the wrong place. This should confuse the fuck out of them!"

Sun-Hee's brother nodded, smiling. The North Koreans Lee had met so far seemed to shrink from profanity, but Sun-Hee's brother clearly understood what Lee meant and seemed to approve. Lee smiled as well, happy that his comment had helped put the soldier at ease a little.

"Look at the lay of the land," Lee added. "There are several valleys running east to west. The shadows get deeper to the west as they lead down toward the sea. We'll drop down below radar and follow one of them out to the ocean."

"And pick up Sun-Hee?" the brother asked.

"No," Lee replied. "We'd never make the border. We need to ditch the helicopter. We've got to draw our pursuers off in a feint, double back and leave by sea. If we can get them looking in the wrong direction, looking for the wrong mode of transport, we just might stand a chance of getting out of here alive."

A soft hand rested on Lee's shoulder. Jason couldn't have heard what was said, but he seemed to be expressing his gratitude for their escape.

Lee breathed deeply.

For the first time since he'd been captured, he had the luxury of relaxing. He was still nervous, but flying was second nature. To be cocooned within the familiarity of the cockpit of a helicopter was understandably soothing for him. A slight vibration came through the cyclic control, renewing the ache in his hand, but it was an ache he welcomed, one he wouldn't try to avoid. He was flying, free. Freedom itself lay a long way off, but to feel the pulsing downdraft of the rotor blades with their steady rhythm was deeply reassuring.

"What's your name?" he asked the brother.

Lee thought he had perhaps five to ten minutes before the North Koreans were able to mount an aerial response. Right now, the biggest temptation he faced was to react too quickly and give away their true intention. He began a slow descent. Something that would be barely noticed on the radar, something that would be incidental rather than important to the various radar operators who were undoubtedly tracking their northward progress. His faux heading had to be convincing, so he made small talk with Sun-Hee's brother, wanting to settle the butterflies in his stomach.

Sun-Hee's brother didn't reply.

Lee looked sideways at him, looking to see if he'd heard him. The young soldier looked back. He seemed distracted. The enormity of what he'd just done was probably only now setting in. There was no going back, and that must have weighed heavily on the young man.

"Seung-Chul," he responded reluctantly.

"Well, Seung-Chul. It's nice to meet you."

There was silence for a few seconds. Lee eased his descent, feeling he was rushing. The helicopter continued to race forward, but the downward motion was slight. In the distance, Lee lined up a gully roughly a mile or so ahead that appeared to wind its way down to the lowland.

"What made you do it?" he asked, adjusting his rate of descent, wanting to bottom out at ten to twenty feet above an open paddock at the base of a sloping hill. By his reckoning, he figured they were two minutes out. Lee was careful to keep his airspeed consistent so there was no indication they were changing heading as they dropped below radar. A forest lay to one side with a large mountain beyond that. With any luck, it would look like they'd crashed at the base of the mountain.

"Honor."

"Honor?" Lee replied, genuinely surprised by Seung-Chul's response.

"Grandfather said he would not rest until you were free and honor had been satisfied."

Lee nodded.

Seung-Chul continued, saying, "Debts must be repaid. Anything less would bring shame and misfortune. Grandfather demanded you be freed. I told him, this would cost us our lives. He said he didn't care. I told him, you must take us to America. That was the only way I would agree to help."

Lee smiled, understanding what Seung-Chul meant. His words were hyperbole, an exaggeration. America was too far away to be literal, but to the North Korean mind, South Korea was as decadent and extravagant as the USA. With US troops stationed across the border, just to make it below the 38th parallel would be akin to reaching America. For Seung-Chul, America meant freedom. Freedom was what he wanted. In rescuing Lee, he saw a means of escape for him and his immediate family.

"And Sun-Hee?"

"She is well," he replied, with a deferential nod of his head. Apparently, nothing more needed to be said on the subject. "She and grandfather await us with a fishing boat in a cove beyond the village."

"Good. Good," Lee replied, noting the way the trees to his right swayed in the downdraft of the helicopter. Judging distances at night was never easy. Rather than relying on depth perception, he sought to use the trees, paying careful attention to how the branches at various heights swayed differently. He could see across the treetops. A few more feet and they would drop below the level of the tree tops, which he figured put them roughly thirty feet off the ground.

"Hold onto the boy," he said. "From here on out, the ride's going to get rough."

Working with his foot pedals, cyclic control and the handbrake-like collective, Lee brought the chopper through an arc to the left, turning west. Normally, he would have allowed the helicopter to drift into a high, banking arc that ensured good ground clearance, but they had to stay under the radar. Now, time was of the essence. Whatever aerial resources the North Koreans had deployed would be screaming in toward this point. He had to put some distance between them, and quickly.

Lee opened up the throttle, tilting the helicopter forward and racing along barely twenty feet above the undulating grassy meadow. He slipped into the gully, keeping to the moonlit side. Their shadow was slightly ahead of them, giving him a good visual indicator of their height.

Seung-Chul had turned to one side. He had his shoulder over the back of his seat, holding Jason firmly as the chopper swayed from side to side in the darkness, following the contours of the gully as they sped through the night.

"Some cloud cover would be nice," Lee mumbled to himself, forgetting he was transmitting. Seung-Chul must have heard him, but he didn't respond.

Lee's eyes scanned the distance, noting the subtleties of the terrain, observing how the river wound its way through the widening gully. He had to anticipate obstacles like trees and cliffs well in advance.

At the breakneck speed they were tearing through the gully, his reaction time was roughly two hundred yards. If he hadn't responded at least two hundred yards before he reached a bend in the river or a stand of trees, it was too late and he knew it. His mind was focused. He barely blinked. Every muscle in his body was tense. The helicopter responded to the slightest twitch of his hands, the softest touch of his feet. In that moment, he and the machine were one.

The angle of the moonlight caused the landscape to look skewed. Shadows stretched to one side, obscuring the actual height of the trees lining the banks, making them look monstrous and hideously distorted. The river swelled in places, providing plenty of space for the helicopter. In other sections, it narrowed to no more than ten to fifteen feet wide, forcing him to pull up above the trees.

For the most part, the hills on either side were well above the helicopter, hiding them from any airborne search. At least there were no power lines, he thought. If he'd tried this stunt in South Korea, the all but invisible power lines would have cut the chopper into strips of metal ribbon.

The gully opened up into a valley, forcing Lee to fly in the dark shadows. There were places where he had no depth perception and no points of reference. In those areas, he eased up on their forward speed, wanting to give himself more reaction time. Against his desire to stay concealed, he eased higher out of necessity.

Not knowing where the North Korean radar stations were located or what search pattern the air force would adopt, he had no way of knowing how effective or ineffective his measures were. For all he knew, they were already following him. They could be sitting a thousand feet up watching his pathetic attempt at escape, waiting for him to put down, or holding off and observing as other air units converged on them.

Lee breathed in short bursts. His heart pounded. His concentration sharpened, focusing on the grainy view before him as his eyes strained to make out details in the dark.

He saw a fishing village well before he got to it, but there was no advantage in changing course. By the time he recognized the dark shape of the huts nestled together on the bank of the river mouth, it was too late. They would have already heard the helicopter. There was nothing for it but to keep going.

The hills parted, revealing the broad, flat expanse of the sea.

As they passed low over the village, Seung-Chul said, "It is OK. They have no radio, no phone."

"Is this your village?" Lee asked, easing the helicopter to the left, following the southern shoreline and speeding away above the crashing waves.

"No. It is Byul-Ma-Ul. It is perhaps ten kilometers north."

"OK, that's good."

The helicopter was low enough to kick up spray with its downwash. Lee knew that that would make them more visible, but since the village had no way of contacting anyone, there was no point hiding from them. It was aircraft and radar that worried Lee.

They rounded the peninsula. Lee was tempted to cut across between the finger of land jutting out into the ocean, but the further he strayed from land the more likely it was they'd be picked up by radar. Instead, he cut back in, continuing to follow the shore as he weaved his way to the south.

"Where's this cove? Where will your grandfather be?"

"It is hard to tell at night," Seung-Chul replied.

Lee wanted to swear, but he didn't. The young soldier had probably never seen the area from the air, let alone at night.

"Can you describe the cove?" Lee asked, slowing his speech, aware his mind was racing as fast as the helicopter. Patience was needed. "Is it to the north or the south of your village?"

"To the north."

"OK," Lee replied. "That's good. I can work with that."

The coastline turned on itself, angling back toward the open sea. They followed another sprawling peninsula, mostly denuded of trees. Jagged rocks and broken cliffs marked the landscape.

"What else?" Lee asked

"There's a cliff," Seung-Chul replied.

Lee had seen plenty of cliffs.

"How would you get there from your village?"

"To get there by land, we would follow the road north along the ridge for maybe five or six kilometers. The cliff has a sheer drop into the water, but there is a pebble beach to one side. A path leads down to the beach."

There was no way Lee was going to be able to spot a path from the air in the dark, but the description of the cliff face was good. Most of the cliffs he'd seen had been formed by landslides or had rocky boulders at their base. Very few dropped straight into the ocean.

"Is the cove facing the open ocean? Or does it run along the peninsula, facing the far shore?"

"It faces the ocean."

"Shit!" Lee cried, realizing they'd just passed the cove as they rounded a rocky outcrop on the headland. They'd begun heading back along the far side of the peninsula. He pulled the chopper around above the land, gaining height as he turned back on his path. There, anchored not more than a hundred yards off shore was a small fishing vessel, just a black dot floating on the waves.

"Look," he said, pointing at the beach. Someone was standing on the beach beside the darkened outline of a rowboat. The man ran for the tree line as Lee brought the helicopter down, setting the craft on the pebbles. He eased the helicopter in, kicking up spray as the chopper touched down.

"Listen," he said. "I need to ditch this chopper out there in the water. Our escape depends on stealth. If they find this helicopter sitting on the shore, they'll know where we left from. I'm going to have to sink this thing."

"OK," Seung-Chul replied.

"Take the boy with you. I need you to pick me up out there, OK?"

"OK."

Seung-Chul opened the cockpit door and a blustery cold downdraft whipped around the cramped cabin. Seung-Chul took Jason's hand, pulling him out. At first, Jason resisted, pulling away from the North Korean soldier.

"Go!" Lee cried. "It's OK. I'll join you."

Reluctantly, Jason followed Seung-Chul onto the pebble covered beach. They sheltered themselves, hiding their faces from the hurricane whipped up around them by the rotor blades as Lee took to the air again.

Lee took the helicopter out over the water. He turned, watching as Seung-Chul met with the man on the beach. That had to be his grandfather.

Lee watched as Jason climbed in the rowboat. He wasn't sure who climbed into the boat with Jason and who pushed the boat back out into the waves, but within a minute, one of the two men was rowing the boat toward the fishing vessel bobbing on the ocean.

"Well," Lee said, working with his foot pedals, easing back on the controls and positioning the helicopter roughly fifty feet away from the fishing boat. "This never gets any easier."

He unbuckled his three point harness seatbelt. He hadn't even been aware he'd strapped it on inside the North Korean army camp, but he had out of habit. Now, he was focused on doing whatever he could to free himself from the helicopter once he'd ditched her. He'd been dragged beneath the waves once before and he didn't want to go through that again. Holding the control stick between his legs, he pulled the headphones off and tossed them to one side.

The rowboat reached the fishing vessel. Jason climbed aboard. His small frame was easily distinguishable in the dark.

"It's now or never," Lee said to no one in particular. What he was about to do ran against everything he knew and counter to every safe choice he'd ever known about flying. Ditching in the ocean was dangerous at the best of times. There was no right way to conduct a controlled ditch. If there was, he'd never heard of it. He decided his best bet was to set down lightly, as though he were landing on the beach again.

Easing the helicopter down, Lee watched as the chopper skids dipped beneath the water. He lowered the chopper further until the water lapped at the door.

Lee kicked the door open, wedging it open with his boot as the cold water lapped in around the foot pedals. Breathing deeply, Lee powered down the chopper, cutting the power to the engine just as he would if he'd set down on land.

The chopper began to sink, gently slipping beneath the waves as the rotor blades still whizzed by above the cockpit.

Water poured in through the open door, chilling him.

Salt water soaked through the bandage on his hand, searing the wounded stubs where his fingers had once been.

Lee froze.

He couldn't leave the cockpit until the rotor blades had stopped turning. The helicopter twisted as it sank, with the open cockpit door tilting down toward the bottom of the ocean. Water rose up around his neck and head, forcing him to take one last breath. The chopper shuddered under the torque as the rotor blades struck the water, and that was his cue. Lee pushed off, diving down and out of the cockpit.

Something caught around his boot. The cord from the headset had wrapped around his left foot. He struggled, shaking his foot as the helicopter plunged into the depths, dragging him deeper. Although the laces on his boots were undone, he couldn't shake the boot loose. Using his other boot, he managed to pry his foot free, and kick toward the surface.

His lungs were burning as he burst up through the waves.

Lee's clothes were soaked. The heavy overcoat he was wearing began dragging him back down into the murky sea. With only one good hand, Lee struggled to stay above the choppy waves. He choked on a mouthful of water.

Suddenly, a hand grabbed him by the collar. He twisted, turning, grabbing at the rowboat and kicking against the ocean. It took him almost a full minute before he managed to clamber into the boat, dripping with sea water. Lying on his back, gasping, Lee looked up into the grinning face of the old man he'd seen in the hut.

"Thank you," Lee said, coughing and spluttering.

"It is we who should thank you," the grandfather replied with a smile, resting his hand on Lee's shoulder.

Escape

After a four hour drive, they pulled up next to a fire station in North Bend. A faded wooden sign outside announced the name of the suburb: *Windsor Park.*

Twilight cast a warm glow over the distant hills. A community baseball diamond across the street had its floodlights on. Parents sat on metal bleachers watching their children play on the grassy field overlooking the sprawling Coos river. The North Bend nuclear power plant sat on the edge of a wide s curve in the river.

"Stay here," Lachlan said, getting out with Stegmeyer and Vacili.

Vacili was quiet. As a cameraman, being introverted probably came with the territory. Jason had seen him filming, running digital video backups and uploads from his laptop, but he had barely said two words to him in the last day. Vacili appeared to be content recording history rather than participating, but the fact that he was there spoke volumes. The very act of accompanying them was dangerous, and he could spend the rest of his life in a federal penitentiary just for being present. Jason preferred not to think about that too much.

Jason had no doubt Vacili knew precisely what he was involved with and was actively supporting them, and yet he left his camera in the RV at this critical moment, surprising Jason.

"Five minutes," Lily said. She didn't have to say any more. Jason knew why they were here. They were waiting for the explosion at North Bend. Lachlan had promised a spectacular fireworks display, lots of special effects without any real damage. Jason wasn't so sure.

Stegmeyer and Vacili crossed the road and hooked up with a local news crew. Jason hadn't noticed them when they had first arrived. A male reporter stood in front of a camera on a tripod with the baseball diamond directly behind him. Vacili spoke with the cameraman while Stegmeyer moved the reporter, positioning him slightly to one side. They were lining up for the shot, ensuring North Bend was visible in the distance. That explained why Vacili had left his camera in the RV, Jason thought. On this shoot, he was the director.

Lachlan jogged over, holding his phone up and calling out something, but Jason couldn't make out what was being said. Lachlan pointed up to the sky, but neither Stegmeyer or Vacili turned to look. They kept their attention on the news crew. The cameraman disappeared behind the lens and the reporter began talking into a microphone held up to his chin. He gestured to the baseball diamond beside him as a Learjet roared overhead, screaming past barely a hundred feet above the bleachers.

The roar of the engine was deafening. The RV shook. The crowd in the stands was visibly shaken. Kids and adults alike screamed in fright. Some huddled together, holding loved ones. A few ran. Others stood, pulling out smartphones and taking pictures or recording video as the Learjet screamed down into the valley.

The jet banked sharply. Its distinct shape, with fuel pods at the end of its wings and high set tail were visible in profile for a few seconds as the craft turned, lining up for its approach to the nuclear power plant. The plane was terrifyingly low to the ground, looking as though its wings were about to clip the streetlights lining the distant avenue. Cars swerved. A bus rode up onto the pavement, crushing a small tree.

Jason couldn't help himself. He couldn't sit there in the RV. He had to see this out in the open.

"No," Lily cried as he darted out the door of the RV. She ran hard on his heels.

Jason came around the side of the huge vehicle just as the jet leveled out, heading for the nuclear power plant. Lily came up beside him.

The cameraman across the street followed the path of the jet. Parents stood in the bleachers watching as the Learjet slammed into the side of the distant nuclear power plant.

A blinding flash of light cut through the deepening twilight.

There was no sound at first, which surprised Jason. He watched as a massive fireball enveloped the twenty story building.

Jason found himself wondering how anything could survive the fury of such a blast.

Silence fell as the fireball mushroomed into the sky.

Cars stopped on the road. Drivers stood beside the open doors of their cars, watching what looked like a nuclear explosion roiling into the heavens.

The billowing cloud seethed with anger. In the midst of the black smoke, reds and oranges glowed like the sun.

BOOM!

Jason felt the blast wave pass through him, rattling his bones. Windowpanes shattered in the fire station behind him. Still, the mushroom cloud rose higher. A long dark column formed a thin stem beneath the fireball. The head of the cloud folded in upon itself, reaching thousands of feet into the air.

Nobody moved.

People stared in disbelief at the sight before them. Armageddon had come, and they were paralyzed. What could be done? Jason could understand how crippling this sight was for them. Even knowing the impact wasn't a threat to his safety didn't stop the helpless feeling from washing over him as he watched the massive explosion unfold.

"Come on," said Lachlan.

Jason hadn't noticed the professor crossing the road. Lachlan, Stegmeyer and Vacili were the only ones on the move. Everyone else stood there spellbound, aghast with horror. Vacili grabbed his camera from the RV.

A child screamed, and that seemed to break the paralysis. In an instant, the din of hundreds of people panicking filled the ballpark. People began running, screaming, trying to reach the illusory safety of their cars.

Lachlan led Jason away from the blast and into a house two doors down from the fire station.

Bellum opened the garage, saying, "We've been planning every detail of this for the past eighteen months. You'll find boots, jackets and helmets already in the vehicle."

As they walked around the large truck, Lachlan explained, saying, "Local fire crews have standing orders for containment at North Bend. Given the size of that blast, they'll have every appliance in the city there in the next half hour."

Bellum busied himself, handing out heavy boots, turnout pants and jackets, and helmets.

"You guys will ride in the back," Lachlan said to Jason and Lily.

The hazmat vehicle looked like a perfect rectangle. It must feel like driving a brick, Jason thought. Every conceivable inch of space had been covered by something functional. Dozens of compartments lined the vehicle, each with labels designating their contents. There were hoses rolled up and stacked against one side and a ladder at the back allowing access to the roof. The truck must have weighed at least ten tons. If it was a fake, it had Jason fooled. Every detail was meticulous, right down to the North Bend city logo on the doors.

Jason and Lily climbed aboard as Bellum turned over the diesel engine. The engine roared to life, shaking the frame of the vehicle. Black smoke billowed out of the exhaust.

Jason sat there with his helmet in his lap. Lily put her helmet on. Her head looked absurdly small in the huge helmet. She turned to him and grinned like a schoolgirl, signaling with her thumbs up. Jason gave her a nervous thumbs up in response.

The others climbed aboard. Bellum waited, watching as two fire engines pulled out of the fire station and headed down the street away from them. He drove the truck out of the garage and onto the street, but didn't sound the siren until they were almost a block away.

Jason couldn't help but be swept up in the moment. He rolled down his window and rested his elbow on the door. The wind whipped through the back of the truck. Cars, buses and trucks all pulled to one side, letting the convoy of fire engines and the hazmat truck through. The convoy slowed as they approached red lights at intersections, but never stopped. Sirens wailed discordantly across the town. Several other fire departments had mobilized. Jason could see additional fire engines joining them on the main road to North Bend.

Smoke continued to billow from the nuclear power plant. The mushroom cloud had dissipated, turning into a dark, ghostly smudge in the clear night sky, blotting out the stars. Fires raged within the compound.

The fire engines raced up to the open main gate. Several security guards recognized the lead vehicle and waved them through. There were already a number of other fire engines at the scene. At least one of them looked as though it was from the plant.

The convoy came to a halt and their hazmat truck pulled to one side as the lead fire truck stopped to talk to the emergency controller on the ground. An overweight man dressed in yellow gear stood beside the front fire engine. He was clearly flustered. He hadn't donned his helmet, leaving it lying on the ground a few feet away. He had a radio in one hand and was gesturing wildly with the other as he barked instructions.

They started moving again, driving around the side of the main building to where the fire was raging. Flames licked at the concrete.

Several firefighters jumped out of the lead engine as they came to a halt upwind from the fire. Jason could see these guys were taking no chances. They were already breathing through the air tanks on their backs.

Out in an open field away from the prevailing wind, another fire engine was setting up decontamination showers. This was a well-rehearsed emergency plan moving into operation.

The hazmat truck pulled up on the far side of the fire engines, parking away from the fire, beside the dome over reactor one.

Water sprayed through the air as the firefighters fought to control secondary blazes that had erupted in the low-lying surrounding buildings. Lights flickered as electricity fluctuated. Darkness descended on the plant. The only light came from the raging fires and the fire engines. The sound of diesel generators kicked in and dim, emergency lighting switched on.

Lachlan and Bellum jumped out of the truck and jogged over toward an enclosed walkway leading to the unscathed dome towering over what was supposed to be reactor one. Everyone else followed.

Bellum was carrying a heavy duffle bag over his shoulder. The sound of metal tools clinked as he ran. He dropped the bag unceremoniously on the ground in front of a set of doors and pulled out a shotgun. Two quick, well placed shots rang out, blowing the hinges off the door and causing the steel frame to fall inward with a thud.

Jason felt as though he were caught in the current of a fast moving stream, being dragged along by the sheer weight of water pressing on his body. He couldn't help but follow. He had to see the UFO. An overwhelming compulsion demanded his obedience. All the fear and reservations he'd had were drowned by the current.

Professor Lachlan was the first one through the door. He had some kind of map in his hand. Bellum grabbed the bag and stepped through after him.

"We've got five minutes on the ground and that's it," Lachlan yelled. "Grab anything you can: hard drives, print outs, schematics, and then get back here. Vacili, stay with Jason and Lily. Record everything that happens."

Before he had time to think, Jason found himself jogging down a long hallway behind Bellum and the professor. Emergency lights flickered overhead. Another shotgun blast blew open the door at the far end of the corridor, and in the confined space, the report was deafening. Bellum's shot had hit the lock and handle, blowing a hole six inches in diameter in the door. He had to be using some kind of solid shot, like a bear slug rather than regular shotgun shells.

Without the main power, the inside of the vast dome looked hauntingly empty. A single spotlight overhead illuminated the UFO. Jason stepped through the door and got his first good look at the craft. He was overcome by the sheer size of the interstellar alien machine.

From where he was standing, the UFO looked roughly circular, like the classic shape of a flying saucer from the 1950s, but it was pitch black rather than silver in color. A series of permanent scaffolds had been erected around the craft, allowing workers to move above and around or below the massive vessel without touching it. It looked as though the UFO was resting on some kind of small base under its center, with the bulk of the disk suspended in the air.

The walkways were extensive and allowed access at distances anywhere from a few feet to a few inches of the dark skin of the interstellar vehicle. The craft was covered in graffiti. At least it looked like graffiti at first glance, but these were the calculations scattered around the vessel. They were drawn at hasty angles. Some of them were incomplete. Most of them were overlapped by some other formula.

Lily gasped.

"There's no time for sightseeing," Lachlan yelled. "We've got to be in and out in five minutes!"

Lachlan ignored the craft, jogging over to one of the split floors that surrounded the UFO. He had a battery powered screwdriver and began the task of disconnecting the many computers. He tossed hard drives in a backpack and then jogged further along the floor. Jason could see he was skipping stations, trying to strip out at least one computer from each section.

Jason shed his fire helmet and heavy jacket, standing there in a t-shirt, bunker pants, and oversized rubber boots. They were far too heavy to drag around, so he shimmied out of them, leaving them crumpled on the floor.

"You'll need these when we leave," Lily said, turning to him.

"You don't understand," Jason replied, gesturing to the craft. "Can't you see it? None of us will leave this place. We won't make it out of here alive!"

Lily looked at where Jason had pointed. He was staring at several phrases carved into the side of the vehicle.

Why? Why? Why?

Why keep coming?

Only death awaits

Jason bent down and grabbed a small hand ax that had been hanging from the belt of his coveralls.

"What are you doing?" Lily asked.

The ax had a blade on one side, a pick on the other. Jason turned the ax around and rested the pick in the O of *Only*. The blade fit perfectly. Slowly, he traced the word *Only*.

"Jason," Lily cried. "We don't have time for this!"

"On the contrary," Jason replied, speaking in a calm voice. "We have a time machine. We have all the time in the universe."

He rested his hand on the side of the vessel as he traced the word *death* with the ax pick, thinking about the implications of the word and the style of writing. With his hand on the skin of the alien craft, a long, low growl reverberated through the air, like the sound of an animal in distress.

The UFO shook.

"She's alive," Jason said.

"That's impossible," Lily replied. "This is a machine!"

"I thought so too," he said. "But she's not. She responded to my touch."

Jason stroked the hide of the massive beast, feeling the hard exterior soften in response to his touch. What had looked like a stone surface had a texture similar to leather. Jason thought the hide resembled that of an elephant, thick and impenetrable.

"Come on," he cried, running along the scaffolding, feeling the metal walkway vibrating beneath his bare feet.

As he ran, he tried to keep contact with the creature. His fingers trailed over the thick hide, skimming over the scars of various calculations and formulas.

"They're telling a story," he said, "the equations," lifting his hand every ten feet to dodge the scaffold support poles, always returning to the UFO.

The scaffolding wasn't level, at some points forcing him higher, dropping down lower at others as he jogged around the massive living vessel. The UFO seemed to breathe, expanding as the chest of a man would when inhaling deeply.

Lachlan had seen the craft respond to Jason and ran over to join them.

"What is it? What's happening?"

"She's alive!" Jason yelled in excitement. He stopped, looking at the formulas and words before him. For the first time, Jason could see the etchings as a continuous whole rather than a disjointed mess, and he understood what he was looking at.

"These markings," he cried. "They're here for us. They're meant for us, so we would understand."

"Understand what?" Lachlan asked.

"I'm still figuring that out," Jason replied. "But this is deliberate and it's meant for us, I'm sure of it."

"Who wrote these words?" Lily asked.

Jason shrugged. He ran his fingers over a series of words.

Beautiful

Lonely

Scared

Hurt

"The formulas," Jason said, letting the words speak for themselves as he referred to a jumble of calculations to one side. "I know what they are. They're not calculations for time travel, they're trying to understand the impact of unshielded travel of regular matter through a wormhole comprised of exotic matter. They're trying to determine the consequences for anyone passing back in time."

Lily had a pickaxe as well. Like Jason earlier, she ran the tip of the ax gently over the scars, tracing the words, seeming lost in thought.

"We need to get up higher," she said, pointing toward the center of the UFO. There was a dome on top of the creature, barely visible from where they were on the rim of the gigantic beast.

Jason began climbing up the scaffolding hanging over the living being. Lachlan and Lily followed. Vacili hung back a few yards, catching everything on video.

Down below, gunfire erupted. Jason caught a glimpse of Bellum firing an M4, rattling off shots in rapid succession. The crack of each round being fired echoed through the dome. Stegmeyer was already heading back for the walkway.

"We have to go," Lachlan cried. "We've got to get out of here while we still can."

"We can't," Jason replied, dropping down from the scaffolding and onto the sloping flanks of the vast interstellar creature. "We can't leave her. Don't you understand? She's waited. She's endured. She's held on for us, waiting for us to free her."

Lily followed Jason, landing just a few feet away from him. She crouched as she absorbed the jump, and came to a rest with one hand reaching out and touching the thick, scarred hide. Even here, numerous formulas tattooed the skin of the animal.

Lachlan hesitated.

"Come on," Jason cried, gesturing with the pickaxe still in his hand. "You want answers. They're all here. They're all around us, written in plain sight."

"But it makes no sense," Lachlan cried. "Who would leave these messages?"

Jason didn't have an answer, but he'd already figured out that all of these markings were made by only a couple of people. Although the carvings were crude in places, they were unmistakably related, as though the same people had written different messages at different points in time. One person had been preoccupied with the science, the other had focused on emotions.

Free

Release

Mercy

Jason watched in horror as the professor lurched forward. A bullet ripped through his shoulder, spraying blood over them. Lachlan struggled to hold onto the railing. He fell to his knees as a second bullet tore through his thigh.

The old man tumbled from the scaffolding, falling awkwardly onto the creature. The massive beast responded to his presence, wailing in a tone deeper than a fog horn. Lachlan slid to one side. He was in danger of rolling off the edge of the wing when Jason grabbed his wrist. A single finger, a thumb and three mutilated stubs grabbed desperately at Jason's hand. Lily grabbed her father's other hand. Together, the two of them hauled the old man further up the steep incline on the flanks of the beast. The thick hide on which they stood trembled, shaking as the creature groaned.

Jason fought to get beneath the professor, hoisting Lachlan's arm up over his shoulder. Together, they staggered up the craft.

As they approached the dome, the gradient lessened, making the climb easier. Down below, explosions rattled the scaffolding.

Jason had no idea how many armed men had stormed the nuclear reactor building, but Bellum was holding his own, that much was clear. Handguns cracked as they fired, rifle shots echoed around them. A flash of light lit up the shaking scaffolding, followed by a thunderous crack.

"No more," Lachlan cried as Jason dragged him roughly up toward the dome of the UFO. "I ... I can't take any more."

Jason swung the professor down, resting him gently against the dome.

The central dome of the creature was easily thirty feet in diameter, but it was torn and damaged. The front portion had been ripped open, but the wound was old. Jason could see inside the cavity. There were electronic monitors and computers set up on tables. Wires snaked their way out from inside the dome, leading over to the scaffolding on the far side of the craft.

Lily crouched by her father, pressing on the wound in his shoulder.

"I'm dying," the old man said.

"Don't say that," she cried.

"They've hit an artery," he managed. "It's just a matter of time."

Jason took his mentor's hand. Immediately behind Lachlan's head there were more words, only this time they were in complete phrases.

You cannot save him

You can save him

Listen to him

Lachlan must have seen Jason staring. He turned to one side, twisting his head and looking up.

"When we first met," he grimaced. "You told me you knew how I died."

Jason held his hand, not saying anything.

"I've always known this day was coming, but I believe in you. You can change this," the dying man said, struggling to breathe. "History doesn't have to repeat."

"Time travel won't allow for paradoxes," Jason replied. "Nothing changes. Nothing can ever change."

"Who says it's a paradox?" Lee said, gasping for breath. "I think I finally understand what this is, what all the scribbling is ... For years, we've wondered about the meaning. We didn't understand—the equations are not the answer, they're the question. A question that has been asked over and over, through thousands of iterations, spanning tens of thousands of years."

The old man slumped against the wall of the central dome. Jason squeezed the dying man's hand gently.

"Feedback," Professor Lachlan said.

"Feedback?" Jason asked, his mind remembering the word he'd seen chaotically spelled out when the photos had fallen to the floor of the RV. "You mean, like a microphone getting too close to a speaker?"

"Yes."

Jason looked up, looking at the scratchings and messages, the words that seemed so disjointed and confused.

"So all this, it's feedback from previous iterations? These messages we see here. These are messages we've left for ourselves?"

The professor nodded. "Each message defies fate. Each etching represents a small, subtle change. Time is dynamic—elastic. There's always a choice."

"So we can break out of this feedback loop? We can end this?" Jason asked.

"Yes," Lachlan replied as the battle raged below them. Automatic gunfire echoed through the vast chamber in staccato bursts.

"Feedback builds until something gives," Jason said, realizing what the professor was getting at.

The old man nodded, saying, "Each time, we learn more."

"But it's too late!"

"It's never too late," the professor said, struggling with those final words. His eyelids drooped. His head bowed, as his hand went limp.

Lachlan was dead.

Jason struggled to swallow the lump in his throat. Tears spilled down his face. He was overwhelmed by the loss of this man. His mentor. His friend. This was the man who saved his life as a child. Jason owed him every breath. So much had been lost in that tragic moment. A lifetime of learning and reasoning, a brilliant mind, but more than that, a friend, a father, a husband, a teacher—gone. The finality of death struck Jason, forcing a lump to rise in his throat.

Jason barely knew the man that had rescued him from North Korea, but he knew he owed him a debt that could never be repaid.

"We should have left," he sobbed, feeling the weight of the professor's death because of his irrational insistence that they stay with the craft. "I'm sorry. You were right. We should have grabbed what we needed and run."

Lily cried. She rested her head on her father's shoulder and sobbed, combing his thin hair with her fingers.

"You and I," Jason said, grasping the professor's hand and squeezing. "We have lived for thousands of years, never able to escape this prison, but this time, it will be different. I promise."

Jason knelt beside Lily, gently rubbing her shoulders, whispering to her. "I'm sorry. I'm so sorry."

Bullets sliced through the air around them, zipping past just inches away from striking them. A battle continued to rage beneath the creature, but there was only so long Bellum could hold out. It was only a matter of time before he was outflanked. Gunmen were moving in from all sides.

In the confusion, Jason had lost sight of Vacili, but the cameraman had been there. He'd followed them onto the wing of the craft although Jason had no recollection of him jumping down from the scaffolding. A blinking red light on the camera told Jason he'd caught Lachlan's last few moments on video.

Jason looked up at Vacili, looking deep into the dark, cold, impersonal camera lens as a bullet struck the back of Vacili's head. An explosion of red sprayed to one side as the cameraman's body crumpled and fell. His lifeless body slid a few feet after hitting the hide of the great animal, while the camera rolled down the sloping wing, slowly gathering momentum before it bounced off the edge and out of sight.

Lily grabbed Jason, holding on to him as though she were desperate not to fall. Jason could feel the terror in her trembling body.

On the distant scaffolding, April Stegmeyer's body lay prone, sprawled to one side in a pool of blood.

The gunfire beneath the UFO ceased abruptly. Bellum was either dead or had been wounded and captured.

"We need to go," Jason said, pulling Lily to her feet.

"Where?" Lily asked.

"We'll go where we've always gone. Back in time."

As the words left his lips, he realized she was going to die. He wasn't sure whether she would die there in the nuclear reactor, within the time stream, or in the dark waters off the coast of North Korea, but there had only ever been one survivor, a boy. And that was the answer to the calculations. What was the consequence of traveling through time with a ruptured shield? The answer was that any matter that travelled through the wormhole reverted to its then current form. But that couldn't be the whole answer. His body had retained its magnificent genetic changes, but where had those genetic enhancements come from? Were they the result of exposure to radiation while traveling through time? But surely, he thought, such radiation would be destructive. There was some other hidden element he didn't yet understand. Some other influence swaying the course of the mighty river of time, and that puzzled him.

"We should run," Lily said, pulling away from him, dragging him from the dome of the creature. "We need to get back to the truck. If you go back in time, this will never end. We need to get back out the way we came."

Jason never saw the shooter, but he heard the shots ring out, echoing around the vast dome.

Lily's body convulsed as three bullets ripped through her abdomen. Bright red blood sprayed across the dark hide of the creature. Lily sank to her knees and fell to one side clutching at her bloody stomach. She screamed in agony.

"No!" Jason cried. Crouching beside her, he raised her head and cradled her in his arms. "Oh, no. Not you too!"

"You have to run," she said, looking up into his eyes. "You can't go back. If you do, you'll never escape. Your only hope is to get out of here."

Her body shook, but the spasms were only from the waist up. Holding her, he could feel her shattered spine. She was paralyzed from the waist down. Blood and fluids poured from her wounds, soaking his hands.

"No, no, no," he murmured, brushing her hair to one side and inadvertently smearing blood on her forehead. "It can't end like this. Please, don't let it end like this."

"Don't you see," she gasped, squeezing his hand. "This has to end. You have to break out of the time loop."

"No," he whispered. "I can't leave you."

"You have to," she said, closing her eyes as she whispered, "Run!"

Like Lachlan before her, Lily's body went limp in his arms. Her eyes flickered open, but they stared blindly up at the vast ceiling of the reactor dome.

"Nooooo!" he screamed, arching his back and tensing every muscle in his body in a futile bid to roll back time, but there was nothing to be done for her.

Run!

Lily's last word seemed to echo in his mind.

Run?

Sitting there, he trembled, trying not to collapse beside her lifeless body. Jason was shaking uncontrollably. Standing seemed impossible, let alone walking or running. Here he was, sitting on a time machine, unable to roll back just one minute to save the young woman. He couldn't explain the connection he'd forged with Lily over those past few days, but it had been severed violently and abruptly, tearing at his heart.

Soldiers dropped onto the edge of the UFO. They were shouting, waving, firing their rifles. Bullets whipped by his head, passing just inches from his face.

"I'm sorry," he said, resting her head gently on the thick hide of the interstellar beast. With two fingers outstretched, he closed her eyelids. It seemed only decent and proper. He couldn't pretend he didn't care. He couldn't pretend that just moments before, her body hadn't been animated, radiating a life he found deliriously intoxicating. The realization that Lily was dead caused a knot to form in his chest. A knife through the heart couldn't have felt more painful, he thought.

Run!

Again, her soft admonition reverberated through his mind. She was right. He had to run.

Jason grabbed the pickaxe and ran. His legs felt weak, drained of strength, but he forced them on. Bullets whizzed by, cracking through the air as they shot past him at supersonic velocities.

Jason ran on blindly, but he was running around the center of the UFO, not away from it. If he wanted to escape, he should have run toward the walkway. His mind felt drugged and lethargic, still reeling from shock.

He climbed into the shattered dome on top of the vast creature.

Immediately, the alien animal responded to his presence. Light began pulsating out from the center of the craft, running in ripples across the immense hide in much the same way as a cuttlefish displayed a variety of colors. The soldiers were thrown backwards, as if hurled outward by a massive electric shock.

Jason got his first good look inside the vast cavity that was the head of the creature. That the beast was organic was not readily apparent because the outer skin was transparent, like a massive windscreen. From the outside, the central dome had appeared dull grey, but from inside the view was clear.

There were controls, at least they looked like controls. Row upon row of lights lit up on a bank in the craft, but the far side of what could be mistaken for a cockpit had an earthy feel. Severed roots and crushed rocks lay in complex matrices, interlaced with each other, connected by thin, sinuous veins. The contrast between the two hemispheres of the dome was stark, giving the impression that they didn't belong together.

The rear half of the alien skull appeared to be sectioned off. A series of hurriedly scrawled formulas scarred the wall. These were the most advanced calculations he'd seen. They were complete. He recognized several portions from the photographs he'd seen in the RV.

The creature throbbed and pulsated. He could feel her lifting into the air. Outside, scaffolding fell away, crashing to the ground. Soldiers were yelling and firing, but where Jason was, there was only silence. They appeared to be acting out some part on a stage without any sound to accompany them.

Jason turned back to the scratches on the rear wall. He fought with his legs to stay upright as the craft swayed in the air.

Lachlan was right. What seemed like a single strand of time to Jason was in fact a time stream that repeated thousands and thousands of times. Each time the outcome had been the same. The only difference was those etchings.

Among the chaos, they were all that mattered. They were the fleeting efforts to steer a new course.

You can save her

You can save all of them

These were messages he'd left himself.

The scratches outside had been from previous iterations of both him and Lily as they fought to understand what was happening to them time and again, but inside this dome, the only handwriting was his.

Standing there, he realized he had a plan. Jason still hadn't quite comprehended what that plan was, but he knew why he went back in time. He couldn't run. He was always going to go back for her. He had to save her. That's what this was about: love.

Jason had gone back innumerable times out of his love for Lily and her father. And he had a plan, he knew he had a plan, a plan that had been formed over thousands of cycles, a plan carved here on the walls of this vast creature, only he had to figure out the messages he'd been sending himself.

The animal continued to pulse, increasing in its frequency and the brightness of the light it emitted.

"I know," Jason said softly. "I understand the pain you've been in for so long. You want to be set free, too. I can do this. I can change this. I can bring about the end. Stay with me, my old friend. Together, we are going to change this and bring you release from the torment and pain."

Jason stepped back, his eyes focused on the back wall, intently wanting to understand the message he'd sent himself.

He knew in past iterations he would have turned because he would have wanted to see the spectacular sight of the creature bursting through the dome over reactor one. He'd have relished the vision of time and space warping around him and the majesty of traveling a wormhole through space-time, but to escape he had to ignore all that. He had to knit the threads of a plan being passed down through time. The answer was right there in front of him, he just had to see it, he had to see it just as he had in times immemorial.

You can save her

You can save all of them

And that was when it struck him. Finally, he understood. He'd never seen these words. If there had been photos taken of these words, they never made it to Lachlan. Perhaps they hadn't been deemed important, but for some reason this message only ever reached him now, although portions of the calculation lower down made it back to him in the RV.

Jason closed his eyes, picturing the photos scattered on the floor of the RV. They'd fallen out of sequence, scattered in a seemingly random pattern, but they'd formed coherent words.

fe ED b A ck

d E st R oY

Opening his eyes, he ran his fingers over the thick hide of the animal as it rose thousands of feet above the Earth, readying itself for a jaunt into the past.

There it was. He recognized the letters, if not the order.

fe fe fe fe ck b ED A ED ck A

To anyone else, these letters would be nonsense, but the first three *fe*'s were there as markers, slowly lining up those two letters over several iterations so they appeared in precisely the right spot within the photograph. Whoever had taken the pictures must have resolved never to show him anything that appeared unsettling, or they hadn't seen any significance in these letters and so ignored them, but either way, this was the only means by which he could talk to himself across the gulf of time.

Each of the letters was part of a multi-iteration attempt to warn himself of what was to come.

E d R st o Y

There was *destroy*.

Jason leaned close, studying several small scratches in the shape of v's and ^'s. Instantly, he understood what he was telling himself. He'd previously calculated where the edge of those photos had been. He'd already mapped out where the final words should go. This was it, this would be the last iteration. With this, he could end the cycles.

Jason held up his pickaxe, looking carefully at the markings and remembering the sequence in which the photos had fallen. Quickly, he scratched two words into the wall, using all the space he felt was available.

ctor 1 Rea

Reactor 1. That was the missing piece of the puzzle,the final portion of the plan. He went back over the R, making sure it stood out clearly. This was what he needed, he was sure of it.

Jason thought back to his state of mind in the RV after they struck the branch on the road. He remembered how he'd wondered about these words, and he remembered the conversation he and Lachlan had, the discussion about the three reactors.

Would this message work?

Would Jason believe someone was talking to him across the vastness of time itself?

Would Lachlan believe in this ad hoc message across the ages?

He knew Lily would.

What would they do?

Would they destroy the dome?

His only hope lay in that Learjet punching its way through the dome over Reactor 1 and destroying the time machine.

Would the blast kill the creature?

He'd seen *Mercy* scratched on the side of the craft, and now he understood why. Standing there in the cranial structure of the beast he knew it desired *release*, yet another message from its scarred hide.

Was that what this was all about?

Was that why this astonishing animal continued to loop over and over within space-time? Was it seeking release?

The alien had been injured. From what he could tell, almost a quarter of whatever made up its brain had been destroyed at some point in the distant past. As best he understood what he'd seen, this magnificent animal was on the verge of being brain-dead. It had suffered for far too long. Yes, he thought, *Reactor 1* completed the message he'd been trying to send for thousands of years. *Reactor 1* would bring about the end.

A cold wind swirled into the open cranial structure of the vast dark beast.

Jason turned, but his vantage point had narrowed.

The pickaxe in his hand looked magnified.

He dropped the ax and staggered forward, his mind reeling from the physiological change that had been thrust upon it.

Thoughts he'd had just moments before were lost to him. There was something he needed to remember, but he couldn't grasp what had seemed so important just seconds before. A few, brief flashes of memory lit his mind, that of a woman dying in his arms, and an old man with a mutilated hand, but beyond that his mind was blank.

Jason's clothes were too big and baggy. He reached out a tiny hand, steadying himself against a bank of flashing lights, looking out into the darkness.

Clouds raced by.

The alien creature banked to one side.

Wind howled beyond the cockpit.

Dawn broke in the distance. The sun peeked over the horizon as the massive craft crashed into the sea, sending up a wall of spray.

Cold sea water flooded into the fractured cavern, washing over Jason and causing him to choke. He spluttered, struggling to swim against the inflow of water flooding the vessel. Frantically, he kicked with his legs, freeing himself from his oversized, baggy clothing and pushing toward the surface.

The craft slipped quietly beneath the waves.

Jason swallowed sea water. Struggling and coughing, he fought to stay afloat, but he was sinking beneath the waves. Suddenly, a hand grabbed him, hauling him up into a rough wooden boat and he turned, seeing a familiar, friendly face, a face he'd seen thousands of times before.

Jason smiled at the aging North Korean fisherman.

He'd escaped, yet again.

THE BEGINNING OF THE END

Εpilogue

The lights in the airlock dimmed as the pressure dropped, slowly forming a vacuum in the chamber. Jae-Sun could feel his spacesuit flex slightly. The pressure within his suit hadn't changed, but the dropping pressure around him forced the material to take shape, swelling slightly.

The interior of the airlock was white. Various touch panels indicated readings from inside and outside the lock. A green light came on, signaling that a vacuum had been established, matching that outside the vast exploration craft. The lighting inside the lock remained dim, ensuring the astronaut's eyes remained accustomed to the low light outside the spaceship.

The iris on the outside of the airlock opened, beginning as a tiny dot and spreading to more than twenty feet in diameter, which was more than enough given that there were only two astronauts preparing to exit. Normally, this lock handled up to fifteen astronauts at a time, including construction equipment.

"You are clear for EVA," a disembodied voice said over the radio com link.

"Roger that," Commander Lassiter replied from opposite Jae-Sun.

The young man grinned from behind his glass faceplate, smiling at Jae-Sun. Such excitement was contagious. For a moment, Jae-Sun could almost pretend he was a young man, but four hundred and eighty-seven years were taking their toll on his aging frame.

Even with gene therapy and rejuvenation sleeps, there was only so much the cells of his body could endure. He wanted to make five hundred, and why not? It was more than just an arbitrary number; it was his life. Jae-Sun was a bio-geneticist before switching to complete a double PhD in physics. He was one of the first to undergo live gene reconstruction in the twenty-first century. There was no known upper limit to the therapy, but his body still aged, just far more slowly. By the twenty-fifth century, he had the appearance of a sixty year old under natural aging.

Lassiter gestured to the old man, signaling for him to leave the airlock first.

Jae-Sun stretched the fingers on his right hand and his spacesuit responded effortlessly, following his every impulse. He twisted his hand slightly, adjusting his orientation and rotated to one side relative to Lassiter. A jet-propelled equipment case mimicked the motion of his suit, staying several feet behind him and off to one side.

Jae-Sun lined himself up with what he thought of as vertical on the distant asteroid. The equipment case aligned itself with Jae-Sun so that it remained behind him to his left, exactly as it had been in the airlock. The white cube was a meter on each side, but Jae-Sun, even after all these years still thought in imperial measurements. To him, it was three feet square, and some. The dials and gauges covering its six faces were overly large, having been designed to be easy to operate with thick gloves, but this was no ordinary instrument array.

Lassiter followed him out of the airlock.

"Keep the *Excelsior* on station in this orbital path," Jae-Sun said over his radio.

"Yes sir," came the distant reply.

"Under no circumstances is the *Excelsior* to approach OA-5772, is that understood?"

"Yes sir."

"Regardless of what happens to me, you are to maintain the isolation of the asteroid and report into sector command."

"Understood, sir."

"Commander," Jae-Sun said, turning toward the young man. "You have command of the EVA helm."

"Roger that," Lassiter replied, tapping on his wrist computer.

Jae-Sun never tired of the majesty of seeing a man or woman in a spacesuit, defying the cold, harsh vacuum of deep space. Over the centuries, the suits had changed from the bulky EVA packs he'd once used on the International Space Station. They were still white, as that was universally recognized as the most distinct color in space. There had been some experimentation with other colors like fluorescent green and Day-Glo orange. Both of these worked from a practical perspective, but they weren't aesthetically pleasing, and in the harsh, hard life of an astronaut, even small concessions were highly significant. White had prevailed. White seemed to link the astronauts of today with those silver suits of the Mercury program, the emergence of EVA suits with Gemini, and the moonwalks of Apollo. White linked far-flung astronauts with a planet few would ever see again. White was important, and Jae-Sun understood that, having participated in space travel ever since the exploration of Mars.

"Setting way-points," Lassiter said. "On your command."

Jae-Sun turned to face the distant asteroid and said, "Go."

Lassiter eased them forward, accelerating slowly. He was more considerate than most of the pilots Jae-Sun had worked with over the centuries, which was the reason Jae-Sun had requested him for this mission.

They pulled away from the *Excelsior*, leaving the three quarter mile long exploration vessel behind them. Within fifteen seconds, the two astronauts had passed the spinning centrifugal cabin used to maintain artificial gravity in deep space. The instrumentation cube followed faithfully behind them. Faces peered out from portholes swinging briskly by. They were better off watching on a vid-monitor, Jae-Sun thought.

Lassiter continued to accelerate, taking them up to a sustained one gravity, allowing them to cross the four hundred miles to the tiny, distant asteroid in less than seven minutes. Jae-Sun's suit was in buddy-mode, matching the flight commands issued by Lassiter.

Jae-Sun felt some grit in the corner of his eyes. He should have cleared it out before the space walk. He closed his eyes for a moment, pinching his eyelids tight and then slowly releasing. While his eyes were closed, flashes of blue and white sparkled on the inside of his eyelids, appearing fleetingly, shining briefly like diamonds. It was Cherenkov radiation, the effect of cosmic rays passing clear through his skull and exiting out through his eyeballs. Astronauts had seen this phenomenon for hundreds of years, ever since the first Apollo missions. Nothing short of the shielding on the *Excelsior* could prevent it. He opened his eyes, and for a second, it looked as though there were blue flashes in the distance.

"Are you OK, sir?"

"I'm fine," Jae-Sun replied.

It took several minutes, but as the asteroid began to loom larger in front of them, the commander reversed their thrust and where once Jae-Sun felt flung toward the asteroid he now felt as though he were diving through water, being held back by some invisible current dragging on his body. Commander Lassiter decelerated as smoothly as he'd taken off from the *Excelsior*.

Looking back, Jae-Sun couldn't make out the exploration vessel against the pitch-black of space. At this distance, she was invisible to the naked eye. A soft yellow light pulsed on his heads-up display, artificially marking the distant ship.

OA-5772 was fifty seven miles long, twenty miles wide, and was shaped like a peanut. She was one of over five hundred thousand celestial objects being tracked in the Oort cloud. The asteroid had a rotation period of four hours, turning lazily before a sun so distant that it looked like Mars or Jupiter from Earth, blending in with the other nearby stars.

"Why this asteroid, sir?" Lassiter asked.

Jae-Sun decided Lassiter deserved to know, but before answering, he asked, "Are we transmitting to the *Excelsior*?"

"No sir. We're on local coms only at this distance. I can align a directional transmission if you want."

"No, no," Jae-Sun replied. "That won't be necessary."

"Is it true, sir? Are you hunting a dragon?"

"How long have you been out here in the deep?" Jae-Sun asked, not intentionally ignoring Lassiter, but wanting to understand a little about the man from a personal perspective.

"Fourteen years, sir. Eight spent in transit, two on station and four on the *Excelsior*."

"What brings you to the deep?"

"I want to get a place on Enceladus," Lassiter replied.

"You like working with bugs?" Jae-Sun asked. "There's nothing down there but microbes."

"My wife, well, my girlfriend, my fiancée. She's a biologist."

"You're a long way from Enceladus, son."

"I know," Lassiter replied as the asteroid grew in size before them, slowly filling the view in their faceplates. "But I figure it's worth doing my time out here. The pay is good. It should set me up for a couple of centuries in the inner system."

"Enceladus is an icy wasteland," Jae-Sun said, probing. "You're not tempted by Mars or Titan? They've got some serious terraforming going on in those provinces. You could buy yourself a nice view of the space elevator disappearing above Olympus Mons, or get an apartment overlooking the atriums in Valles Marineris. I guess you like Saturn, huh?"

"Saturn's beautiful," Lassiter replied. "But not as beautiful as my Peg."

Jae-Sun laughed softly in reply.

"So," Lassiter asked again as the craters and mounds on the asteroid came into view. "Are the rumors true? Are there really dragons in the deep?"

"Yes."

"And you've seen them?" Lassiter asked.

"No. Not with my own eyes, but I've been tracking gamma ray bursts out here in the Oort Cloud for almost two hundred years, narrowing down the possibilities.

"At first, I didn't believe the old spacer stories. No one did. But after eliminating all the other possibilities, the only possibility that remains is the presence of extraterrestrials skirting the edge of our solar system."

"So now you believe?" Lassiter asked.

"It's not so much a question of belief. It's about accepting the evidence," Jae-Sun replied. "Science is the realization that natural phenomena have an explanation independent of beliefs and opinions."

"But dragons?" Lassiter asked ironically, his skepticism clear in his voice.

"What do you know about them?" Jae-Sun asked, watching as the rugged terrain of the asteroid slowly began to reveal its torrid, chaotic past. Boulders the size of an apartment came into view, casting long shadows over the dusty surface of the asteroid.

"Just rumors," Lassiter replied. "I didn't think they were real. They just seem like the stuff of myth and legend."

Jae-Sun listened carefully to the young man as he looked around, marveling at darkness that surrounded them. Tens of thousands of stars fought against the pitch black void, pinpricks of light shining in defiance of the eternal night.

At a distance of just over a light-year, the sun's rays had lost most of their potency, making the asteroid appear bathed in dull starlight. Photon amplifiers in the spacesuit helmets compensated for the low light, but those areas in shade appeared pitch black.

Jae-Sun marveled at the stark contrast between the grubby asteroid and their crisp clean spacesuits. He replied to Lassiter, saying, "The majority of the science we're doing out here is to try to catch one of these aliens. The placement of probes, the scanners and patrols, we're looking for telltale signs.

"Oh, the official line is that we're monitoring the stability of the cloud to keep long-cycle comets from threatening the inner system, but that's just a cover. Sure, there's the potential for mining vessels to disrupt orbits, but it's a low risk and one that would take thousands, perhaps millions of years to form a credible threat."

"But dragons?" Lassiter whispered softly.

Lassiter seemed unusually flustered. Jae-Sun realized he had his undivided attention. Central command might consider the existence of dragons classified, but Jae-Sun didn't care. The ever changing whims of bureaucrats were an annoyance to the old man. He'd lived to see *Homo sapiens* escape the shackles of Earth and fight off the concept of death, extending human life by a factor of ten. As one of the theoretical physicists that made the space-time compression drive possible, he had a certain amount of latitude. Some called it irreverence.

"It's not that much of a surprise when you think about it," Jae-Sun said. "The Oort cloud is impossibly large. There's more pre-organic matter here than there is in all the planets combined, but it is so broadly spread out that it appears insignificant. The Oort cloud drifts on the edge of interstellar space, held loosely in place by the weakened pull of the sun, over a light-year away.

"To us, the Oort cloud seems like a far-flung, desolate, rocky, icy shell surrounding the sun, an unlikely place to find life. But think about space as a biological environment. Stars are like tar pits, sucking in any creature that strays too close. But out here, we're on the edge of the tidal zone. Out here, a nudge one way or the other can send you to the Oort Cloud of dozens of other stars with very little exertion."

Lassiter asked, "And these dragons? They inhabit the Oort Cloud?"

"Yes. Although dragon isn't the term I'd use," Jae-Sun replied. "Dragon conjures up images of fire and damnation raining down from some dark, winged monster. No, I'd call them celestial cetaceans or migratory birds. If we're going to use some kind of terrestrial analogy, we should make it one befitting their character."

"Birds? Whales?" Lassiter asked.

"Yes. Both of them are renowned for their astonishing migrations, and from what I've observed these dragons, for lack of a better term, have a similar mode of being."

"Are they intelligent?"

"I suspect they're more intelligent than we believe." Jae-Sun paused before adding, "They may be more intelligent than us."

"Then why don't they make contact with us?" Lassiter asked as the two astronauts slowed to barely fifty miles an hour and began skimming over the surface of the asteroid toward a predetermined waypoint. Due to the undulating nature of the asteroid, their altitude fluctuated anywhere from a few hundred feet to almost a thousand feet.

"Why don't dolphins learn English?" Jae-Sun asked. "Why doesn't an octopus learn how to use a crowbar? Why don't chimps have a mastery of fire?"

He paused for a moment, letting those thoughts sink in before continuing.

"It's not in their nature. Contact may be a biological imperative for us, but it's apparently not for them. If anything, they seem wary of us. We're the aggressors, escaping the gravitational confines of our planet and encroaching on their natural habitat. From their perspective, they have every reason to avoid us."

Lassiter slowed their forward momentum, dropping them closer to the asteroid as the waypoint approached. The instrumentation cube slowed in tandem with Jae-Sun.

"But you've found one?" Lassiter asked.

"I think I may have found one," Jae-Sun replied. "It's hard to be sure. These things can move through both space and time, but they leave a trail. Each time they warp, they emit high-energy particles. And they follow a pattern, in the same way that birds will follow the same path to escape the coming of winter."

Lassiter pulled them to a halt, lowering them down to within two feet of the asteroid. Jae-Sun watched as he established buoyancy, ensuring their suits automatically counteracted the weak pull of gravity from the asteroid.

The two astronauts were side on to the asteroid, so the surface appeared like a wall in front of them, with the distant sunlight running left to right. Pin pricks of light edged around the raised, stippled surface, while long black shadows stretched away from them.

Jae-Sun reached out his gloved hand. His fingers sank effortlessly into the fine powder on the surface of the asteroid. He moved his fingers in a figure eight and watched as the fine powder swirled as though it were suspended in water.

"Never lose your childlike sense of wonder," Jae-Sun said, turning to Lassiter. "When you go to Enceladus, don't lose your appreciation for how astonishing it is to walk on another world. Even the humblest of microbes on that small moon represent billions of years of evolutionary change, and that's not something to be taken lightly."

Lassiter nodded inside his helmet.

"First contact protocols necessitate that you wait here," Jae-Sun said. "Is that understood?"

"Yes sir," Lassiter replied. "Buddy mode is off."

Lassiter's gloved hands tapped at his wrist computer, returning local EVA control to Jae-Sun.

"Whatever happens," Jae-Sun said, already drifting away from him. "Do not follow me. If I fail to return, you are to initiate the containment plan and deploy robotic probes. Understood?"

"Yes, sir."

Jae-Sun stretched out his hand and thrust away from Lassiter. The white cube raced after him, keeping pace beside him.

Jae-Sun checked his wrist computer, watching the readouts relating to altitude above the rocky surface, way-point distances and signal strength. The pitted surface of the asteroid glided beneath him.

At a hundred yards, Jae-Sun slowed to a halt and turned, looking back at Lassiter in the distance. The astronaut floated above the dusty surface, his spotlights illuminating the rough surface.

"Com check," Jae-Sun said.

"Coms are good," Lassiter replied.

Jae-Sun raised his gloved hand and waved. The white suited astronaut waved back in reply.

Jae-Sun turned and continued on. He brought up a topographical overlay in his heads-up display and began moving to a second way-point, one known only to him.

After crossing a ridge and skirting the edge of a large crater, Jae-Sun knew he had moved out of line of sight. Neither Lassiter or the *Excelsior* could see him as he'd moved over the horizon from their perspective. Coms would still work, but the signal would be degraded. This was part of the plan. He'd convinced them there was a need to be coy in the initial approach to these creatures. Dragons had proven elusive for hundreds of years, since they were first spotted by the miners on Pluto. Now that one was at rest on an asteroid, the last thing anyone wanted to do was to spook the creature, and that played right into Jae-Sun's hands.

Being one of the pioneers of manned interplanetary space flight had its benefits, he thought. No one else could have gotten away with this without dozens of questions being raised from generals across the command structure, but Jae-

Sun was trusted. Jae-Sun knew he was about to betray that trust, but he had a higher purpose than the capture of one of these aliens. He had a promise to keep. Where others struggled to understand the mechanism by which the dragons moved and how they evaded observation, Jae-Sun already knew their secret: they moved through time.

A chasm opened up beneath him. The readout on his wrist computer indicated the probability of finding the alien within the dark canyon at 78% based on available readings and the various, faint electromagnetic emissions. Scratch marks lined a rock wall, appearing as though something large had scraped against the dust and rocks.

"I'm moving into a chasm," Jae-Sun said. "I may lose coms."

"Roger that," Lassiter replied. Already, his voice was breaking up with the low signal-to-noise ratio. "Still receiving telemetry."

Jae-Sun felt no fear, no sense of trepidation. He'd been waiting for this moment for hundreds of years.

Most people thought it was only the past that was set, but Jae-Sun understood time was a dimension every bit as fluid as any of the three spatial dimensions of up and down, left and right, forward and backward. The past and future seemed distinctly separate from a human perspective, but that was an illusion. Jae-Sun already knew what the future held. He was determined to make different choices.

He flew down a yawning hole that opened into the asteroid. Darkness enveloped him. His spotlights were feeble, barely illuminating the canyon walls as he descended out of sight and into the heart of the asteroid.

As he drifted deeper, he punched several commands into his wrist computer, deactivating the array of sensors on the white cube. These were supposed to record the interaction with the alien creature. They were largely passive, intended to avoid appearing intrusive to the alien. Had the scientists on the *Excelsior* known what he was doing they would have been horrified, but Jae-Sun had a plan. The instrumentation crate was carrying a payload other than probes and monitors.

"I've lost telemetry," Lassiter said. "Do you want me to reposition?"

"Negative," Jae-Sun replied. "Hold station. I'm still recording."

He was lying, but Lassiter had no way of knowing that.

Jae-Sun reiterated his command. "Hold your position. That is an order."

"Roger," Lassiter replied.

Jae-Sun cut his com-link, cutting himself off from the universe outside. Lassiter wouldn't move and neither would the *Excelsior*. They held Jae-Sun in too high regard to disobey. It wouldn't occur to any of them to question his judgment. No one would have believed this wasn't Jae-Sun descending into the inky depths of a lifeless asteroid.

Jason had lived so many years as Jae-Sun his own name sounded strange. The real Jae-Sun was on Titan analyzing readings from the deep space array and relaying advice and recommendations via the deep space network. Well, Jason thought, real was a relative term when it came to time travel. They were both real. They were both one and the same person. The split in the timeline meant they were effectively identical twins. How that worked from the perspective of conscious awareness, he had no idea, but it did.

"Where are you?" he mumbled to himself. "Come on, baby. I know you're down here."

Above, a handful of stars shone in the thin sliver of the eternally dark sky. An inky pitch-black gloom surrounded Jae-Sun from every other angle, and he felt as though he were descending into Sheol, leaving one universe and falling into another.

Darkness surrounded him. The dim light on his wrist computer read 120 meters and still the darkness seemed to be without end. Rather than the sensation of claustrophobia, with the jagged walls closing in, the intense darkness gave him a feeling of floating within eternity. Instead of being trapped inside an asteroid, he felt as though he were floating free in a void without end. Occasionally, his spotlights lit up a craggy rock drifting silently by in the dead of night. The cavern seemed to open out into a vast empty chamber beneath the chasm.

A smooth edge appeared below him, curving away in an arc as it disappeared into the darkness.

"I see you," Jason whispered, slowing his rate of descent.

Although he couldn't make out the entire craft, his navigation computer had already analyzed the shape, providing him with a three-dimensional wire-frame model of the UFO oriented in the same manner as in the view before him. Jason didn't need the image.

"It's been a long time," he said softly.

Memories flooded his mind, the lost fragments of previous encounters from tens of thousands of time loops.

Gently, Jason reached out and touched the skin of the massive alien vessel hidden in the darkness. Through his gloves, he could feel the structure tremble.

"Easy, girl."

Already, Jason felt confident in his assessment. This wasn't a vehicle or a spaceship, but a living organism. Rather than dealing with a technologically advanced alien species, they were dealing with a biological entity. While humanity had reached the stars inside machines, evolution within a stellar environment had enabled these creatures to survive in space.

Slowly, he drifted over the smooth skin of the alien creature, sinking further, descending into the darkness like a deep sea diver. His fingers disturbed a thin film of dust and he watched it swirl as though it were sediment being stirred up in the depths of some murky ocean.

As his lights illuminated the hide of the creature, he noticed changes in the skin texture. Images flooded his mind. Memories he had no previous awareness of suddenly seemed so clear. He blinked and could see scratches. Words and formulas had been carved into the hide of this magnificent animal. They weren't real, he understood that, but once they had been and now his mind replayed them, recalling each pattern as he drifted over the creature.

His gloved hand skimmed over the hide of the interstellar beast as he sunk deeper into the asteroid. He could almost feel the phantom sketches, the symbols and letters he remembered from another lifetime. They had scarred the creature's thick hide, having been hastily carved into its skin. He'd never understood these formulas. Jason knew what they were but why they'd been carved into the creature had puzzled him. All he could think of was that they were some multi-cycle attempt at comprehension spanning the vastness of time itself.

He and Lachlan had only ever lived through one iteration. Jason was only consciously aware of his singular passage through time. He'd avoided the feedback loop. Jason knew these ghostly memories weren't his. They were from another Jason, one that existed in a previous time loop.

Memories flashed through his mind, glimpses of formulas and words, sometimes entire phrases carved into the skin of this magnificent animal. Jason had never seen the creature before in anything other than photographs, but thousands of previous iterations had etched these figures in his memory in defiance of time travel. He understood he existed in a vortex, with his life reset time and again, and in the deep recesses of his mind, he could still remember.

For Jason, the critical moment had come in the RV so many years before.

Rain had lashed the windows.

The dark night seemed to stretch on forever.

Their recreational vehicle had hit something while driving along an interstate and the cabin skewed sideways as the driver slammed on the brakes. Broken branches flipped up beneath the underside of the vehicle, slamming into the chassis and puncturing two of the tires.

The specifics of what happened next were lost to him, but he remembered being left alone with Lily.

Photos lay scattered on the floor of the RV.

They spelled out a dire warning.

fe ED b A ck

d E st R oY

Rea ctor 1

At the time, it had been hard to believe. How could photos taken in the past, falling in a chaotic, random manner, form a deliberate message? The implication was that the etchings represented not only the past but the future. Somehow, someone in the future knew that those past photos would fall in that exact manner and used them to send a message to the present, but that was impossible. Or was it? Jason thought the answer lay in the first word, feedback.

Jason had realized the etchings weren't all the same age. The scratchings in the *R* of *Reactor* were lighter in coloration than either the *E* the *R* or the *Y* in dEstRoY, and each of them was still lighter than the *ED* in *feEDbAck*. The implication was that they'd been written at different times in a different feedback loop.

He had debated the mechanics of time travel with Professor Lachlan for almost three hours after that, stopping only when dawn reminded them they'd lost a night's sleep. There was a reporter, Jason had forgotten her name after so many years, but she was the first to accept the idea.

Feedback, Jason had argued, meant there were two time streams, a primary and a secondary line. Time would appear identical in each loop. The actors on the stage would have no idea what was happening. For them, time only transpired once, but the markings revealed secondary events existing within time. The carvings were proof they were caught in a feedback loop within space-time.

"But we can never know for sure!" Professor Lachlan had argued. Even some four hundred and sixty years later in the dark depths of a distant asteroid, Jason could still hear his mentor uttering those words.

"No, we can't," Jason had replied in what seemed like a dream to him half a millennia later. "It's not just these words that reveal the feedback loop, it's their timing. Why did they appear now? Why at this precise moment? This is no accident."

"Of course this was an accident," Lachlan protested. "Are you seriously suggesting someone staged this by throwing branches on the road?"

"No, no," Jason protested. "The words. They're no accident. This is deliberate. They hijacked this event to get this message to us."

"They who?" Lily asked.

"They—us," Jason replied. "We are the only ones that knew this would happen. We are the only ones that could have staged this."

"You're saying we sent this message to ourselves?" Lachlan asked. "That we sent a message back from the future?"

"Yes."

"But how could that work?" Lily asked.

"It's a time machine, right?" Jason had replied. "If you have a knowledge of the past, and you're looping back into that past over and over again, you have an opportunity to influence past events."

"So this is a hidden voice in our discussion," Lily said. "We're warning ourselves."

"Yes," Jason replied. "We knew this was the critical moment. We knew we would have this discussion and we sent a message to ourselves, one that would be received at precisely the right time."

"But … But," Lachlan protested, "that would take an astonishing amount of precision. These photos are from one spot within the interior of the craft, but they're out of order, they've been scattered randomly."

Jason agreed, saying, "It would take an astonishing amount of patience, probably over several iterations through time. You don't pull something like this off in one shot."

"But what if there's another way?" Lachlan asked. "I mean, why destroy the UFO? What about if we just leave it there and run?"

"We can't," Jason replied. "Whether its now or in fifty years, any contact I have with that craft is going to result in the same outcome. If I come in contact with this thing, whether willfully or forced, the feedback continues.

"It doesn't matter how big or small a feedback loop is, if it always returns to the same point you always have the same problem.

"We don't know how long this has been going on. There's no reason to assume every trip back has started at the same point. We could have had this conversation thousands of times already."

Lachlan thought for a second, before saying, "You're right. It's a chance we can't take."

Lachlan delayed the attack by 24 hours to allow time to arrange their escape from the United States. That they would be hounded by law enforcement was beyond dispute. Rather than exposing the UFO to the media, they were going to destroy it.

"You'd better be right," Lachlan had said the next day.

"There has to be a reason we told ourselves to destroy the reactor," Jason replied. "We have to trust ourselves when we're the ones telling ourselves there's no other way."

The inky black darkness inside the asteroid was mesmerizing, and Jason found his mind running to the past. He could remember the Learjet banking as it approached the nuclear reactor. There had been several large explosions at North Bend after the plane punched through the roof over reactor one.

A dark cloud seething angrily had risen above the shattered remains of the dome like the mushroom cloud from a nuclear detonation. Sporadic smaller explosions rocked the power plant for almost an hour afterwards. Finally, a brilliant blue-white explosion ripped out of the heart of the reactor with such ferocity that it blew apart the dark clouds looming overhead.

Their escape from the US had been carefully planned. Air travel was out of the question. From Oregon, they fled north to Seattle and on to Canada, traveling overland from Vancouver to Montreal. From there they boarded a merchant ship traveling to Cuba via Bermuda.

DARPA had burned enough people over the years in relation to the UFO that Bellum had no problem creating a false trail. His contacts left clues of an escape by land through Texas and into the lawless northern regions of Mexico surrounding Monterrey, keeping federal investigators off their track.

For almost two decades they were considered fugitives, but eventually the truth came out. Evidence of the UFO had surfaced quite early on in the FBI investigation, but it wasn't believed. Several high-profile leaks in the subsequent decades revealed the extent of DARPA research into the craft along with DARPA's plans to exploit the technology to allow the US to leap thousands of years ahead of other nations. Even the most diehard patriots could see such a concentration of power would be abused.

When the truth about the murders of Mitchell Jones and Helena Young were finally revealed, public opinion swayed toward the North Bend Six, as they were known. It took another seven years before they were granted amnesty.

During that time, Jason and Lachlan had made clandestine contact with the original Jae-Sun. He was born and raised in Orange County, Los Angeles and appeared to be the same age as Jason.

Jason had struggled with the realization that he was Jae-Sun. This wasn't some stranger divorced from him. They weren't twins. This was him in his infancy. Only the term infancy was a euphemism, as Jae-Sun was the same age as Jason, but for Jae-Sun nothing had happened yet.

Jason could remember the look on Jae-Sun's face when they first met. Rather than staring at a mirror, he felt as though he were looking at a video of himself.

"How can this be?" Jae-Sun asked, sitting across the table from Jason under the shade of an umbrella at a small cafe on the boardwalk in Havana.

A bright sun burned through the cloudless blue sky. Sunlight reflected off the waves in the harbor, blinding Jason, but he removed his sunglasses anyway so Jae-Sun could get a good look at his face. Lily sat beside him sipping a Piña Colada. She seemed taken by the concept of seeing two Jasons.

Even then, Jason felt as though theirs was a love that would last a hundred years. Little did he know at the time that medical advances would allow their love to extend over five hundred years. And if he had known, he would have smiled even more on that bright, sunny day.

Lily caught sight of this distracted look and returned a smile more radiant than the sun. They were here to meet with his doppelgänger not to bat their eyelids at each other, but Jason struggled with the realization that he was originally Jae-Sun. Even with all he knew, there was a surreal feeling about the meeting. Seeing Lily's smile grounded him. He didn't feel as though he could have ever actually been the seemingly identical twin sitting across from him talking to the professor, and yet he knew he was. Jason understood it must have been even harder for Jae-Sun to accept.

Jae-Sun turned to Professor Lachlan, saying, "I appreciate you sponsoring my work, but ... but you want me to believe I'm looking at myself? That's just not possible. Is he like a twin, or something?"

Jason found it strange to hear himself being described in that way, as though he were somehow less than human. It was the "or something" that cut to the bone. In Jae-Sun's mind, Jason was a freak of nature.

"I assure you," Lachlan replied. "Jason is your future self, dislocated in time."

Jae-Sun didn't look convinced.

Jason sat there quietly as the professor explained, "Time travel rolls back the clock, but without proper shielding, a time traveller is not excluded from that process. Just as there's no preferred location in space, there's none in time, and with the alien craft damaged, you reverted back to your age at your destination time and again."

Jason pulled a computer tablet out of his bag and handed it to Jae-Sun, saying, "Perhaps this will convince you."

"Yes, yes," Lachlan added with some excitement.

Jason gave Jae-Sun a moment. His doppelgänger turned the tablet around so the dark screen faced him, and looked up as if to say, so what?

"It's locked," Jason said, gesturing for him to turn it on.

Jae-Sun pressed the small button at the base of the tablet and the screen came to life, showing an icon in the shape of a thumbprint with a thin green line scanning slowly down the print.

"Go ahead," Jason said. "Swipe your finger. Open it!"

Jae-Sun swiped his index finger down the screen and the tablet unlocked, revealing a selection of application icons in a rainbow of hues.

"Finger prints are like snowflakes," Lachlan said. "They're wonderfully unique, even among twins."

"If you had an identical twin," Jason began, but Jae-Sun finished his sentence.

"He would not be able to open this!"

Jae-Sun put the tablet down carefully, as though he were handling a priceless Ming vase. He ran his hands up through his hair, grabbing at the strands and pulling on them. Jason understood the gesture implicitly, he'd felt much the same way when he first learned of the UFO.

During that first visit, the three men talked long into the night, showing Jae-Sun all they knew. As unbelievable as it must have been for Jae-Sun, the fingerprints were the proof he needed. They couldn't be faked.

Knowing they had to keep their origin secret, Jason and Jae-Sun conspired to wear different hair styles and clothing types, as well as to avoid being seen together to reduce the likelihood of being discovered.

Over the next few years, they developed the theory behind the space-time compression drive, which helped to sway the political opinion increasingly calling for the pardon of the North Bend Six. The prospect of losing such research to the Russians or the Chinese had the US Congress in an uproar. Like Von Braun in the 1950s, all was forgiven for the sake of space exploration.

In the dark vacuum of space, the only sound was that of his breathing and the soft whir from the circulation vents on his helmet.

Jason's gloved hands stirred up dust, causing it to swirl before it sank into the depths, disappearing beyond the range of his spotlights. Without meaning to, he'd halted his descent. His memories were so vivid, he felt unstuck in time. He could have been flitting back and forth across hundreds of years in the quiet of the pitch black void.

"How long have you waited?" he asked of the alien, not expecting a reply.

Time was all important to *Homo sapiens,* but to a creature that could move through time, what was a moment? A day? A year? Was a century of any consequence? From his calculations, he thought the creature had only arrived recently, but in the dark depths of the asteroid he wasn't so sure.

"It's me," Jason said, still running his fingers gently over the creature as he sank lower into the dark abyss. For the creature, this was first contact. It couldn't have known him, could it? Or did the concepts of cause and effect blur for an animal that lived its life traversing time?

Who was he? Jason or Jae-Sun? Names didn't really matter anymore. He was both. He'd always been both.

Mentally, he identified as Jason, but being here with the creature, he understood he was taking the place of the original Jae-Sun, and he felt as though that were in more ways than just by his physical presence. He could feel the same temptations that had once stirred Jae-Sun. A desire to change the past, to fix things, to correct the mistakes and travesties of humanity and avert suffering. It was well intended, but Jason had always understood such intent was folly.

"How does this work?" he asked as he descended, his equipment cube keeping pace behind him.

There was no answer.

"If I prevent myself from going back, if I take the place of the original Jae-Sun and refuse to return to the past, what happens to me? Will I cease to exist?"

His breath condensed on the glass faceplate of his helmet. Immediately, a cool, dry draft circulated from the rim of the helmet, clearing his view.

In the darkness, the skin of the creature looked slightly stippled beneath his spotlights.

"Are paradoxes possible?"

He was talking to himself, he understood that. Reasoning through the logic of time travel as he slipped slowly further down the gentle arc of the creature's hide.

"In any other dimension, we ignore the paradox of direction. A skier ignores a mountain climber, even though their motion is contradictory. Is this the same? Is time just another direction? Is time a mountain slope so steep we only ever go one way? Are paradoxes a matter of perspective?"

He drifted down to the center of the alien creature, his fingers still brushing over the dark skin. As the dome came into view, he noticed dim red lights within the gigantic fractured skull. Carefully, he negotiated his way into the gaping hole in the side of the dome, again reliving flashbacks from previous iterations in time.

Jason looked toward the back of the creature's skull. Hundreds of years ago and in a different time frame, he'd thought of that hard, smooth surface as a wall, but as he floated there in his spacesuit, he could see it was a partition, a membrane segmenting the skull into quarters. His spotlight swept across the smooth surface. Once, words had been etched into that thick membrane.

You can save her

You can save all of them

Now, though, the wall was empty and those words seemed like ghosts from the past.

Jason understood that the overwhelming feeling of deja vu was from having stood here hundreds, perhaps thousands of times while trying to break the cycle.

His white equipment cube drifted through the jagged opening and inside the dome. In the glare of his spotlights, its sterile surface and hard lines looked alien inside the organic creature. Jason switched off the tracking system, leaving the cube floating beside him.

As his spotlight swung around, light rippled over the rough texture of compressed brain matter on the other side of the skull.

Rows of tiny red lights flashed in the vacant front-left quadrant of the dome. This front quarter was the only vacant space within the central dome.

"I'm sorry," he said, not sure if the creature could hear him or even if it would understand. Perhaps he was speaking just to assuage his conscience. Perhaps this was a confession, one spoken to no one but himself in the bitter darkness.

"I wish there was another way."

The empty void remained silent.

Jason reached out and keyed a code into the equipment cube. A compartment opened and he pulled out a clunky device that looked somewhat like a metallic basketball with tiny pipes and wiring wrapped around it, hiding its explosive shell and plutonium core.

To his surprise, he was breathing heavily. Physically, there was no reason to, but the stress of the moment preyed on his mind.

"Why didn't you run?" he asked, arming the nuclear warhead with his stubby gloved fingers. "Why did you loop over and over again? You had all of time and space. Why did you return to Korea time and again?"

A soft green LED turned red, indicating the bomb was armed.

Jason breathed deeply, sighing as he exhaled. It all seemed so easy in their planning. Time travel was too dangerous for humanity. Nuclear weapons had once brought the world to the brink of annihilation. What would a mastery of the very fabric of space-time afford this infant species still reaching out from its parent star?

This was a mercy killing, he told himself. The alien was brain dead. That was the only possible explanation he could conceive to explain why the creature had been locked in a time loop. He had no choice. He couldn't let this alien fall into anyone's hands. He had to destroy the creature, regardless of his own sentiments. Eventually, others would stumble upon these dragons of the deep, but perhaps by then humanity would have reached beyond adolescence.

"Farewell, old friend," he said, using his suit thrusters to move forward and position the nuclear bomb so it was wedged between the console and the dome. All that remained was for him to return to the *Excelsior* and remotely detonate the device. He had to leave. He couldn't remain there. He had to see the plan through and end the madness of time looping over and over again.

There was something about the console that looked strangely out of place, and that distracted him for a moment, taking his mind off his singular purpose of destroying the creature.

Jason turned, drifting under power, controlling his motion with deft skill as he looked around within the alien skull, wanting to understand what had happened to drive it into this abyss. He reached out and grabbed at the strange console as his spotlights pierced the transparent outer dome, lighting up the sloping front of the creature.

"What have they done to you?"

In those few seconds, he understood something quite profound, something that had escaped their attention for centuries. There were two alien species involved, not one. These magnificent beasts, capable of migrating through space and time were being hunted by some other alien culture, one capable of taming and controlling them. The console was a horse bit, a harness, some kind of biotech designed to control the creature, to transform it into a mule.

"Lobotomy," he whispered in horror.

For all the interest *Homo sapiens* had in the fabled dragons of the deep, it seemed the real alien monsters were still hidden from sight. Someone had attacked this creature. To the best of Jason's knowledge, this was the first occasion in which there was any inkling of an aggressive, conquest-driven interstellar species that could represent a real threat to humanity.

He turned his attention to the ruptured section to his right. The membrane had burst and spilled into the empty quadrant. He could remember seeing this mass set like stone when the creature had been housed in reactor one.

Jason reached out and touched the dark, grey goo. Although it looked soft, it was as hard as a rock. As his gloved fingers ran over the bumps and undulations, images burst into his mind, except these weren't his displaced memories from the past, they were coming from the alien creature.

Large clouds of hydrogen billowed within a stellar nursery. At first glance, they seemed cold and menacing, and yet Jason felt at ease. Then he understood. The creature was sharing images and feelings with him.

Jason felt trusted. He couldn't explain why, but he knew there was no one else the creature trusted, and for the first time Jason had a glimpse of why it had circled so long through time trying to escape: there was no one else the alien felt it could trust.

His hand drifted away from the brain matter and the connection was broken. Immediately, he thrust closer, making contact again.

A thin, gaseous nebula surrounded the dark cloud, emitting a kaleidoscope of colors more beautiful than any rainbow.

Starlight lit up the tip of the molecular cloud, exciting the gas filaments and blowing the dark edges away like the wind eroding a sand dune. Judging from the surrounding stars, the cloud easily spanned a dozen light years or more. Several sections had broken away, floating like islands against the azure blue nebula.

A new born star lit up one corner of the cloud, pushing back the dark swirling mass and breaking free from its stellar womb.

"Home," Jason whispered, understanding what he was seeing.

Given the sheer size of this stellar nursery capable of birthing hundreds of stars, was it really such a surprise that it should not also give rise to life? Jason could feel himself smiling with delight. Within that molecular cloud was a cocktail of chemicals containing more mass than anything found on ten thousand planets like Earth.

The dark cloud was deceptive, hiding the complex chemical reactions sparked by interstellar radiation. What was sunlight to Earth but the radiation of a nearby star?

Jason saw Earth in a different light.

Earth was exceptional among the planets surrounding the Sun, but perhaps it was exceptional on an even grander scale, being the exception to other celestial processes by which organic chemistry could form life. In that moment, he understood that the conglomeration of molecular clouds and the multicolored nebula that surrounded it like a cloak could give rise to countless lifeforms.

Was it that unlikely? He wondered. Life had arisen on Earth when it was a hellish, seething volcanic wasteland. The newly formed moon orbited so close that it caused tides hundreds of feet high. The atmosphere choked with toxic fumes, almost entirely devoid of oxygen. The heat was unbearable. The planet was bombarded with tens of thousands of asteroids, causing earth-shattering impacts, some leaving craters that would have spanned most of the

Continental US. And yet in the midst of all that, life arose. Perhaps life in space was more of a natural occurrence than anyone had ever dared imagine.

The vision before him was surreal.

Although his hand was outstretched and his thrusters continued to maintain pressure against the brain mass of the creature, the view before him was one of being transported across the universe. He could see his white spacesuit, with his gloved hand apparently pushing against nothing. Looking down, past his feet, the nebula continued to bloom below him. Had it not been for the resistance to his suit's gentle thrust, Jason would have sworn he was there, beholding the majesty of the nebula firsthand.

A flock of the alien creatures passed overhead. He could see them spinning about each other, playful and vibrant with life. Their saucer like shape seemed more fluid and organic than mechanical. They looped and twirled, like a litter of puppies playing, with their disc-like bodies flexing and twisting as if they were stingrays undulating through the ocean.

From his perspective, he seemed to be tracking along next to them as they approached the nebula, only the backdrop of the nebula never seemed to change. Its sheer size and the distance between them and the cloud made it seem as though it had been painted on the backdrop of the heavens.

Michelangelo and Picasso could not have rendered a masterpiece so grand.

Then, without warning, a javelin shot through the air. At least, that was the impression Jason had. It was difficult to think of the colorful rainbow of gas clouds as a cold void, a lifeless vacuum at -455F.

The javelin moved in an arc, reminding Jason of the motion of a spear or an arrow on Earth, only in zero-g that meant its flight was powered, being guided onto its target.

The alien creatures had the appearance of stingrays without tails. They broke away from each other, dispersing with a sudden burst of speed. Blue lights flashed around them, peppering the nebula with blinding strobes as they disappeared into space-time, fleeing to the safety of some other place, some other time. One though, flipped on its side, wounded by the javelin.

"That was you," Jason said in a voice breaking with emotion.

The wounded alien creature tried to escape. Flashes of blue light strobed around its circular hide, but several more javelins struck the animal. Was it an animal? We're all animals, Jason reminded himself, regardless of how civilized we try to appear. He had no doubt those that hunted these magnificent alien creatures somehow depersonalized their barbaric acts just as humanity had done for centuries when hunting whales or apes.

Another dark saucer-like creature appeared on the edge of his vision, with a row of javelin darts attached beneath its shell, strapped on like missiles on the underside of a warplane. The intruder rushed at the wounded creature.

Jason watched as spider-like aliens launched themselves from this marauder, thrusting through space and landing on the crippled alien. Some kind of particle beam erupted from one of these pirates, searing the central dome and creating the massive scar he'd floated through just minutes before when he found the alien in the darkened crevasse deep within OA-5772.

Jason could see that the spiders were capable of operating without a spacesuit. Their exoskeletons must have shielded their internal organs in much the same way as his spacesuit protected him.

Jason found himself wondering about the energy requirements of such celestial creatures and the need for their metabolism to maintain an internal temperature in which their biochemistry could function properly. That space was poor at convective heat transfer must have helped, but the extreme differences between starlight and shade would have made it difficult for any biological creature to negotiate. Perhaps this was why these creatures stayed well clear of the stars, he thought. Perhaps it wasn't the gravity wells they were avoiding, but the excessive heat. Or maybe it was both.

Jason wanted to study these creatures. He was fascinated by the possibilities filling his mind and he could understand how Jae-Sun would have once felt the same way.

His viewpoint closed in on the fractured, smoldering dome of the creature and he could see one of the hunters setting up the console he'd seen glowing in the darkness.

The wounded creature fought, bucking like a bronco. Strobes of light continued to burst around it as the pirates set about breaking their captive's will. Jason found himself willing the alien to flee and in a flash of light it was gone. The marauders were left without their prey, drifting aimlessly through the nebula in response to the shockwave that reverberated when the wounded creature fled.

Jason was again in the darkness of the chasm deep in the shattered asteroid, only his viewpoint had shifted. Although his outstretched hand still pressed hard against the mass of brain matter, he appeared to be floating near the back wall of the skull. He watched as another astronaut sailed in through the gaping wound and at first he thought it was Lassiter.

A white spacesuit drifted before him. Spotlights flashed around the darkened interior of the skull.

"That's me!" he said, almost expecting to see himself responding to those words. It took a moment for him to realize he was seeing Jae-Sun in the original time stream.

His doppelgänger turned, looking through him, not seeing him.

Several more astronauts drifted by outside the creature, floating past like scuba divers in a dark cave. They attached cables to the outside of the animal.

The view before Jason flickered and suddenly the empty brain cavity was flooded with light.

Jason blinked as his eyes adjusted to the sudden influx of light.

Several men walked around within the brightly lit skull of the creature. They were dressed in clean-room suits, hermetically sealed with their own oxygen supply.

That the men walked meant they were under the influence of gravity, and Jason wondered whether this view was onboard the *Excelsior* or on Earth. Their movement was too fluid for either Mars or Titan, where they would have appeared to rebound more, but either way, this view revealed a much more distant, future time.

Jason could make out Jae-Sun's features through the visor of one of the suits. He'd aged considerably. Given that they were both already almost five hundred years old, that could only mean Jae-Sun had reached the limit of genetic renewal. As Jason understood the process, that would have made Jae-Sun almost a thousand years old.

"The collar is in place, but the damage appears too great," one of the men said.

"I'm convinced we can do it," the older Jae-Sun replied. "I've studied the design. I understand the physics."

"But the dome would need shielding," the other man said. "Without protection, you'd be exposed to the radiant energy within the wormhole. We have no idea what that would do to human tissue."

A woman spoke. Jason had assumed all three scientists were men, because their baggy suits hid any hint of gender.

"You're going to hit a backwash of energy, not unlike when a river opens out into the sea. Both sides of the timeline are going to pour energy into the void, trying to close the hole. I don't see how anyone could survive given the damage to the alien dome."

"And yet this creature survived such a trip to get here," the aging Jae-Sun insisted. "Don't you see? If we can harness this power, we can change time."

Jason was shocked to learn he could be so arrogant. This magnificent interstellar creature had once been nothing more to him than a vehicle to exploit. He'd given its life no more consideration than a child would stepping on a bug.

"Think about what you're saying," the woman pleaded. "You're stealing fire from the gods!"

"Ha," the elderly Jae-Sun replied, clearly surprised by the comparison with the fabled Prometheus. "Think about how society advances. We learn from our mistakes. We learn the hard way. What if we could learn the easy way? What if we could learn without consequence and avoid heartache and ruin? What if we could fix our mistakes?"

"But consequences are unavoidable," the woman replied. "Time will not permit paradoxes. You cannot play God!"

"God was an amateur," the old Jae-Sun snapped, his voice booming as he became more bellicose. "God knew the future and never changed a thing. But us, we have a real shot at turning back the clock and resetting the tragedies of mankind. We can prevent billions of deaths in the War of the North! We can avoid the loss of tens of thousands of other animal species to our own stupidity. We can undo extinction itself!"

"You are mad," the woman stated firmly, raising her voice in defiance. "You're drunk with power."

He recognized the voice.

"Lily!" he whispered, reaching out with his hand.

The woman turned her head to one side as though she heard something from the rear of the craft, but that was impossible. They were separated by hundreds of years, and this was an illusion, a projection, a fabrication. In that instant, their eyes seemed to meet, but it wasn't Lily. The eyes were too narrow, the jawline too broad.

The woman turned back to the older Jae-Sun, pleading, "This is wrong. Don't do it!"

The aging man stood there, proud and defiant. He began to reply, but in real time, Jason pulled his hand back briskly, breaking the neural connection and returning himself to the darkness of the asteroid.

Jason was repulsed by what he had seen. He didn't want to see any more. It wasn't that he was in denial, but rather that he found it difficult to watch himself being swept up in the hubris born of time travel. The cavalier attitude he'd witnessed sent a chill down his spine. This was the egotism that defined evil across generations: Stalin, Hitler, Mao, Pol Pot, they all shared the same self-absorbed arrogance and myopia. They saw everything clearly, and they alone held the answers. It was the classic trap: blind stupidity and hubris.

For a moment, Jason wasn't sure quite where he was. The visions he'd had were overwhelming in their clarity, fooling his senses and leaving him uncertain of when and where he was, but he quickly became sure he was back in the quiet of the present.

"I didn't know," Jason whispered to himself, realizing he couldn't separate himself from Jae-Sun. They were one and the same person, the only difference between them had come from thousands of iterations through time.

"I thought I understood," he pleaded to the empty vacuum. "But I didn't."

It felt strange to be defending actions Jae-Sun wouldn't make for hundreds of years. Defending? Was he being defensive? Or repentant? Even Jason wasn't sure at that point.

"That was a different time," he insisted, feeling as though the silence of the creature somehow condemned him.

What was this magic? How could he see into a future that hadn't happened yet? He had to destroy this device lest its magic fall into the wrong hands.

Magic! Yes, he thought. What else was this but sorcery by human standards? There had to be some science to the animal's motion, but humanity was so primitive by comparison that this magnificent creature seemed almost divine, like one of the fabled cherubim that wept over the mercy seat on the Ark of the Covenant.

"It doesn't have to be this way."

Jason wanted to believe those words, but the red LED flickering on the side of the nuclear bomb spoke only of violence. It pulsated, casting an eerie glow in the open brain cavity.

"I can change this," Jason said to the ghosts echoing around him in the darkness.

As he turned, his spotlights lit up sections of the wall in the skull. Words and equations had once scarred those surfaces. He could still see them in his mind's eye.

"I can fix this!"

And with those words, he realized nothing had changed. This was the same hubris that had led Jae-Sun to travel back in time in the first place.

Looking at the rear membrane, he saw words once carved in desperation.

You can save her

You can save all of them

Her?

All this time, Jason had thought he understood the message he'd been sending himself across the vast expanse of space-time, but he hadn't. For hundreds of years, he'd missed the real meaning in the messages he'd left for himself over thousands of iterations.

He'd never intended to save only himself. He'd never intended to save just Lily or even Lily and Lachlan. He'd always wanted to save them all, including this remarkable alien creature. It wasn't that he'd previously assigned a sense of gender to the alien, but that he'd only ever thought of her as a ship and so had spoken of the UFO using the feminine pronoun: her.

There was much he didn't understand about the feedback loop, but he understood the creature was somehow locked into a certain point in space-time, always returning to that stormy night off the coast of North Korea. But why?

At the time, all Jason could think of was that the injury to the alien's neural compartment had rendered it essentially brain dead. But now his opinion had changed. He had seen an astonishing amount of cognitive function as the creature had shown him visions of its home, visions of its capture, and of the future.

The alien was wounded; of that he was sure. The damage to its skull was clear. The bit and bridle sat before him as a strange alien console with faint, exotic markings.

This dragon of the deep was crying out to him for help. She could see both the past and the future. Why had she continued circling over and over? Why return to that dark night off the coast of North Korea thousands of times? What was she waiting for?

Finally, he understood. She was waiting for him. She needed him to understand what had to be done at this precise moment. She wanted him to set her free. It had taken thousands of iterations to bring him to the point when he could help her.

In the original timeline, Jae-Sun had been selfish, self-centered. Now, though, Jason knew what she needed him to do.

In the vision of the nebula, her fellow creatures had fled through space-time, leaving in their wake flashes of pale blue-light. And he'd seen this earlier today. He'd thought it was Cherenkov radiation breaking before his retina, but it wasn't. They were out there, waiting to effect a rescue.

This was the answer he was looking for. This was an alternative that could break the time loop. All he had to do was to lead the *Excelsior* away and leave her to her kind.

This wasn't part of the plan, but to hell with the plan, he thought.

"I understand," he said, gently touching at the brain mass that had revealed those visions to him. Everything they'd gone through, it must have been all she could do, all she was capable of in her injured state, desperate to escape.

He drifted forward and removed the nuclear device, deactivating the bomb. The red LED switched to green as he packed the bomb back into the equipment cube. His gloves were clumsy, or was it that his fingers were trembling? Jason couldn't tell, but the realization of how close he'd come to destroying this intelligent alien shook him.

"This," he said, turning to face the strange console. "This must go."

While working with the equipment cube, he had drifted sideways and somewhat upside down relative to the floor of the cavity. The floor itself sloped down at an angle of roughly seventy degrees within the asteroid, and yet in the near weightlessness he could convince his mind that the angled surface was flat. Slowly, Jason aligned himself with the floor, grabbing hold of the console.

"Let's get this off you."

The console looked like a mesh of smooth, brushed aluminum with organic branch-like edges weaving down into the floor. There were dozens of tiny lights, barely visible in the darkness. As his spotlight drifted over them, they seemed to disappear. At first glance, the console seemed to be part of the vessel, but Jason had seen how brutally it had been set in place.

He planted his feet on the floor immediately below the console and grabbed at the thick edge. Flexing with his thighs, and keeping his back straight, he pushed off, trying to pry the console loose. There was a little give, but the console remained stuck.

Working hand over hand, he moved to one end of the console. Jason positioned himself carefully and instead of slowly increasing pressure, he thrust downward with his boots while pulling upwards with his hands. His head and neck arched back as he strained to pull the console loose. He could feel this end of the console starting to budge.

"Come on, you bitch!" he cried, jerking at the alien device.

Pulling himself along with his gloved hands, he moved to the other end of the console and pried at the structure. This end moved more than the other. Slowly, he was jimmying it out of place. He repeated this several more times until the console drifted just a few feet above the floor, still held in place by thin tendrils reaching out like roots.

Jason was sweating. His suit compensated for the exertion, lowering the temperature and circulating dry air to draw off the humidity produced by his perspiration.

Lying on his back, he reached under the console, grabbing at the roots. Lying there, he felt the vertigo of spacewalking. He could have been lying next to the floor, leaning against a wall or drifting close to the ceiling. All possibilities were equally valid, but for his sanity he chose to think he was lying there, even though he was floating inches above the floor.

The creature shook as he jerked at the roots, tearing them free like loose wiring.

"I'm sorry," he whispered, pulling the debris away and watching as the console toppled slowly, propelled forward by his jerking motion.

With the console floating freely within the skull cavity, a rainbow of colors began appearing on the surface he'd thought of as the front windshield.

"You like that, huh?" he said, smiling to himself.

Jason grabbed the console, using his maneuvering thrusters to drag the console toward the fractured opening. The computer controls in his suit struggled with the center of gravity being shifted to one side, and he quickly powered down, arresting his motion before he spun out of control. The only way he was going to get this out of here was by using the equipment cube to drag it, as the cube was designed to retrieve collection samples and its navigation systems could deal with more complex maneuvers.

Attaching the console to the cube was easy enough.

It was time to go.

"Goodbye, my dear friend," he said, taking one last look at the kaleidoscope of colors pulsating through the cavity. "Take care of yourself."

Slowly, he drifted out of the yawning hole in the skull cavity, watching as the cube followed automatically behind him. The console caught on the edge of the skull, but the cube adjusted its motion, working the console out of the gap.

Jason couldn't look back. Tears welled up below his eyes, sticking to his cheeks like globs of glue in the low gravity. He shook his head, shaking them loose so they would be drawn away by his helmet vents.

His spotlights illuminated the sloping body of this majestic creature as he ascended, but he couldn't bring himself to look at the central core. Above, a handful of fleeting stars provided the only hint of the universe beyond this dark cavern.

As he approached the top of the fracture in the asteroid, the dim light spilled in around the edges of the yawning canyon. Again, he could see the scratch marks where the creature had scraped against the dusty, rock walls while fleeing for the safety of the darkness.

For a moment, Jason floated above the crevasse. Chunks of dusty blue ice mixed with rocks and boulders. The dark crack beneath him looked more ominous than familiar.

"Farewell," he said, accelerating away from the fracture in the asteroid.

The equipment cube mirrored his motion, following behind him with the console in tow. If he changed direction or came to a halt to examine his wrist console, the cube darted around, compensating for the added mass it had to deal with.

He cleared the lip of a vast impact crater and returned to the way-point set by Commander Lassiter. His surreal experience inside the darkened fracture seemed almost like a dream out here among the stars.

Jason steeled himself. As far as the universe was concerned, he was Jae-Sun again, in demeanor and attitude. He had to play this part once more, one final time.

Jae-Sun activated his coms and caught the tail-end of chatter with the *Excelsior*.

"—roughly two hours, but he—wait, I've got him on radar," Lassiter said.

Jae-Sun could see the young man in the distance, just a speck of white drifting above the murky grey asteroid with its pits and boulders, craters and cracks.

"Did you find her?" Lassiter asked.

"Her?" Jae-Sun replied, his mind still awash with all that had happened. "No. There was nothing down there. But she'd been there. I found some debris, part of a control panel."

"Hot damn!" Lassiter replied with excitement.

Jae-Sun found it strange trying to mimic the young man's excitement. He smiled as he sailed up to him. Yes, he thought, I should be excited about finding evidence of an intelligent alien species.

Lassiter came around beside the equipment cube, drifting by the console as he examined this strange and curious alien device.

"Unfucking believable!" he cried. "We hit the jackpot!"

"Yes," Jae-Sun replied softly. "Yes, we did."

Would he ever be able to tell the true story? He wondered. Would he ever be able to reveal all he'd seen? It wasn't the dragons of the deep humanity needed to be wary of. What were those spidery pirates? Where were they from?

What would happen when humanity first encountered this hostile alien race?

Whatever was to come, they had the past to build upon. Perhaps this console would give them a glimpse into the nature of these other alien creatures. At some point, he'd have to reveal what he knew, but not now. For now, it was enough to know these dragons were benign.

In the distance, hundreds of miles behind Lassiter, there was a faint flicker of blue light. The dragons were coming for her. In his mind, Jae-Sun remembered those ghostly words from within the alien skull.

You can save her

You can save all of them

In the end, he really could save them all.

Afterword

Thank you for taking the time to read *Feedback,* and for supporting independent science fiction. Please take the time to leave a review online as your insights and feedback are invaluable (no pun intended). Independent authors thrive on word of mouth advertising, so if you've enjoyed this story, please tell your friends and recommend they grab a copy.

Thanks go to Brian Wells and John Walker for their assistance with the scientific aspects of this novel, and to my editor, Ellen Campbell, for her patience in working through the seemingly endless revisions, and to Jae Lee for his insights into Korean culture. The cover art is by Jason Gurley. Thanks also go to those beta-readers who helped fine-tune the content before the general release: Damien Mason, Bruce Simmons, Jamie Canubi, Tomi Blinnikka and TJ Hapney.

The world of publishing is changing rapidly. Whereas once big name authors dominated the best seller lists, now days there are more and more independent writers climbing the charts. If you liked this story and would like to be a part of its success, please tell a friend about it and take the time to leave a review online. Reviews are the lifeblood of independent fiction. Your thoughts and insights help others decide whether this is a novel they'd enjoy.

Several years ago, Professor Stephen Hawking pointed out that time travel is impossible because of feedback. If you tried to connect any two points in time with a wormhole, the energy from both the past and the future would pour through the gap, rushing through and causing a feedback loop much like a microphone being left next to a speaker.

In this novel, we explored the concept of a broad feedback loop, where the start and end points in time are separated by decades and the feedback comes not in the form of energy but in knowledge. In both cases, though, feedback builds until the loop is broken.

Although the bulk of this story traces only one iteration within the feedback loop, the following image shows the entire sequence of events as described in the epilogue. Rather than timelines splitting into parallel universes, *Feedback* relies on the idea that space-time is plastic and malleable, with time being as flexible and robust as any other dimension.

For us, paradoxes don't occur because time is linear, but should a time machine ever be invented, paradoxes could occur as easily as they do in any other dimension.

This image shows the timeline followed by Jae-Sun/ Jason

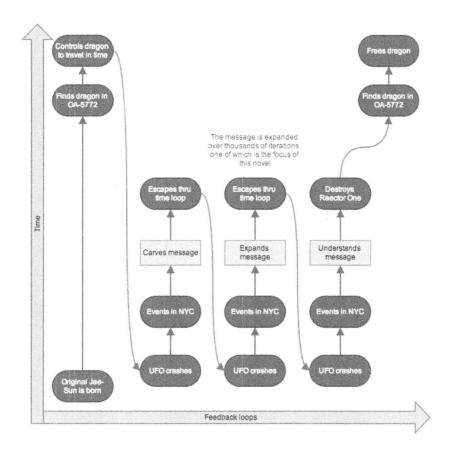

Made in United States
North Haven, CT
25 January 2023

31602301R00251